CO

AUTHOR'S NOTE..vii

New York City, 1938 1

New York City to Hull, England..28

Hull to Prague 34

Prague, August 1938..37

Hello Prague 42

Emergency 52

October 1938 57

Settling for the Unknown...61

Christmas 1938..80

New Year 1939 85

The Inquiry 90

The Quaker Lady 98

Revelations..102

Uncertainties 110

Spring 1939..126

My Twenty-Second Birthday 1939 131

The Unexpected 138

Stolen Moments..143

Parting 158

Leaving...163

Onward 173

Arriving 180

Settling In 192

Unsettling 197

The Piano 201

New Events 203

World's Fair 1939 209

New Endeavors 211

Changes 233

A Wanted Arrives 244

Social 246

Christmas 1939 250

Discoveries 254

Terror 257

February 1940 266

Fears 268

Bad News 273

Other News 277

Summer 1940 280

November 1940 282

Then It Came 285

Raison d' Être 290

Other Places 294

Anja's Birthday 296

War 299

1942 305

Making Do 306

Grim Events 308

Alex 311

A Big Surprise 314

Rationing 318

Alex in England 323

New Moves for Anja and Other News 326

Happy News 330

Sad News 331

Sad Missive 335

Doing It 339

1944 343

New Adventures 354

Five Years of War in Europe 364

Battle of the Bulge 368

1945 373

The Front Line — 23 December 1944 406

Another Rite at the Front 411

Afterwards 413

An Ending 415

Aftermath 419

Good News 420

A Beginning 427

Studies 442

Lessons 446

Dissolution 462

Friendship in Remiss 466

Changes 468

ACKNOWLEDGMENTS 483

ABOUT THE AUTHOR 485

AUTHOR'S NOTE

The years of World War II 1939–1945 were like no other in our world history.

Some eighty-five million people, men, women and children who were never to know their lives any other way, died in this time. The miracle is that during the horror and madness of this war, some people were still able to nurture the human instinct of caring and love, even at the risk of the highest price possible. The characters in this story gave that love, each bearing the cost.

Ingrid Wolsk

The Secret of Anja is a work of historical fiction. Apart from the well known actual people, events and locales that figure into the narrative, all names, characters, places and incidents are the product of the author's imagination or are used fictitiously. Any resemblance to actual persons, living or dead, the events or the locales is entirely coincidental.

All rights reserved.
Copyright © 2017 by Ingrid Wolsk
ISBN: 978-1-54392-763-4 (print)
ISBN: 978-1-54392-764-1 (ebook)

In Memory of my Mother

THE

SECRET

OF

ANJA

INGRID WOLSK

NEW YORK CITY, 1938

THE YEAR WAS 1938, another year of the Great Depression. The country was still suffering its effects in all sectors of life. It was a time when the hope for a job in your chosen field was narrowed to the hope of maintaining a slim daily subsistence on whatever work was to be found. I was lucky to have a father that did not believe in banks or the stock market. He had kept the family assets safely squirreled away, and they appeared to meet our needs as required.

As a young twenty year-old woman, I escaped a lot of the misery of the times, mostly due to my father's financial planning and the warmth and security of family life they showered on me as their only child. I had led a protected existence, one that did not demand much of me to reach beyond what I seemed capable of at the time. My father saw me as his jewel and my mother tried to protect me from the unnecessary bruising of the slings and arrows that life could inflict. With my mother's staunch Swedish upbringing she at times would tow the line with me when she saw things too differently from what she expected of me. Now, I was looking for something in my life. I wanted it to be big, but at that point I had no idea of where to look. My degree was in English literature, I saw nothing big in the offing there.

I chose something to awaken a new interest. Reading through New York University's course catalog, I found that the description of 'Art in Architecture' piqued my interest. 'This course is an introduction to the architecture in New York City that has incorporated some of the finest art of its kind. This little-known subject will be explored both in the classroom and on foot in the city. This non-credit course will awaken your interest in art far beyond the stone, steel, and mortar it houses.'

Something small for starters, I thought, so I signed up for the course, which started in January, and committed my next six Saturday mornings from nine to eleven to 'Art in Architecture'.

It was just after half past eight on a Saturday morning when I arrived at the school cafeteria with the slim text written by the lecturer, and with a cup of coffee, I sat down to steel myself once again as a student. I had just opened the textbook when I heard the chair opposite me pulled out. I looked up to see a good-looking young man. He asked, "Do you mind if I join you? I like this table."

"No, of course not. I'm just about to leave anyway."

"I haven't seen you here before. Are you new?"

"I signed up for just one course, 'Art in Architecture'."

"Would you be a new architecture student?"

"No, I've come just for this class. Just a six-week Saturday morning effort," I smiled.

"I know this lecturer. He's a bit of a drone in his delivery, but he does know the subject. I was already enough interested in it to do well, I'm an architecture student normally."

"Are you taking a course in this field as well?"

"No actually. I'm taking a course in the language department. It's a beginner's course in the Czech language. My parents are Czech and I grew up speaking it, but now I want to be able to read and write it as well."

"That sounds hard. Is it?"

"I'll be able to tell you next week. Come early for coffee and we can compare notes. I guess I better get a move on I wouldn't want to miss the first of, 'My name is.' By the way, my name is Alex." Smiling, he extended his hand to me.

Returning the smile, I offered mine, saying, "I'm Karin."

He bounded off to his first class with an energy I found intriguing. When I went to my class, I found he was right about the droning voice of the lecturer, but I too was interested enough to remain attentive. Little did I know then that this casual meeting was to dramatically change my life forever.

Going home on the bus, I reviewed my perfunctory notes, which left much to be desired because the lecturer so far had made no statements worthy of note. What I remembered most of that first morning was meeting Alex. I recalled his enthusiasm and his nice smile, and how easily he talked. I hoped I would see him again next Saturday.

I walked into the cafeteria the following Saturday morning to find Alex at his—and, at least for now, my—favorite table. I put my books down as he rose to greet me. We hadn't even gotten coffee when he said with a smile, *"Jak se máš? Moje jméno je Alex."* 'How do you do? My name is Alex.' That is a direct translation from the Czech I learned last week. I can even write it and read it, and beyond that my true purpose remains to be fulfilled." Smiling, he asked, "How did you like your first class?"

"As you forewarned me, he is indeed a bit of a drone, and I was expecting it to be more interesting than it was. I guess once I warm up to his delivery, I'll enjoy it more."

"I have an idea. I'm studying architecture, and I know this subject well. How would you like to meet me on a Sunday, and I can walk you around the city and show you some of the gems to be seen? I promise not to drone on! I will make it interesting for you, and I hope you will warm up to my delivery of the subject. What do you say?"

"I like that idea! When were you thinking of doing this?"

"Tomorrow, if that suits you. We could meet at Grand Central Station, say nine o'clock?"

"Are you sure?"

"Yes, I'll see you there at nine sharp, in the main hall under the clock." He grabbed his books off the table and dashed off. I am still taking in the suddenness and directness of it all as I too walk to my classroom.

SUNDAY MORNING, I RUSHED INTO THE MAIN HALL OF Grand Central Station and walked around the information booth that housed the huge clock. I was looking around for him when suddenly I almost walked right into him. "*Dobré ráno, Karin. Jak se máš? Moje jméno je Alex.* Good morning, Karin! How do you do? My name is Alex." He laughs, "That's what I learned yesterday, and now I can faultlessly read it and write it in Czech. And what did you learn?"

"The only thing I learned yesterday was that I would be here on time today," I said.

"Oh dear, I better make my best effort to be warm and interesting. Let's go for some coffee, and I'll tell you about this building." Seated with a cup of steaming coffee, he shared many amazing things about Grand Central Station, one of America's most historic landmarks. I wondered how he kept all this in his head when surely there was a lot of other stuff going on in there at the same time.

Perhaps noticing my attention turning inward, he broke off. "How am I doing? Not bored yet?" He laughed.

"No! Not at all." I was on the border of boredom, actually, because of the overwhelming amount of information. I was charmed by him and his warm delivery.

He continued. "As for the famous four-faced clock where we met, this is probably one of the most poignant features of interest."

By that time, I had already decided that he was the most poignant feature of interest.

"It's where assignations take place. Where new lovers meet and, sometimes, where old lovers part. It marks the time of beginning and ending of arrangements of people's travels and lives. They somehow get swallowed up in these cavernous halls of constant movement."

I couldn't think of anything to say, other than, "I'm astounded by your knowledge."

He smiled and reached for my hand saying, "And I for my intent."

We went out into the brisk morning air, with my cold hand held in his warm hand. He suggested, "We could go to the Horn and Hardart Automat to warm up and have a bite to eat. Its Sunday, after all, a day of rest."

And that was how it all started. For the next four weeks, we met briefly on Saturday mornings before class, and then on Sunday at the four-faced clock. Each Sunday, Alex took me on a jaunt to another building of interest. On the last Saturday of my class, Alex stopped at our breakfast table briefly, only to say, "Meet me here at the table after class so we can talk."

TODAY, THE LAST DAY OF OUR CLASS, the lecturer took us on a field trip of some notable buildings around the city known for their artistic installations. The Chrysler building was outstanding. I returned to the school later than I expected, and I hurried to the cafeteria. I was relieved to see Alex at our table, writing in his note-book and mouthing words in Czech. When I arrived, he stood, took my hand, and to my surprise, leaned over to give me a quick kiss on the cheek.

His relief was visible as he said, "I thought you might not come."

I shook my head, saying, "I thought you might not wait. I was on the final field trip, worrying the whole time about being late."

" I'm glad to see you. What would you like to eat? They close the food counter here shortly."

"Nothing, thank you. How's your course going?"

"I'm working hard at it, and the only distraction I have is when I think of you, which is often. Tell me more about yourself! I know so little about you."

I try to hide my blush with a wave to minimize his ques-tion. "I guess these days my most outstanding feature is that I have a part-time job as an assistant in the art department of the Works Progress Administration."

"That sounds impressive."

I laughed. "It isn't, really. I paste together visual presentation segments for proposed art projects that the WPA is considering funding. I'm lucky to have it, though."

"Did you study art?"

"No, English literature, but there isn't a great demand out there for my reading list."

"What will you do?"

"Pray to keep this job and hope that President Roosevelt will continue to fund the WPA arts projects." I paused and thought on this for a moment, and then I asked Alex, "And you—what do you do?"

Alex made a face as he said, "I'm studying to be an architect, but I can't afford to get my degree here. My parents are Czech-born, so I can go to Czechoslovakia and continue my studies there for a pittance of what it would cost me here. That's why I'm taking this Czech reading and writing course. I plan to apply to the university in Prague. I have two aunts and an uncle there with whom I can live, and so it should all be possible. I was a lot happier about all of it until I met you."

"Me? Why is that?"

"Now I can't imagine weekends not seeing you."

"You'll have an exciting new life to look forward to! Although I will miss our walks and talks, too."

"I haven't gone and done it yet."

"Well, you most certainly should, with such a good plan, and I have a feeling you will."

"Okay, enough heavy stuff. I'd like to take you to the Fulton Fish Market. There's a great seafood bar where we can eat. I can't afford the lobster, but we can share a Pompano and fries." He gathered his belongings, and mine as well, and we took the bus all the way downtown to Fulton Street. In the bus he sat with his arm around the back of my seat, and every now and then he gave my shoulder a little rub and a small squeeze. It was the last day of my class, but it was also the first day of something I didn't expect. I was soon to learn that most of life is taught that way, and with my classes now over Alex wanted to continue the Sunday meetings.

Before we realized it, May had arrived, and with it came some truly beautiful days. One Sunday when it rained, we went to the movies. We sat through a double feature, a cartoon, and a serial, with Alex holding my hand. When the Movie Tone News reels came on his grip moistened and tightened as we watched lines of fleeing refugees leaving areas I never even heard of before.

The newsreel commentator spoke of the possible incorporation of the Sudetenland into Nazi Germany, and that this action would leave the rest of Czechoslovakia weak and powerless to resist subsequent occupation. I never even heard of the Sudetenland before this—I didn't know if it was a separate country or a region of one of the surrounding nations. As time would prove, I had a lot to learn. It seemed that some distant parts of Europe early in 1938 were in uncertain political conditions when it came to interpreting Germany's actions, which were still unclear in nature. Alex didn't say anything, and I didn't ask, because we were not affected by these events. For me, at least, Germany's actions were just a passing newsreel item.

When we left the movie theater, the sun shone brightly as the clouds broke apart, and the streets glistened and the air felt freshly washed. We walked for a while, chatting about the features, when Alex told me he had gotten a job in an architectural firm.

"My sole task is to draw heating duct ways and ventilation carriers for a proposed office building. My job is to reproduce the drawings and to make the corrections given to me from time to time. It's boring work, but I am so lucky to have it so I can save up for Prague. I have decided that I want to do that. This job has prompted me even further in that direction."

I didn't say anything. He took my hand again and turned to look at me. I continued walking looking down at the sidewalk. He was quiet as well. Finally he asked, "What do you think of that?"

I gave a small shrug. "I don't know, Alex. I don't know what to say."

In a sudden spurt of enthusiasm, he said, "Well, I've been thinking about it, a lot in fact." He stopped walking and turned me to look at him. "Why don't you come with me? You said you've never been to Europe, and I know you'll love it! We could travel during school holidays. We get along really well, and we like each other. You could live with me at my aunt and uncle's house. It could be your great adventure."

I laughed as I shook my head. "That sounds like a fantasy to me."

"No, no! It's not. We can go over on a freighter. We can work our way over there, so it won't cost us anything. We'll just need to get from the last port of call in Europe to Prague. I've thought it all out. We can do it!"

I couldn't believe what I was hearing. We hardly knew each other. I was at a loss for words, when I next heard myself say as if this crazy idea were even a possibility, I said, "Well, I've never been away from home alone before."

"You won't be alone! You'll be with me. Just think about it. Let the idea sink in, and I'm sure it will seek its level of acceptance. Give it that chance. Please, promise me you will?"

Level of acceptance? That sounded strange, but I said, "I promise to think about it, but nothing more than that."

"That's all I ask!"

"You ask a lot of me, Alex, when we hardly even know each other."

He looked me right in the eye and said, "I know I want to do this with you, and that's all I have to know."

"Please, not another word about it for now."

Alex nodded. "Okay, we can talk about it next Sunday."

"Oh, next Sunday there's a problem. I can't next Sunday."

"Are you rejecting me already?" he asked, pulling a sad face.

I laughed. "No! It's my birthday, and my mother usually does something special, along with a nice dinner. I could invite you. Would you come for dinner with us? No gift, please, just you."

Alex smiled, but said, "I'd feel better if you checked with your parents first. Come to the school cafeteria next Saturday at eleven and we can decide what to do."

We had reached my bus stop at this point, just as the bus was approaching. Alex quickly put his arm around me and gave me a hurried kiss on my cheek. "Till Saturday then," he said, and stepped back as I stepped into the bus. I numbly found a seat, considering the conversation we'd just had. The escalation of our friendship made my mind spin, so much so that I missed my stop. I jumped up when I realized I had gone two stops beyond where I should have gotten off. I wondered if that was a metaphor of my current predicament.

At dinner that evening, my mother asked me how I had spent the day. Over the past several weeks, I had told them a little about Alex, but not all that much. When I said I would like to invite him for my birthday dinner, my mother and father exchanged a look that said, "I told you so " and then my mother said, "Yes, we would like to meet him. Dinner will be at six, but he can come earlier if he'd like."

I thanked them. "He's nice; I think you'll like him."

My parents quickly moved on to other topics. I was puzzled that they didn't ask me more, but I was also relieved.

All week, my burdened mind kept nagging me about major decisions that would all too soon come up for discussions. All that came to mind whenever I thought about it, though, was Alex's positivity about not only his studies in Prague, but also about the idea that I would accompany him. Sure, he had a goal at the end, but what was mine to be? What would I do there, and why would I even want to go? Prague was not part of my life's plan, not that I had one—and if I had, I would want it to be of my choosing, not an unknown tag-along with a near stranger. Who knew? Maybe this was exactly that big thing I was looking for in my life, however well disguised it seemed at the moment. Still, I wished such a big step stemmed from my own desire and not from the pressure of someone else's fantasy.

ON SATURDAY, I SAT AND WAITED FOR HIM IN THE cafeteria. He was late, which was very unusual. I decided I would wait until noon. *If he doesn't show up by then*, I thought to myself, *I'll know that he thought everything through and decided it wasn't such a great idea.* I pulled my coat around my shoulders to ward off a sudden chill when I heard running footsteps behind me. I turned, but didn't see anyone. Imagine how I jumped when Alex surprised me with a quick kiss on my cheek! Alex said, "I'm sorry I'm late I was taking a quiz and the teacher went over the most common mistakes the class made. I wanted to tell her the worst one I was making was leaving you to wait for me. She was still talking when I left. How are you?"

I laughed as I imagined the scene. "I'm glad to see you. My parents have officially invited you to my birthday dinner tomorrow at six; mother said you should come early if you wish. I suspect there will be a pre-dinner grilling of Alex!"

He laughed. "Maybe I should have a pre-dinner drink to marinate myself for the occasion. Do you think they'll approve of me?"

"Not if they know you want to steal me off to Prague."

He smiled. "Let's keep that for another time then."

"Yes, I would like to as well."

"I knew this wasn't going to be easy," Alex admits as he reached for my hand. Then looked up at me and said, "I find liking you this much is the easy part, but then that has been going on for a while, so I'm well practiced. I don't have as much practice putting it into words."

Not terribly surprised at hearing that, I said, "I've been learning about that myself as well, but it's not as easy for me because I lack your initiative. I find myself responding to them, though."

"You haven't responded to all of them," he said with a warm smile.

"I need more time."

"I'm thinking of leaving in about a month from now."

"A month! Alex, I don't even know your last name."

He straightened formally. "It's Forman, I'm Alexander Forman, and I'm very attracted to Karin . . . ?"

"Wilson. Karin Wilson."

"Alexander Forman is entranced by Karin Wilson. Who needs to know more?"

"My parents, for instance, and I run a close second."

"You're such a stickler for details! Do you know that about yourself? I do."

"If I am, it's to support the fluff with which you so easily dispense reality."

"Do I really give that impression?" Alex asked, in mock dismay.

"Kind of, at times."

"Are you forgiving of it?"

"I'm afraid so—most of the time, anyway."

"Well then, given that, maybe we should know something more about each other. I'll go first as a warm-up. I have a brother, Greg, two years older than me, and he's in medical school. My father is an engineer, although an out of work one. Medical school is expensive, so my father did a creative job change. This is a family secret, so you become part of the family when I tell you he got involved in rum running from Canada. He had limited involvement; he did the communications in Czech between himself and a Czech Canadian, so the authorities did not understand the communications. He didn't handle the goods or traffic them, and he wasn't armed or involved in any rough stuff. It paid well, but my mother was so worried that if he was found out he could go to jail or, even worse, be deported. She begged him to stop, and finally he did. My mother is a theatrical agent; she works for an artist management bureau. That's it for us. Now it's your turn."

"I'm an only child. My mother is Swedish, and she was a classical singer, but she now gives voice lessons. My father is English; he is also a musician and teaches piano. They met when my mother went to England as a young voice student to audition for the music conservatory, and the person that was supposed to accompany her got sick at the last minute. She would have missed the audition if it weren't for my father, who bravely volunteered to accompany her. She was so nervous; they were only allowed time for one run-through, even though they'd never played together before. To calm her he said, 'Don't worry, I won't let you down. I'll follow you.' He has been doing that ever since. My mother is lively and adventuresome, my father less so, but he follows her lead.

"Now that we know so much about each other, we can face the world!"

"Let's just meet my parents first, then, maybe, the world."

He laughed. "You worry too much"

"And you should worry more! Here's my address. Just press the apartment button and I'll buzz you in. Wait for me in the lobby, and I'll come down to get you."

THE DOORBELL RANG SUNDAY AT FIVE THIRTY, AND I buzzed Alex into the lobby. The elevator seemed to take forever as I waited for it to arrive, and the ride down lasted an eternity as well. Then I saw Alex waiting by the door, holding flowers. "Happy birthday, Karin. This is for you," he said, bending down and giving me a kiss, "and the flowers are for your mother. I have a little something for your father as well, its some wine,—don't worry, my father made it, that's allowed."

I took his hand and we stepped into the elevator. He put his arm around me and said, "There, now I feel better. How do I look?"

"Irresistible!" We both laughed.

As I opened the door to our apartment, I heard my mother coming down the hall to welcome us while my father is waiting nearby in the living room. My mother extended her hand and said, "How nice that you could come." Alex handed her the flowers and said, "Thank you for inviting me."

The three of us moved a little awkwardly to the living, where I formally introduced Alex to them. My mother smiled warmly, but my father was holding back. Alex handed him the bottle of his father's wine and said, "My father makes this with a friend who has a press. My father thinks they are making a good non-vintage wine. I hope you like it."

My father nodded, still without a smile. "Please thank your father. We'll have it with dinner tonight."

I wondered how this was going to go when my mother, sensing that a slight thaw was needed, said, "Please sit down, Alex. I've made a few appetizers, so let's have a glass of your father's wine with it." I felt that this invitation to sit was the start of the pre-dinner grilling of Alex. I worried about how he would handle questions from my father, and how his response in the face of adversity might affect me here or anywhere else I could possibly find myself with Alex. Outcomes are transient no matter where you are.

My father looked at Alex with a critical eye as he fired the usual opening salvo of questions. "So, tell me, Alex, what do you do?" Alex told him with more detail than he had shared with me. I tried not to stare at Alex, but I was pleased to see that his handsome face was in total control as my father held him in the witness box for further questioning. At that point, the judging was far from over. My father continued. "What does your father do?"

"My father is an engineer. His specialty is bridges."

"I've never met anyone who does that. It sounds technical and demanding."

"It is, but at the moment he's out of work."

"Ah, yes, as so many others. Does he do anything else in the meantime?"

"Yes, he had a job in refreshment distribution." Quickly followed by, "My brother is in medical school, and my father took up the job slack to pay tuition. But then my brother got a part-time job in the hospital lab, at which point my father thought it best to go back to pursuing jobs in engineering."

Having taken a sip of the wine, my father said, "This is a nice wine. Please thank him for us."

My mother, full of questions that I'm sure were far too personal to ask, instead asked, "What does your mother do?"

"She's an agent for a theatrical artist booking firm."

"Ah, we are in the arts, as well, music to be exact. Thankfully we have managed fairly well through the hard times. People still want and take music lessons, and we love what we do, so we consider ourselves fortunate. Karin has sidestepped the tradition by going into the literary arts; in time she may want a degree when things settle down." I'm starting to fidget a little at the topic of discussion. Just before I melt into the couch, a reprieve came when there was a ding from the kitchen and my mother said, "I think we can come to the table now. Dinner is ready." I looked at Alex, thinking the condemned man is about to have his last meal. I took the warm hand of my gladiator into my cold one and, with the formalities over; we followed my parents into the dining room.

The flowers Alex brought were on the table, and father lit the candles as mother and I brought in the roast duck along with my other favorites. Mother told Alex, "A friend of ours raises ducks on Long Island, and so we benefit from her skills on special occasions." Mother quartered the duck and served Alex and my father, then me, and herself last. The roasted potatoes and stewed red cabbage were passed around. Wine was poured and glasses were raised in a happy birthday toast to me. During dinner, conversation was a bit guarded on both sides. After the dishes were cleared, I sat back down next to Alex, who smiled at me as he rested his hand on my thigh. I gave him a warning look, but he ignored me. It occurred to me then that Alex was a bit of an opportunist. Alex probably saw it as his reward for his earlier fortitude during the pre-dinner grilling. Father brought the coffee from the kitchen, and mother carried the cake with twenty-one candles as they sang happy birthday. With the cake in front of me, my father said, "Before you blow out the candles, be careful what you wish for—it may come true." I smiled at him, closed my eyes for a moment, then took a deep breath and blew them out, all except for one. Mother put the plates and the knife in front of me as I reconsidered my wish and then quickly blew the straggler into darkness. As I took the little candles out of the cake, I saw the little black holes they left behind and I wondered how they will be filled.

We talked about the hopeful prospects for the year ahead, reassuring ourselves that things can only get better. It was nearly ten o'clock when Alex said he should leave, hoping he has not overstayed his welcome. He thanked my parents for a lovely evening, and they said they hoped to see him again soon as I helped him into his coat. I went with Alex down to the lobby. While we were in the elevator, he reached into his coat pocket and pulled a small package wrapped in brown paper. He said, "I know you'll enjoy this, but don't open it now. Wait until I've left. I'll see you on Saturday." He gave me a kiss and said, "Happy birthday, Karin." And then he was gone. Sitting down in the lobby, I opened the gift. It was a book, *The Art of Architecture in Prague*. I wondered about the wish I made and my father's words.

Back in the apartment, my parents were at the piano, warmed by the wine, playing and singing a duet. I walked to my room and put the book away. I quietly went into the kitchen and closed the door to wash the dishes without interrupting their performance. I saw that Alex had left a few sips of coffee; he was the only one who did not take cream. I raised the cup to my lips, drinking from the same spot where he drank, finishing the remainder and wondering with new apprehension where all this was going. Our casual friendship had rapidly turned into something more than I could handle. Alex was nice, and he was fun to be with, although he could get pushy with his assumptions that I would be a part of his plans. My life hadn't exactly been lived on the edge of excitement, at least not until now.

The week felt unusually long, but then Saturday seemed to come too quickly when it was time to meet Alex at the school cafeteria. I had just started to unbutton my coat when Alex came up behind me and said, "You can button that up again. I'm taking you home for lunch." When I spun around and he saw the surprise in my face, he continued, "Yes, to meet my parents, one good turn deserves another. They are expecting us."

"You can't just do that." I gasped. "I'm not dressed to meet company."

Alex waved his hand dismissively. "They're not company, they're my parents, and with luck my brother Greg will be there as well."

"You keep springing things on me with no forewarning."

"That's what life is—you are meant to live it with no forewarning."

"Do they speak English?"

"Good heavens, yes. Their grammar is better than mine."

"What have you told them about me?"

"The truth!"

"And what might that be?"

"That you are the most beautiful, the most intelligent, the smartest, and the funniest girl I know. And that I like you a lot."

"Oh, thank you, and how am I supposed to live up to that?"

"Just be you!"

"I'm afraid that's all I can be on such short notice."

We entered a nice older building on the upper west side with some iron filigree work supporting the stairwell bannister. I was sensitive to things like that now. On the second floor, Alex opened a door with his key, calling out, "We're here."

A woman with short wavy hair in a stylish bob and bright red lipstick came bustling down the hallway of the apartment, hastily tying the belt of an embroidered silk robe in the Oriental style. She greeted me energetically, saying, "I'm sorry, I was still getting ready for your visit." Alex gave her a quick hug that she returned with a quick kiss on his cheek.

"Come in, come in Alex, make your friend comfortable while I finish dressing."

The living room was in a state of total confusion. Books were piled everywhere, on the coffee table, on the end tables, and there were several stacks on the floor against the wall. Alex plumped the cushions of a chair for me to sit in, then he pulled over a footstool and sat down in front of me. Alex smiled at me, and I relaxed a little, enough to smile back at him. We hesitated with any conversation when his mother bounced into the room and said, "I sent Harold out for lunch a while ago, I don't know what's keeping him." Alex got up and let his mother sit down on the stool, still buttoning her blouse. She said, "Come now, Alex, introductions, please."

"Mother, this is Karin."

"Oh, yes, you did tell me that." She turned back to me. "He's fond of you, you know, but I guess you already know that, so naturally we are happy to meet you. Alex, dear, put some wine out, the glasses are already on the table." Turning back to me again, she went on,. " Now tell me, how did you two first meet, and where was it? Alex must have told me, but I'd like to hear it from you as well."

She delivered all of this in slightly accented English with an air of flightiness. Just as I began, the apartment door opened and a man I presumed was Alex's father arrived laden with delicatessen packages. She jumped up to relieve him of the packages. She called over her shoulder, "Excuse me, Karin, while I attend to this."

Alex's father came into the living room, "You must be Alex's friend that we have been hearing about."

"Yes," I smiled. "That might be me. Hello, Mr. Forman. I'm Karin."

"Welcome to our home, Karin," he cast a furtive glance around the piles of books. "Such as it is."

Just then Alex came and said, "Greg just called, he can't make lunch today."

There was so much activity in the apartment that I was afraid to start a sentence, thinking it would be interrupted before I could finish it. Alex's mother called from the kitchen, "Okay, children, lunch is ready!" Alex and his father ushered me to the dining room we enter a scene of tranquility. His mother had set the table with a beautiful embroidered tablecloth and elegant plates and silverware. Filled wine glasses await us as we sit down.

"Alex, would you get the horseradish for the roast beef sand-wiches, please? Aside from that, I think we have everything. Karin, I hope you aren't a vegetarian—I should have asked."

I smiled. "No, I'm not. I eat everything except organ meats."

"Well then you're safe." She laughed musically as she passed large sliced dill pickles and pickled vegetables. The only non-human sound to come from his mother is her wrist full of silver bracelets which seemed to speak for her in her rare moments of silence. On the other hand, his father was rather quiet; probably accustomed to the likelihood that any of his sentences would also be interrupted. He looked at me and, when Alex's mother had taken a bite from a sandwich, asked, "Have you known Alex long?"

"I guess he told you we met at the university some months ago."

"Oh yes, I do remember that now. Do you want to be an archi-tect as well?"

"No, I studied English literature, but I find that of little use at the moment."

"Oh, no, Karin," his mother says, "you mustn't feel that way, literature is the backbone of culture. I recently became interested in philosophy, and I now read all I can on the subject. I don't understand it all, but then, that's the point, isn't it?"

"I don't know much about the subject, I can recognize some of the big names. My literature studies at the time didn't dwell on it in any depth."

"You see, that's how it is these days. It should be part of everyone's studies, and it is after all the cornerstone of learning."

"Now, Bettina," his father interrupted, "it takes more than one cornerstone to make a building, and that's only one of them." He smiled at her as if in apology for imposing a different view of the subject.

Her response was "Alex, please make us some coffee and bring the dessert in please." Alex looked at me and smiled as if to say, 'I'm the dutiful handmaiden of a son' as he left for the kitchen. His mother turned to me and said, "He's so nice, we love him dearly. I'm sure with his fine mind he will be a great architect one day." Resting her chin in her cupped hand, she held a stray stand of hair away from her face and asked, "Don't you agree?"

"Oh yes, I'm sure he will be."

Mr. Forman added, "Whether great or not, he'll be a fine architect." Looking at me, he said "When he sets his mind on something, he sees it through, obstacles be damned."

Mrs. Forman added, "Well, yes, most of the time, anyway, but he does have a habit of changing his mind when one least expects it. Sometimes himself included!" She laughed.

Alex returned with a tray of plates with a creamy vanilla pudding and cups of fragrant coffee that was richer than I was used to. Mrs. Forman passed a small pitcher of a strawberry sauce she made

21

and instructed me to pour it over the pudding, saying, "It's a refreshing and harmonious mingling of flavors. The tartness balances out the sweetness."

I was struck by this description because of how well it applied to Alex's family at every turn, including the interrupted sentences.

Alex finished his coffee a little more quickly than customary and said, "I promised I would see Karin home."

His mother said in protest, "But we are just getting to know each other What's your hurry?"

"I have a lot studying to do, so I have to get back."

Mr. Forman raised a hand to gently restrain his wife's protests. "Bettina, I'm sure we'll be seeing Karin again, so for now we'll have to let them go."

Alex's mother looked crestfallen until Alex bent down and kissed her cheek, saying, "I'll be back soon." Alex quickly pulled my chair out, and I had just enough time to thank them for lunch and my visit when Alex was shuffling me down their hallway to the front door. At the elevator he said, "You were a big hit thank you for coming on such short notice."

"Everything you do is on short notice," I replied dryly, and he quickly planted a kiss on my lips as we got into the elevator. These quick kisses were just one of them.

From the time that Alex and I met to meeting our respective families, there hardly seemed to be enough time to reflect on these events and where they were going. Mr. Forman's words about Alex came to mind, ". . . and obstacles be damned!" How prophetic.

THE NEXT TIME I SAW ALEX, HIS FIRST QUESTION WAS, "Do you have a passport?"

"No, I don't. Why would I want one?"

"To go to Prague! Remember, we talked about it?"

"I only remember you talking about it."

"Yes, and you were to think about it. Given the amount of time you have had, I assume that has been done and we are now ready to get our passports."

"I haven't come to any decision how could I?"

"Well, while you're in the process of deciding, you can get your passport. You don't have to use it right away."

We met during the week and went to apply for our passports. An alarmingly short time later, I received mine at home. When I opened mine to sign it, my photo had captured a surprised look on my face, a look I was sure to match if I ever used the passport.

One day, not long after the passports had arrived, we were sitting in Horn and Hardart when Alex brushed our coffee cups aside. He laid out some papers on the table, flattening them with the side of his hands. He quickly looked at me with a smile and said, "I've been looking into our overseas passage possibilities. I have found a good prospect for us. We can work our way over," he ran his finger along a line on the page, saying, "Here we are, on the SS *Stimins*. It's a freighter sailing in late July. I called them and we can book with them. I can go as a deckhand, and you can assist the cook in the kitchen. It may make some unscheduled stops after it leaves New York, but it will get us to Hull, England, from there we go on to Prague, mostly by train. It's perfect timing for us."

Speechless, I couldn't even look at him. I stared at the empty cups he had moved aside for this display of an impossible series of events in which he has me playing a key role.

I sat twirling a small hank of my hair between my fingers, a habit I use as some displaced energy in times of indecision, such as now, and I felt like the whole world was awaiting my decision.

"I haven't even said I would go with you," I said quietly.

"You've been with me so far, why stop now?"

"Alex, you assume far too much, too fast, too often."

"I like you, Karin, and if even for just now you like me, the rest could follow."

"How can you be so sure of yourself?"

"Karin, if you don't like it once you are there, you can come back. I'm not tying you to anything. Just try it for a month as a vacation. If you want to come home after that, I promise I won't pressure you to stay."

"Alex, one thing I do know about you is that you excel in pressure."

"Give it a month, you'll love it."

"I have to speak to my parents first."

"Of course. But do it quickly."

"You see, Alex, that's just what I mean." He took my hand and gave it a squeeze; I felt that more than my hand was being squeezed.

That Sunday, as my parents and I started our second cup of coffee, I brought up the dreaded subject of Prague. My father, who was reading the paper, tipped the top corner of it over. Looking at me over his reading glasses, he said, "Surely you haven't been keeping up with the news. Parts of Europe are in turmoil, and that may just be the beginning of it." He suddenly dropped the paper into his lap, crumpling it with his hands, which was very unlike him. "I don't see this as an auspicious time to visit Europe. It's just too uncertain to be playing tourist."

"I would not be a tourist, I would be living with Alex's aunts and uncle. Besides it's only for a month."

My father harrumphed. "A lot can happen in a month!"

My mother's Swedish sense of neutrality rose on my behalf. "Thomas, I'm sure she'll be fine. Alex will look after her, and it is only for a month. It will be her great adventure. That's what youth is for; before one gets bogged down with a family and responsibilities, let her spread her wings. She's an American citizen; she can always come home if your views become real concerns."

"Yes, but who will look after her? Alex is just a young man. She could get bogged down over there with more than family to worry about. Let her spread her wings here." At this, he turned to me. "I won't forbid you, Karin, but I won't approve either. You're twenty-one now and must be responsible for your actions. That's my last word on that."

Mother patted my hand and made a small grimace with a quick tilt of her head toward my father, who had gone back to reading the paper. I noticed a slight tremor as my father turned the page of the newspaper.

My mother got up and cleared the dishes. I stood as well and joined her in the kitchen. There she turned to me and said, "Do be careful, and we'll want to meet his parents before this goes any further." I nodded, both grateful and terrified at her support and my father's comments.

I invited Alex and his parents over for coffee and cake the following Sunday morning. It was staged to be sure. Two sets of parents in flux over a pair of children who wanted suddenly to leave the nest with untested wings, while their parents engaged in the eternal questions of readiness.

The parents on both sides shared a few similar concerns about Alex's reassurances. The Prague relatives are more of a comfort to my mother than to my father. Overall, there was a general feeling of "why not," and the newspaper's concerns about turmoil in the region seemed like unrealistic worries. The meeting in the overall went well, despite remaining reservations, mine included.

Later that week, when Alex and I met for lunch, he said, "I want to hear a final yes from you. Also, I forgot to ask, did your parents like me? Or worse still, did they dislike me?"

"It's not a matter of liking or disliking, really. They only have one of me, and they have centered their concerns on that, rather than on you."

All doubts aside, maybe this was to be the big something that I was looking for in my life. Other than that, I have little idea what prompted me to say, "Yes, for a month."

"I can't ask for more."

"But you will, I know."

He put his hand on my shoulder and said, "You won't regret it, Karin. We could even get married, you know." We both laughed at that.

"No, one life-changing event at a time, please. You've pushed your luck way too far already."

Alex's excitement was barely contained. "Our next task is to book the jobs on the SS *Stimins*. I'll take care of that. You need to pack just a few warm clothes, and prepare for rain as well."

I caught my breath, realizing what I had just decided. So much of it now increasingly out of my hands.

Alex didn't notice. He was already thinking of the next things to do. "Can you get home on your own today? I have things to do for us."

I nodded and said, "If I can't get home on my own, we are both in a lot of trouble, and I had better not even think of going to Prague."

On the bus ride, I looked out the dirty rain-spattered window and tried to see beyond it. I couldn't.

New York City to Hull, England

WITH THE RESERVATIONS MADE and some others brushed aside, one morning at seven a.m. Alex and I arrived at the docks. We sought out the SS *Stimins* and found a well-worn, weathered freighter. As we walked up the gangplank of the SS *Stimins* a hot muggy wind blew in off the water. We were shown to the captain's cabin. He was a large man with a dark bushy mustache and eyebrows to match. Seated at his desk, he gave us a hard look as he reached out for the papers and passports Alex passed to him. Before he looked at the papers, he spent a little more time looking at me. Then he asked, "Are you prone to seasickness?" Alex assured him we weren't. Another rash assumption on his part, made in haste on my behalf. The captain stamped the two sets of papers, one of which he kept and the other Alex pocketed. Addressing Alex, the captain said, "You are deckhand to anyone needing it, and you, Miss, will be at the service of our cook, Olga. Also, you two do not leave the ship until we reach Hull, England. Is that understood?" Alex nodded again for both of us, a surety since the captain held on to our passports. The captain called someone in to show us where we were to drop off our belongings before we reported for our duties for the crossing to England.

I met Olga, my new advisor, in the galley. She was a large woman from the Ukraine, and she wore a sleeveless less-than-pristine white blouse that exposed her flushed, heavyset upper arms and had a pronounced strain at the buttons from her ample bosom. She wore once-white pants under an apron that had clearly seen a great deal of kitchen work. She showed me to our shared sleeping quarters, where I was to have the top bunk in a claustrophobic cabin with a single small light. She showed me a locker in which I could put my things, although much of the space was already taken up with her belongings. Then we went to the galley, where large pots of water were set to boil. She showed me a sack of potatoes to be washed for the pot. This small hot cramped kitchen was to be my workspace for the uncertain days to come. I learned that we would be doing all of the hot water cooking and deep-frying in port. Food cooked in this way was reheated in the oven for meal times at sea. She emphasized that the lurching of the ship at sea required this routine. She offered no words of comfort for me as an untried ocean sailor. Breakfast had already been served that day, so a deep metal sink with dishes, pots, and pans from that meal awaited me. Alex and I had only allowed enough time for a quick cup of coffee before coming to the pier, so I was quite hungry by the time I finished washing the pots and pans. When I was done, Olga gave me a thick heavy mug of coffee and a slice of cold buttered toast. The potatoes were at a full boil when she threw in a handful of salt, saying, "You must step back when you do this." I jumped back as the water frothed with the addition of the salt. I wondered what Alex was doing, and if he were now living his dream up on deck.

The galley was not spared the ship's noises, of which there were many—banging, clanging, whistles, and horns, all of which were part of the workings of the ship. Just when I thought I had heard them all, a loud long blast announced our departure. Olga smiled and said we were about to leave. My knees felt weak, and so did my resolve for what lay ahead. Olga's body threw off nearly as much heat as the oven did as she showed me where things were and told me the sequence of my duties. The crew ate in shifts in the small table/bench area set aside in the galley. The captain ate in his cabin or, in stormy weather, in the wheelhouse on the bridge of the ship. When she said we were getting ready for lunch, I moved to set the table. Olga just looked at me, saying, "This isn't a restaurant. The tin plates are stacked there. Each person takes one, and I dish out the food. They take their places and eat without talk, and then go back to work. One reason for the quiet is that not all have the same language." I waited to see Alex, but he was one of the last to come to eat, looking exhausted. He smiled at me and gave me a two-fingered salute. Then he sat down to eat as silently as all the others before him, the only difference being that he gave me a kiss before he left.

These routines were repeated with little variation for several days, when Olga brightened one morning and said, "We're coming into port now."

Thank God. I was grateful that we had avoided storms at sea. When I told Olga I would pack to get ready to leave, she laughed. "Not yet, you don't, —we're pulling into Halifax, Nova Scotia, England is on the other side of the Atlantic."

I can't remember ever feeling so much disappointment over unexpected news. I again felt my knees go weak.

"Come on, Karin. We have to start boiling, cooking, and fry-ing." I looked down at the well-used apron she had given, wadded in my hands. I pulled it back on and let out a sigh of frustration. In port now, the floor of the galley practically bounced under our feet as heavy wooden crates were hoisted into the hold of the ship.

"A little bouncing is okay in port, but tossing at sea is not." Olga said.

We worked feverishly in the galley, boiling, cooking, and frying as if our lives depended on it. Who knows, maybe they will. In addition to the cargo already taken on, we took on a full load of coal and provisions for the rest of the trip across the Atlantic. I had just thrown a small hand full of salt into the potato pot when I heard Alex's voice outside the galley door asking Olga where to put crates of fresh produce, dairy, and meat. When he finished, Olga handed him a mug of tea the color of weak coffee, and she put a tin of sugar and a can of condensed milk on the table in front of him. She saw me eyeing Alex and pointed at the stove, where I resumed boiling, cooking, and frying. I turned to look at Alex a few times, and between sips he gave me a small smile as he slowly shook his head. He put his cup in the sink and leaned over and gave me a kiss as he was leaving. Olga said, "Do you have one of those for me, too?" He blew her a kiss and left as Olga gave me a sideways glance and laughed.

Some five hours later, some heavy sea swells rocked the ship heavily. I held onto anything that was not hot, of which there was little in this galley. The instability gave credence to Olga's in-port routine. As I sat down, feeling green about the gills, Olga looked at me. "Tsk, tsk, tsk, this is nothing, little one! Don't you get seasick in my galley, you hear?" I was holding onto the table's edge, hoping desperately to comply with her last command.

The day's routine for us started by getting up at four in the morning to get breakfast ready for the first shift at five. Olga heated up the large iron sheet griddle and whacked a large glob of bacon fat to bubble. Once it had melted and spread out, she dumped a huge supply of chopped onions. Next to the onions, bacon was frying, and I slid sliced cold boiled potatoes into the sizzling bacon grease. Eggs

31

were fried on demand. The intense smell of the onions in this small hot space made me feel nauseous. Olga nodded toward the entrance and said, "Get a breath of air." When I stepped out into the fresh air, however, the movement of the ship made the horizon seesaw, and I got sick on the spot. I was holding onto the doorframe when Alex appeared. Seeing what happened, he fetched a pail of water and washed away my *mal de mer*. He embraced me and said, "This is the worst of it, I promise." By now I knew to take Alex's promises with a handful of salt. It wasn't the worst of it, but I did get used to the pitching of the ship, and my resolve strengthened as my life at sea flowed slowly behind.

It was almost smooth sailing across the Atlantic Ocean. We experienced one bad storm, where we served cold food a day and a half.

Once, on one of those days with calmer water, I went out on deck for a breath of fresh air. I leaned my arms on the railing, focused on my folded hands, and in a panic state of mind, I asked myself, Why am I here, why am I doing this? Everything and everyone I love I have left behind to leap into the unknown with someone I hardly know. How will I handle myself and how will I get along? I looked at the framed scene that my arms and hands had made over the vibrant ocean below. Alarmed at the energy of the water as it slapped at the side of ship and reminded of how far and fast I was being transported, I wondered, if I would find that big something I was looking for.

Olga was now looking for me, calling me into the galley, where I asked no questions, but simply followed instructions, as was expected of me. When I turned to go back to work, I wondered if Alex had any misgivings of what we were doing. I almost never saw him to ask him about his thoughts, except at meal times when our mute exchanges were brief. I so much wanted to get off this freighter, no matter what awaited me. After that, however, I labored constantly under Olga's directives. As the days wore on, I was sure I was at one with those birds that were reputed to never land but to fly all their lives. One morning Olga said, "We're approaching Ireland," which had no meaning to me aside from Irish stew. We had just a quick stop in Cork to load and unload some goods, then we sailed out into the Atlantic again and on through the English Channel. After bouncing around in the North Sea we came to Hull, England, the land of redemption for me. This was where I folded up my well-seasoned apron and bid Olga a fond farewell. I think toward the end she liked me, because she wrapped her ample arms around me. Pressing me into her bosom, she gave me a kiss and said, "Take care little one, and have a good life. Maybe we'll meet again."

Quietly I thought it would not in fact be a good life if I had to relive this experience. My feet were anxious for terra firma, and they hurried me down the gangplank to wait for Alex to retrieve our passports and me. It felt as if the ground I stood on was in motion. Just then Alex came bounding down the gangplank. He rushed up to me and said, "We made it!" The immigration officer stamped our passports, smiled, and said, "Welcome to England."

HULL TO PRAGUE

ALEX EXPLAINED that we would take a ferry from Hull to Rotterdam in Holland. When I groaned, he said, "As paid passengers this time." On the ferry I relaxed into his arms and slept, the quietest and longest sleep since I left New York City.

Upon seeing our American passports, the customs and immigration officials stamped them and handed them back to us with a smile, saying, "Welcome to Holland."

We moved quickly across Holland, and we entered Germany after a warm welcome at the border. For the next fifteen or so hours, we traveled by train, changing three times along the way. After wending our way through Germany, we finally arrived at the Czech border. There we were asked the purpose of our visit. Alex said we were tourists, and after carefully looking us over and closely examining our passports, the Czech customs and immigration officer stamped them and handed them back to us without a smile or any sense of welcome. This was my first taste of the Europe I was to be in, and beyond the wonder of it all, it left an unpleasant aftertaste. I couldn't quite put my finger on it, but it lingered. I decided it was just the weariness from some 26 hours of travel since we had left the good ship SS *Stimins* before finally arriving at the train station in Prague.

Alex called his aunt, and he was told to wait in the train station for them to come for us. As we sat and waited, we compared notes on our stint aboard the SS *Stimins*, since we hardly talked during the voyage. Alex's hands were rough and a bit raw from his deck-hand jobs. My only souvenir of the crossing was the baked-in smell of fried onions and bacon grease in my hair and on my skin. We both needed a good head-to-toe soak in a hot bath. As we waited, we took in the newness of our surroundings. For me, of course, the language was completely new, and the subdued colors of the clothing and the homogeneousness of the people was also quite different from New York City. I did not see any people of African or Asian heritage, or any other noticeably ethnic people. I think we were the most ethnic foreigners present. I had never realized what it meant to live in the melting pot that was New York City.

All of a sudden, a middle-aged woman rushed up to us, followed by a friendly looking man. They had recognized Alex from photos sent from his parents. It is his Aunt Beata and his Uncle Jiri. Repeated hugs and kisses take place as Beata wipes her eyes, and Alex introduced me. I could pick out my name, but I have no idea what else he said, because he said it all in Czech. Despite surprised looks, I was warmly embraced as they both greeted me in English. A big relief!

Looking down at my shoes, spattered with food and grease, I thought that surely the worst was over, and that we both would get that hot bath to wash away all of those memories I didn't want to evoke ever again. They relieved us of our baggage and we followed them out of the train station to a hub of streetcars. After boarding a streetcar, Aunt Beata sat next to me while Uncle Jiri and Alex stood in front of us. Uncle Jiri was talking to Alex, and I supposed it would be the latest news and updates to our arrival. Aunt Beata patted my hand and said in halting English, "This must be all strange to you, even us. But you will get used to it, and to us too, we hope." She had a nice warm welcoming manner that felt reassuring as I looked up at Alex and smiled. He leaned over to my ear and said, "Welcome to Prague."

Prague, August 1938

OUR HOST AND HOSTESS motioned for us to follow them as they stepped off at the next tram stop. We entered a lovely tree-lined street in the old part of the city, with well-cared-for older houses and gardens. We turned into one of them. When we came in, the other aunt, Sabina, greeted us warmly. I felt she had a special smile for me, maybe it was just that she hadn't been expecting me. Alex was embraced as a long-lost nephew. This was their first meeting of Alex, and it felt like a momentous event for everyone. Beata interrupted by showing us to a table set for a late lunch. There was smoked fish, pickled herring, and open-faced cheese sandwiches accompanied by slightly chilled bottles of pilsner beer. It felt so nice to sit down at a table with a tablecloth and flowers, to drink out of real glasses and eat from real china plates once again. During lunch, Jiri was kind enough to speak to Alex in English, mostly talking about school and the papers that had arrived for him to fill out before registering at the university. Jiri told Alex I don't know how many times to be sure to take his passport with him. I was also told to have mine on my person at all times. Nobody elaborated on the reasoning for this, and neither Alex nor I thought to ask about it. Alex updated everyone about his parents, how they were, what they were doing, and how much they wished to see them. Sabina told us that the three of them had planned to immigrate to America after his parents, but when they delayed because of her bookstore, they had missed the quota when they were finally ready to go. So now they were not able to go to America. Aunt Beata made coffee, and the heavenly aroma of a dark roast in beautiful china cups and accompanied by a creamy cake was sheer ambrosia after our trip across the Atlantic.

Surely, I would get used to everything here even more quickly than I had anticipated. Some things would require discovery; for example, that hot bath could not happen at the turn of the hot water tap. Taking a bath required a bit of planning. The first step was to turn on a gas water heater above the end of the tub; after an hour or so, it heated just under half a tub of hot water. Hair was washed at the kitchen sink, using a small hot water heater above the sink.

Their house was old, and it had been in their family for three generations by that time. It was originally built as a pension, what we would call a rooming house, where single rooms were rented and, if meals were included, they were served in a small dining room off the kitchen. They tell us that their rooms are now difficult to rent because those seeking rooms look at the more modern accommodations with better facilities in the newer parts of the city. So the small dining room housed Jiri's piano and violin, instead, and he gave his music lessons there. At that time, in addition to Alex and me on the second floor, they had just one roomer above us on the third floor. They described the young man as a music student who only rarely ran into them at the kitchen table for breakfast. To lower his rent, he helped out in the house and garden. The aunts tell us his name is Simon and he is quiet except for his practicing his cello, which of course they love and hope we won't mind.

Beata showed us to our room. I didn't know what Alex told them about me and about us, but it must have included something more than friendship to his open-minded aunts and uncle. After they left us to get settled, I looked at the narrow bed and then at Alex, who smiled sheepishly and said, "They're not prudes, and I hope we aren't either." He meant only me, of course.

"And if I were, where would a prude sleep?"

"In the bed and I on the floor, but thank goodness that's not the case." Once again, he had rushed to judgment and I didn't know how I could respond. That was the last word on the subject from either of us. Our room on the second floor was in the back of the house, with a window looking out on a small garden with two pear trees. *I can do anything for a month*, I told myself. We put our things in the wardrobe. Alex held up his stiff paint-spattered deckhand pants and said, "What do you think?"

"I don't think there's any water heater big enough to make those wearable again." He laughed and asked, "Should I save them for the return voyage?"

"Definitely not!"

I liked the big kitchen, which was the hub of family life. Jiri kept the dining room door closed when he gave lessons, but one could still hear if it was a beginner or someone who had been studying for a while.

While Jiri and Alex worked together to complete the university papers, I put in my bid to have a bath and wash my hair. Beata showed me how to light the fire under the bathtub water heater. Washing my hair turned out to be a surprising introduction to the hard water of Prague, in contrast to the soft water of New York City. My straw-colored hair took on the texture of straw, one of the many things I would have to get used to here. With the smells of Olga's galley washed away, I happily helped with dinner, which was a curried lamb stew with root vegetables and a salad of tomatoes and onions. Sabina made a vanilla pudding that was served with a strawberry sauce, shades of lunch at Alex's house, but here, the wine was bought. At dinner they told me about Sabina's used English books and music shop, and how it came into being after Sabina's piles of her own books filled their house. I again thought of Alex's mother— some things truly run in the family. I smiled and laughed. After dinner, Jiri read the newspaper, just as my father did.

By that time, the kitchen sink water heater had recovered from my earlier draining of it, so we had hot water as we did the dishes. They used a little wire cage with a handle that contained a bar of brown soap that they swished around in the dishpan of hot water. When Jiri and Alex were done with the papers and we with the dishes, we drank some coffee that was sure to keep me up through the middle of the night. After coffee, Jiri played his violin for a while, and Alex and I said goodnight. We slowly walked the stairs to our room to the strains of a nocturne. The toilet was down the hall in a separate little room, where I found the old wall-hung water closet over an antique wooden toilet seat. The toilet bowl had the words Stoke on Trent imbedded in it in blue. When I came back to our room, Alex said, "I'll toss you for it!" but then he said, "I'm too tired for that tonight. Should we just call it even and go to sleep?"

I was too tired to think another thought as I climbed into bed after Alex. I slept the night through and woke up to birds singing in the garden. Alex was already up, so I was alone for a few minutes as I came fully awake. Soon after, Alex came in with a large cup of tea for me. As I sat up in bed, he said, "I'm off to the university to register. If you go out, take this with you, it's the address here, either that or leave a trail of bread crumbs I'll see you later, Goldilocks . . . or was it Gretel that did that?" He shrugged and gave me a quick kiss, then said, "Take care."

As Alex left, the sound of the closing door made me think of the harsh, spring-loaded closing of the narrow metal cabin door on the SS *Stimins*, where night after night I laid on the hard, narrow top bunk attempting to visualize a beautiful breezy meadow so that I could fall asleep. It was incredibly difficult in the stuffy air of the cabin, laden with kitchen smells and shaken by Olga's reverberating snores.

I felt a smile come over me as I stretched my legs on the recently vacated bed. I thought about why I was here and not in my own bed at home. *It could be the big thing I've been looking for*, I told myself. That thought faded slowly as I looked around the room. I liked the window that let in the sunlight and the sounds of a bird singing its praises in the back garden. There was a small desk with a lamp and a chair by the window. My eyes wandered around the room, past the faded green-flowered wallpaper to the old wooden wardrobe with inlays of lighter and darker woods twisted into wreaths on the outside of the double doors, while the inside of the door held a speckled mirror. There was a small table next to the wardrobe draped with a pretty linen cloth with blue birds stitched in an oval. The aunts had put a blue vase with flowers on this table to welcome us. On the next wall was a two-cushion settee with a floor lamp next to it, then came the wall where our bed and two nightstands stood. On the floor next to our bed was an old Persian rug. The room's door had two coat hooks on it and a small-framed mirror for adjusting your hat. This is my new home.

I got out of the bed and stretched again, a full-body stretch like that of a cat waking from a nap. I opened the window to the back garden, dressed, and made my way down the creaky stairs to the kitchen.

HELLO PRAGUE

MY FIRST FULL DAY in Prague had begun. In the kitchen, a nicely set breakfast table greeted me. We ate fresh crispy rolls with home-made pear jam. It was so good that I could have eaten it by the spoonful. We also had strong coffee, poured along with heated milk into large coffee cups.

Sabina was ready to start her day in her used books store. She looked elegant in a rayon Art Nouveau print dress. She wore a neck-lace of large amber beads and under it a beautiful folded lorgnette on an elegant silver chain. Wide orange and green Lucite bracelets adorned her wrists. Her hair was pulled up in a loose topknot with an elegant Art Nouveau pick nestled in it. Her soft makeup comple-mented the look beautifully.

"Well, dears, I must go. I'm sure to have more sellers than buy-ers again today."

She put her hand on my arm and said, "Enjoy your first day in Prague. It's a beautiful city. I'm sure you won't want to leave at the end of a month." She patted my arm, got up, kissed Beata, and left.

Beata said, "Isn't she lovely? She has such an air about her. I'm just a crone compared to her."

"I wouldn't say that," I protested.

Looking up from his newspaper, Jiri said, "I can't count the times I have said the same, but now she has two people she won't listen to."

Beata traded her apron for her hat and jacket. Taking two shopping nets off a wall hook, she turned to me and said, "Are you ready for your first experience in Prague?" I nodded excitedly.

We walked the clean and quiet tree-lined neighborhood streets. Beata said, "At times, if you look up at the second story of some of the four-story houses, you will see beautifully painted scenes between the tall windows." They looked like delicate watercolors, but their themes of nature and figures had little to do with the facades. They seemed to have been put there just for the beauty of it. Then we turned into a street with some shops. I followed Beata into a bakery, where the lady greeted her warmly. Beata glanced at me every now and then as she mentioned my name. They were speaking in Czech, so I presumed she was telling her who I was. The lady smiled and gave me a wonderful marzipan strawberry. I admired it for its likeness to the real thing, and she motioned for me to eat it. I nearly forgot to separate the paper stem and leaf before it disappeared into my mouth. I wished I could tell her I have a weakness for marzipan. Beata bought more of those crispy rolls and some pastries.

Our next stop was the butcher shop. Beata again introduced me in Czech, after which there was a bit of conversation before Beata bought some veal sausages and quarter of a kilogram of salami. Then we went to the green grocer, where the lady behind the counter came out to greet me, looking me over from head to toe. I wondered what she thought of me, since Beata wasn't translating anything for me in the shop. Beata bought tomatoes, onions, a cucumber, and half a head of cabbage. I carried the shopping nets, both of which were nearly full.

We made one more stop where the specialty was coffee. The shop owner roasted the coffee himself, and he ground it to order right in front of you. Conversation here was limited due to the noise of the grinder, but I enjoyed the store nonetheless, with its delicious aromas. Our nets full, we walked home.

When we returned, Jiri left on his bicycle wagon to buy more wine and beer. Beata cut up the cabbage, which was put on a slow simmer with caraway seeds and a bay leaf. The custom in Prague was to have your biggest meal of the day at lunch. Beata said it was often the only hot meal of the day as well. That day, we had cabbage and potatoes, veal sausage, and beer followed by a bit of goat cheese.

Alex still had not returned when the three of us sat in the garden with coffee and shared pastries. They wanted to hear all about New York City, and about me and how Alex's parents were doing. I could tell from their expressions that they truly missed Alex's parents. Talking about it all so did I, but then again, I figured I would be back in a month telling them all about Beata, Jiri, and Sabina. *Would I long for Prague then?* I wondered. The three of us retired for a nap. I slept well until I felt a hand on my arm. As I opened my eyes, Alex said, "I found your trail of bread crumbs." He leaned over to kiss my forehead.

I sat up and asked, "How was school?"

"Confusing and much more rigid than my previous university. They copied down all my personal information as well as the information from my passport. Oddly enough, they asked me my religion. I wanted to say I am an atheist, but sensing the already heavy atmosphere I said none. That did not suffice. They asked if I were baptized, and where and in what church. I told them, and that seemed to fill the allotted space. So, I start tomorrow at nine! I have to go out to buy some books and supplies. Will you come with me?"

Alex had a city map on which Jiri had marked the streetcar lines. He also helped Alex with his list of where to go and what to get. We went into a utilitarian textbook store, where Alex asked if any of the books were in English. The nasty reply was, "No, and not in German, French, or Russian." Alex paid, and we left with his new tomes. The help at the next store was nicer. I guessed that they saw the list of items and figured he was new. Here, he got his notebooks, rulers, pens, nibs, and inks for his pens, as well as pencils and a slide rule. The clerk suggested a conversion table from metric into standard, a purchase Alex would later cherish. On our way back, we got lost once in the network of choices.

That night we dined on a tomato salad and well-buttered rolls with cheese, mustard, and salami, along with beer. We finished with coffee and pastries in the garden.

My first full day in Prague was drawing to a close. Tonight, Alex seemed less concerned about our sleeping arrangement than he did about his choice to study in Prague. I think he already sensed that it would be harder than he thought. It was still unclear how long he would be attending university here, but I knew that I would be going home in a month's time. In bed Alex took my hand and put it on his chest, saying, "What do you think of all this?"

"I think it is different. Some of it will take getting a bit used to like, the different venues for the completion of my ablutions," I laughed, "but with a bit of planning I'll get the hang of it. I like your aunts and uncle, they try so hard to make me feel at home, aside from us in the same bed, that is—that is still foreign to me."

"It needn't be, you know. Some things get less taking used to than others."

I blushed in the darkness and hurriedly said, "Good night, Alex!"

THE NEXT MORNING, I TOOK A WALK AFTER BREAKFAST to see what I could absorb on my own. I passed small shops that displayed some unusual and beautiful items in their window. I passed some people pushing a baby carriage filled with personal items, which seemed strange even for Prague. From what I could tell, there was a great regard for old and beautiful things, and many shops catered to people who were interested in buying or selling such things. I caught my breath when I came to a shop specializing in crystal ware. A huge crystal chandelier filled the large shop window. Its eighteen white candles lent a hint of another time period. Who could have owned it and why was it here, so out of place? I thought about how my parents and I had promised to write each other. It seemed like a good time to do that. I had the SS *Stimins* stories to share, as well as the wonderful things I was experiencing in Prague.

The next few days were long as the daily routine repeated itself. Then one night, over dinner, Alex asked me, "Have you seen Sabina's book store? That could be a fun outing for you."

I shook my head. "I don't read Czech, I would only be in the way."

Sabina jumped in. "Oh no, I specialize in used books in English, and I sell old sheet music as well. I would like you to come with me. Do you like to read?"

Alex interjected, "Karin has an English literature degree, so yes, she likes to read. She has a wide range of interests."

Sabina's eagerness brightens at this. She said, "You can help me put order into what is becoming an overwhelming task for me these days."

"I don't know how helpful I would be, but I would love to come to the shop with you."

The next morning I left the house with Sabina, feeling a little plain next to her bright fashion choices. The door of her shop read, "Specializing in used books in English and sheet music." The shop interior itself was as old as the building. Sabina gave it her touch of originality; she had hung once colorful, now faded, Chinese accordion paper swags from the ceiling. She had an old toy monkey hanging from the ceiling as well, just above her cash register, holding a faded Welcome sign. She showed me around the shelves, saying, "Some are catalogued, but when they come in so quickly I just put them on the shelves by subject. I'm sure you can put some order into the mess I have made."

"You certainly have an eclectic collection to deal with."

"This is nothing! Come into the back room," she exclaimed.

Stacks of books tied with string were piled haphazardly all over the storeroom. Little white slips of paper were stuck under many of the knots. Looking at some of the titles from one of the bound piles, I saw that the books ranged from gardening to stories of the great operas to a few volumes with the medical titles, such as *The Duodenal Ulcer, Its Diagnosis, and Treatment*. I looked at Sabina and pointed at that particular book. She shrugged helplessly and said, "Yes, I never know what will come in."

"But where do all these books come from?" I asked.

"These are troublesome and difficult times for some people. Those who can, try to sell everything to prepare to flee the danger."

"Who are these people, and why are they fleeing? What danger?"

"They're Jews mostly, worried what the future will bring."

"What's happening here?"

"The German anti-Semitic policies have spread and are making the lives of many difficult, and in some cases, even impossible. They sell whatever they can to get out."

"Where do they go?"

"A lot go to England, others will go anywhere just to stay one step ahead of persecution."

"But here in Prague?"

"We're neighbors to Germany, you know, and as all neighbors do, they tend to share their ideas over back yard fences. At times one doesn't even have to go to the fence; there are some Czech sympathizers here to carry that nasty message further into the society. Don't worry, Karin, you will be all right. You're an American, and you aren't Jewish. Besides, America is not involved, nor does it want to be. Now, how would you like to help me catalog the less controversial authors, such as Beatrix Potter?" That was a sobering shift from her earlier words.

With blank cards in front of me, she read out each title. "*The Tale of Peter Rabbit* by Beatrix Potter. Do you know anything about her?"

"Only that she was English, and she was a wonderful illustrator and a well-respected nature scientist. Among her many writings she also wrote a highly respected scientific work on mushrooms that she illustrated with beautiful watercolors."

"How wonderful. Would you write that down, please? Next, we have a book by Robert Southey. Can you tell me about him?"

"I'm no expert on children's literature, but I do know about him because of his associations with other famous English authors of his time. He was a prolific letter writer and literary scholar as well. He knew Portuguese and Spanish and translated some of those books into English."

"You are a treasure trove, I think it is called. Please write all of that down on the card. This book of his is *Goldilocks and The Three Bears*."

"Well, now you know about him," I said.

"Yes," said Sabina, turning and leaning on one of the less precarious stacks. "And now I would like to know more about you."

"There isn't much to tell, I'm afraid."

"Oh, I'm sure that isn't true."

"Let's go through the rest of the children's books before I bore you with my own story."

The children's books took the rest of the morning. We closed the shop for lunch and went home to a hot meal. As we had our coffee, Sabina again prodded me for my personal history.

I told them just enough to satisfy them before we went back to the shop. That evening at dinner, Alex said he wanted to resume our Sunday city walks. We enjoyed our first Sunday walk in Prague, although Alex more or less followed the way he knew from his daily ride to the university. On the way home, he had an idea of buying a used bicycle to get to school, which would be more convenient and would save time. It sounded like a good idea until he came home the following day with a bicycle and a job refurbishing old bicycles to be sold in the shop. He was now going to be at the university six days a week, and our Sunday walks were put on hold while he worked in the bicycle shop. Alex's studies were stressful, I think even more than he had anticipated. A mathematics class on statistics in particular worried him. He suffered evening after evening with things like standard deviation. He said he thought this would be difficult enough for him to grasp in English, let alone in Czech. I felt sorry for him, but he was still prepared to tough it out, no matter the cost.

On the next Sunday, the aunts tried to make it up to me by taking me along to church. Aside from the several crucifixes in the house, I had felt no religious fervor from any of them. I went along just for the company and the experience; the added incentive was that we stopped for a cognac and coffee on the way home.

I had been here just over a week and a half when I felt that this situation with Alex left us too little time together. He was always at school or working at the bicycle shop. Even when he was at home, he was always either studying or being tutored in Czech by his aunts and uncle. I looked forward more and more to going to the bookshop with Sabina and spending days with her as she told me bits and pieces of their lives. She told me she had a daughter from a previous marriage, and she was married and living in a town some seventy miles away. Her son-in-law was in the army, and she now worried because her daughter was about to have her first baby and would need help. She said she planned to be with her and hoped it was still possible before the baby's arrival.

"How long would you be gone ?"

"For as long as she needs me."

I was sure to leave here in just over a few weeks, but I suddenly offered to keep the shop open for her, at least for the time I still had left. She was overjoyed at my suggestion.

"I can close the shop if you aren't back when I have to leave."

"Yes, that would be fine. Thank you so much for your kind offer." She kissed me on my cheeks in gratitude. "I can leave in about two days then, and I will keep in touch with you."

In the next two days she showed me the running of the shop and how to make out a chit with a number on it and to the name and the book's value in a ledger, so that when someone came in to sell books I could give them the chit, since she had run out of money to buy them outright. She said they would get paid for any sold books when they were back in Prague. The people weren't happy, but what else could they and she do? They left their books at the shop, and they left with a chit—this was all she could offer them. Sabina left me in charge and I hoped it would all work out until her return, or my departure, whichever came first. The bookshop became my little world of discoveries, not only about books but also about people. I learned the chit system, and despite the disappointment of my having to hand them out in exchange for their books that the often-distraught people came in with and then left with the sobering resolve of a chit. How could I possibly know what was going on in their lives.

I saw Sabina off, hoping that my English and a smattering of high school French would be enough to handle any situation. As I dealt with the customers of used English books and sheet music, the sheet music was the easy part.

EMERGENCY

═══════════════════════

ABOUT A WEEK LATER, as we were sitting down to breakfast, Alex got a phone call. His brother Greg had terrible news. Their parents had been hurriedly crossing the street against the light and just as they stepped onto the streetcar tracks their father had a fatal heart attack. In her attempt to get him off the tracks of the oncoming streetcar, their mother was hit by the streetcar. Greg reported that she was in the hospital in a comatose state. Greg said the prognosis is unknown and that she had not yet regained consciousness since the accident. In view of the situation, he urged Alex to come home right away. Alex, shaken by the news, turned to me. "What am I going to do? I would have to fly back home, and I don't even have enough to pay for the trains back to Holland." Beata, Sabina, and Jiri were beside themselves with grief, thinking they would never see their sister again. Jiri poured us each a stiff cognac as they tried to console each other.

Later that night, lying awake in bed, I looked up at my one piece of luggage on top of the wardrobe that held the one hundred dollars my father gave me with the instructions that it was to be used for an emergency purpose only. I got up and walked to the wardrobe, and then I pulled my luggage down, and opening it, I reached into the lined lid pocket and took out the envelope. I held it for a moment and then quickly nudged Alex, saying, "Alex, here, this is your ticket home." I explained what it was, and what it was for. He looked at me and then at the envelope and said, "I can't take this, this is yours."

"Alex, I'm sure everything will work out as it is supposed to, but now you have to go home to be with your mother. Call Pan Am and see if you can get a seat on the Clipper. Don't worry about me—just get back here as soon as you can, or I will follow at some point as soon as I can."

"I will. You are a life saver, I shall never forget you for this."

"I hope you never forget me here for any other reason."

Alex put his arm around me and said, "I won't."

The next day we pooled all our available resources. Pan Am told Alex that the Clipper was all booked to New York, so now he would have to sail home. Alex left the following morning with boat arrangements and promised to call as soon as he could. I was grateful for the responsibility of the bookshop, because it gave me enough of an outlet for my anxiety over recent events.

One day, maybe a week later, Jiri handed me a letter from my parents when I went home at lunchtime. It had been written before the accident with Alex's parents. It was terribly alarming as my father warned me about the increasingly hostile escalation of political events in Europe. He went so far as to say that I should think about leaving earlier to come home. I couldn't even consider whether I should heed his suggestion, because I now did not have my father's emergency money. Alex and I had saved up our earnings at home to help pay our way in Prague. I had enough saved to see me perhaps through the month, but not much more.

I wrote back to my parents, saying I was fine and that the conditions here did not warrant alarm of any kind. I did not know much about what was happening in certain parts of Europe, even though Jiri kept me informed to some extent by translating the Czech headline stories. I never followed politics at home and had even less interest in it here. "Thank you, Jiri, for keeping me informed, but I must say I am not interested in politics. It is so futile for those who are not directly involved. My belief lies where I can actually do something of my own free will to make a difference. I'm not sure what that would be, but I would give my all, of that I'm certain."

Jiri looked at me incredulous and at a loss for words. Time would prove that my words were to be deeply etched on my consciousness. As time went on, however, the little that I knew combined all that I saw in the shops and at Sabina's bookshop, so that I could see that Prague was becoming a city besieged with an ideological division of thoughts and allegiances. People were starting to turn against each other, and people who were once friends now no longer were or were cautious with one another. It had a cloak and dagger aspect to it that was beginning to make me uneasy. Later on, some shortages of foodstuffs and fuel only added to the uncertainties.

A few days later, while waiting for the streetcar to take me to the shop, I heard some shouting across the street. I saw a man look over his shoulder at three men who accosted him. They pushed him until he fell on the sidewalk, and I saw them start to kick him, just as my streetcar came in and blocked the scene from my view. I rushed onto the streetcar and looked out the window in time to see the three men run off. The man on the ground held his stomach and rolled from side to side. I wondered what the man had done to provoke such a blatant attack. When I mentioned the incident at lunch, Jiri said, "Yes, these things happen now and then."

"What things?"

" A rabid element here is showing their hand publicly more and more these days."

"What rabid element are you talking about?"

"There are Czechs who identify with the Nazi doctrine of anti-Semitism. These days they feel especially free to express their opinions. This is even more alarming because Prague has the oldest Jewish community in Europe." A chill ran down my spine when I heard that. Those words haunted me all the way back to the bookshop. My father's warnings bore new meaning for me now. There was nothing I could do about it, however, until I heard from Alex again. I certainly did not want to ask my father for money, so I could come home; he had already been more than generous in giving me the one hundred dollars. It forced me to think more seriously about my situation. What if I were stranded here? I now knew that I had to earn enough money for a boat ticket home. I couldn't possibly do that in two weeks' time.

That evening at supper, I mentioned the idea of giving English lessons here at the house in the evenings. They offered the music room, Jiri saying he was willing to reschedule as many of his pupils as possible.

The next day I put a notice advertising English lessons on the shop door, and one on the counter as well. It wasn't long before I got inquires. Each day I closed the shop at five, so I could have my first pupil at six. If I could work until nine, I could have three paying pupils each evening, and maybe I could have some on the weekends as well. There was quite a lot of interest, more than I had expected, from teenagers to people in their late 50s and 60s. Jiri advised me what to charge. While I thought it was a bit steep, the people never questioned it. I enjoyed my time teaching conversational English, mostly dealing with practical matters, as many of the pupils said they had travel in mind.

The month of my planned stay here was now nearly up, and aside from a quick call from Alex to say he had arrived safely, I knew little of the situation back home. He promised he would let me know when there were more facts, and until then I was to sit tight. Other than that, I had no news from him. I still had some distance to go to make the price of a boat ticket home, so I know I had to stay in Prague until something changed.

OCTOBER 1938

THE SECOND WEEK OF OCTOBER found me still at the book-shop, where I continued to spend nearly all of my days. Some interesting people appeared on any given day, although there were more people with books to sell than wanting to buy. When a buyer did appear, they got my full attention. I liked roaming the aisles of books, and by now I knew where just about everything was. Nearly everyone who came in either understood or spoke some English, and I enjoyed the work. The only task I disliked was when I could only offer a chit for their books. They generally took the chit resignedly and then left in disappointed haste.

I tried not to feel any further anguish after Jiri informed me that now German troops occupied the Sudetenland and that the Czech government had resigned. I too resigned my fate to whatever I would have to face next, given the uncertainties of these events. What had I gotten myself into?

One day at lunch I received a letter from Sabina enclosed with a letter to her sister and Jiri. She needed to stay longer than anticipated with her daughter and new baby. She wrote that I was to shut the shop whenever I needed to. She also wrote how grateful she was to me for having helped her. She made no mention of when she might come back.

There was another letter from Alex, as well. There had been no change in his mother's condition; he felt a clear need to stay in New York City. He had gotten his old job back at the architecture firm and was once again drawing heating and air ducts for large proposed building projects. For the present we both had to settle into a holding pattern. As soon as he could save enough money, he would send me the price of a boat ticket home. I wrote back telling him what I was doing. I lamented that we were at a standstill, in terms of both our location and whatever our relationship was. While it was unfortunate, to be sure, it was understandable, considering his grief.

Jiri shared news of the conflicts surrounding the Sudetenland, and aggression between the Germans and the Czechs. Things were heating up because of it, but in my naiveté, I thought these two adversaries were just venting old vendettas that would quiet down with time. I couldn't have been more wrong. Before long, Jiri uttered a stern warning, "Observers in the field have long ago warned of the German military buildup. There were voices trying to shout a warning message, but they only landed in the abyss of apathy. Now it is time to pay the piper. When the Spanish fascist dictator Franco and his Falangists in 1936 sided with the Nazis and massacred the Spanish people from the air and on the ground, it was only an exercise, just a rehearsal for what we will soon have with the Nazis. And this time for us it won't be the hand-to-hand combat of the trench warfare of World War I. Now it will be fully mechanized, to our great disadvantage. It is just a matter of time, given how things are going, until it will all end." Jiri was the family harbinger of the direst possible outcomes. I hoped that time and the events to follow would prove him wrong in every case. Beata and Jiri reassured me that I was going to be fine, no matter what happened, because I was an American and so not involved. Both were true, for the moment at least.

When Vienna welcomed the German annexation of Austria on March 12, 1938, with cheering swastika-waving crowds, one did not have to wonder how that would end or where, considering the Sudetenland issue. From the outlying towns of Prague and far more distant places, Jews were now beginning to flee to Prague, seeing it as a place of departure to other countries. That made little sense to me, since on that very morning, as I rode the streetcar to the shop, I saw swastika flags flying from several buildings. Jiri dismissed that as a further display of Czech sympathizers. Even more disturbing, however, were boycotts of Jewish-owned shops as a show of support for Nazi anti-Semitism. The alarming thing to me was how quickly all of this was happening, from day to day. I tried to put these thoughts to rest each day as I went to the shop. More and more people were coming in now with books to sell, but what surprised me and frightened me was that rare and valuable first editions were being relegated to chits. This pointed to the people's desperation. These books belonged on the shelves of specialist biblio-antiquarians, not on the musty back room shelves of a used bookstore. They may have tried other avenues before we became their last resort, or could it be that perhaps time snapped at their heels. I treasured the fine leather bindings and carefully relegated them to a special place on the top shelves in the back room with their spines facing the wall to hide their value. Now even works by Heinrich Heine were not on open display.

My parents and I continued to write letters to each other. My father's letters were laced with alarm about the political situation and how it could possibly affect me, and mine in answer to him reassured him that we were fine in Prague. I did not deny the political dissidence, but I assured him that life here continued pretty much as it

59

had before these events, and that I was enjoying my stay. I cheerfully detailed my working at the book shop. My mother's letters were of a chattier nature, but they always ended with "Please take good care of yourself." Alex's letters were concerned with what was happening in New York, including the hope shared with his brother that their mother would regain consciousness soon, at which time he would return to Prague. He was nevertheless saving up for my return ticket.

Settling for the Unknown

THE SHOP AND MY ENGLISH lessons kept me occupied as the days rolled into weeks. More and more refugees wanted to learn or perfect their English, hoping to immigrate to England. Every two weeks, after my living contributions to the household were deducted, I counted my savings for the ticket home. I was making very slow progress.

The bed was now bigger without Alex in it, but I missed him and his assurances. The weather at the beginning of November became more wintery, weather I had not planned on being here for, nor did I have appropriate clothing. The old house lacked a central heating system. Rooms were heated separately by square or round cast iron or porcelain tile-faced heaters using wood or coal. One of these sat in the corner of my bedroom, but I rarely used it because I was gone all day. Even when I returned in the evenings, I usually spent time in the warmed kitchen. We were also very mindful of the supply of wood and coal. At bedtime, I made quick work of changing into a nightgown and getting into bed in the cold of my room.

Since my mostly summer wardrobe of thin cottons and rayon were inadequate for this cold weather, Beata and I went to a used clothing shop where I got some things to see me through until my as yet unknown departure. There were some surprisingly high-quality and stylish clothes to choose from. I found a pair of beautiful black leather ski mittens with removable wool linings. I hoped I wouldn't be here long enough to need to wear them as intended, but that seemed more and more likely, considering I was spending part of my savings just to stay warm.

Many of my pupils asked me about England, about the food, clothes, and especially housing and travel. Some knew I was American and some didn't. I had little information to offer them.

ONE DAY EARLY IN NOVEMBER A MAN CAME INTO THE shop with a little girl. I recalled seeing him on occasion, looking into the shop window at the display of books and sheet music or through the upper glass of the door. Whenever I noticed him, he had turned quickly and left, but today he came into the shop and greeted me with a small smile, holding the hand of the little girl. He asked, "May I just look?"

"Yes, of course, you're welcome to look around."

He and the little girl walked up and down the aisles. After a while, he said, "Thank you." And then they left.

A few days later, I saw him looking in the window and then at me, and with a small-embarrassed smile, he waved and left. I put interesting books in the window of varying subjects to entice people to come in and at least look at what we had to offer.

Two days later, he came again with the little girl. This time he came in without looking at the books in the window. Smiling, he asked me if I had any children's books that she could look at while he browsed the shelves. I told him that we did, and that we had a special section just for children. Jiri had built a little alcove near the back of the shop with low shelves and a little table for two small chairs that he had painted in bright colors.

The man bent down and said something to the girl that I could not hear. He walked her over to me, and I extended my hand to her. She hesitated, and then looked up at whom I assumed was her father. He smiled at her and nodded, and then she cautiously took my hand and I led her to the children's alcove. I showed her to one of the chairs and took out a few books, including *Peter Rabbit* and *Goldilocks and The Three Bears*. I put them down in front of her, but she only stared at them without touching them. I pulled out the other chair and carefully settled into it. I opened *Goldilocks* and set it in front of her, standing it up on her lap. She stared at it and then at me. I moved closer and shared the book and began to read. She looked at me wide-eyed and then at the page. She had not said a word the whole time. I pointed to Goldilocks and said the name. The little girl looked back at me and then at the page. When I introduced the three bears, she had the same reaction. I turned the pages, pointing to the characters and reading the story, she sat quietly, occasionally looking up at me with her large dark eyes as if to make meaning of me as well as the characters. Having finished the book, I picked up *Peter Rabbit*. I decided to give this story a more dramatic reading. As I read the story, she snuggled up against me. When I got to the page where Peter Rabbit runs to escape Farmer McGregor with rake in hand after stealing the lettuce, she suddenly hugged my upper arm and partially hid her face from the unexpected anger of the farmer. She still had not uttered a word. When I looked up, the man was standing by the sheet music bin, looking at us and smiling. He came over to fetch her. He thanked me, and then they left. This continued for a time, and soon I came to greatly enjoy the frequent visits of my new non-selling, non-buying customer. I looked forward to their visits, while I found the little girl's continued silence puzzling.

THE MOST RECENT LETTERS FROM MY PARENTS WERE even more insistent that I come home. My father reminded me more than once of the safety net he had given me for just such a purpose. The safety net of course no longer existed, but I could not tell him that, nor could I ask him for more help. I was resolved to get out of this on my own. My leisurely trips to explore Prague felt like the distant past because I took every person interested in English lessons. I noticed that most of my pupils were Jewish. They were, every one of them, anxious and hard working in their lessons. I became more and more aware of their plight as our conversations, which were meant to practice English, centered on their reasons for wanting to leave the European continent. A few even asked me if I could teach them Spanish as well. I was certain it figured into some sort of a backup plan they were contemplating. As time went on, and as I learned more about what was happening throughout Europe, I realized that the chances of Alex returning to Prague were near nil—in fact, financially, emotionally, and politically speaking, it was virtually impossible.

I finally admitted to myself that I was stranded. The only saving grace was my American citizenship and American passport, which would let open the path for me to leave and go home. The only obstacle was money. I fully realized my fate in late November as I leaned into the biting wind, crunching through icy snow, to go home for yet another English lesson. Everyone was learning something except me.

At the shop I could count on visits from the man with the little girl. One day he entered the shop and came directly over to me. It was the first time he had come near me, and so it was the first time I saw him up close. He had the same large dark eyes as the little girl, and he spoke in halting but well-schooled English with an accent that I could not identify. He also had a fresh gash on his left cheekbone. He looked straight at me, and I had looked at his coat lapel to escape his intense gaze. I noted that the lapel had a thread sticking out of the stitching at one end of the buttonhole. He said, "Excuse me. I'm fond of Nevil Shute's novels. Do you by any chance have a copy of *What Happened to the Corbetts?*"

"I'll see, but I doubt it," I stammered. I nervously pulled the inventory index card file toward me, aware that he was staring at me. When I found the author card, I was pleasantly relieved. "Oh, here he is, Nevil Shute Norway. I remember reading about the one you are asking for in the *New York Times*. This was months ago. In the States it was retitled, *The Ordeal*. The publishers do that sometimes, you know. He released it earlier this year to be published, so it most likely will appear early in 1939. We certainly would not have it, not for quite some time. I'm sorry."

The man gave a solemn nod. "Well, thank you for checking. I hope you won't mind if I check with you now and then, just in case a stray early copy finds its way to you?"

"No, of course not."

"May I have the phone number of the shop?"

I wrote it down for him, and as I handed it to him he said, "May I have your name as well?"

"Oh, don't worry, I am the only one here," I said, gesturing to the otherwise empty shop.

"Nevertheless, I like to know who I am talking to."

I told him my name, to which he replied, "Is there a last name to Karin?"

Flustered, I said, "Yes, it's Wilson."

"Are you English? You don't sound English."

"No, my father is English, but I'm American."

He extended his hand to me and said, "How wonderful." Then he quickly added, "How nice it is to meet you. Thank you. I'll keep in touch." He then took the little girl's hand and they left. I was mystified by how well informed he was about Nevil Shute's new novel, and I realized he was now a little bit more informed about me as well as I watched him shut the door behind them.

Two days later he came in again. Upon seeing him, I with a laugh, "No new Nevil Shute yet."

"I didn't expect it so soon, but maybe if I browse, I'll find a waiting substitute. May she see the children's books while I explore?"

"Certainly." By now he didn't have to ask; she and I had developed a routine of going to the alcove in back, where I read to her. Her favorite was *Peter Rabbit*. As was her occasional custom, when I finished she turned the pages back to the beginning. I was on my second reading to her when I heard the bells above the shop door sound. I called out, "I'll be right there." I handed her the book and walked out to the counter. I saw no new customer. I called out, "Can I help someone?" There was no answer. I looked at the aisles of bookshelves, but I saw no one. Then I realized that the little girl's father was also nowhere to be seen. I quickly walked up and down each aisle, calling out. The shop was empty. I stood in the middle of the shop, trying to make sense of the bells that announced someone coming into the shop. I soon realized that this time they had announced someone leaving. I thought perhaps he had gone outside for a smoke. I opened the door and looked to the left and right. No one was there. I stepped out into the cold air, looking further down the street. I saw a streetcar at the stop just down the street, and a man with the same overcoat, the one with the loose buttonhole thread, stepped up onto the running board. The streetcar clanged its departure and left. My mouth went dry as I gasped in the cold air. When I walked back into the shop, I saw a package tied with string on the floor by the door. I looked wildly from the package to the back of the shop, where a beautiful little girl was sitting in the alcove. I tried to compose myself as I walked to the alcove. She was closing the book as I walked up to her She held her hand out so I could guide her back to her father. I took her outstretched hand, and we walked back out to the front of the shop. I couldn't think of anything to say. When we came to the counter, she looked around for her father. Not seeing him, she uttered the first words I had heard from her. She called out, "Papa, papa?" When there was no answer, she ran around the shop calling out with increasing panic. "Papa? Papa?" She came back to me, and she looked at the door, and then at me. She seemed to understand what the stricken look on my face, combined with her father's disappearance and the package that likely contained her clothing, meant. She became even more frightened and, crying, she tried to open the door, but the old round knob just turned back and forth. Her little hands couldn't turn the knob enough to open the door.

"Papa, papa!" she cried, stomping her little feet rapidly in place repeatedly and working the door knob in her little hands. I noticed a little puddle on the floor at her feet, and my heart finally broke wide open. I lifted her up and held her close to me, hugging her and kissing her on her tear-wet cheeks as her sobs continued. I took her behind the counter so I could slide off her wet panties as I opened her coat, I saw a note pinned inside. In what I had come to think of as European handwriting, I read the words, "My name is Anja. I am three years old." That was all. At first, I thought it was intended to help her if she were lost, but then I reasoned that it would have been sewn in, and would have included more information, if that were the case. The man must have pinned it there earlier that day. I looked at my watch. It was half past five, and I should have closed the shop thirty minutes ago. I decided I would wait till until seven before leaving. My mind tried desperately to find reasonable explanations for the situation. Perhaps he simply had something to take care of, and once settled he might come back for her. Or perhaps he would call me, since he had the number here.

The only sounds from little Anja were her heartbreaking cries for her papa. Nothing more. Her terrified eyes glistened through her tears and her rapid breathing gave her the look of a frightened rabbit about to be taken.

I called Beata to say that I was awaiting a customer who could be back by seven. I asked her to please tell my pupils that I was delayed and would see them the next day.

I carried little Anja in my arms while she laid her head on my shoulder and sucked her thumb. Her little chest convulsed intermittently with her sobs. She was as light as a feather in my arms, but a heavy burden on my mind and heart. I could not fathom what happened here to us. With glances every now and then at the shop door, we spent the next hour and half in that way. At seven o'clock, I finally buttoned her coat, put mine on, shut the lights and picked up the package by the door, and locked the shop, then, with Anja in my arms, I took the streetcar home. I sat with her in my arms, examining every man even close to his age, looking at the left cheekbone for a fresh gash, at the overcoat buttonhole. I kept hoping that he might appear on the streetcar and claim her once again, but much to my dismay that never happened.

When I came home, all I could do was kick at the door to be let in with my new burdens. Beata stood in the doorway, looking at me with an incredulous stare. Seeing the weight of what I was carrying, she quickly stepped aside and followed me into the kitchen. Jiri was just finishing his supper as I walked in. When he realized what he was seeing, he slowly lifted his napkin to absently wipe his mouth.

I sat down with Anja clinging to me and staring fearfully at the new faces and surroundings.

Jiri was the first to speak. "What is it? What has happened? Who is this?"

I sighed. "I wish I had an answer to all of that, but I don't." I told them what had happened. They shook their heads as I spoke, looking at each other as if doing so would lend some clarity.

Beata lifted the package from where I had dropped it and cut the string. She folded back the paper to reveal a note laid on top of some clothes. Beata unfolded the note and handed it to me. I read it silently to myself and, after a loud gasp, handed it to Beata, who read it aloud.

> My dear Miss Wilson,
>
> I must ask you to forgive me for what I have done. If I had any other choice, please believe that I would have taken it. Her name is Anja; she is three years old, and that is all I dare tell you. My life is in great danger, and I fear my little Anja's may be as well. I am in no position to protect her. I look to you, whom I have carefully chosen, to keep her safe, to protect her, and to give her all the love she deserves. I know she will have a safe life with you. It breaks my heart to have to do this, but she is my only gift to the world, and now to you. Please keep her to yourself and love her with all your heart.

I pray that Anja and God and you will forgive me, and that He will protect us.

Anja's father

Beata fell back into her chair with the note loosely held in her shaking hand. "Oh, Karin, do you know what this means?"

I shook my head. "No, not really, not yet."

Jiri said, "But you know nothing about her, who she is or where she comes from."

Quickly, as if by some instinct, I say, "I will care for her and keep her safe, whoever she is. Do either of you speak German?" They nod, and I asked them to ask the girl for her name in German. They did this, but Anja gave no response.

"Please try it in Czech," I urged. Again, no response. "So far she hasn't said anything except to cry out for her p-a-p-a." I spelled it to avoid upsetting her any further.

Jiri said gravely, "No last name, no information at all. You may have to turn her over to the authorities."

I frowned at Jiri. "No, I will not do that! Her father thinks she is in danger. I don't know what that could be, but I don't want to put her at risk, not after all this."

Beata said, "No, no, you were carefully chosen for her. You, as an American with your blue eyes and blond hair, are to be her safety. I think he did this to save her when he knew he could not even save himself. A gift from God for you," she said with a weak smile, patting my cheek. *A gift with a weight*, I thought. I hoped God would also endow me with the strength needed to bear it. I didn't have the faintest notion whether I was capable of being entrusted with the life of this helpless soul. Anja clung to me as if her life depended on me, which I was terrified to realize was true. I was overwhelmed by the tearful heartbreaking little life that was given to me out of desperation for her survival. Nothing in my twenty-one years of life ever prepared me for this.

Jiri cleared his throat and said, "We should talk about it again in the morning, when we are over the shock."

"I don't think I will ever be over it," I said quietly.

Beata put a plate of sandwiches in front of me. I took a bite and offered it to Anja, but she just looked at it as if she would burst out crying again. I hugged her close to me.

Beata looked through the contents of the package. On the table, she laid a child's hairbrush, a toothbrush, some underwear and socks, a nightgown, cotton stockings, slippers, a bathrobe, and a small well-loved stuffed rabbit nestled into a small blanket and pillow. Anja grabbed the stuffed rabbit and clutched it to her chest; it is now her only small comfort from home. There was also a beautiful hand-knit sweater and a wool dress. Beata asked, "Should I take these things up to your room, or keep them here where it is warmer to change her?" I shrugged in confusion, and Beata indicated she would simply leave them in the kitchen.

Beata helped me change Anja into a nightgown before I carried her upstairs and into my cold room. I knew that the bed would be frigid, so I got the wool liners from the mittens I had bought, I and put them on Anja's feet. I snuggled her into the eiderdown so that I could change quickly into my nightgown, but she pulled my hand to her chest. I laid down next to her and softly hummed to her; she looked at me intently with her big questioning eyes, as if she wanted to know if I would still be here when she awoke. Still holding my hand, she began to suck her thumb. Before long, she closed her eyes and with her tear soaked lashes fell asleep. Sleep lightened her grasp on my hand, so I carefully got up and sat in the chair next to the bed for a time, watching her sleep and trying to make sense of it all. I finally got up and changed into my nightgown and bathrobe, tonight not even aware of the cold. I carefully got into bed next to Anja. I turned off the table light; I listened to the comforting sound of Anja sucking her thumb. My growing fears of what I was to do and how I was to handle this plagued me through the night, and I slept poorly.

I was awakened early the next morning by movement; it took a moment to remember that I was not alone. Anja was sitting up in bed with her little fists on her eyes, ready to cry. With my warm hand I gently rubbed her chilled back. My heart broke all over again when she started crying. I sat up and hugged her close to me. I wrapped the eiderdown quilt around her and eased her down next to me. It was only a mild comfort to both of us. After a while I got up and dressed, and then I put her clothes inside my sweater to warm them. She stopped crying and moved to the edge of the bed where I could dress her. Maybe she thought I would take her to her father. Oh, how I wished I could.

We were up before anyone else in the house, so I began to make breakfast. Anja watched my every move as I scrambled some eggs and made toast. I was mindful of the primitive toaster, having learned the hard way that the perforated tower sitting on the stove top would burn the bread very quickly if unattended. I buttered the toast and put pear preserves on it; I heated milk and sweetened it with cinnamon and honey. When I served this to Anja, she just looked at it as if unsure what to do. I picked up the fork and offered a bite of the eggs to her. She barely opened her mouth, but her eyes were as wide as they could go as they watched my every move. I cut up the toast for her and held the cup of milk up to her mouth. From what little I knew of small children, she was probably capable of feeding herself, but she wanted me to feed her as if to prove that I would nourish her, dress her, and comfort her. I didn't know anything more about children except for faint memories of having been one myself, but I certainly had never been in a similar situation. How will I learn to care for her? At best, I decided I would imagine that she was me, and I asked myself what I might want just then. The only one thing that came to mind was "papa."

Anja cautiously tasted some of her breakfast on her own while I made myself some coffee. When I sat down next to her, she pulled my hand and my cup to her lips. She took a sip and wrinkled her nose, looking at me as if I had played a trick on her. I smiled at her, and I suddenly realized that we had begun to communicate with each other. It was a soundless communication on her part, but it was nonetheless communication.

I heard footsteps on the stairs, and Beata joined us in the kitchen. Seeing us, she asked, "How is it going?"

I shrugged. "I wish I knew."

"Has she spoken yet?"

"No, not a word. I wonder if she is speech impaired, or too traumatized to talk. Maybe she is deaf."

"We will find out soon enough," Beata promised.

I tried my primer school French. "*Comment t'appellee, ma petite cher?*" It was my best try, but no answer.

I had another idea. "Beata, try to get her attention." While Beata made silly faces at Anja, I took a heavy book from the kitchen bookshelf. I opened it roughly to the middle and, standing behind Anja, I slammed it shut. Anja jumped and turned around to look at me quizzically. "Well, she's not deaf," I said relieved.

Beta said, "Let me try something." Beata turned her back to us and spoke in a language I had never heard before. "*Baruch atah*

Adonai, Eloheinu melekh ha'olam, asher kideshanu b'mitz'votav v'tzivanu, l'had'lik neir shel shabbat."

"No response. What was that, Beata?"

"It's a Jewish prayer said each Sabbath night at the lighting of the dinner candles. If she were Jewish, even if she doesn't know what it means she would recognize it."

"How did you know that?"

"When I was young, I had a Jewish friend. She and her family invited me for dinner at times. I thought it was a poem and I asked my friend teach it to me." Beata had a faraway look for a moment, but then she asked, "What did Anja's father look like? He might be— rather, maybe they are Spanish, or Belgian, or French?"

"I can't really say. He spoke English fairly well with an accent that I couldn't place. He was handsome, but not in a way that made me think of any particular country. He also had a fresh cut on his cheekbone."

"Handsome, could be from anywhere in the world, and a fresh cut on his face . . . these do not make a good combination for finding someone. Whatever language she might speak, we'll have to teach her English, now that she is yours."

The words *Now that she is yours* made me feel as if the Karin I had always been had suddenly disappeared, dissolved into a Karin I did not know, one who was to be made over into someone much wiser and stronger than I felt. Beata seemed to understand. She took my hand and shook her head, adding "Poor her, poor you."

A FEW DAYS GO BY, AND ANJA HAD ONE CLEAR AND CON-stant need, and that was to never let me out of her sight. When I went to the toilet, she always came with me and held my hand in both of hers, as I did with her, so she wouldn't fall in. This poor, beautiful, terrified little three-year-old girl sat in my lap whenever possible, pressing herself against my chest and holding tightly onto my hair as if she wanted to hide under my skin in the warm darkness, away from the terrors in her life that only she could know. I did my best to release her from those terrors, but no one could answer how I was supposed to comfort and care for this little soul. I often thought that I was as frightened of the prospects as she was.

Anja comes with me to the bookshop every day, where I keep hoping her father will reappear. I always felt that Anja held the same hope. Behind the shop's counter with the register there was a U-shaped area. I set up a large pillow on the floor for Anja, where she could sit or lay down with a blanket. Every day I gave her some children's books. *Peter Rabbit* is always among them, but she did explore nearly all the children's books in the shop. She turned the pages slowly, looking at the pictures and occasionally getting my attention to share one of the pictures with me, but she never spoke a word.

One evening at supper, Jiri said, "Karin, what are your plans for the two of you?"

I thought about this question almost constantly, but I was ashamed of my answer. "I haven't any, Jiri. I'll wait a while longer before I consider anything, just in case he shows up."

Jiri frowned thoughtfully. "And if he doesn't, I worry about the two of you. Alex is surely not coming back, but I think you know that by now."

I nodded, surprised that I am as certain about this as Jiri is. "Yes, I know."

Beata said, "You know, Karin, I have been thinking about that letter her father left for you, and the words. He said his life was in danger, and hers as well, and that he could do nothing about it. Do you know what I think?"

"No, tell me."

"I think they are Jewish. It makes sense in these times, don't you think?"

I nodded sadly. "It worries me to no end as well, and to hear you say it as well, I am afraid, too. How can I protect her?"

Jiri said, "I think the time has come for you to create some credible information about her as your daughter. Give her your last name and come up with a birth date."

I paused for a moment, thinking about Jiri's suggestion. It made sense, and it would afford Anja all the protections that I had as an American citizen. "He left her with me on the tenth of December. I remember the date because I had to check it earlier that day when I wrote a letter to Alex. Her birth date will be December 10, 1935."

Jiri nodded at the sense of my thinking. "That is only the beginning, Karin. Beata and I have been talking about it, and we think you must plan to leave with her as soon as possible."

"I will, but now I need to earn enough for two passages. That will take a while longer, no matter how many English pupils I can find."

Beata's eyes glistened with tears as Jiri went on. "I wish we could give it to you, dear Karin, but we are managing day to day as it is."

My heart filled with love for these strangers who had become family to me. "I know that only too well, and I know you would do that if you could. This is to be my burden, not yours. I am thankful that you can keep us as it is."

The telephone rang shrilly in the following quiet. Jiri went to answer the call, and within a few moments he hurried back into the kitchen. "It's for you, Karin. It's Alex."

I went to the telephone. I took a deep breath, but before I could speak, I felt Anja's hand in mine. I smiled down at her. Then I said, "Hello, Alex."

"Hello, Karin! How are you? I've been getting worried that I haven't heard from you in a while. When are you coming home?"

"I'm fine, Alex. I sent a letter just a couple weeks ago, but perhaps it hasn't reached you yet. I am giving English lessons, as many as I can, and I'm saving as much of that as possible so that I will be able to come home soon."

"Why is it taking so long? Is there anything stopping you besides the money? I'm beginning to worry that some handsome Czech has snapped you up out of my grasp." He laughed at his own joke. "That's funny, isn't it? Please tell me it's funny."

"No, Alex, nothing at all like that. I'll come as soon as I can. I'll be sure to let you know when. It would help if you could send me some of the money you owe me."

"Okay! Don't forget to write. Wait, I'm at your parents', they want to talk to you, too." I wondered if Alex had heard my last statement.

Mother was the first on. "Hello, Karin, how are you? Is everything all right? Are you well?" I could hear curiosity, concern, and love fighting each other in her voice.

I smiled at hearing her. "Everything is fine, Mother, and yes, I am well. It has gotten a bit colder here now. How is the weather there?" It was lovely to hear my mother's voice, but I engaged in the chitchat to avoid some of the larger issues at hand.

"It's cold here, and we had some snow yesterday. We have Alex over for dinner every now and then so we can share your letters. They have been a bit sparse lately, so we worry."

"Don't worry mother, I'm fine."

"Please write, dear. I do miss you so. Daddy is waiting to talk to you—here he is."

"Hello, Daddy, how are you?" I braced myself for his predictable comments.

"I'm fine, but, how are you? I don't like what I'm reading in the papers about what's happening in Europe. I want you home, Karin."

"Daddy, we're fine here in Prague, really. Everything is okay. I've just gotten used to living as a European, and I'm enjoying it."

"I want you home and I want you to attend to that now. If you need money, just say so. Please just come home as soon as possible." His voice was commanding which I knew was a measure of how concerned he was for me.

"Okay, Daddy, and I'll write more often than I have been." I paused for a moment and then said, "Hello? Hello, Daddy, can you hear me?"

I heard him clear as a bell. "Yes, I can hear you, so it must be at your end. I'll hang up now, but we will continue this conversation soon again."

I placed the receiver back on the hook and hung my head. I could not say more and still be truthful, so I chose to fake a bad connection rather than lie to my father. With Anja's little hand in mine we walked back to the kitchen where Beata and Jiri waited for me.

That night after Anja fell asleep, I had troubled thoughts about her father's letter. If Beata and Jiri were right and Anja was Jewish, I feared what the discovery of his letter would mean for her.

I took out of my suitcase a pair of underarm dress shields that I had never used. I carefully folded the letter into the same half-moon shape of the dress shield and sandwiched it between the two halves of one of the dress shields. Then I carefully picked the stitching of my bra's inner lining and inserted the two shields, one on each side for balance, one containing the letter. I meticulously stitched them back as they originally were. Now the letter would be safely hidden on me at all times. I just wouldn't be able to wash my bra for only God knew how long.

Christmas 1938

CHRISTMAS WAS APPROACHING, my first ever away from home. Standing at the window and looking at the bare pear trees silhouetted against the steel gray-blue of the sky, tears welled up and blurred my vision. Beata said from behind me, "We can cheer up that view for Christmas." I wondered what could possibly cheer me up.

One day, as we were coming home from the bookshop, Anja was sitting on my lap as usual and looking out of the street car window when she suddenly pointed to the sidewalk and called out, "Dada, dada!" She quickly slid down from my lap and ran to the streetcar door. I caught up with her and took her hand as the conductor shook his head, pointing ahead to the next stop. When he opened the door, Anja almost flew out the door and ran to the sidewalk, pulling me behind her. That was only the second time she had spoken, so I was sure she had spotted him on the street. I ran with her for a few blocks when she suddenly stopped in front of a run-down antique shop, pointing excitedly at the crowded show window. Anja pulled me into the shop and tried to climb into the window. The owner came rushing over. I held onto Anja so she couldn't climb into the window, and she kept pointing at an old rocking horse in the window.

"Dada!" she said, again. When I addressed the dealer in English, he said, "Ah, it's the rocking horse she wants."

"But she said 'dada,' I thought it was her father she saw on the street."

He looks at me puzzled and says, "No, 'dada' is French for rocking horse."

All this further puzzled me as I watched him take it out of the window. He set it on the floor and lifted Anja onto it.

She leaned forward and hugged the moth-eaten mane. The owner chatted with me, saying, "These days I never know what will cross my threshold. I no longer deal solely in antiques because so many other items find their way here. I am hard pressed to handle it all, and still I usually can't say no."

When Anja sat up from hugging the horse, the owner lifted her off and offered her to me, her legs and arms still frozen in position from being on the horse.

I took her into my arms and said, "I had best leave quickly with her before it breaks her heart."

He looked at me with a sad little smile. "I think it already has." He then saw us out of the shop. We got back on a streetcar and continued home. Anja was sad at not having the rocking horse, but at the same time she did not seem a stranger to disappointment. I am sad about it as well; if I'd had the money I would have bought it, but my greater sadness is that it was not the discovery of her father on the street. *What about her mother?* I wondered. *Was she French? Where was she?*

Some days later I went to the bakery shop with Anja, and the baker's wife had just slid a tray of freshly baked sugar cookies glistening with colored sugar into the showcase. Seeing that, Anja got excited and, pointing to them, said, "Papa young!" She smiled at me and, tapping her tiny finger on the glass case at the butterfly-shaped cookies, repeated, "Papa young!"

I remembered that *papillon* in French meant butterfly. The baker's wife smiled adoringly and handed one of the cookies to Anja. For the first time that I could remember, Anja smiled a wide happy smile as she nibbled away. I too was happy to hear another word of speech from her.

That evening, when I mentioned it to Beata and Jiri, we were all frustrated that all of this was still so little to go on. The questions of who she was, where she was from, and what language she spoke or understood, other than the few words she has so far spoken, were still unanswered. I noted that, while she spoke some French words, when she cried out for her papa it was not with a French inflection, but more of a Germanic one, deepening the mystery even further. When it was time for bed, as always, I sat next to her and held her hand until she was asleep. Jiri often played his violin in the evening; tonight he played the piano instead. Suddenly Anja sat up and jumped out of bed. She hurried down the stairs to Jiri at the piano. She climbed on his lap and put her hands on his as he played. She was totally absorbed as she kept time to the music with her little feet in my black mitten liners with the empty thumbs wiggling. We are astounded, and Jiri thinks that she was used to this happening in her life. From that day on, whenever Jiri played the piano, Anja joined him. We could only wonder about what it meant.

During supper about a week before Christmas, Beata said we were going to dress the pear trees for Christmas. She put a pile of old newspapers on the table and some scissors and glue, and she showed us how to make garlands of stars for the pear trees. Anja had fun folding and tearing odd shapes that we fastened into garlands.

After we made a pile of them Beata said, "Tomorrow we shall dress the trees."

Sunday morning, Beata baked Christmas bread that we sliced and covered with pear preserves. After coming home from church, we took the garlands out to the pear trees, and Jiri followed with his tall ladder. Our breath made little clouds before us in the frosty air as Jiri began to decorate the trees. Anja jumped up and down with excitement and clapped as our garlands encircled the two trees. At the lowest branches, he held Anja up, so she could put her garlands on the trees, and she was enthralled the whole time. When we were finished, we stood back and admired them. Beata crossed herself and said something in Czech, and Jiri smiled as Anja nestled in my arms.

The next Saturday was Christmas Eve. We celebrated with an early candlelit supper, and then presents appeared. Jiri played St. Nicklaus when he handed me a package from home. I felt tears well up, knowing I was thought of. I also felt guilty, because I had not sent them anything other than a card. I undid the outer wrappings and found a gift from my mother, along with one from my father and one from Alex. My mother had sent a big tin of Swedish cookies that she made every Christmas, as well as a little metal carousel with angels that spun from the heat of the small candles that we lit under them. Anja was mesmerized as they twirled and danced round and round. When I opened the tin of cookies, their fragrance brought tears to my eyes, tears that dropped on the note my mother had laid on top of them. In both Swedish and English, it read, *God Jul, Karin* and *Merry Christmas, sweetheart!* I held the greeting and passed the tin around. Anja saw that I was sad, and she held a cookie up to my lips. It was the best present she could have given me Then Jiri took Anja by her hand and led her to the music room, where he showed her to cover her eyes. I had to help her while Jiri carried a large blanket-covered object from behind the piano. Putting it down in front of her, he said, "Okay, look!" She and I took our hands from her eyes, and she stared in disbelief at the old rocking horse. She got her dada after all! Jiri lifted her onto it and she leaned forward into the moth-eaten mane and hugged it. She began to rock gently back and forth, humming something we couldn't make out.

Jiri sat down at the piano and played Christmas carols. Before long, even though she clearly loved the rocking horse, Anja climbed up on his lap and bobbed her head to the songs, some of which I recognized and some I didn't. The music transported me back to my Manhattan home, where my father did the same for us at Christmas. For me it was a bittersweet celebration. My parents called me on Christmas Day, another wonderful treat. We kept the conversation light as far as my departure was concerned, but on hearing their voices I had to choke back tears. I heard them in my mother's voice as well.

New Year 1939

THE NEW YEAR was ushered in with some misgivings, the sort that my father would have raised as a red flag of alarm. Here, the red flags with the black swastika on a white circle are to be seen more and more now. While some cheered at the sight, many others jeered, and it was clear to me now that I was caught in the cross-fire of political events. My fears for Anja became even more of a concern.

My continued inertia saw the days and weeks and months roll by. Just before mid-March, we had a heavy snowstorm, the kind that blankets everything and quiets the air to stillness, where even the smallest sound can be an intrusion.

I was awakened by a distant heavy rumbling sound that seemed to be coming from the bowels of the earth. The rumble seemed to be coming closer and closer. It was nearly dawn, and Anja was fast asleep. I quietly slipped out of bed and hurried to the end of the hall to look out the window that faced the street. The floor beneath my feet vibrated as I looked down, where I saw tanks rumbling heavily past our house. I wondered whether the Czech army had come into Prague in a stance of protection.

I went downstairs to where Beata stood by the partially opened door. We moved aside as Jiri stepped back in from the icy cold wind outside. He said, "They all have black and white crosses on them—they are German tanks. We are finished!"

Beata put her arm around me, "Come, I'll make us some coffee."

It was a stoic response to the inevitable outcome that the conquered must embrace in order to survive. We sat at the kitchen table in stunned silence until Jiri looked at me and said, "Now, if it isn't already too late, you have to get out with Anja. I'll try to find out whatever I can for you. Until then, we have to go on living, but keep your head down. We have our weak little president Dr. Hacha to thank partly for this. Of course, his quiver is empty now, but even if it were full, he wouldn't know what to do with it. We can also thank the French and the British for their lack of support, a go-ahead sign to Hitler that we are the sacrificial lamb in all this." Before he had the chance to go on, Beata poured him a stiff brandy to calm him down a bit.

Just then I heard Anja crying. I hurried upstairs. I bundled her up and we went down to the somewhat warmer kitchen. Today, she and I would stay home. The rocking horse saw some mileage as we tried to keep her and ourselves busy as life as we knew it unraveled.

Jiri left in the morning to join the crowds that blocked the streets to see what was going on. When he returned, he said that most of what he heard could only be considered rumor. There were so many flying around, however, that very little was known for sure except for the obvious fact that we have been invaded. That changed radically in the next few days. While the German occupation itself appeared peaceful enough, other signs were not. We learned quickly via radio that all the Czech ministries were now under German control, including the ministry of defense and the ministry of foreign affairs and communications. We were told that gatherings and political meetings were banned. Added alarm came when we were told that all Czechs were to have new identification documents proving that they were not Jewish or Roma. This proof had to go back to their grandparents. Signs were even appearing on some shop windows declaring that they were not Jewish. We were informed that strict rationing would take place as well as blackouts, with a nine o'clock curfew at night.

It was clear that citizens were trapped, because no one could leave or enter the city now without a permit to do so. Huge Nazi banners hung everywhere in the city. In the streets one could see SS men, as well as the regular army officers and soldiers. It was a massive, well-planned sweep that overwhelmed any effective preparatory resistance.

Students at the universities were being arrested for unlawful assembly, and there were rumors that some active protesters were shot. We heard that the university was being shut down. We heard rumors of names being put on lists, but for what purpose one could only guess. Alex's aunt and uncle, who enjoyed going to the theater, no longer went. The old town market became a scene of occasional clandestine exchanges of words and goods. Even the familiar street musicians who played for contributions no longer dared to come out. Life had changed overnight for everyone.

In addition to my own fears about my status and that of Anja, I worried terribly about what my parents must be going through, reading and hearing about all of this. My father's next call to me was short and direct. "Go to the American embassy and get yourself out of there. Call me when you have left Czechoslovakia. Your mother is in a state, and my anger level has reached new highs. Alex seems to think you'll be all right, but we don't. Karin, do this today, and call me with your news." His concern was no longer only his, but mine as well. One by one, my students had stopped coming, and Sabina had called saying that she was trying to apply for a permit to come back to Prague but the lines in the bitter cold for that were endless.

That evening, the three of us sat down to construct a scenario that would get Anja and me out of Prague. We finally agreed on the soundness of my presence with Anja here. That I had come to Prague with my husband Alex and daughter so that Alex could get his degree in architecture at the technical university, and then when his parents in New York had the accident, Alex returned home to help, thinking his mother would recover and get well enough for his return to Prague, to Anja and me. I continued to wait for him to return and did so because Anja was on his passport and not on mine. It was clear now that, since the university had closed, he would not be coming back, so I now had to secure exit permits and travel and transit permits and transit visas for my daughter and myself, as we were both American citizens. We saw no flaws in this story, and we hoped no one else would either.

When I went to the American embassy for assistance, I was told that it was in the process of closing down and the ambassador had been instructed to cease all official duties. On April 6, he would be leaving his post. I was given the name of the chargé d'affaires and was told to pursue my request with him. He in turn referred me to the American Consul. At that office I spoke to an assistant, who pulled me aside and asked me what exactly it was that I needed. When I told her, she gave me the name of an American woman here in Prague who was connected to The American Friends Service, that she was a Quaker, and in a position to help. "She knows me, just mention my name."

I sincerely hoped that this contact would be our safety net, and that she was still in Prague. While I waited to make contact with her, I continued to work at the bookshop, all the while feeling as if I were standing here on the sandy edge of the Atlantic Ocean as the water sucked the sand from beneath my feet.

As Jiri said, we had to continue living. Very few people were coming into the shop, but I continued the routine as best I could. The information people now needed was not to be found in any book on my shelves here.

THE INQUIRY

ONE DAY, AS I LOOKED OUT the shop window from my counter, I saw a German in a gray army cap looking at my window display. He suddenly stood up straight and came into the shop. As he approached me, it was with an assurance that weakened my ability to speak. The sound of his booted footsteps on the old unfinished wooden floor intimidated me further. Beata's words flashed through my mind, "We think they are Jewish." My God, had her father been found out and picked up by the Nazis, and now were they here for Anja? Why else would a German officer come to an out of the way used English bookshop? There could be no other reason. I felt my blood drain down to my feet as the young officer stood before me at the counter.

He looked at me for a moment, and then he smiled. I looked away to steady my nerves. To my surprise, he asked me in perfect English if I had a copy of Shakespeare's sonnets. Was this just a ruse to throw me off my guard, or was this his real intent here?

"I might have," I stammered, pulling the card file box hurriedly toward me. I had a fair number of books by and about Shakespeare, but only one that contained some of his sonnets. I told him where to look, adding that he might see other books of interest there as well. He smiled and thanked me, and then walked toward the aisle

I directed him to. I watched his back, which even under his heavy overcoat suggested a young trim fit body. Yet he had a softened military bearing, supported by his booted gait as he walked past the bookshelves. I was sure my heart was beating loudly enough to be heard. When he found the book, and spent some time looking it over, he came back to me and spoke again in well-polished English, "Are you familiar with his sonnets?"

How I kept the tremor out of my voice, I'll never know, but I said, "No, it has been a long time since I studied them in school."

"It couldn't have been that long ago." He smiled.

When I say nothing, he put the book down and patted it, saying, "I think I'll wait until you get a complete anthology of his sonnets. Thank you for your help." I watched him as he walked to the door. As he opened it, he turned and tipped his hat to me. Then he was gone. I took a deep breath, wondering whether this was just a scouting visit, with far worse yet to come. My first encounter with a German, and hopefully my last.

I continued trying to contact the American Quaker lady, but I'd had no luck. Anja was still speechless, but she seemed to be adjusting to me with less anxiety. I called my father to let him know that I was working on leaving here, making the contacts to have that happen. He said he was happy for a better connection this time and that I should keep them informed. "Alex said one of his letters to you had been returned for insufficient postage. He says to tell you he is sorry, and that now it is once again on its way to you. He says there is no change in his mother's condition and that he tries to put in more work hours. Mother is at the dentist, so I send you her love as well as mine. Take care, Karin. We love you and miss you." I felt much better after that conversation, at least about their end of it.

I continue trying to get hold of the Quaker lady. Anja still speechless seems to be adjusting to me with a little less anxiety as time goes on. The snow melts a tiny bit but then just before evening freezes up again. Winter seems interminably long, as does everything else.

SEVERAL DAYS LATER, I WAS ABOUT TO CLOSE THE SHOP for lunch when the bells on the door announced a customer. It was the same German officer from the other day. Walking over to me he smiled and said, "Hello again, today I am looking for something different. Would you have a German/Czech dictionary?"

I tried hard to hide the fear in my voice as I replied, "We had some, but lately they have been in great demand."

"Yes, I could see why that would be."

I hesitated a moment before saying, "I'll take a look and see what we have."

He followed me, and I could sense the length of his stride as we walked to the language section. All that was left was a thin translation pamphlet for tourists, with requests for "where is," "how much," etc. He stood so close to me that I could smell the sharp cold air he had brought in on his heavy woolen overcoat.

He smiled at the pamphlet. "Not what I need at the moment. Is there any chance you might get something better than that?"

I attempted to put some bravado in my voice when I said, "These days, not really, but I'll keep you in mind if I should get one." I cringed inside, hoping he didn't take this as an invitation to return.

He followed me back to the counter, saying, "I also need a good bilingual conversation manual."

In my nervousness I blurt out, "Actually, I have set aside, and have been holding for over a month now, a good German/Czech dictionary and a good textbook on German/Czech conversation. I have not heard from the gentleman since his first inquiry, so I think it is safe to say he either has forgotten or no longer wants them." I took them out from below the counter and handed them to him. As he took them from me, I noticed that he had nice hands. Hands had always held a special fascination for me.

He looked them over quickly and said, "Yes, thank you! This is exactly what I need. May I buy these?"

"Certainly. In fact, this will be my first sale of the day." I smiled nervously.

He smiled again and said, "By the way, before you said 'we' when you spoke of the shop, yet I never see anyone else except you here."

"Oh, I'm only helping out as a favor to the owner. She has gone to be with her daughter who had a baby in a town some distance from here."

"Well, in that case, I hope she is no hurry to return, because then I would miss seeing you." His smile deepened took on a personal quality with this compliment.

For the first time I admitted to myself that the little crinkles that appeared around his beautiful blue eyes when he smiled, and his dark hair further accentuated his uniqueness and captured his appeal for me, regardless of his uniform. I seemed to be speechless as I thought he was just too good looking for comfort.

He patted the books and said, "Thank you for all your help. I must be off to start studying again. I have not forgotten the sonnets; I will look in from time to time, if you don't mind."

"No, of course not. I'll still keep my eyes open for a copy of them for you."

"I'll keep my eyes open as well." He smiled warmly again and tipped his hat to me as he left. His words could of course have had other implications, but I thought that wasn't so bad; maybe this is just a harmless book-buying customer and not what I had feared since he first came in. His English was impeccable, and his usage was certainly much more formal than mine, giving him an added charm. He softened the formality with his friendly voice and warm smile, both of which I am becoming used to.

In the afternoon a few days later, when Anja had settled down for her nap behind the counter, I saw a gray cap at the door hesitating just a moment before opening it. I looked down at the small desk below the counter and busied myself with the card file. I heard him walk over to me and stop. He didn't start speaking, so when I couldn't avoid it any longer, I looked up to see him smiling at me. He said, "It is nearly as cold in here as it is outside. Can you take a break and come and have a coffee with me at the café just down a few doors? Would that be possible?"

I responded quickly, "Thank you, but I can't, my little one is asleep." He leaned over the counter and looked down at Anja, fast asleep on the cushions on the floor. A wave of fear shot through me and I regretted having mentioned Anja's presence, because now he had seen her as well. I had to hope for the best while I feared the worst.

"Yes, of course. Perhaps another time then." He smiled and left. About fifteen minutes later, he reappeared, followed by a young man from the café carrying a covered tray. The officer took the tray from the young man and thanked him, and then he set the tray down on the counter. It had two cups of coffee, cream, and a sugar bowl, and

94

two small pastries. Looking at me, he said sincerely, "I realize that being with me in public may be an embarrassment to you, but, as you see, where there is a will, there is a way. I see this as the next best thing." He smiled broadly as he gestured to the tray, saying, "It's just coffee served with a little sweetness, nothing more. I only hope you will see it as such." Then he extended his right hand and said, "My name is Ernst. May I know whom I have the pleasure of meeting?" I did not extend my hand to him in return, stunned as I was by all of this. He said pleasantly, "Well, maybe next time then."

I let out a breath I didn't realize I was holding. I slowly reached out and shook his hand. I quietly said, "Thank you, I'm Mrs. Wilson."

"Ah, a pleasure." He looked down at my hand and, seeing no wedding band, said, "I would not have guessed you were married. Perhaps I should have known because of your little one, but then one can never know these things for sure. I hope I have not offended you."

I tried to hide my embarrassed smile by shaking my head. "No of course not."

He put his cup down after a few sips and politely asked, "May I ask how it is that you have a child and no wedding band?"

Quick to deceive him, I said, "I take it off when I do laundry."

"You must do a lot of laundry then." He smiled. "I meant nothing untoward when I said I would like to stop in now and then to see if a stray copy of the sonnets should appear."

I nodded, glad for this innocent direction of the conversation. "I'll keep my eye out for you for a collected edition, if you'd like."

"Yes, I'd like that. Thank you." He finished his coffee, once again formal. As he pulled on his gloves, he said, "It was nice seeing you again. And now I should go."

I watched him leave. He seemed nice, although he is much less afraid of asking bold questions of me than I am in answering them.

I wondered how impressive my deception had been, if it had been at all. I told myself that time would tell—I just hoped that in my anxiety I wasn't too transparent in my answers.

I finished my coffee and wrapped the two little pastries in a napkin to save for Anja. The young man returned for the tray and left without looking at me even once. I was sure there was no new flag hanging from his house.

When I got home, Beata said the lady I had been waiting to hear from called and said she would be in touch again in a few days. I was both relieved to know I had not been forgotten and fearful that I missed her call.

On Sunday morning, just as we are about to go to church, Jiri said in disapproval, "Say a prayer for all of us, since the Catholic priests blessed the German troops at the occupation. And don't forget one for Cardinal Schulte in Cologne, who praises Hitler, so many prayers for so many Germans, and so little time for it all."

Even going to church was now an eye-opening experience because among the usual congregation there were now a number of German soldiers. This sight was staggering, considering what was going on outside. I looked back at when Alex and I arrived here, when things did not seem as threatening as my father had feared. My world was quite small, consisting of the little house on the tree-lined street, meals with Alex's aunt and uncle, and the bookshop. I made few exchanges with others, mostly due to my lack of the language. Whenever I did venture out I would hear even more foreign languages—after all, Prague was a cosmopolitan city that drew many to live here, not a place that one would flee from. Things had changed, but the German invaders were well disciplined and friendly, if one set aside the true intent of their presence here. I would see these soldiers, usually in groups of two or more. I wondered if that was for their companionship, or for intimidation for us, or for their own safety as they walked around sightseeing. They took photos of the astronomical clock in the square, doing what any other tourists would do, only they were not here for only three hours, or three days, or three weeks; rather, they had imposed themselves indefinitely. I shuddered to think of Anja and myself in their light.

Despite my concerns, I reassured myself that, as an American, I was safe, that Germany and America had no quarrel at hand. I felt America would not go to war—how could they, even if they wanted to? Three thousand miles of ocean separated them, it just wasn't feasible. Besides, earlier on the American authorities had presented no obstacles to some Czech Jews who were not political and who wanted to leave. Every country they sought out had a quota, but still, as I found out later, nineteen thousand people left in 1939. As of now Anja and I weren't going anywhere. I now have another small life to protect at all costs, and so my efforts continued in that direction. It continued to snow heavily, well into spring.

THE QUAKER LADY

A FEW DAYS LATER, the Quaker lady called. "I'm sorry that you had to wait to hear from me again, but I'm glad to speak to you at last. I must see you. Can you meet me tomorrow at the other side of the bridge? There is a small shelter there by the little sausage kiosk? Can you be there at eleven? I'll be wearing a black coat with a red wool scarf."

"Yes, I will be with a little girl. She is three years old and I'll be carrying her small blanket."

"We won't miss each other, I'm sure. See you then."

When I met her, she greeted me warmly. "I know nothing more about you, but that you need help."

I bought Anja a sausage and we went to a bench in the little shelter. We cleared the snow off the bench and sat down. I told her I could hear in her voice that she is from New York City.

"Yes, Morningside Drive. And you?"

"I live in the Village on Perry Street, with my parents."

After this little bit of chitchat, she grew serious. "I notice you have referred to me as the Quaker lady. I'm used to that; it even gives me a lower profile, which can be an asset in what I do. Tell me your situation, and I'll see what I can do for you." When I told her the whole story, she shook her head and said, "After all this time, I was sure I had heard it all, but never, never anything like this. Okay, here is how I see it. You, as a U.S. citizen with a valid U.S. passport now, and I stress now, can only leave Prague with an exit permit and all the other needed travel permits and transit visas so that you can make your way home. The little one here is a different story. By the way, from now on her name should be Anna, as in Anna Wilson. Anja will raise an eyebrow or two. Remember, she is an American now minus the proof, as far as you and anyone else is concerned, but still, without papers the best I can do is get her assigned to a refugee group of children to go to England. The golden rule, however, is that a parent may not accompany a child in a refugee group. These children are assigned to families once in England. That is how it works."

I shook my head emphatically. "She could never be separated from me. She has been so traumatized; she doesn't speak but a word or two. I don't even know what language she understands! She would never survive separation from me. So that's out of the question. What are the other options?"

"I am offering salvation and emigration, and I am allowed to operate only under these conditions, for as long as they allow me, which can change at any given moment. Other than that, there are no other options. Aside from that, the only other possibility is very risky, as much for me as it would be for you and her. You would need to get falsified exit permits, travel permits, to leave Czechoslovakia and the same along with travel visas for Germany, Holland, and England for her and you. Then you could travel with me in the train car neighboring that of my child refugee charges. With a bit of luck you might make it through Germany and on to England. Once in London, I could arrange for you to be escorted to Southampton and onto a ship for the United States or possibly Canada. If it goes to

Canada rather than the United States for some reason, there could be further complications. This is an all-around risk, and it would take time and money to get falsified exit permits and travel permits and visas. How prepared are you for that expense?"

I was crestfallen. "Not at all."

"No, I didn't think you were. But then, that is where I am connected, better at some times than at others, I might add. Do you want to give it a try and travel with me? There are no guarantees for any of it till you are safely in England. It is up to you, and I will do all I can to make it happen. What do you think of the risks?"

"Yes, I'll risk it. I don't see any other way for us."

"Good, I'll get to work on it. It will take some time, but I never know how long. In addition, I am often away ferrying children out of here. Don't worry, I won't forget you. By the way, Mrs. Wilson, get yourself a wedding band." She smiled at me when I gave her a hug and thanked her for meeting with us.

I wrapped the blanket tightly around Anja and carried her across the bridge, now a metaphor for our survival together.

Sabina is also bogged down with red tape and long lines for her permit to return to Prague. We are adjusting to daily life with new restrictions and rationing. After sharing what the Quaker lady had told me, I asked Beata where I could buy a used wedding band. She shook her head and went to her room. She came back to the kitchen and pressed a ring into my hand. "Sabina has no further use for this, but now you have. Try it on. "

It is a bit too big for me. Beata took it back and thought for a moment. Then she took a spool of heavy linen thread and wound the thread around a section of the band. Giving it back to me, she says, "Try it now." I slip it onto my left hand, and it fits snugly. I am now a proper-appearing Mrs. Wilson; I can't decide whether my mother would laugh or cry at that. Beata said, "Karin, it belongs on the right hand."

I shook my head. "In America we wear it on the left hand, the heart side."

She laughed. "You Americans are so romantic."

REVELATIONS

———————

A WEEK OR SO LATER, the German officer returned to the bookshop. "Good morning, Mrs. Wilson?"

The uneasy shiver returned as I said, "Good morning."

"And where is Mr. Wilson?"

I feel this is not a social call or a book request, but something more official.

"He is back home in America, attending to a serious family illness."

"When will he be back?"

"I am awaiting the answer to that any day now." I feel myself grow pale, and for the first time really afraid. He must have sensed that, because after a pause he said, "Well, Mrs. Wilson, I hope things go well for you. These times are troubling enough as it is. I was on my way to an interview, I just thought I would stop by to say hello. Please do remember me if a copy of those sonnets should grace your presence." He smiled, tipped his hat to me, and left. I shuddered as I wondered if perhaps I was the intended official interview. Now more than ever I hoped to hear from the Quaker lady soon.

The same day, the letter from Alex arrived. The envelope had official stamps all over from being processed twice. Reading it, it is clear that he has no idea what life is like here. I won't write to him about that, because Jiri told me about a rumor that the mail was soon going to be opened by the Germans—perhaps they already were at that point. I wondered how safe phone calls out the country were, and I decided that the less that was written or said about life in Prague, the better. What amazed me is that I had adjusted to all this with relatively easy acceptance. I would not have thought it previously, but I supposed that one just goes along to get along, so long as you were not Jewish or Roma, that is.

I heard from the Quaker lady the next day. The weather had warmed a bit, and the streets were fairly clear of ice and packed snow. As I crossed the street to the market square, I saw the etched white scrapes in the cobblestones left by the Nazi tank cleats, scars that would remain for a long time to come. For the first time I feared how deeply etched this all may yet become for my leaving. I grasped my coat collar tightly around my chin as I tried to step over a deep rut to step onto the sidewalk. I saw a gloved hand extended to me to assist me onto the sidewalk, and without looking I accepted the help. When I looked up, I saw it was the German officer from the bookshop.

"What a pleasant surprise," he said. "Surely you have time for a coffee to warm you up, if nothing else. There is a nice little café just a few streets down; I have a coffee there once in a while when I need to get out of the office." Without waiting for an answer, he took my elbow and led me along the sidewalk.

"I have just a quick minute before I do my errands and before I open the shop," I invented as he whisked me toward the café.

He opened the door for me and followed me into the simple café. As we sat with our cups of coffee, he pointed to the café's wall murals. "That is one of the charms of Prague. Even a simple place like this is adorned with beauty. The bookshop as well, when you are in it. Please, enjoy your coffee—things cool down so quickly in this weather." I did not have my ration books with me, so I could not feign shopping. More importantly, I feared that I would miss my appointment with the Quaker lady, and I couldn't even let her know why. He must have noticed my increasing anxiety. He said, "Can I drop you off anywhere? I work just across the street and am parked nearby." I looked out the café window across the street and stifled a gasp. The building was one of the Czech ministry buildings, but it now served as headquarters for the Gestapo, the German secret police. Buttoning my coat, I managed to get out the words, "No, I think I'll attend to my errands some other time, thank you. I was just out for a hurried breath of fresh air before being in the shop all day."

"I have to go to work as well. Take care, and do be careful crossing the streets. There is still a lot of confusion on the streets with the change of left hand traffic to right hand. These days you have to be extra cautious." He got up and, tipping his hat, said, "Until later." He left without a backward glance. I saw the coffee waitress looking at me and shaking her head. A few other patrons went back to reading the café's newspapers, held fast in their wooden rods, while a couple older men placed the papers back in the rack for others to discern the day's fact from fiction. I felt caught at every turn now, but this event left a quickening in my gut as I watched him walk into that building.

I hurried home and called the Quaker lady, leaving a message for her that I was unavoidably detained, but I hoped to see her at her next earliest convenience. When I sat down, Anja came rushing over and climbed onto my lap with her well-worn bunny. She had gotten a bit better now about my leaving her for a short period of time, hugging the bunny and the rocking horse in my absence.

Beata and Jiri asked me how it went. I told them about the German officer, from his first visit at the bookshop to today. This is the first time I have mentioned him, and Jiri looked at me with concern. He said, "This is not a good thing to be happening for you."

I let my hands drop into my lap. "I can't control it, and besides maybe knowing one of them could be helpful at some point."

"Or not!" Jiri sneers.

"If she calls, please give her the number of the shop and the hours when I am there. I didn't want to leave that information in my message."

Jiri turned his back to me and said, "I think you are trusting the wrong people."

Suddenly a loud backfire sounded from a truck just outside our door. Anja jumped off my lap and with frightened wide eyes she put her finger to her pursed her lips and ran to hide behind the piano. Beata, Jiri and I looked at each other.

"Poor little thing, she is petrified," Beata said as I gathered Anja in my arms. She was shaking with fright. No wonder she didn't speak; the fear of making a sound had been etched into her psyche. *Is that how she lost her mother?* I wondered. Was she alone in hiding when she saw her mother taken? It was only conjecture on my part, but there was a wide area of missing information about her, so that one guess could be as valid as another. Holding her close to me, I said, "Anja, it's okay, it was only a truck." I knew she didn't understand a word of what I said, but the gentle calmness of my voice was reassuring enough to her as she leaned her head on my shoulder and sucked her thumb, holding my hair tightly with her other hand.

I realized that I was being pulled in too many directions at once, each bearing its own responsibilities and consequences; sleep did not come easily that night.

THE FOLLOWING DAY, THE GESTAPO OFFICER CAME TO see me. He was smiling and as friendly as usual. Still reeling from yesterday's discovery, however, I was not.

"Good morning," he said cheerily. I said nothing. "You appear upset. Have I said or done something to upset you?"

"No, not really."

"Well, then, what is it really?" he asked gently.

Unaccountably, my fear lessened as I blurted, "I didn't know where you worked, not until yesterday." Then I was embarrassed and afraid again, and I looked at the floor.

"Please look at me. From the moment I saw you when I walked into your bookshop, I hated this uniform, because I knew it would cause a gulf between us, one not of my making, one that I would have to bridge so that we could be just two people meeting each other without any symbols of distrust on either side. I told myself after seeing you that I would find a way for that to happen. I want you to know that I have nothing to do with the Gestapo or the SS in that building where I work. I am a member of the *Wehrmacht*, that is to say, the regular army, just as any other country's army. In fact, the Gestapo, the SS, and the regular army have a distinct distrust and dislike for each other. They don't trust us and we don't trust them, and they don't even trust each other. So you have nothing to fear from me. Quite the contrary, in fact."

His words hung heavily in the air. I finally said, "I don't know what to say."

"Just say what you feel."

He waited, and when I said nothing he went on, "Back in Berlin, I had been practicing law when the government decided I must go into the army. I am not even a party member, which displeased them, so I was surprised that they made me an officer. I guess they wanted

106

a lawyer to do their paperwork, even though I see little fine print to be interpreted. I sit in a small windowless room and fill out papers all day. I am a supply officer. That means I order everything that keeps them functioning here. Yesterday I requisitioned all the meat and potatoes needed for the next month. Today it will be diesel fuel and tires—nothing more sinister than that. If I had my wish, I would be back behind my desk in Berlin pursuing the letter of the law. I did not choose my present state, and the only good about any of it is that I have met you. That is my only defense, and you will have to judge me on that. I hope the outcome is in my favor. I'll leave you with that for today, but I want to come back tomorrow to face your verdict." He leaned over the counter and quickly put a very light kiss on my cheek, saying, "That was my last plea." He turned and left.

Having been here a while now, I had discovered that one did not need to be German to be a Nazi, and that a German is not necessarily a Nazi. I also learned that not all Germans are party members. Now I was confronted with coming to terms with my feelings and the facts. I wanted to trust that he was who and what he said he was, and I wanted to believe that he was no danger to Anja or me, and that he could possibly even protect and help us. I realized that I had already reached my verdict, subject to future proof coming to light. Wanting to believe it and actually believing it were not the same thing.

The following morning, I had just opened the shop when he came in. He stopped just inside the door, putting his hand over his heart and taking a deep breath. Then walked over to the counter where I stood.

"Like a condemned man, I did not sleep last night, I'm here for your verdict." The slight smile on his face faded, it gave away his uncertainty. When I cleared my throat and took a deep breath, then I said, "You are the first German I have ever met or known, except for my high school math teacher. If I didn't understand something that he had laboriously gone through for the class, he would look at me and say, 'Math is and isn't like poetry. You can understand the basic parts, but together the meaning eludes you. It's first only when you grasp the overall concept, when they coalesce, then it has meaning.' It was his way of relating the material that I didn't understand, my impoverished ability to do math was further confused. I knew what he meant, and yet I didn't get it." I laughed. "I think you are pretty unusual, too, being so fond of Shakespeare's sonnets."

"Well, I hope I don't plague you with any unsolvable problems. He sounds like a good teacher, although perhaps a bit advanced in his explanations for high schoolers."

"I'd like to know, as a German, are you an exception?"

"My mother is convinced I am," he laughed, "but I am much more reserved than she on the matter. And you? Are you a typical American?"

"I'm not sure there is a typical American. We're firm believers in freedom of the self. We are and can be anything or anyone we want to be, if one is willing to work for it and you don't harm anyone else in the process. Our revolutionary war freed us from the British class structure; that is how we won our democratic pursuits of the individual." I hoped my pompous garble did not put him off.

"You make it sound easy, but I'm sure it wasn't."

"Anything worth having is worth fighting for, and that is never easy."

He nodded. "You could say that about you and me, too, I suppose. Am I to suppose your verdict favors me?"

I nodded. "Yes, but I don't know what more I can say."

"Again, just say what you feel."

"I like seeing you, and I miss you when I don't." At this point there was more surety in the words than in the feelings I had.

Smiling he took my hand in his and said, "That is a good beginning. That is how it started with me, too, you know." He leaned over and quickly kissed my cheek. Then he said, "That's for encouragement to further those feelings."

"I'm not sure I need that much encouragement," I smiled.

"You see, it's working already!" He stepped closer to me and gently took my hand. "This is only a reminder that gulfs can be bridged."

His warm gentle touch on my hand passed a feeling to me that I was not prepared for. I was still trying to think about his verbal and visual messages to me without these new physical ones. He did not say anything further on the subject, and neither did I.

Uncertainties

===

ALEX'S LAST LETTER was full of questions, to which I dare not give answers. He also talked about work and the loneliness in the apartment, he says when thinking about me, he said that he has regrets for having talked me into going to Prague with him.

I wrote back that all I could think about and work toward was coming back as soon as possible, and again, could he send me more of what he owes me.

The Quaker lady called me today to arrange another meeting over the lunch hour at the shop. I was so glad to see her as she hurried over to me. She asked if it was all right to talk, then we briefly exchanged some information. Hers was that she was trying to get papers for Anja and me through a faster but more uncertain route. Then she told me something even more uncertain. "For now, it is only a rumor at best, but these days, rumors with bad news bear listening to. There is now a condition called 'stateless persons;' you of course are not one, being that you are American, with a passport, but as for the little one that is uncertain." The word "uncertain" raised fear in me as much as "stateless persons" did.

"Since you don't have any documentation for her, the authorities could declare her to be whatever they wish, and then the whole situation may be out of your hands. People are disappearing in the night, and I want you and Anna to be one of them, only under my protection." At that point I told her about the German officer. She stared at me in disbelief, then said, "Keep all our talks and contacts private. Do not tell anyone about our arrangement, otherwise it could be the end of it. I have to continue to walk a tightrope in what I do here, and at any time the authorities could pull it out from under me as they see fit. So many lives are at stake, so please be very careful. Don't write or talk about any of this, because these days you can count on the Germans reading and listening to anything coming into or going out of Prague. I'll be in touch with you as soon as I have more news. I have to go now. Please be careful." She squeezed my arm and left. I went home for lunch with Anja, newly alerted to our situation.

By now I have stopped looking for men of a certain age who might have a scar on their cheekbone and a loose buttonhole thread. I was sure that the man I was looking for will not appear. In the weeks that have passed, we kept having more snow. I didn't think it could get much colder, and then it did. On a day that felt colder than any other so far, I considered leaving Anja home, but I knew she would not tolerate that. I kept an extra little blanket for Anja in the shop as she settled into her little nest of pillows and blankets on the floor and played quietly.

Early that afternoon, after Anja and I had returned from lunch, Ernst came in with a bundle and set it on the counter. He said, "This is for Anna, an extra blanket. She'll need it in the coming days of colder weather." Ernst had continued to stop by often for short visits. Through our conversations, I learned that he was a lieutenant in the *Wehrmacht*, and his last name was Möller.

"Thank you for the thought. I am sorry to say that I cannot afford it, and I have no coupons for it."

"None of that is necessary. Consider it a gift from 'the administration' he smiled. "And now, I have a surprise for you. I have tickets for a string quartet performance this evening; I would be honored if you would be my guest. We could have a bite to eat before, if you can make arrangements for your little one to be cared for."

This was not something I had prepared myself for. When I did not answer, he said, "Don't worry about the curfew. You will be fine, because you will be with me."

He left me no way out, yet I can hardly believe it when I hear myself say, "I think I can arrange something."

Ernst was genuinely happy with my response. With a warm smile he said, "I'll come by for you at five when you close."

I worried about all the possibilities that this entailed, most of them frightening. One worry among many others was that he would know where I lived. What had I done? I called Beata and told her what was going to happen.

"Don't worry, we'll take it in stride. We have to hope Anja will, too."

As I was getting ready to close the shop, I was folding up the woolen blanket Ernst had given me. I noticed a label in the corner of it: Lt. E. Möller. He had given us his blanket! I'm sure he had replaced it from the army's inventory, but for Anna this one was irreplaceable.

At a few minutes before five, Ernst appeared at the door. I closed the shop while he watched, then I carried Anja as we boarded the streetcar to go home. I was not at all at ease being in the company of a German officer. After we were seated, the ticket taker came over to me. Ernst pointed to Anja and me and then to himself, at which the ticket taker raised his hand to his cap in a civilian salute and moved on to collect other fares. A few people looked at me side-ways, giving me looks of disapproval, while others smiled at us. The lieutenant took my hand in his as if we were a couple, and he smiled and nodded at the people. As soon as I dared, I retracted my hand to gather my coat collar around my neck; I looked out the window past the people and told him this was my stop. He stood up, and to my surprise he gently took Anja from my arms and carried her off the streetcar. I followed behind them. Seeing him carry her away from me gave me the worst kind of a fright, one of helplessness despite having sworn myself to safely care for her. We walked the block and a half to the house. I opened the door and then took Anja from him. He followed me inside to be out of the cold. Jiri was at the kitchen entrance, holding his newspaper with his reading glasses on the tip of his nose. He looked over his glasses at the officer and then walked back into the kitchen. Beata stood there, looking pale. She held Anja's bunny tightly. I put Anja down and Beata started to unbutton her coat. She looked up at us and said stiffly, "Have a nice evening."

I left quickly with Ernst, feeling like I was on that same tight-rope as the Quaker lady.

He took me to a small Hungarian restaurant. As we sat down, he said, "The wine here is as stout as the best Hungarian goulash in Prague." I felt so nervous that if the wine hadn't gone to my head quickly on an empty stomach, I don't think the goulash would have made it off my plate.

At dinner Ernst told me a bit about himself. "I was fond of literature in school. Perhaps that was my true calling. I know that the military isn't, but there I have no choice. Maybe when it's all over I can go back to Berlin and follow my true passion, at least one of them." He smiles, pouring me more wine.

The concert was all Mozart, an enjoyable escape for me from an otherwise tense evening. During a short intermission, Ernst said, "I like Mozart, even though he wasn't German at all. Did you know, he was born a *Salzburger,* an Austrian? Well, we see him as one of our own. He came to Munich once, to play when he was just six. He died when he was thirty-five, only ten years older than me. I can't imagine being dead ten years from now, having lived only half my life. What a dreary thought! Back to Mozart. His opera *De Entfurung aus dem Serail,* which is translated as 'The Abduction from the Seraglio,' was an instant success and brought him fame through all of Europe at the time. The words of his I like most are 'Love, love, love, that is the soul of genius.' In the opera, when she sings 'I shall be freed by death,' Mozart understood the torment of love only too well. I don't mean to lecture you. If I sound a bit pedantic, I'm sorry to have done so. Oh look, here they come again."

The lights lowered, but my anxiety did not. His discourse seemed all too similar to what I saw as current events. Or was I looking for hints and messages that weren't there?

When the lights lowered, he gently took my cold hand into his warmer one and drew it over to him. There was no eye contact, only new warmth between us that was easy to understand. When he turned the wedding band on my finger, I wondered if the linen wrap gave him pause. As he held my hand, the music became a muted background for me. For some time, I felt that his warmth was binding me to him in a way that I have never experienced. Whenever Alex held my hand, it was nothing compared to this. This simple act by Ernst raised a new emotion in me. I don't know what was happening, but I let it happen anyway as the music of Mozart came to the fore once again.

After the concert he invited me out for a cognac and coffee. He took me to a nice little place filled with smoke from cigars and cigarettes and the laughter of well-brandied voices. "It's a bit dense in here, but we won't stay long. Just a quick cognac to round out the evening."

I was glad that he didn't ask a lot of questions about me, but then I worried that maybe he already knew the answers. The cognac was quick, and we bypassed the coffee for some fresh air. When we came outside, it was snowing heavily. We linked arms to keep our balance as we walked along the now snow-covered icy sidewalks. He knew just where to get the streetcar home from here. When we got to the passenger island where the streetcars stopped, he turned his back to the cutting wind and unbuttoned his coat. He drew me to him and enfolded me in it, wrapping his arms around me to keep me close to him and his warmth. He leaned down as he looked at me, and when our brandied breaths met, he kissed me warmly. Being held by him and being kissed awakened a new intense feeling for him—then the clang of the approaching streetcar as it swung around the corner to this stop put an end to the moment. He backed away from me and buttoned his coat again, and we once again linked arms to navigate the icy stop into the streetcar. It was dimly lit, and there were only a few people sitting at the far end, probably shift workers with permits to be out past curfew.

He got out with me at my stop and again held me close as we navigated the treacherously icy sidewalks. I wished I lived some streets further on from where I did. He saw me to the door and said, "I have enjoyed being with you this evening so very much. I know that it must cause you some anxiety, being seen with me in public. I wish it were not so, but I can not change that. I hope that whatever the distress, it did not spoil your enjoyment of the evening."

"Ernst, I am no stranger to anxiety or distress, so I try to handle it as it happens. I enjoyed your company and I, too, had a very nice time tonight. How will you get home in this cold with so few street-cars running at this hour?"

"I have my thoughts of you to keep me warm on the way." Then he put his hands on my waist and gave me a quick kiss on my cheek. He turned up his collar, tipped his hat to me, and said, "I must let you go now. Goodnight, Mrs. Wilson." He turned and walked down the street into the cold darkness, while he had become the warmth and the light in my life.

I walked into the kitchen to see Beata holding Anja fast asleep on her lap. Beata smiled at me, but Jiri did not. And so, the evening ended.

I TRIED TO ORGANIZE MY THOUGHTS AND ESTABLISH A clearer picture of this young German, I felt at times he was as nervous about me as I was about him. He seemed to genuinely like me, and that too was worrisome as I thought of my chances of leaving here, which were clouded. I remembered how he held me at the streetcar stop, and our kiss, and the intense yearning I had for him to continue embracing me. It was a desire that I had never known before, and it swept over me again and again. By the time I was ready to fall asleep, Anja had pressed herself up against me, her face buried in my neck. I remained on my side as I fell asleep, my mind crowded with foreign affections.

At breakfast, Beata asked, "How was the concert last night?" I told her a bit about the evening while Jiri ate his breakfast. Jiri didn't look at me, and he hadn't greeted me when I came to the kitchen. I felt chastised by that message of disapproval; he did not have to say a word. I addressed it by saying, "I did not ask for any of this. I don't want to ruffle any feathers or call attention to myself. I just want to work my way home."

"Is that what this is?" He asked as he held his newspaper in front of him. Anja and I left for the bookshop. Leaving the house, I wished that today could be a normal, uncomplicated day, even though I couldn't remember anymore what that might be like.

Ernst came into the shop mid-morning. When I said good morning he said, "There have been better ones. I'll be away for a few days I am going to Kutna Hora, about an hour from here. It's all about paper work and more paper work."

Hearing that, I wished I could give him Sabina's address in hopes that he might help her get back to Prague. I decided against it, thinking it would be best not to involve the family. My own involvement was troublesome enough.

"I'll see you when I get back. Try to keep warm." He reached in his pocket and handed me a bar of chocolate, saying, "For the little one." He smiled, tipped his hat, and left. I looked at the bar of Swiss chocolate, wishing that Anja and I could be where that chocolate had come from.

Several quiet days later, the lieutenant returned on Friday afternoon. He walked up to the counter, smiling at me. He said, "I have missed two things. The sonnets that I have been trying to recall over the click clacking of the train ride back to Prague, and your smile. When I think of you, I can only remember one of the sonnets. I wonder if you know it. I think it goes, 'But woe is me! Too early I attended a youthful suit, then something, then O, one by nature's outwards so commended, that maiden's eyes stuck all over his face. Love lacked a dwelling and made him her place, and when in his fair parts she did abide, she was new lodged and newly deified.' Did I get it right?"

" You have a good memory."

"But did I get it right?"

I nodded. "Yes, the Bard of Avon would have been delighted."

"But the real question is, are you?"

I knew only too well what this thinly disguised love poem he had chosen to recite alluded to. I tried not to look flustered or flattered when I said, "Shakespeare's words are a true delight to hear."

"One of the things I like most about Shakespeare is that he is a dance master of words. Do you agree?"

"Yes," I said, smiling broadly. "I would have to agree."

"You too know how to dance around a direct question, but do I hear an answer in the dance? "

"You do me far too great an honor comparing me to Shakespeare." I laugh.

"Oh, but my honor for you stands alone, not to be compared with anyone else."

My embarrassment appeared as a rising blush, caused by his personalized meaning. He had such a way with words, and on the wooing scale he was definitely escalating.

"That said, and now in clear English, I wish to invite you out for lunch on Sunday. Do you think you can arrange care for your little one?"

"I don't know, at the moment. Can I call you when I make arrangements?"

"I'm sorry, but I will have to call you. Would you prefer me to call you here at the bookshop? And must it always be 'Mrs. Wilson?' You haven't told me *your* first name."

"It is Karin—Karin Wilson. Yes, at the bookshop would be best." I gave him the number, and to my surprise he said, "Yes, thank you, but I already have it." I knew I had never given it to him. That brought up inquiry alarms in me; did he also already know my first name?

He tipped his hat and said, "I have to go. Try to remember, if you can, the words in the poem that I forgot. I'll call you. Goodbye for now, Karin Wilson."

At supper I asked if I could leave Anja with them for a few hours on Sunday for lunch. Beata looked away and said, "Yes, that will be fine, as long as it's after church."

Jiri said, "Anja and I will play the piano and go to the zoo, two of her favorite things to do when her mother is otherwise occupied. Yes, Karin, it is fine." Once again, I hear the reproach in Jiri's words. I felt guilty about leaving Anja, and about putting another burden on Beata and Jiri. I resolve that I will not allow this to become a habit.

Ernst called on Saturday and we arranged to meet on the street corner near the house.

The next day, I saw Ernst leaning against a car as I approached the corner. He stood straight and tall when he saw me. When I reached the corner, he said, "I have a car today. I know of a nice little inn just outside the city. I hope you like it." He opened the car door for me and I got in to yet another nervous unknown chapter in my life here in Prague. It was a cold, clear sunny day as we headed out past the city limits into the sprawling countryside. I realized that I was seeing this for the first time since I had come to Prague. Just before we left the city center, we were stopped at a red light. He pointed down the cross street and said, "You see that corner building? Well, the one next to it is where I am quartered. I think it used to be a boys technical school before they converted it into officer's quarters. It is clean, it still smells of fresh paint; it is warm and dry, and the food is rather good. I wish I could show you my room there, but ladies are strictly forbidden."

"Good heavens, did you walk from my house to here that bitter cold and snowy night? It is at least a mile from where I am!"

"The imagination is a wonderful thing at times. I thought of you the whole way, and I barely noticed the cold. Only my feet were unhappy, protesting the need to walk away from you."

"That is quite an imagination, even by my standards." We laughed at ourselves.

"How has your week been?" he asked.

"I have been trying to keep order on the shelves and in my card file."

"It sounds a bit like what I do."

"Often times people will take a book from the shelf and then don't return it to where it was."

"Yes, I can understand that, but then they must have been distracted by you, as I was."

I waved away his compliment. "I don't know, but it keeps me busy."

"In my case, the distraction quickly became an attraction; one *I* can't be blamed for." He smiled at me. Embarrassed, I quickly turned to look out the side window to avoid looking at him. After a minute, he said, "We are nearly there." He soon pulled into the yard of a country inn. He said, "I hear they have a fine menu and wine list."

He opened the car door for me and showed me into the inn, which looked more like a hunter's lodge inside, with a crackling fire in a huge fireplace. We were shown to comfortable seats by the fireplace, where we were to wait until our table was ready. Ernst looked over the wine list. He ordered in German, and soon a bottle of wine arrived, along with freshly baked bread and goose pâté. He said the specialty here was wild fowl. I had never been in a setting like this to say nothing of this wine and appetizer. The crackling and snapping sounds of the logs in the fireplace filled a strained silence between us. He suddenly said, "I hope you aren't a vegetarian, in which case this is a very poor choice for lunch. But I seem to remember you did eat the goulash, so I think I have chosen well."

"No, among my many flaws, that is not one of them." I felt a flush of heat on my cheeks, but I couldn't tell if it was the wine or the fireplace or something else.

Ernst said, "I'm glad to know that you are not a vegetarian, but the flaws that you claim surely are not based in fact." At that point, the waiter came over and handed us menus. The Lt. spoke German to him, and then he asked me, "May I order for both of us?"

"Yes, please."

He ordered in German, and when the waiter left Ernst said, "The house specialty is partridge prepared to perfection—at least, that is the claim. I hope you will like it."

"I have never tasted partridge before. All I know about it is that at Christmas time we sing about one that sits in a pear tree." We both laughed, and I realized that the wine had thawed the earlier tension.

"What did you think of the goose pâté?" he asked.

"I liked it, but then I like goose as well. My mother is Swedish, and when they can afford it, she roasts one for Christmas dinner. She inherited that custom from her mother, who was German."

"Oh, we have more in common than we first thought. My mother too made one for Christmas dinner. And you have a German born grandmother?"

"Yes, she married a Swedish ship builder and never returned to Germany."

"Women do that, they—marry and then follow their husbands. Tell me, why did you not go back to America with your husband?"

I explained about Alex's parents. Then I said, "And now I need all the required papers like everyone else to leave, and I don't know how to do that, or if the authorities will even let me leave, because I hear that the authorities will keep my passport in order to get that exit permit. I was told in the United States when I got my passport to never to give it up to anyone. My daughter is on my husband's passport, but now he can't return to Prague and I can't return to America. My little girl is so traumatized by all this I fear for her well-being."

Ernst nodded gently. "Don't worry, things have a way of working themselves out, given the time."

Just as I put my wine glass down, the waiter came to show us to our table. It was beautifully set, and the pristine whiteness of the tablecloth lit up our faces as the waiter lit the candles. I thought of Jiri and Anja at the piano and at the zoo, and for just a moment I wished I was with them. Our plates arrived with the partridge slices covered with a rich cream sauce, along with Brussels sprouts and roasted potatoes, and a compote of red berries that reminded me of cranberries, and we were presented with a new bottle of wine.

The food was delicious. The lieutenant looked at me and asked, "I hope it is to your enjoyment, because we can end it with a dessert that defies description." I nod wordlessly, letting my reaction to the delectable food speak for itself. Dessert was a light creamy pudding over which a strawberry sauce was poured. This dessert is familiar, but I can't tell anymore how it compares to this than I can about anything else right now.

We had an after-lunch espresso, but I declined the brandy, feeling that the wine had already transported me to a guilty place of selfish enjoyment. My thoughts were interrupted when Ernst said, "I keep thinking of that sonnet poem I recited to you and the missing words that I would like to find. I have a collection of his sonnets at home. I asked a man who makes handmade books to make me a fine leather binding containing equally fine paper on which the sonnets were beautifully printed. With or without luck that binding will out-live me. I left it at home, too valuable a treasure to be subjected to the rigors of military life. But that sonnet is an ode to love, one so ten-uous it could disappear any given moment in our lives, one that we are only able to touch upon now and then, and only if we are lucky enough to have even met with it once in our lifetime."

The waiter came over and placed a silver plate with a slip of paper on the table. Ernst glanced at the slip of paper and then depos-ited enough money on the plate to nearly pay for Anja and me to travel to New York. It shamed me to think that I had consumed that in wine and food. The waiter bent close to the lieutenant's ear and said, *"Wünschen Sie ein Zimmer zu bestellen?"*

I got the gist of the waiter asking if Ernst wanted to reserve a room. Ernst replied, *"Nein, danke."* No, thank you. We got up from the table and made our way back to the room with the large fire-place. The waiter brought our coats. Ernst laid his across a chair and took mine from the waiter. He helped me into my coat, and then the waiter helped Ernst with his. As I started to button my coat, Ernst said, "Please, may I do that? I want to know I have contained your warmth." He buttoned my coat and took my hand as we left. The waiter bowed, looking at me as we walked by him. When we are back in the car, but before Ernst turns the motor on, he said, "You have given me great pleasure. Today is a day that I shall remember. Thank you." He leaned over and kissed me. As we head back to Prague, he asked "Mrs. Wilson, how long have you been in Prague?"

"Please, you can call me Karin. I came in August of last year."

"Longer than I. You were here for the transformation. Did that come as a surprise to you?"

"I don't speak or read Czech, so I did not keep up with events as they were about to happen. So, yes, when the tanks arrived on that March morning, I was surprised."

"You must not worry. We are here only to administrate the city. I know it's hard for the civilians to grasp that. But once things are in place, everything will run more smoothly. It has to for normalization. I am new to all of this, but that is what has been promised us. What do you find the most troublesome?"

I wanted to say the large red Nazi banners everywhere, and some of the stories I have heard, but I didn't. "The shortages affect us most in everyday life. My husband's aunt and uncle deal with most of that for me. I'm glad I have only to go to the bookshop every day."

"Yes, so am I." He smiles, "You'll be fine here, I'm sure of that."

"For someone like me who is so uninformed, that is reassuring." The truth was I was more informed than reassured.

He patted my hand, which was resting on my knee. "It has been a hard winter, but we are coming into spring, and it should warm up soon. If ever I can do anything for you, please, you have only to ask."

"Thank you."

The cold gray steeliness of the sky hovers over us again as we enter the outlying ring of Prague.

"Would you like me to drop you off where I picked you up?"

"Yes, that would be fine. Thank you for the exceptional lunch in the countryside."

"It was my pleasure, Karin. I'll come by the shop to say hello."

"I'll be there."

"Please, if I am to call you Karin, you must call me Ernst. Shakespeare would have it that way, you know." He laughed. Then, taking my hand as I moved to leave the car, he said, "Karin, thank you." I smiled, and then stepped onto the sidewalk. I closed the car door, and I knew he was watching me. Only when I turned the corner did I hear the car's engine start.

The sound of my key in the door brought Anja running to me. She pulled me into the music room and stood at the piano. She played a single octave scale with her little right hand. It was a struggle for her little fingers, but she was ecstatic and so was I. Jiri looked at me and said, "Something good has come out of today after all." Beata smiled as she resumed making potato dumplings.

After supper I wrote to Alex and my parents. I believed that now no news of any substance from me is good news and worth repeating in either of my letters. In bed that night I reviewed the day's events. Some brought back a smile, while others did not.

Spring 1939

WE WERE WELL INTO April now. The days were getting longer, and the sun was able to warm us a little if we walked in its path. I also noticed a new feeling that came over me whenever the lieutenant appeared. Just seeing him walk toward me gave me a heightened feeling of wanting closeness with him, an intimacy like an emotional fever just at the sight of him. I had feelings I shouldn't have for this man, who had suddenly stepped into my life out of the cold. I didn't know anything about falling in love, if that's what this was; admittedly I had never had any intense feelings for Alex. But this now had a grip on me, one I had to deal with.

A daily worry on my part was the fact that Anja still would not speak. She did not even call me by my name. Under certain circumstances, that might have been a good thing, but whatever had caused her trauma still had its hold on her—and thus on me.

One day Ernst arrived with a small package of sliced salami, rolls, cheese, and two bottles of beer. He also had a sweet for Anja. I had gotten used to his frequent short visits, and by that time we had little anxiety together and were happy to see each other. I think he was as lonely as I was. He told me about a dog that wandered into his office from the street. It had just sat there, looking at him. "He would not allow me to pet him." Ernst said, "I'm convinced he came as a messenger with a secret message, that I was to come to see you, and so here I am." I laughed, but even in this telling he showed shades of poetry about him that I was drawn to. After a while he leaned over the counter and kissed my cheek, took the empty bottles, and left. He made my days here more bearable yet, at the same time, unbearable.

The Quaker lady called and asked, "How old are you?"

"Chronological or emotional?"

She laughed, "You choose."

"I'll be twenty-two next month."

"What is your eye color?"

"Before or after crying?"

Another laugh. "Your choice."

" A watery blue."

"Do you have any scars or identifying moles?"

"Yes, I have a three-year-old daughter."

"I gather the scar is the lieutenant, then? I know your hair color, just keep it the same. I need the same information for Anna now." When I gave her the information, she said, "That's all for now, Mrs. Wilson. Don't forget to wear that wedding band; they leave impressions and one on your finger as well which may be looked for in any part of your journey."

"How soon?"

"I don't know. I'm bogged down with paper work for hundreds of children; as soon as you are papered, I'll let you know. Take care." She hung up. For now, Anja and I were descriptions in her paper networks.

I got a package that day from my parents. My mother had sent me my flowered rayon blouse, which I liked to wear in warm weather. I held it to my face, feeling an overwhelming longing as

I inhaled the smells of home, again and again till the dampness of my breath dissolved them. Even now I could hear my father's key in the door, quickly followed by, "I'm home!" Mother had also sent my heavy linen skirt, a pair of sandals, and some socks. In the skirt pocket were two letters, one from Alex. My parent's letter was newsy and with lots of questions for me that I couldn't answer. Alex's letter was one of impatience, implying that I was purposefully staying here to be away from him. If he kept this up, it may become true. I wrote to my parents in appreciation.

To Alex, I sent a picture postcard of the old astronomical clock in the town square. I wrote, "Alex, mark your desired time of my departure and I'll consult the heavens for a date. I'll alert Copernicus to make the reservation, upon payment from you! Karin."

His reply came quickly this time. It was a picture postcard of the Statue of Liberty. "Just keep your attention focused on this. I'm glad to see you haven't lost your sense of humor, but I wasn't amused. Alex"

Well, that put our current relationship on an equal footing. Thank goodness for the Quaker lady, my one anchor in reality.

On a nice warm Sunday afternoon, Ernst invited Anja and me out for a picnic lunch in one of the many parks in Prague. Sitting on the bench as he unwrapped the boxes' contents, he spread a napkin on the bench and he set out roast chicken, a tomato and onion salad, and wonderful rolls and cheese. Anja leaned on my lap nibbling away; it was good to see her eat. The fresh air did me a world of good as well. After lunch she cuddled in my arms and fell asleep. Ernst sat close to me, and he put his arm around my shoulders as we sat there like any other married couple with a child for a lunch outing. I saw him looking thoughtfully at Anja. Eventually he said, "It's odd, I think, that she doesn't look like you much at all. She isn't as fair-skinned as you, and she doesn't have your blond hair and blue eyes." Hearing that worried me, because I had not really thought of it until now.

I said, "You're right, she doesn't. She looks just like her father, same dark hair and eyes."

"I'm sure though, she has inherited your gentleness and sweet smile."

"I hope she will develop more than just that," I quickly add. "As she gets older, I mean. My next one will probably be a boy with blond hair and blue eyes."

"Yes, if chance has anything to do with it, that could happen."

I looked at other couples and wished for once that I were not the exception. We watched a boy running with a kite and his dog chasing after. It is peaceful and serene, I sit with my eyes closed and my face tilted up bathed in the sunlight, when I feel Ernst's lips on mine. When I opened my eyes he said, "I did not mean to disturb your moment of bliss, but I selfishly wanted so much to be a part of it."

I moved some hair away from my face and said, "Like a sonnet revisited."

He smiled warmly, then, looking straight ahead, he said, "I wish I could go home now and take you with me. What would you say to that?"

"It can't happen. You see, I don't speak a word of German." I smiled.

"You wouldn't have to, I would teach all Berliners English, because I would do anything for you, possible or impossible. Now, what do you say?"

I laugh and say, "I believe you, and I would say that would be the ultimate of transformations."

Just then Anja stirred and woke. I straightened her up and we went for a walk. Ernst carried Anja, and she rested her head on his shoulder and nodded off to sleep again. We walked on the tree-shaded path, just like any other couple.

As we left the park, I saw a sign in Czech and in German posted on the entrance pillars. When I ask Ernst what it said, he replied, "It's to inform the citizens of the new regulations. It says, 'Entry forbidden to Jews.'" I could hear the distress in his voice as he read it to me. "The administration has plastered these signs all over public and not so public places. Do not worry, it does not affect you in any way."

It did in fact affect me to know that I must never enter such places with Anja; someone could stop us, just on a whim. While I did not need to act like a disenfranchised citizen, I knew I needed to think like one at all times now, and sometimes act like one. I wondered what Ernst would say or do if he thought that Anja was Jewish and that I was harboring her. It was my duty never to put it to the test—not ever, under any circumstances.

That evening I told Jiri and Beata not to take Anja to the zoo or parks anymore, and I explained about the warning signs. Jiri, who had disregard for all the new German edicts, acquiesced and offered to build Anja a sand box in the back yard and a swing to replace the off-limits zoo and parks. The new worries we have to face are everywhere now.

My Twenty-Second Birthday 1939

AS I READ THE WARM MESSAGES from my parents, I was struck by the fact that my birthday is May 13. Who would have thought I would be spending it here? Certainly not I!

Ernst came by this afternoon. After saying hello, he said, "Close your eyes for a moment." I did, and after a rustle of paper, he said, "You may now open them." He held a small violet colored box in his hand. It was slightly larger than his palm. He held his hand over the top of the box and said, "Allow me to help you open it." There was a rosette of violet tissue paper on the inside and under it lay a nest of handmade Swiss rum truffles. He didn't know it was my birthday; in fact, not even Beata or Jiri knew. I was so touched by the gift my eyes flooded a bit when I thanked him. He leaned over the counter and gave me a kiss, saying, "Nothing is as sweet as that." He tipped his hat and left. I looked at the lid he had covered. It was from a chocolatier in Bern, Switzerland. I took one and closed my mouth on a creamy rum truffle the likes of which I had never tasted before. I had one for Anja; when she woke up, she would have her first rum truffle, too. When I went home that evening, I told Beata and Jiri about it. Beata beamed when I offered her one, but Jiri snapped his newspaper closer to his face and said, "Too bad it had to come from

Switzerland through German hands." His hostility only increased when Beata told me she had gotten a job through a friend of hers to cook hot lunches for the soldiers. They were hiring civilians to perform some of the domestic jobs. Jiri cleared his throat behind his newspaper when Beata said, "I like it. I work with my friend and we have a hot lunch, and can take any extra lunch perishables home, in fact, we have goulash for supper tonight that my friend made. It also pays well." At suppertime, Jiri drank a beer and ate bread and cheese instead. When Beata was finished eating, Jiri wiped her bowl with a piece of bread and said, "One day we'll wipe them off the face of the earth." He poured the rest of his beer and went back to his paper.

While Beata and I were slowly adjusting to things we could not change, Jiri was not. The only joyful sound in the house these days were the piano, where Jiri and Anja practiced daily. Anja had now accomplished a two-octave scale, with her little fingers working twice as hard as Jiri's. That night as I lay in bed listening to Simon's sonorously haunting Bach etudes for cello float down from his room upstairs, I thought of Ernst, his unknowing birthday gift of rum truffles, and the kiss he gave me on parting. He was a mix of things, but then so was I, as I drifted off to sleep.

After our terse exchange of picture postcards, Alex stopped writing, until one day, when Beata and Jiri got a letter from him with the message that they were to send me home without further delay. Alex suggested it was they who kept me there; when I heard that, I begged them that under no circumstances were they to say a word about Anja. My parents and Alex still knew nothing about her and now with the chance opening of the mails, I wanted everyone ignorant of my true situation and what kept me here. Jiri only said, "I'll leave the correspondences to Beata. Alex would not appreciate my contributions at all." A few days later, Beata showed me the casual letter she wrote in answer to his. She had written it in halting English, which kept it brief. I cringed whenever I thought of my parents or Alex asking me to come back, and how I had to continue to put them off.

The last time I had spoken with the Quaker lady, she had told me there would be another short delay in procuring the needed transit visas for Holland and England, but that it was all in the works. My whole life is now in the works, with possible changes expected at any time.

Today the lieutenant came by with a small bouquet of flowers. He said, "I walked in the park earlier and saw the new spring flowers. I was tempted to pick some for you, but then I decided against giving you contraband, so these are from the florist," he laughed. "I cannot vouch for where he may have gotten them, however. How are you?"

"A bit tired. It must be the warmer days of spring. Thank you for the flowers."

"I notice you haven't been doing as much laundry lately, so that can't be it. There is a band concert in the park tonight, would you like to go?"

"I'd have to bring Anna. She hates it when I leave her." I was sure that being with a German officer Anja and I would not be questioned if we were out past the curfew or for any other queries.

"Yes, of course, bring her blanket and pillow, and I will bring some food and wine. You can relax; I will come by for you at six. I'll meet you at the corner again. I will have a car. I'll see you then." He leaned over and gave me a quick kiss on my cheek and left.

I enjoyed his fun spirit and warm friendship, and I was beginning to like him more and more, too much perhaps, because the word "like" is now an understatement.

Anja ate a snack at home while I told Beata that Anja and I were invited to a band concert in the park along with supper. Beata smiled; Jiri scowled.

We met Ernst around the corner. Anja liked the car ride, and I enjoyed the beautiful chestnut trees, which were about to bloom on the boulevards. Anja was very excited to see us entering the park. Ernst brought a large blanket—I wondered if it was the replacement of the one he gave us—and spread it on a flat spot away from the bandstand. Anja ran after some pigeons before coming back to sit down while Ernst unpacked a supper of cold chicken, sausage and cheese, wine, and an orange drink for Anja. She sat between us, munching happily. Ernst looked at her and smiled. He said, "She seems happy in her silence. Have you asked a doctor to look at her?"

"No, but I've talked to someone about it and the feeling is that once she is in a familiar, stable family situation, she will regain her desire to speak."

"Does your husband know about her silence?"

"No, he worries enough without that."

"If I may, I don't agree with you about keeping it from him. Of course, I play no part in this. If I were her father, however, I would want to know. Exactly what, now, is keeping you here?"

"I need the paperwork to leave and I don't have it. It's as simple as that."

He said nothing and, so I had the feeling he is disinterested in my dilemma. Really, why should he be otherwise? He opened a bottle of wine and poured us each a glass. "What shall we drink to?"

"Happier times," I suggest.

He shook his head. "No, I think these are the happiest of times, for me anyway. A crust of bread, a glass of wine, and thou, that is how I will remember this evening and any others I have had or will have with you." He looked into my eyes then, and said, "To the times, then. *Prost!*"

I quickly took a sip of the wine, and then I handed him the glass. I put Anja's pillow down, and she lay back on the pillow, curled on her side. I covered her with her blanket, and she closed her eyes to the strains of a Viennese waltz. I lay down next to her, as is our routine. Then Ernst lies down next to me, resting his head on folded hands. He said quietly, "I can see us dancing to this at the pavilion by the lake in Berlin. I can feel the gentle breeze brush your hair against my cheek and feel the evening chill leave us as I hold you even closer." He then turned on his side to look at me. "But that is the ideal, one I can only wish for." He gently put his hand on my arm saying, "Karin, I am falling in love with you, and I don't know how to stop it. I must, because there is no future for us. You are married, and so none of this should be happening. And you will leave Prague and Europe altogether soon. I do not belong in your life, but you have inextricably entered mine and I don't know what to do about it. I have tried to reason myself out of it, but as you can see, that has not happened. It is such a beautiful feeling I have for you, one I want to feel even more intensely every time I see you. I simply cannot let you go. I did not intend to complicate your life, but I think we have done that already." There were two things I could tell him that, if they didn't stop him, would at least slow him down, but I said nothing.

"I didn't want this to happen, none of it—not the army, not you, especially not you in this impossible situation, because I know it can only end sadly. I never chose any of it, yet I also have not the power to stop it. Loving you has been the sweetest price to pay for all of it; without the army, I would never have met you. You are the other side of that coin, the most valuable of all and that will never change for me, no matter what the other side has in store for me. The other day,

I told myself I would try not to see you. I walked past the shop, but before I had reached the end of the street, I turned around and came back. You see, that is how undisciplined I am when it comes to you. From the first time that I came into the shop and saw you, I have not been able to stop myself from going back again and again."

Hearing this, I tried not to look at him. I wished I could be as honest with him as he was with me, but the risk was too great. Anja's safety was foremost in everything I did or said. Every time I was with Ernst, I had to pay that price, again and again.

With him next to me in the cool spring air, I wished for him to be even closer. I wanted to say, no, I'm not married, not at all—but I don't because I can't. I held his hand in mine, and with my other arm I covered my eyes to hide any betrayal that I feared could be seen there as he leaned over me and, stroking my hair, kissed me. Then he stopped and suddenly sat up, then patting my leg he said, "Well, have we had not enough wine to drink, or have we had too much?"

I looked up at him sadly and said, "Maybe some of both."

I wished he hadn't been so respectful of my non-existent husband, because now I, too, had feelings for him that I didn't know how to stop.

MAY HAS SLIPPED AWAY AND JUNE IS UPON US. AT TWEN-ty-two years old, I seem none the wiser where Ernst is concerned. If at any time he were to suggest a room for the afternoon at the inn, I would not hesitate to go, not even a second. But he didn't. His sense of honor put mine to shame, and I added that to my already long list of shameful behaviors. I do believe that for the cause of them I will be forgiven, but by whom? Or do I have to do that for myself as well?

Ernst and I saw each other as often as possible, and it became harder and harder not to give in to our feelings, which grew deeper and more binding each time we were together. I was not sure we will outlast the temptations we have for each another.

The Unexpected

IT IS THE MIDDLE OF JUNE when the Quaker lady called to tell me that she expected the transit visas for Holland and England to come through at any time. When that happened, I would have to put all my energy into applying for exit permits and travel permits from Prague, and for transit visas for Germany, which I should already have been doing, because if I were without them I would need more doctored papers, which could take even longer. I didn't say a word to anyone about this; I had to weigh one burden against the other. I couldn't imagine never seeing Ernst again; I wasn't convinced that either of us were actually trying to stop that feeling.

One Sunday in June, Ernst invited Anja and me for a ride in the country. I loved these Sundays with Ernst, within or outside of Prague. They made leaving feel less urgent, even though all the while I knew it was a bubble that had to burst one day.

When we met him, I was shocked to see that he was wearing a pistol. He saw my reaction and said, "Late Friday evening, a group of protestors entered the building. I was still working when I heard the commotion. They were stopped, of course, but after that, we were warned to wear our pistols at all times. We should have been anyway, but some of us were lax about it."

How strange that Jiri, who was eager to keep me up to date on the latest transgressions of the invaders, had not mentioned it. Maybe the Germans wanted to keep it out of the newspapers and radio newscasts, or, maybe, the event never happened. It was a reminder of the might of the occupation we were under, which made me think back some days earlier, when Ernst and I were walking together. Coming toward us down the street were two SS men. Ernst leaned down to my ear and whispered, "Remember what they look like. These are dangerous men, and you must avoid them at all costs." Then he guided me into a small shop before our paths crossed. I felt relief at his warning, and I hoped I could at all times avoid them. I realized that Ernst never took Anja or me to the fancy places where the SS liked to congregate. Aside from the inn outside the city and the concert in the park, we went to small, out of the way places.

I shook off the dark thoughts and returned to the bright sunny Sunday as he drove us out into the countryside. Anja was delighted to see cows and horses, pigs, and chickens on farm after farm, and suddenly I realized that some of this was familiar. As Ernst pulled off the road into the driveway of the inn, my head spun. What was he thinking? I couldn't think of anything to say as we walked out of the hot bright sunlight into the darker cool of the inn. The same waiter greeted us, and upon seeing Anja his disdainful looks for me softened. We were seated at a table immediately this time, and Ernst said, "I thought a refreshment was in order. I hope you don't mind?" I shook my head and smiled, and he ordered some drinks and sweets for us. The question of a room would not come up because we had Anja with us. Ernst said, "I just wanted to be here again with you, perhaps for the last time."

I was quiet, trying to sort the whirlwind of thoughts about all the different things that "perhaps for the last time" could mean. What was he thinking?

We finished our drinks, and I wiped the last traces of the fancy ice cream dessert from Anja's lips. He paid the waiter, and we went back into the heat of the afternoon. He suggested I sit in the back with her out of the sun, so she could nap. Every now and then I saw him look at me, in the rear-view mirror. The idea that not all love stories ended happily troubled my mind; I could only hope that ours would not end tragically. He drove for a while longer, eventually pulling off the road when we came to a shady forest. I looked down at Anja asleep in my arms as he got out of the car and opened the back door.

"Karin, please put the little one on the seat and come out with me."

I feared the worst—was he going to shoot us? —But all I saw in his hand was his blanket. He opened the other doors to let the breeze cool the car, and then he took my hand and we walked to a large oak tree. He spread the blanket out beneath it. Then he went back to the car and gently lifted Anja out from the back seat. He placed her on the shaded blanket, then stood again and stepped next to me. He said, "Karin, I wanted only one more private moment with you, we have so few of them. Today I wanted to take you out into the cool green of the countryside and away from Prague to unburden some of my thoughts to you, but now I fear I will have burdened you hearing something unwelcomed. If you want me to end this, just say it. Please say it now, if you do."

I feared the worst was about to happen. I looked at him with a soft smile when he drew me nearer to him, with his arms around me. He said, "When I knew I couldn't stop loving you, I wanted all of you for me to remember for the rest of my life, but this is as close as I dare come. Anything more is not my right." He then squeezed my hand and said, "I'm sorry, Karin."

On the way back, Anja searched the fields for more farm animals, while I searched for a quietness that my heart and mind needed to go on from here.

THE NEXT DAY, I WAS LOOKING THROUGH A BIG BOX OF books and some sheet music that had been donated by a secretary when the American Embassy had packed up to leave. To my delight, I found *Begin the Beguine*, a favorite of mine. I held it up and sang the lyrics as I danced around the shop. Anja watched with great interest. I was so absorbed that I did not see Ernst at the door. He had paused before opening the door, knowing that the bells would disrupt the scene. I saw him at the door as I finished, and when he came in he said, "Would you sing it again so that Anna and I could dance to it?" He held her in his arms and danced around as I sang. She laughed with glee. When the song was over, he put her down on the counter and took me in his arms. "I think I am practiced enough to try it with you now." He cleared his throat and continued, "When you do dance, I wish you a wave o' th' sea, that you might ever do nothing but that."

"Ernst, Shakespeare is never far from your thoughts."

"It is you who are never far from my thoughts."

We danced while we softly sang the melody together. Anja was entertained by it all. Then he went to her and, taking out a small bakery box, he asked me if she could have some marzipan. I nodded, and he opened it for her. There was a miniature pear, strawberry, and banana, painted with food color to look like the real fruits. Anja picked one up and looked at me, and when I smiled and nodded, she took a bite. Her eyes widened and the rest of it disappeared into her mouth.

"Ernst, they are expensive! You shouldn't spoil us like that."

"Nothing is too good for my little family. I hope we can *Begin the Beguine* another time soon, but now I have to go. I'll see you soon." He leaned over to kiss me, and then he left.

STOLEN MOMENTS

WHENEVER ERNST STOPPED BY to see me, I felt more and more drawn to him. I can see the same in his eyes as well. One day, as we sat in the little café, holding hands, he said, "People are being transferred from my building. I don't know whether I'll be one of them. Little notice is given, sometimes no notice at all—they just leave. I'm telling you this because there may come a time when I will be gone. I want you to know that it is not because I have stopped wanting to be with you. I would never stop wanting that."

"I will also have to leave one day, Ernst. When, I don't yet know, but it will happen."

He nodded sadly. "Yes, I know that, Karin." Then he lifted his head and smiled. "But now, let's move on to a happier subject. There is a dance tomorrow evening at one of those pavilions I mentioned. Would you accompany me?"

"I'll see if I can get care for Anna."

"I'll call you at the shop after lunch tomorrow. I have to go back to work now. I'm drowning in paperwork these days."

When I asked Beata that evening she simply said, "Have a nice time."

Jiri on the other hand responded somewhat ominously. "Ah, Karin, do you know that these nice times will end?"

Beata chided him gently in English, "Jiri, listen to me, she is young, and she has no friends here. She doesn't speak the language. Don't deny her a little harmless fun." He looked over his glasses and said nothing. He simply shook his head and went back to the newspaper.

Wearing my favorite flowered blouse and the heavy linen skirt, I dressed for an evening of dancing with Ernst. When I got into the car with him, he leaned over and kissed me. He said, "Now that will put me in a mood for more than dancing." He smiled as he turned on the motor. The dance pavilion was on a wide lawn in a park, with a bandstand decorated with colored lights and paper lanterns; there was a bar and several tables with food. Ernst had bought two tickets, which entitled us to a small table, dancing, and the purchase of food and drinks.

When we sat down, he reached for my hand. "You are looking very beautiful tonight, Mrs. Möller." He grinned sheepishly and went on. "The 'Mrs. Möller' part I made up, wishful thinking, but the rest is true."

I tilted my head to the side and said with a smile, "I am so happy when I'm with you."

"So am I, even more than I dare admit."

When the band began to play, he took my hand and led me to the dance floor. We danced a few numbers and then sat down. He looked over the drink menu and said, "From what I see here, I suggest the white wine. Shall I get two glasses, Frau Möller?"

"Yes, please." He was having fun this evening and so was I. He returned with the wine and raising his glass to me, said, "Here is to you, Frau Möller. We've very nearly earned that right, you know, very nearly."

The evening was lovely from start to finish. I felt care free in his arms, moving to the music and flush from the wine. At one point, while I rested for a moment, he went to the musicians and talked to them. When he came back he said, "I have a small surprise for you, I hope." I saw the musicians hold a short conference amongst themselves, and then I heard a familiar sound. Ernst took my hand. "Shall we?" As I followed him, I recognized the opening bars of *Begin the Beguine*. I felt safe and protected as I danced with him, and I returned the feeling when he sang the lyrics "Darling, I love you." I did not want the evening to end but, as with everything in life, it did.

EXCEPT FOR THE HEAT, MY MIND COULDN'T ACCEPT that it was now mid-July. Ernst and I saw each other nearly every day, and I miss him when I don't. He came into the shop one morning waving two tickets. He said, "Guess where we are going tomorrow night?"

I smiled and said, "The bull fights?"

"Certainly not! We are going to the ballet."

"The ballet? How did you manage that? I hear people have to wait months now to get in to see a performance."

"Where there is a will there is a way, remember?"

I laughed. "What are they doing?"

"Something different. It is to be an evening of famous *pas de deux*."

"That is different. It sounds exciting."

Ernst made a humorous quick bow. "An evening out with you always is. Can I pick you up tomorrow at five thirty, at the corner?"

"I'll be there." A quick kiss and he was gone.

When I told Beata and Jiri about the ballet, she asked, "Do you know why it is an evening of only *pas de deux*? It is because they can't stage a full-length ballet anymore because the backstage manpower is gone, drafted into less entertaining work."

Jiri looked over his paper at me, "To do the heavy lifting for the Nazis, of course!"

Beata said "The dancers will still delight the senses."

"Yes, even for those who have lost most of their own." Jiri is becoming increasingly hostile to me over my seeing the German officer.

AFTER THE BALLET, I CAME QUIETLY INTO THE KITCHEN. Anja was fast asleep on Beata's lap. Jiri said angrily, "I trust you had a good evening at the ballet, while others in Prague tonight did not. What's the matter with you, Karin? Get off your romantic naïve cloud and take your blinders off to these new 'administrators' of Prague. Jews are disappearing, and protestors are imprisoned, and some have even been executed. That is what is going on while you look the other way for an evening out with your officer!"

Beata scolded him. "Jiri, enough now. It's late."

"Yes, I'm afraid it is, too late." He got up and stomped out of the kitchen.

Beata apologized for Jiri as I lifted Anja from her lap.

"Yes, I am sorry, too. Thank you again, Beata."

I felt swept away by the maelstrom of emotions.

EARLY IN AUGUST, ERNST CAME INTO THE SHOP WITH AN idea. "I would like the three of us to go to a professional photographer to have our photos taken."

"That sounds costly. Can't we just borrow a camera?"

"I want a good professional to do it. Can you be ready for that tomorrow?"

"I suppose so. Are you sure you want Anna in it, too?"

"Yes, by all means! She is part of us."

The following day the three of us were sitting in a photographer's studio. Ernst told the photographer exactly what he wanted. Ernst turned to me and said, "Please don't smile. I want you *au natural.*" Anna and I each sat for a number of photos alone. Ernst hadn't sat for any photos. Then he said, "I would like one of the three of us together." He took off his cap and jacket and asked me to sit next to him. I moved to put Anja on my lap, but Ernst shook his head. "Please have her stand between us. That way I can see more of you." When Anja stood between us, he put his arm around my waist and crossed his other arm in front of Anja, taking my hand so that we are both holding Anna together. He said something in German to the photographer, and then he said, "It's okay to smile for this one." A few more poses were photographed, and then we were done. Ernst paused to give further instructions to the photographer, and then we left. "Thank you for that, Karin. Now let's find an ice cream for her and something more celebratory for us."

A FEW MORNINGS LATER, ERNST BUSTLED INTO THE shop and hurriedly said, "Bring your passport to the shop with you tomorrow and any documents you have for Anna and yourself."

It was very unlike Ernst to be worked up like this, so it made me nervous. "Why?"

"You'll see, just do as I ask. Please don't look so worried! I'll see you tomorrow." Before leaving, he squeezed my hand and said, "Until then. I'm sorry I can't stay longer, but I have a lot to do." I watched as he left; now feeling far more worried than I looked. He wasn't his usual casual self, and his words had come with a commanding edge to them, even as he held my hand.

What had happened? What had changed? Was Anja's father picked up? Do they know about Anja now, and what I have done? The rest of the morning passed in a haze of fear.

When I went home for lunch, Beata said, "The Quaker lady called. She'll call you again tomorrow."

I now hoped tomorrow would not be too late. That evening at dinner, Beata said I looked pale, and I could only manage a cup of tea. She said she hoped I wasn't coming down with something, just then there was a quickening in my gut and I rushed to the toilet to rid myself of its watery contents.

In bed that night, I held Anja in my arms, hoping it would not be the last time as I recounted the day's events. I could not escape the very worst thoughts of what might happen. It was terrifying to think that I had allowed myself to become a patsy in exchange for some affection from a German officer. Was I so deprived for such attention that I unthinkingly risked Anja's well being and life by tapping this unknown source? Had I really been that blind and selfish all this time?

I did not sleep, and I thought of what Ernst had once said of himself, days after we had met so long ago, when he awaited the verdict of my judgment of him. Was that all a ploy to put me off my guard? Did he know about Anja and me from the very beginning? Morning could and couldn't come soon enough.

Ernst arrived just after I had opened the shop. At the counter, in an official voice, he said, "May I see your passport?"

My hand shook as I handed my passport to him. Then he asked, "And what about the little one?"

"I have nothing for her. She is on my husband's passport, which is in New York, with him. That was part of my problem here."

Ernst's face softened, and he said, "Karin, was I the other part by any chance?" I slowly nodded my answer, but would it be enough to save us? I watched my passport in his hands as he looked carefully through it. For a terrifying moment, I felt a pall of doom as though the high wire were about to give way under me.

Ernst reached into his breast pocket and placed an official envelope on the counter. The Nazi insignia seemed to scream at me at the top of the envelope, which was nearer to me. My heart thundered in my chest as if to fail. He looked at me and said, "I have a surprise for you." As he took a small stack of papers from the envelope, I saw official papers, some with a photo of Anja and me. I felt dizzy as my blood drained to my feet. The only thoughts on my mind as I watched him lay out the papers on the counter were dire indeed. When and where had I made the fatal mistake? I had been so careful with all my fears surrounding Anja's safety, but had I somehow betrayed the greatest of trusts given me? Was the man before me so much better at deception than I was? Was it all over for us now? That was my last thought as he looked up at me and, turning the papers so they were upright in my hands, he gave them to me. He said, "You have here exit permits for you and Anna, and a set of travel permits and transit visas from Prague and to Germany, and another set of transit visas for Germany to Holland."

The photos I had seen were those that we had taken a few days ago. The photos were attached to each permit by two grommets that went through the photos to prevent tampering. They all bore official stamps and signatures. He looked through my passport once more and took the papers back to make some entries on the documents. He reviewed them carefully and slowly, and then, signing them all, he handed me his pen and said, "For your final permission."

I was speechless, while what he had done for Anja and me sank into my frightened mind. My hand slowly reached for his pen. I mutely took the pen, still warm from his hand, and signed the documents for our freedom.

Ernst put the documents back in the envelope, along with my passport. "These permits are good for one month only, so you must use them within that time, or," he paused and reached for my hand, "or not at all. Be sure to be in Holland by then. I urge you to leave as soon as possible, because there will likely be delays along the way." He reached into his other breast pocket for another envelope. I recognize the photographer's name on the envelope. Ernst took out the photos, the ones where we had posed together. "I have made one for you and one for me to keep." It was a truly perfect picture of the three of us. He put one back into the envelope and handed it to me. "Please keep this separate from the others—perhaps closer to your heart would be a good place for it. If ever you doubt your memory, just look at us."

Then he took my hands in both of his and said, "I must tell you something for which I hope you won't hate me. This paperwork is also part of what I do in that building. I could have done these months ago for you. But I wasn't strong enough. Loving you, I did not know then and even now, I do not know how to stop, and so I wanted to keep you here for as long as I dared. I hope you will forgive me for that. Your husband is a very lucky man; I envy him and hate him at the same time. Karin, I only wish I had met you before Mr. Wilson did, and under very different circumstances."

I stepped from behind the counter and took his warm hands in my cold hands and led him between the book cases. I embraced him, leaning my head on his chest and silently praying for my own forgiveness. He folded me in his arms, and when I looked up at him he said, "Now, Frau Möller, I have to transform you into Mrs. Wilson. This I do against my will, as my mind but not my heart tells me I must. I have to tell my heart that this is for the greater good, and so it shall be. Once you have your transit visas for Holland and England, you can leave by train from Prague. I'm sorry, but I cannot arrange those for you. Let me know when you have them, then I will have two train tickets for you and Anna, my parting gift to you, so that I may see you safely off. I have to go back to work and do what I can to provide these same documents to perhaps a few others of the many hundreds seeking what I have given you." He took me in his arms and kissed me as if for the last time. Then he left. I returned to the counter and leaned heavily against it. I looked down at Anja and said a silent prayer of thanks and forgiveness for all I have and have not trusted in Ernst and myself.

I called the Quaker lady to tell her I had some paperwork for her to look at. She told me she had gotten some for me last night and would come by the shop right away. When she arrived, she paused at what must have been a strange expression on my face, if it reflected just a small portion of the conflicting emotions I was feeling. She asked what had happened, and I handed her the envelope with the Nazi insignia on it. She gasped, "Oh my, what is this?" She pulled out the documents and looked them over. She gasped again, and then a third time before she spoke again.

"Good heavens, do you know what this is?"

I held my breath after I whispered, "I think so."

"These are not only the valid documents, but they have a high priority rating. Not many people get this. With this classification, no one seeing it will dare question you. Whatever did you have to do to get this?"

"For starters, I had to trust someone whom I shouldn't have, trusted."

"That must have been the hard part."

"It was, the hardest."

"Well, my dear, I have here two sets of transit visas for you and Anna, one set for Holland and one for England. You and Anna have everything you need to leave at any time, and the sooner, the better. I have a group of children I'm transporting to England, and we are leaving on Saturday, August nineteenth. You can travel with me in the next train car."

"Saturday the nineteenth? That's fifteen days from now."

"Yes, and I would be on that train with me if I were you. I say do it!"

I nodded. "It's just that I've wanted this for so long, now that it's here, it's a bit scary."

"It'll only get more so the longer you wait. Look, guard this packet with your life, because ultimately it could be worth just that much, and Anna's. See me at the train station no later than half past eight on the morning of Saturday the nineteenth. I'll look for you. If you're delayed or change your mind, contact me right away. I have to go now, see you there." As she closed the shop door behind her, the bells sounded louder and longer than I knew them to be.

That evening I told Beata and Jiri the news. Beata smiled through tears as she hugged me and said, "I will miss you and little Anja, but I am happy to know you'll be home soon."

Jiri reacted as if a thorn in his side was about to be removed. He irritatingly said, "It hasn't been easy for anyone, but you got what you wanted, so I guess that justifies the effort." As Jiri lost his patience with me, I felt more and more like Alex's undesirable leftover. After all, they hadn't planned on me when they offered the room to Alex. When I arrived with him, they must have thought a month would be all right. But then Alex left, and I stayed, and when Anja was added to the mix, of course it was more than they had bargained for. I also didn't blame Jiri for his disdain after Lieutenant Möller entered the picture. I tried my best, and I hoped Jiri would remember the pleasant times we had together. "Thank you, Jiri. I will miss you, too." His hard face softened at that, and a smile passed between us.

That night, as I lay awake trying to see myself in the coming events, Simon played the Bach etudes again in the room above, but now they had a heavy sad sound, one that only I could hear.

Now the other concern was Anja. How could I communicate to her and she to me about leaving? It would have to play itself out for both of us. I had often watched her interacting with Beata and Jiri; they were close and loving despite the lack of speech. I would have to face taking her away from what had come to be family and home for her, as her father had done once in her life already. Only time would tell, but my fears for her going through it once again continued.

Ernst made only a brief visit to the bookshop the next day. He said, "If I make a room reservation at the inn, will you come with me tomorrow?"

"I'm sure I can have Beata take Anna for the afternoon." My words came out before I completely grasped what he had said.

"Wonderful. Have a bite to eat before I come to get you, I don't want to waste any of our time in the dining room. I'll pick you up at noon here." He kissed me and left.

I realized I had made two commitments in the past two days, both of them sure to be heartbreaking for both of us. Life wasn't getting easier as I had hoped it would, and it was sure to get even harder when I told him that I would be leaving in fifteen days. As I thought about going to the inn with him the next day, and what getting a room will involve, a frightening thought occurred to me. At some point he may well discover that I am a virgin. I know I will. I would have to figure out how to explain away my immaculate conception. I will have to take that as it happens and so will he. Right then it was just a white heat of unknown magnitude.

The next day, Beata came to the shop at lunchtime and picked up Anja with a mimed promise for an ice cream. Anja smiled and then waved to me and went off with Beata. We were both going to indulge in one more of Prague's enjoyments today, mine surely with much greater apprehension.

ERNST CAME INTO THE SHOP SHORTLY AFTER BEATA left with Anja. We walked hand in hand to the car. He opened the door for me and asked, "No last-minute regrets, Karin? You can say so at any time."

With more conviction in my voice than I would have expected, I said, "No, no last-minute regrets."

We drove into the countryside to the inn that would become a memory that would spread itself over a lifetime, mine certainly, and even his. At the inn he parked in the shade and said, "We're here, but it still isn't too late."

"Yes, it is," I said as I got out of the car. He held my hand as we walked up the carpeted flight of stairs to a room with a chilled bottle of champagne awaiting us. Ernst closed the door and said, "Welcome home, Mrs. Möller." He embraced me and said, "These few hours will be my lifetime with you." He poured us each a glass of champagne and said, "A note of joy to begin."

Our room had a small sink. Ernst went to it and shaved. I watched him, as he shaved, having never watched a man other than my father shave. He smiled at me. "I will only do this for you, shaving twice in the same day." He laughed.

I was leaning against the door frame when I asked, "Does that hurt?"

"Only if I am suitably distracted, which could happen at any moment now."

I laughed and left him to finish his shave.

When he had rinsed the cream from his face and dried off, he embraced me again. He looked at me with a small smile and said, "I think it is a little too late now." He slowly undressed me, and then he undressed himself. He took off his ID tags and put them on the night table. He smiled at me again and said, "Don't worry about my ID tags. If I die of happiness here, only you will know the true cause."

Thanks to my mother, I did know a few things about what was about to happen. As I lay in his arms, he must have felt my tension. "It's all right, Karin, just relax. We can stop whenever you want." I shook my head no. I was committed. Even though he was loving and gentle with me the whole time, womanhood came as a surprise to me. He searchingly looked at me and asked if I was all right. I assured him I was. Later, when I got up to use the bathroom down the hall, it was clear that I would have a few things to explain when I returned to our room. When I came back in I went to him. He reached out his hand to me and asked, "Are you all right, Karin?"

"Yes, I will be."

Lying side by side, we didn't say anything for a little while. Then he said, "I'm sorry, Karin. I didn't know. Please tell me about yourself, about your husband and the little one."

Even now, after making love to Ernst, a new fear swept through me upon hearing those words. I felt like a moth attracted to a beautiful bright light, only to discover it was a searing hot flame that threatened to consume me as I got too close. My mind began to race again, switching into survival mode. As if I were separated from myself, I heard myself say, "My husband was never able to consummate our marriage. I don't know if it is physical or emotional. I asked him to have it seen to by a doctor, but he refused. I wanted children, or at least one, so when it was clear that he could not father a child, I chose to adopt. Anna was not even three when I finally got her. She was this beautiful but frightened little girl; she was and still is a traumatized child. She is capable of speech but does not speak. Her background is a sad story, but I loved her even from the start when I first met her. That is my story. I hope you don't feel deceived by me."

"No, not at all! I feel that I am your true husband now, and I would marry you right now if I could."

"Yes, in a real sense you are that."

"What will you do now?"

"I must go back to see if there is anything that I can salvage from the marriage. If not, I will leave him. He wasn't connected to Anna, even from the beginning. I think she must remind him of his own inadequacies." I was shocked at my ability to fabricate, and at the content of my fabrication. I hoped that Ernst would not try to unveil them.

"Karin, he doesn't deserve what you are trying to make of the marriage. He doesn't deserve you at all. If we were married, I would be a loving husband to you and a good father to Anna. We will soon have that ocean between us, and as things are now that will be a lot harder to bridge. But I will—by God, I will." He took up my left hand and said, "I wish I had put that wedding ring there."

"So, do I."

"Now, I think the champagne is still chilled, and we have two new events to celebrate now," he laughed, hugging me. "Karin, I'm so glad I was your first. It is said that you never forget your first."

"I will remember you, Ernst, and for much more than that, because you will be the first in my heart and mind as well as in my body." We spent the next few hours in happiness I had not even imagined existed in my twenty-two years of trying to be me, who I now finally had become.

Parting

════════════

WE HAD ONLY DAYS LEFT together, during which we saw each other as frequently as possible. At times we could only speak of trivial matters, other times were filled with silence because we didn't dare say the final things a couple like us must say. Most couples could say that they would come back to each other, but we knew that was terribly unlikely to happen for us. The silences between us protested on our behalf against the unfairness of life.

Late one night, with Anja asleep and pressed onto my back, I convinced myself that what I told Ernst at the inn was a cocoon of safety that I had spun around Anja to keep her safe. I heard her sucking her thumb as if in agreement. I was ashamed at the overlay of a new lie upon an already established lie. But Anja was my priority, and only when I have gotten her home safely to New York would I be able to unravel the lies to bare the truth. At least I hoped so.

PRAGUE WAS SUCH A BEAUTIFUL OLD-WORLD CITY. I'M sorry I didn't get to see more of it in my time there, but with the occupation and Anja at my side constantly, I dared not travel around the city for fear of being stopped with her. I settled for the same scenery every day, the places and neighborhoods I have come to know so well, except when Ernst arranged an outing. One evening he promised a surprise. He brought the car and we drove to another residential district. He parked the car and we walked a short block to a church where there would be a concert of music by Smetana and Dvorak, two of Czechoslovakia's most loved composers.

Ernst was very excited. "This small orchestra will undoubtedly play with their best national pride. I especially like that they will be playing selections from Smetana's symphonic poems." I was touched that he had brought us here, especially since the locals stared icily at the German officer in their midst. I was uncomfortable about it, but I relaxed once the music began. He took my hand in his and closed his eyes.

After the concert, we walked slowly back to the car. We had been sitting there for a few minutes, talking about the concert, when something hard hit the back of the car. A moment later, something else hit the car even harder. Ernst quickly turned the motor on and sped away. Luckily he had a good sense of direction, because the street lights were already out for the blackout and the approaching curfew. Ernst was completely aware of where we were and how to get back into the center of Prague. When we had both calmed down from the fright, he said, "It's a sign of the times, and I must get used to it. I'm glad you are all right, other than being a bit shaken."

"I feel safe when I'm with you."

"You can count on me to keep you safe. I want you to know that."

"I do." I hoped hearing this that it would hold up no matter what was in store for Anja and me. He leaned over and kissed me. We spoke little after that until he got me home.

I SPENT ALL THE DAYS LEFT ME HERE IN PRAGUE IN THE bookshop, awaiting Ernst's visits. I still had not told him that I was leaving on August nineteenth. I told him a few nights after the concert when we went out for dinner. He lowered his head slightly and reached for my hand. Holding it, he said, "I'm partly responsible for that, I know. I have no choice but to let you go home to someone who can never know the love I have for you." He looked up at me and said, "Shall we just leave here and walk for a while? I wish to be alone with you right now, in the dark night air, so that only our footsteps speak for us and I will not have to search for the words for my feelings. I don't know if there are any that can speak of my despair about your leaving."

We walked silently, my hand in his. "Will you come to the inn with me as often as you can arrange to do it, so we can be together for the little time left us? I already regret all those moments that I let pass without being with you. I know I ask a lot, but there is so much of you I will never have otherwise." We had stopped walking, and he said, "I shall love you forever." He kissed me and, with a heart wrenching heaviness in his voice, said, "I had best get you back to your little one now. I have to go back to work, but I will see you tomorrow, and the day after and the day after and after that, for as long as we have."

IN THE DAYS THAT FOLLOWED WE WENT TO THE INN again and again, where after our lovemaking we lay in each other's arms in that warm after glow. Sometimes we spoke at length; at other times, we spoke little or nearly none at all. One time, with my finger on his lips, I asked him how he had gotten the scar just above his lip. He laughed and said, "It's funny now, but it wasn't so funny at the time. For my eighth birthday, I asked my father for a pair of skis. He thought I should wait a year, but I disagreed. My brother Karl was eight years older than I was, and we adored each other. I wanted to be just like him in everything he did. Skiing was only one of the many things he excelled at. Well, with my birthday wish granted, my father took me skiing. Being bolder of spirit than of skill, I insisted on going higher than he thought I was ready for. We did go higher, and on the way down I took a bad tumble. My ski flew up and clipped me on my lip. I guess I haven't changed that much since I was eight years old. I'm still reaching out far beyond my ability to achieve my goal, for a successful outcome, to excel at something I love; such as I have with you. I remember Robert Browning's words: 'Ah, but a man's reach should exceed his grasp, or what's a heaven for?' He must have suspected that I would appear at some point to fit them. My ability to be with you has the stumbling block of a Mr. Wilson, which I can't overcome. I have to give you up, no matter how much it pains me, and that will also leave a lifetime scar. Karin, I promise you and myself, one day I will see you again. I will come to America. I promise, because this can't be the end for us."

I kissed his chest and murmured, "However it happens, I will know that you gave me the joy and the pain of being in love with you, and that you bridged that gulf even before I knew it was happening."

"That was no heroic act. You made it so easy, just being you— that is all it took. I guess I should tell you that even my earliest visits to the bookshop, my literary questions were just a pretext for me to see you and speak with you."

We were still for a while then, until I asked, "Do you still ski?"

"No, not any more. But after that fall, I went with my brother Karl, who taught me more and more of everything, and not just skiing."

"Why did you stop? Did something happen?"

"My brother died of pneumonia when he was seventeen. I was nine years old at the time. Skiing without him was unthinkable; just being alive without him was hard enough. I still miss him."

LEAVING

BEATA WAS WONDERFUL in caring for Anja while I spent so much time away from them to be with Ernst. My conscience weighed heavily when I thought of Anja and me leaving here.

I left the packing till the very last moment. Anja had just come into the room when I had pulled the suitcase down off the wardrobe and began putting my clothes in it. She came over to me looking very perplexed and frightened when she suddenly ran to the dresser and pulled open her drawer and gathered her clothes in a pile and came to the suitcase and threw them in, she again ran back and took the rest out and stuffed them into my suitcase. When I took them out and folded them neatly and put them back in the suitcase she put her little hand on each piece as if to anchor it there. Lastly, she put her little pillow in and lay her bunny on it and covered him with her little blanket. She was prepared for whatever would happen next. So was I.

ON FRIDAY, AUGUST EIGHTEENTH, I CLOSED THE BOOK-shop for the last time. As I slid the key out of the lock, I felt a pang in my heart. It was here that the two defining events of my life took place. Anja and Ernst. From an innocent beginning to a scarred ending that will be with me for the rest of my life.

The days at the inn had ended for us, and now the hours were dwindling as well.

On morning of the nineteenth of August 1939, Jiri and Beata accompanied Anja and me to the train station. When the ordered taxi appeared, and Jiri put my suitcase in the trunk Anja grew agitated. I picked her up and hugged her. She quieted down when Beata and Jiri got in the taxi with us. At the station when the taxi driver put the suitcase down Anja immediately held onto it. When we reached the train platform, I saw Jiri stare ahead to where the train was waiting. When I followed his gaze, I saw Ernst standing by the train, waiting for us. Recognizing that this is where they would say goodbye, Beata hugged Anja tightly, and then hugged me tightly. Wiping her eyes, she said, "Have a safe trip, and write to us as soon as you get home. Tell us how our dear sister is, and tell Alex he must write to us more often." She pressed a food parcel for the trip into my arms. She had baked little cakes that Anja liked and looking at Anja she smiled and rubbed her tummy when she handed them to her. Jiri swept Anja into his arms with a big hug and kiss, when he put her down he gave her a rolled-up paper held with a ribbon, he pointed to the paper and then at her with a big smile nodding at her.

Jiri put his hands on my shoulders and said, "I'm sorry I was so grumpy. I am set in my ways and views, but now I wish you a safe voyage home. We won't walk you to the train, for I see the lieutenant is here to see you off." He hugged me then, a warm, fatherly hug, and I was tearfully happy. "Now go," he said, "and teach Anja a three-octave scale. She is capable of that next step, and so are you. Goodbye, Karin." He led Beata back into the taxi; I turned once for a final look, and I saw Jiri hold up a hand of farewell as the taxi drove off.

When I turned around, Ernst was walking toward us, carrying a small package.

"Do you have all the papers?" he asked anxiously.

"Yes."

"I will see you onto the train." He lifted Anja in his arms and taking our suitcase, I followed. Instead of going into the coupé section of the car itself, he walked to the opposite side of the car entrance. He put Anja down next to me and said, "I did not know how extremely hard saying goodbye to you would be. I knew it would be difficult, but not this painful. I don't like the word goodbye; it has such a ring of finality to it. I prefer to say *Auf Wiedersehen*, which means, upon seeing each other again." He pulled a slip of paper from his pocket and handed it to me. "Here is my address. Write to me when you get home, please. I want to know you are safe. Can I write to you? Will that cause you difficulties?"

"No, it will be fine. I'll give you my parents' address." I wrote my address on a scrap of paper, my handwriting sloppy because my hands were shaking, and I had tears in my eyes. I handed it to him. Even then I had to fight the terrible urge to tell him there was no Mr. Wilson.

He read the address back to me to be sure he could read it correctly. He said, "I will miss you terribly, Karin." He took his hat off and bent down to kiss me. As he pulled me closer to him, I wanted to tell him to come with us.

But I didn't. Instead I reached into my bag and took out my parting gift for him. "I want you to have something to remember me by. I wanted it to be something special. While this doesn't look like much, it is special to me." I handed him a worn compass. "My father gave me this on my twenty-first birthday. He said, 'Knowing your poor sense of direction, I want you to have this, so that you will find your way in life and may it bring you back home."

Looking down at it as I handed it to him, Ernst said, "I will keep this with me so that when the time comes it will guide me back to you, because you must know, as I do, that this isn't the last of us. It can't be. Prague will not be the end of us."

He reached into his breast pocket and took out a fountain pen. "I want you to have this to remember me. It means a great deal to me. My father gave it to me when I graduated law school to sign my name on all those legal documents. Now, because of you and Anna, I have even signed a few illegal ones as well, all with the same pen. See, it has my initials on the gold clip, E.M., so you will remember to write to me often."

I tried to give the pen back to him. "Your pen is such a valuable gift. It means so much to you, I don't dare take it from you."

"No, I want you to have it. Consider it a loan. Let us say that, when I am out of the army, I will come to see you, guided by your compass. I will then give the compass back to you because it will have done its job successfully. And then, if you wish, you can give me the pen in return. We will have a goal then to look forward to, for us, after Prague."

"You make acceptance so easy for me, Ernst, and resistance impossible."

"It might be that I learned something else on that ski slope after all. Without chancing a desire, a love would not be known." He drew me close to him and cradled my head in his hand to his shoulder. When he leaned his head down to kiss me, I felt wetness on his cheek. He wiped his eyes with the back of his hand, saying, "There is so much soot in the air here from the trains that leave."

"Yes, I feel it, too."

He bent down to Anja and said, "Be good little one. I wish I could be there when you give up your silence." He gave her a kiss on her forehead, then straightened. "I have to let you go. I'll walk you in, though." He took Anja's hand in his left and took my hand in his right, and he led us into the coupé. Just before entering he reached into his breast pocket and handed me the two train tickets, saying, I nearly forgot, the final papers of severance." When we entered the coupé he saw the Quaker lady waiting for us, he said to her, "Take good care of them, and see them safely on their way. I know you can do it, because you are so well practiced at that." He put my suitcase up on the luggage rack then he turned to me and squeezed my hand, saying, "I look forward to the sonnets, the ones you know the words to and I don't." He kissed me again, then he stood resolutely and put his hat on, the visor shielding his eyes. He took a long last look at me and then turned on his heel and left the coupé. I looked out the window and saw him hurry away from the train. The departing whistle sounded, and when it had faded away, the Quaker lady said, "Yes, that was high priority wasn't it?"

"Yes, he is."

I looked out at the platform as the train began to move, and I saw him in the crowd. He stood there, looking at me with his hand over his heart, then he put it to his mouth and then turned his palm to me to bid me his final farewell as he faded from my sight.

After the train left the station, the Quaker lady said, "I know him. He's one of the good ones. On occasion he was sent to do the head count against my manifest. One of those times I had taken seven children with me who were not listed. They were from two families, their ages from two to seven years old. I knew he saw the issue; it was clear from the way that he counted and recounted, comparing his count to the paperwork. After a moment, he signed my manifest and handed it back to me, saying only, "There you are, Quaker lady." Then he quickly said into my ear, "Only next time, tidy up your sums. Have a safe trip." "He tipped his hat to me and left. He put himself at great personal risk signing away seven extra children, but he saved those lives, and I got them through just fine, thanks to him."

All I could say was, "One never knows about someone, one can never be sure of their content."

I picked up the package he had left on the seat for me. Upon opening it, I found an envelope addressed to me laying on top of a lunch for Anja and me. I put the envelope in my purse and looked out at the scenery rushing by while Anja stood at the window and waved, she kept waving well after the train had left the station. It had seemed to me as if she was waving our good byes to Prague and the lives we had there. She turned to me and pointed to the suitcase, I took it down and she wanted it opened. She saw not only her pillow and bunny but I had tucked in a surprise for her, a small package of her favorite butterfly cookies. She took out her bunny, pillow and blanket and after neatly arranging them on the seat; she opened the little package and shrieked with joy when she saw the cookies. She put her arms around my neck and gave me a hug before she took one of the cookies and sparingly retired the rest. She offered me the first bite and then she took a small nibble as she motioned me to put the suitcase back. She nibbled away, hugging her bunny as she showed him to wave out the window. Soon from the rocking of the train Anja had nestled into a nap amongst the cookie crumb covered bunny. So far, so good. But there was still much ahead of us.

I asked the Quaker lady to keep an eye on her for a few minutes.

"Are you all right?" she asked.

I nodded. "I will be. I just need a few minutes alone."

I walked to where Ernst and I had been standing, and I took out his letter. Unfolding the plain stationery, I read:

"My dearest Karin,

Just like in that sonnet, I can't find the words to express what I feel today, having to say goodbye to you while fearing that I will never see you again. I have this terrible feeling that I won't—I do not say I may never see you again, because that would imply choice. The Bard would not have approved of anything less than the truth. After the train has left with you, my heart will be a desolate place, with only my memories to remind it of our times together. That will be my only relief. I fear there could be even more terrible times that could pull us apart, but for now there is none more terrible than saying goodbye to you here and now.

All of my love to you,
Ernst

The letter shook in my hand, and it was not from the movement of the train. I turned to the window and looked out through my tears at an even more blurred landscape as the train took me away from Ernst, west through Czechoslovakia to the border with Germany. I put his letter back in my purse, swallowed hard and steadied myself back to the coupé where Anja slept. The Quaker lady told me she had to go to the next car to check on her charges and their escorts.

I sat down opposite Anja, who was still asleep, and looked at her, trying to fix in my mind what I had done. What I had done was not in my mind, however, but in my heart, just as it had been with

Ernst. I wondered if this little sleeping soul would be in my life for the rest of my days.

When the train lurched to a stop at the Czech-German border, German officers boarded it for inspection. Two of the German inspectors entered our coupé, asking curtly *"Papiere!"* When I took out the envelope with the black-winged eagle holding a wreath with a swastika in it, the Nazi logo of the Gestapo, one of the Germans gave the other a quick look. I did not produce my U.S. passport; Ernst had instructed me to do that only if asked specifically for it. I handed them the Prague exit permits, the travel permits, and the transit visas for Germany. The men took a cursory look at them and quickly handed them back to me, saluted, and left. Now I knew the effect of a high priority rating. It was as if Ernst were sitting next to me and had waved them on. When the Quaker lady came back, she said, "Well, they sure left in a hurry, courtesy of your rating, no doubt."

I smiled and said, "Yes, and I hope it's smooth sailing from here on out."

She laughed, "It will be once you get to Southampton."

The train rolled over the border and stopped once again. The check on us was repeated, and my papers produced the same results, with a heel click for emphasis. The train slowly rolled through the German countryside before picking up speed. The train ran at speed until our first stop in Dresden. While the border patrol checked documents again, I saw mail bags and newspapers being dropped off and taken on. It felt unreal to be in Germany. I watched some German officers board the train as passengers; I desperately wanted Ernst to be one of them.

We passed through cities, towns, and countryside at varying speeds, and I wondered how different their lives might be from ours, what the everyday business of living and making a living was like under a tyrannical government that was to dominate them in the weeks, months, and possibly years to come. I felt fortunate that this was not my homeland, and I was sorry for those whose it was.

Our next stop was Leipzig, where our papers were checked again. We passed many towns and cities until we came to Dortmund, where again newspapers and mail bags were dropped off along with the German officers. After that, we did not stop again because we were on an express train going to the Dutch border. After Dortmund, the train barreled along at a fast clip as if it were in a great hurry to unload an undesirable cargo. We talked and ate from our food parcels and dozed to the rhythmic click clacking of the steel wheels on the tracks as we again made our way to the German-Dutch border. At the border, the Germans once again checked our papers; we left the large train and boarded a shorter train for our transit through Holland. Before long, we were once again speeding on to Hoek van Holland, where we were to take the overnight ferry across the North Sea to Harwich, England.

Finally, we settled in the darkened lounge of the ferry. We were too tired for anything but sleep, yet we were so near the end of the stressful trip across Europe that sleep eluded us. Only Anja slept heavily on my lap. Helen Arnsworth, the Quaker lady, remained quiet to let me sleep, but I broke the silence by asking, "Helen, may I ask you a personal question?"

"I hope I'll have a personal answer as well."

"Have you ever been in love before?"

"Oh yes," I heard a little laugh. "A few times, at least."

"Are you now?"

"Oh yes, very much so!"

"How do you know when you are in love? I mean, really in love. I don't know what it takes to love someone, and we only met six months ago."

"It could have been six weeks ago, or six days ago," she laughed again. "If you're a quick study, even six hours ago—the point is that time isn't the factor. It's chemistry, it's that moment you see a face across the room; it just happens. In fact, you don't have much say in the matter. Something new inside you comes alive. It's the presence of someone else, it's irresistible, it's an attraction, a desire, and it's beautiful in its own tortuous way. It just happens, sudden happiness arrives, or the hope of it at least, and you are in turmoil, lots of turmoil, especially the first time. It's real and serious when you feel these things. It looks to me as if you have been stricken."

I nodded. "I have the added weight of the complications that you can well imagine, knowing me and my situation."

"Life is amazing. I have learned that the insurmountable is often there just for us to take it one step at a time, each challenge to be resolved to make way for the next one. It will be so for you, too, so try to put your misgivings and fears aside and give the process a chance. It does work, I've found, every time. We should try to get a little sleep; tomorrow will be a busy one for us. Just one of those steps to resolve in time for the next one."

I closed my eyes, but my thoughts and fears of what lay ahead paced anxiously in my mind all night long.

ONWARD

ANJA WAS NOT WELL as we boarded the train from Harwich to London. She slept a bit of the way, and I hoped I would not have to carry her too far once we got there because my energy—mental, emotional, and physical—were giving out. In London it felt good to get out and away from the bouncing and swaying of trains and boats to where Quaker Helen situated us while she attended to all the assignments to the families taking in the refugee children. It took a long time, but it gave Anja and me a respite after the rough North Sea ferry crossing. Anja clearly was not a sailor, and I worried how she would fare on the ship crossing the Atlantic with no stops on the way. Time would tell. Some ladies from the welcoming committee for the refugees came over to me with some sandwiches and a hot chocolate for Anja and tea for me. We did indeed feel welcomed as well. The London train station was noisy and crowded, but everyone was gracious and helpful, especially when Anja threw up in the reception area. When Helen, our saviour Quaker was finally finished, she came over and apologized. "I'm sorry for the wait. One never knows how long these things can take. Now how about some fish and chips? On second thought, maybe just some broth instead?" she smiled kindly.

"Broth would be nice and best, thank you."

"From here on in, everything will be best."

"Yes, I think a lot of that has already happened."

"Indeed! From here, we are going to catch the train for Southampton, where I'll put you and Anja on the ship bound for New York. Hopefully it will not be redirected to Halifax instead."

I remembered all too well the last stop in Halifax a long year ago. That memory also triggered the thought that until now I had not thought of Alex in quite some time.

"Karin, are you listening?"

"Yes, I'm sorry."

"At Southampton, you and I will part company. I will turn you over to Thomas Brixley. He is our stalwart fundraiser, operating mostly in New York but he keeps up with well-connected purse strings here in London as well. He is one of those angels one can never find big enough wings for. You'll like him—beneath his steely ways as a fundraiser beats a warm heart, and he has a great sense of humor as well. He warms my heart whenever I see him. He's always trying to ensnare me in his pitch line, saying, 'You'll have to stop doing all of this, Helen, because I want you to sit home with one or more of ours.'"

I laughed. "That sounds warm-hearted to me. When would you be ready for that?"

"When there is no longer any allowance or a need to get children out of harm's way. After all they have been through, including separation from their parents, we want them to have a life after that. They are the next generation, and they must survive the one before it."

"You've done so much for Anja and me. How can I ever repay you?"

"The only things with a dollar figure attached are the two transit visas, for Holland and England, and the boat tickets."

"You mean those visas were forged?"

"The only real ones for you and Anna for your trip are the ones in that Nazi envelope. For the most part, mine usually are legitimate, but there are exceptions. People doing what I do rarely, if ever, work in isolation; we network the life of every child into safety. It's how I account for my spiritual life among other things." She smiled. "If you want to help, I can let you know what your two visas and boat trip home cost, and if you can fund raise for our rescue efforts once you are home, I'll let you know where you can contact Thomas."

I opened my purse and took out the envelope with the Czech money I had earned and saved for the trip home and handed it to Helen and said, "This is for the efforts you have made for Anja and me and while it does not nearly cover the expenses I would like to give it to you on account for us. I'll do everything I can to pay back the remaining costs plus more for the cause."

"You sound like a new recruit, Karin. I'd like to count on that."

I nodded emphatically. "You can."

Once off the train at Southampton, she greeted another helper. "Harold, over here. Please come, give us a hand."

"Good to see you again, luv. Thomas sent me this time. He's doing some preload paperwork at the ship. This trip is overbooked, so he wants to be sure they get on without a slip up."

Helen nodded and gestured to Anja and me. "Harold, this is Karin and Anja."

"All the way from Prague? Good heavens, you've put in a lot of travel already!" As Harold loaded our things in the car, he continued, "Hop aboard for the next to last leg of your travels. The ship isn't far from here."

By now, Anja was so exhausted that she was barely able to walk on her own, she is that beyond the pale, and I was feeling just about the same. When we arrived at the ship's pier, a large, jovial man approached the car. Opening the door, he said, "Thank God, I'm so glad you made it. I needed to produce some creative last-minute paper work for your two passengers and myself." He still has not seen us in the back seat of the car as he helped Helen out of the car and said, "Now, first things first," and he bent down to kiss her.

I looked away and collected Anja in my arms. Seeing this, he leaned into the car and said, "Let me give you a hand, and without a second thought took Anja from me. I climbed out of the car and, after introductions; we followed him up the gangplank. It was the twenty-first of August 1939, when we boarded the ship for home. The official at the little table examined my papers and passport, and Thomas handed over his as well. The official made his notes and stamped the passports, and then Thomas showed us to a small cabin. Finally putting Anja down, he said, "Please excuse me for a moment while I pursue one of my other agendas with this lady." He smiled at Helen and said, "I have to tread lightly because she's afraid I'll shanghai her. I'm not above that, you know, but she always manages to jump ship just in time." They walked off to behind the steps, probably looking for a quiet corner for a few moments together. Soon after, the ship's horn gave off a departure warning blast, Helen came back to assure me she would wire my parents with details of my arrival. She hugged us both and said, "I'm sure I'll see you in New York. I don't know just when, but I will."

"Thank you so much for everything, I have one last favor to ask of you. When you have a chance, would you please let Lieutenant Möller know that we got on the ship safely?"

Helen nodded and smiled warmly. "I will. I'm sure he'll seek me out on his own to hear just that. We did well you and he and I, didn't we?"

"Incredibly so, yes."

She left the ship quickly, and Thomas waved to her until she was no longer in sight. Then he turned to me and said, "You'll be home some seven days from now. I'll see you all the way over. I'm only two cabins down from you; so, don't hesitate if you need anything, any time. I'm on duty day and night," he laughed. "I'm sure you both could do with a nice long nap. I'll see you later."

It was not the beginning of an ocean voyage as one might see in the movies, with beautiful people laughing and toasting one another with champagne. Anja and I were exhausted, and we both needed a nice warm bath and a good long sleep. Some restorative food would have been wonderful. The papers that celebrated our journey were not colored paper streamers but permits in a Nazi envelope. Thus, with a heavy heart and an uncertain mind, I began the long voyage home with more than I left with.

The crossing was long, both inside and outside our cabin, as a storm at sea made the Atlantic Ocean rage under and over our ship for two full days. Anja had to be put in the ship's infirmary and at times given a sleep aid to quell her seasickness and sleeplessness. Thomas tried his best to keep my spirits up as well; he even sat with me in the infirmary while I held Anja when she couldn't sleep.

One evening when she was asleep, Thomas and I had dinner together in the dining room. We sat listening to dinner music, sipping a glass of wine to a nice dinner.

"What will you do when you get back?" he asked.

I shrugged. "I don't know. A lot depends on how Anja and I are received."

"That shouldn't be hard to imagine."

"No one at home knows about her yet. I haven't told anyone. It seemed easier that way. I could only take one giant step at a time, and the biggest was being able to leave Prague with her. All the rest will follow as this is doing, with little expectation. I'm still hoping for the best."

"I'll give you my address and phone number in New York. If you need any help or even a place to stay, my apartment in New York doesn't see that much of me anymore."

"Thank you for that kind offer. My parents and I are close, and I hope we'll still be after I arrive."

"How could they not be?"

"I'm providing them with one reason not to be. After all, they said goodbye to a daughter who now comes back with a granddaughter."

"You'll put twice as much joy in their lives."

"Are you always this optimistic?"

"Only when it's called for." He laughed. The dining room had a small dance floor in the middle, and the band has just begun to play *Blue Moon*. Thomas extended his hand to me and asked, "Mrs. Wilson, may I have this dance with you?"

"It's Miss Wilson, actually, and yes, I'd love to." The wine, the nice dinner, and a dance to an American tune gave me a feeling of normalcy, and I couldn't remember the last time I had felt this, if I even ever had.

On the fourth day of the crossing, the sea became calmer. The morning sun warmed the deck, and I took Anja up onto the promenade level. We sat in one of the deck chairs and she nestled into my arms, sucking her thumb, a sign that she was returning to her normal self.

Thomas found us and sat. "We'll arrive in four more days. We'll be at anchor if we have to await the morning tide, and then we'll dock. I'll help and see you safely off." Looking at me with kindness, he leaned over and said, "It'll be fine, Karin. I know it, and you'll just have to trust my wisdom in these matters. In all the time I have been doing this work, I found that the heart is always ready to step up to the plate for the next inning." Stroking Anja's arm he said, "And she will score well for you, you'll see. Look at her, she is already looking and feeling better, and so should you."

Anja was feeling well enough now to eat a bit at each meal-time, and she liked walking the deck with me. I had to tell myself more than once that the tough part was behind us. We spent the next few days enjoying Thomas' company; he was good at amusing Anja as well, who was feeling better with each day. I took the rolled-up paper out of my purse that Jiri had given her and handed it to her. She beamed a big smile at me as she took it and I helped get the ribbon off. What she unrolled was a paper piano keyboard that Jiri had made for her little hands, she was thrilled as I stretched it out on the bed and anchored the ends as she fingered her scales, she was intensely occupied as she remembered her scales and hummed softly to her hands commands. A perfect gift, perfectly timed, just as she had been.

Standing at the ship's railing, I watched the white-capped waves approach the ship only to be dispersed by the wake of the ship's course like aqueous apparitions of Ernst now disappearing on our way to freedom and safety. Still I could feel his energy in all my thoughts of him. The ocean that separated us was becoming larger and larger by the hour.

ARRIVING

ON THE MORNING of the twenty-seventh of August 1939, the ship safely completed its Atlantic crossing with us and berthed in Manhattan shortly after breakfast. After docking, Thomas took us through the disembarking process, where we were cleared to leave the ship. I carried our few things while Thomas carried Anja off onto the pier. Once off the gangplank, I stopped to catch my breath and marvel at the idea that I was finally back home. Thomas said, "Come on, Karin, let's go find them."

We hadn't gone far when I heard my mother's voice, "Over here, Karin, we're over here!" Just hearing her voice again made my legs feel like wet noodles. I hurried past the wooden fence and nearly fell right into her arms. We were both crying happily when I felt my father's arms around me, too.

His voice was thick as he murmured, "Thank God you're back."

Thomas stood a few steps behind me, holding Anja in his arms while we hugged. When he put her down next to me, she clung onto me, hiding her face with my skirt, from all the loud excitement as I tried to introduce Thomas, but I couldn't speak for the happy tears and utter trepidation of the moment. Thomas put out his hand and said, "How nice to meet you. I'm Thomas Brixley. I was Karin's ship companion. This is where we part ways."

He looked at me and said, "Goodbye, Karin. It has been wonderful to meet you. We will stay in touch." He gave my parents a casual salute and hurried down the dock. I saw the surprise on my parents' faces when he left without Anja. Mother looked down at Anja and then at me and asked, "Has he left his daughter here with you for some reason? Do we need to wait for him to come back?"

I couldn't find any words in that moment, so I simply shook my head to say no to both questions. My father took our things and said, "We should hurry to find a taxi." I picked up Anja and followed my father, and my mother fell in step behind me. Anja had her head on my shoulder and I could feel, if not see, my mother's eyes on her the whole time. In the taxi, my mother asked, "Who is she? Have you brought her over for someone?"

"No, mother. She . . . she's mine. It's a long story, one for later, please." My father gave me a look that, when I was younger, meant, "tell me now, what you have done." I looked at my parents and said, "I'm so glad to be back. You can't imagine how I've waited for this moment."

My mother overcame her confusion and said, "I think we can, Karin. We have been doing the same; nearly from the time you left. By the way, Alex sends his apologies, but he couldn't get away from work to be here."

"That's okay." I said, looking straight ahead. She looked at me; I think she was expecting more disappointment.

It was a short taxi ride from the pier to our apartment. When I entered the building, it was like remembering a story I once read before, but now only bits and pieces came to mind. When my father opened the door to the apartment, we were greeted with the pleasant smell of a Swedish cardamom cake that my mother had freshly baked. It was my favorite, and the scent was layered on top of all the other smells of the apartment that I loved, the smells of home.

Father immediately carried my suitcase to my bedroom. Mother said, "Lunch is ready whenever you are, Karin. Welcome home."

I took Anja to my room, where we took off our coats and changed into clean clothing. We both needed a bath, but that could wait. Anja seemed to be holding up well, although she insisted on sucking her thumb, which she normally only did while she slept. I brought her back out to the dining room after a few minutes, and my parents were waiting for us. At the table, Anja sat on my lap, taking small morsels of what she was offered. She kept her eyes on the table, giving quick furtive looks at my parents, especially at my mother.

"Does she speak and understand English?" mother asked.

"No, she doesn't."

"What does she speak and understand?"

"I don't know. She has been traumatized and stopped speaking."

"What does she call you?"

"Nothing, she doesn't speak at all."

My mother looked at my father, and my father looked at Anja and me. He said, "Don't worry, it will all sort itself out." It could have been an empty promise, but coming from my father it filled me with comfort.

When lunch was over, mother said," Your room is just as you left it, as I carried Anja back to my room and put her on my bed. I tucked her in for a nap, and I sat on the floor near her as she sucked her thumb and stroked my hair and then held onto it until she fell asleep. My mother sat on my chair looking at me down on the floor and said as she pointed quickly at Anja,

"That must be quite a story."

I nodded and said, "It is, but I too will be speechless if I don't get into a hot bath this instant. Would you please keep an eye on Anja? If she wakes, please just bring her in to see me."

I filled the tub with steaming hot water, just to know that I could, and then I cooled it down until it was tolerable. I immersed myself up to my nose, reveling in the warm weightlessness. The closest I had come to this feeling since my last bath here was when I lay in Ernest's arms.

I washed my hair at the kitchen sink with an endless supply of hot water. I was feeling close to my old New York self again, with a few major changes that were to last me a lifetime. That night too, when I again took off my white grayed with wear bra, I gave a huge sigh of relief. I looked down at my breasts and said, "Thank you girls, well done!"

I rubbed my midriff nearly raw with reliefe to have the dress shields off me after so long. Then I unpicked the bra lining and removed the well-shaped letter and I put it in my dresser drawer, hiding it beneath my undergarments. I did not have the heart yet to throw out the bra itself, it was after all my undercover so to speak and I was now so glad to be rid of it on my body. I thought I might keep it as a souvenir of my stealth. With or without the bra, I would forget little of it. How could I?

LATER, WITH ANJA ASLEEP FOR THE NIGHT I TOLD MY parents only some parts of the story, from getting on the SS *Stimins* to our first weeks in Prague. Anja didn't wake, and we continued to talk well into the night.

I woke up early the next morning, happy to be in my own bed once again. I was surprised to find Anja fast asleep with her back turned to me. That was the first time I could remember that happening. Could it be she too now felt secure enough to let go of me, at least in her sleep? Or was she expressing her disdain for me for having taken her from her father to this strange new place? Just then her steady breathing paused as she rolled over toward me, still asleep. It was as if she were forgiving me for what I had done. I too had left someone whom I loved, behind and forgiveness was yet to be found. I realized that, because I no longer feared for Anja's safety, I could allow myself to feel what I had struggled to suppress during the latter months in Prague. I thought about how much I loved Ernst, despite the unknown fate that awaited us of our situation there. I thought about how he had given so much more of himself to me than I was able to give him in return. His love for me was unconditional, unlike mine at the time, when I felt so insecure about everyone and everything.

AT BREAKFAST THE NEXT MORNING, THE COFFEE HAD an unfamiliar taste. After I had a few sips, mother said, "Karin, we have to ask. What were you thinking when you took on Anja as your own? Did you even once consider handing her over to someone more suited to have her? Did you think ahead to consider how you would manage this? How do you see your father and me fitting into all of it?"

I could feel anger toward my parents at these questions, and I heard it when I replied, "What was I thinking? I have to tell you that I felt frightened and alone. It was not a matter of thinking, because I had no choice in the matter, none at all! I wasn't consulted before he left her with me. I had a customer one minute, and then I had a frightened little three-year-old the next minute. Yes, I worried about all of it. Did I consider handing her over to someone, like a mis-addressed package to be rerouted into the unknown? No, I did not consider handing her over. If she is Jewish, her fate would have been sealed, as much by me as by the Nazis. There was no one better suited than me in her father's eyes—and do you know what! He was right! You ask how I will get on with this. I came home to you as my shelter, if not loved for it at least understood for it. I see you as her grand-parents, the only ones she'll ever know. And perhaps she's the only grandchild you'll ever know."

My mother looked at me reproachfully. "Karin, you're twen-ty-two, unmarried with a three-year-old. Young men considering marriage want a virgin, also without a child."

I put my hands flat on the table, struggling to contain my anger. As calmly as I could, I said, "Well, Mother, then I will disappoint them on both counts." My mother pulled her head back as the full mean-ing of my response sunk in. Her hand went to her mouth as her eye-brows slowly rose. She gave a little cough into her hand as she leaned back in her chair. At least I had cleared that up. I took another sip of coffee that turned bitter in my mouth, then I said, "You brought me up to be a caring, loving warm human being. Now that I have lived up to that, I am chastised for it. I'm not sure what I expected to hap-pen to Anja and me when we came home, but now I feel unwelcome in the one place where I thought we could be safe after all we have been through." I thought I might have to call Thomas Brixley after all. My mother sat frozen with guilt, but my father got up and came to my chair. He held my head to his chest and said, "Our daughter Karin is now safely home, and so is our granddaughter."

My mother started to cry. I put my hand on her arm and said, "Don't worry, Mother. I'll put a want ad in the paper: 'Deflowered twenty-two-year old with a three-year-old child seeks a handsome, young, loving, understanding, healthy, well-paid professional, seeking the immediate titles of husband/father."

Mother coughs, wipes her eyes and said, "You left out the word 'beautiful.'"

It was only still morning, but my father opened a bottle of spirits to lift ours.

Before I took my first sip I said looking at my mother, "Should I notify our mailman to deliver the mail bags with replies directly to our door?"

She gave a small laugh. "Yes, he definitely should be notified."

QUAKER HELEN ARNSWORTH'S DICTUM ABOUT INSURmountable challenges now came to mind: "You take them one step at a time." I just took a huge leap into motherhood.

Anja never having heard me raise my voice in anger became frightened and was afraid to approach me. I reached out for her and sat her on my lap with a warm hug and kiss to reassure her that I was still a safe haven in her life. She sucked her thumb and held onto my hair. My mother looked at her and smiled, Anja turned her face to my chest and cried. Work was needed to be done here for us to fit in, I only hoped that I was up to all it would require.

I felt there was a floating resolve about my return with Anja. This is the first time in adult life that I had taken on my mother so vehemently. It troubled me that I had; it troubled me even more that her feelings were so harsh and that she had voiced them with so little consideration of my feelings. I wanted her to embrace Anja and me and comfort us in our time of need, not question and attack me.

Before going to bed, mother gave me a glass of wine and said, "It will help you sleep."

I doubted that, but I saw it as her peace offering, so I drank it.

After Anja was asleep I busied myself with routine things, brushing my teeth and hair with unusual vigor. I searched my face reflection in the mirror for imperfections, all the while knowing they were inside me, only to be felt and not seen. I finally turned off the light and got into bed, trying for sleep among the other things I could not shut off.

There is looseness where we hover between the world of the conscious and that of the unconscious, the path we take as we drift into sleep. Tonight, this path led me into a nightmare. I dreamed I was on a large ship on the ocean. Suddenly there was a loud bang. I found myself in the water, and as I looked around I saw the ship sinking. I looked for Anja, and I could hear her crying, but I could not see her. Then I saw her little bunny float past me, slowly sinking below the surface as he soaked in ocean water. I flailed my arms wildly, trying to stay afloat among the waves that tried to pull me down into the ocean's depths. I called out for Anja again and again as I heard her crying. In the widening distance, I saw my mother and father in a life boat. My mother reached her hand out to me, calling, "Hurry, hurry swim to us." My father rowed hard toward me, but the waves pulled him back further and further until they disappeared. I woke up in a panic, and I heard Anja crying in the dark. When I turned to her, she wasn't there. The panic rose even higher. I turned on the light, the relief I felt in seeing her on the floor made my muscles go weak. She had simply fallen out of bed. I picked her up and cradled her, taking her back to bed. She sucked her thumb and held onto my hair while her little chest convulsed, just as it had when we were given to each other in the shop that day. It took us a while to go to sleep, to approach that looseness once again.

Anja's morning bath in a tub of warm water took a bit of hand holding. It was the first time she'd been in such a large tub of water, since we had always bathed in less water in a smaller tub or at the sink in Prague. It took a lot of reassurance for her to trust that she would not dissolve or sink. Mother produced a rubber duck from her supply of "it'll come in handy one day" items. Having the duck as company in the tub made Anja compliant for a soapy rub down. I washed her hair at the kitchen sink, however, and Anja handled that much better, all the while clutching her new rubber friend. Despite her aquatic apprehensions, all went well, and we even resolved a few conflicts as to the necessity of the application of all this soap and water. How we did it without a common language remained a mystery, but it seemed that instinct continued to be a good arbitrator for us. Anja had a lot to get used to. She explored the apartment room by room, she liked the kitchen where someone was always doing something or making something. She was most interested in the room where my father had his piano, and how strange for her to discover that my mother had one in the living room as well. She was still leery of my mother especially when they were alone in the kitchen. Anja took to my father's warmth instantly. On my mothers plus side Anja responded with happiness when my mother made her a slice of raison toast and hot chocolate. Anja discovered all sorts of new and different things to eat and drink. Jelly donuts were a special hit, as the oozing jelly and glistening sugar introduced one of the sweeter newness in everything she was to discover here.

After breakfast that morning, my father asked if I had let Alex know when I was returning. I shook my head in the negative.

My father asked delicately, "Where is he in all of this?"

"I think he is out of it, but I'll know for sure once I try to see him tomorrow."

Mother looked from my father to me before saying, "I'm not sure I should say this, but after what you just said, I will. Daddy saw him the other day standing on the opposite subway platform with his arm around a girl."

I paused for a moment, then realized with relief that this fact didn't hurt me at all. I said, "He and I have no commitment to each other. He's free to do as he wishes."

My mother nodded. "How about you invite him for dinner tomorrow night? Daddy and I will eat early and go to the movies, and you'll have a chance to deal with it in private."

"Thank you. I'll call him today."

THE CALL TO ALEX WAS FULL OF SURPRISE AT MY RETURN, and he seemed happy enough to come to dinner the next night. Mother made Swedish meatballs, my favorite; Alex wasn't particularly fond of the dish, but I saw that as an appropriate kiss-off dinner. He arrived well after my parents had left, and he was empty handed. When I let him in, he hesitated for a moment, looking at me strangely, and then awkwardly gave me a quick kiss on my cheek. He said, "It's been a while." I just nodded.

As we ate, he droned on about his life since returning from Prague. He didn't inquire about mine. He said, "My mother died, did you know? It was an all-around blessing in the end, as there was no hope of recovery."

"No, I didn't know. You never wrote. I'm sorry, Alex."

He shrugged. "Well, it was a while ago."

Just then I heard Anja whimpering in my room as she woke from a late nap. I excused myself, and when I came out with her, he asked, "Who's that? Or should I say, whose is she?"

"This is Anja, and she's mine. A special going-away present from Prague."

Alex was stunned for a moment. Then he said, "I don't know what that's all about, but you seem to have your hands full." That was about all he had to say.

I was again relieved that his unenthusiastic response caused me no pain. "Well, Alex, I guess we won't be seeing each other that much anymore."

"Right. Well, I wanted to say something about that. We started out as friends, and I'd like to think we stayed that way. You came to Prague with me for a month's vacation and were going back, while I made plans to stay for the next three years to get my degree. We didn't have any arrangement other than that. I want to be clear when I say that I did not then, nor do I now, consider anything more serious. I'm not ready for that, much less with an inclusive family. I can barely support myself, let alone a wife and child."

"Whatever gave you the idea that I was looking for that from you, Alex? While your supposition is touching, I would not even consider it. I have never asked anything of you, nor do I now. Anja and I will be fine; we have each other and a loving family. I'm glad we've had the chance to clear things up, it was long overdue."

Alex nodded in agreement. "Speaking of due, I still owe you some of that hundred dollars. I think I sent you everything except twenty or thirty of it."

I shook my head. "No, you still owe me seventy dollars."

Alex looked surprised at the firm confidence in my response. I had to admit, I was a bit surprised myself. Then he nodded again. "I'll get it to you as soon as I have it. I had better go now; I'm meeting a friend from work for a drink."

I saw him to the door, carrying Anja. As he turned to say good-bye, Anja turned her head away. I smiled at him, though the smile was my agreement with Anja: Alex was not father material.

That night, after Anja went to sleep, I sat down to write a letter to Ernst. I gently picked up the pen he had given me, running my fingertips over the beautiful initials E.M. on the gold clip. I could feel my love flowing from my fingers and through the pen as I wrote:

August 31, 1939

My dearest Ernst,

I hope you have heard by now that Anna and I made it safely onto the ship and have safely arrived in New York, all thanks to you. Coming back has been difficult for me. You are constantly in my thoughts, and I long for you more than I know how to control. Our parting at the train is still so fresh in my mind and my heart. As I write this, I know these are the first words this pen has written without it coming from your hand. It, as well as I, will have to get used to being without you somehow. Please write to me as soon as you can. I hope you are well and safe in Prague.

Your loving,

Karin

SETTLING IN

OVER THE NEXT FEW DAYS, my parents, Anja, and I fall into a fair routine. Since the day we left Prague, I had developed a cough that seemed to be worsening as time went by. My parents grew concerned about this, and my mother insisted that I go see her doctor. She also insisted that I leave Anja with her while I went to the appointment. I reluctantly agreed, hoping that Anja would understand that this was like the times I left her with Beata and Jiri while I saw Ernst. My mother's doctor was concerned about the cough, and he insisted that I obtain a chest x-ray to check for fluid in my lungs. When I returned to our apartment, I was grateful to see that neither Anja nor my mother seemed the worse for wear while I was gone. Anja had made great inroads when she put her paper keyboard on the kitchen table and began to do her scales on it. My father seeing this was so delighted he smiled at her and led her into his music room and sat her down at the piano. She smiled at my father who began to play the C scale for her. She cautiously put her hand on the keys and played it. From that moment on they were fast friends for life.

THE FOLLOWING DAY I WENT THE HOSPITAL FOR THE chest x-ray. While in the waiting room, Alex's brother Greg walked by. We recognized each other even though we had only met briefly a few times prior to the Prague trip.

"Hello, Karin! I heard you just got back—welcome home! It can be a long wait here. What do you say I check you in, and then we can go for coffee?" I agreed, and we went to the cafeteria. I found a table for us, while Greg got the coffee. He set two cups of coffee on the table and asked, "How are you? What are you being x-rayed for?"

"I have a cough that my mother's doctor wants further checked. I'm sure it's nothing, but he wants to be sure."

Greg nodded. "They do that, —there's a lot of TB around, and they're trying to keep it in check. I can't stay but a few minutes, but I'd like to see you again."

"Why don't you come for dinner tomorrow night, and we can catch up?"

Greg raised his eyebrows. "Do you think it's, all right? I haven't seen your parents since my mother's funeral."

"I'm sure it's fine. Can you be there by six?"

"I have tomorrow off, so I'll be there. Give me your address again."

"Alex has it."

Greg made a small frown. "I don't see much of him these days."

So, I wrote the address on a paper napkin. Greg thanked me, and then he walked me back to the x-ray waiting room and then headed off about his day.

DURING DINNER THE NEXT EVENING, GREG ASKED, "HAS Anja been seen by a doctor since you arrived?"

"No, should she be?"

He nodded. "A lot of refugee children are not as well as they could be. A friend of mine at the hospital is a pediatrician. Would you like to have Anja checked over?"

I was very grateful. "After what you said, I think it's a good idea."

"I'll set something up and call you." I thanked him, and after he left my parents and I marveled at how Greg was so unlike his brother.

Greg met Anja and me at the hospital entrance and took us up to the pediatrics department. Greg waited with us, and when we were called he came to the examination room with us, where he introduced us to Dr. Grace Hamilton. Then he excused himself, saying he was due to start his shift.

Dr. Hamilton was sweet, and Anja took to her very nicely while I gave the little background I knew about Anja. Grace made some notes and then put on her stethoscope. She was very gentle and kind with Anja as she listened to her heart and lungs. She looked in Anja's ears and eyes and mouth, and she weighed and measured Anja, making notes throughout the process. Anja lay quietly on the table while Dr. Hamilton checked her abdomen. I was surprised at how compliant Anja was. When she was done with her exam, Dr. Hamilton said, "Since you don't have any immunization records for her, I'll look into what we can give her and when. I think it's a good idea to give her all the shots a three-year-old would have by now. But certainly not all at once! In the meantime, keep her away from other children and playgrounds. She should have the pertussis and diphtheria, to be sure. I do not see any sign that she has been vaccinated against smallpox either, so I will arrange for that as well. I would also like her to have cod liver oil. Please watch her diet; no sugary sweets, only fruits and the occasional ice cream. Give her plenty of vegetables and lean meats and fish. I know it isn't easy these days, but we want to build her up from where she is now."

"Do you think she is so small because she is undernourished?"

"No, not at all! She is just a normal delicate little three-year-old with a naturally small frame. If she were a bird, she would grow up to be a sparrow, not an eagle." We laughed. "As for this not speaking, I would like you to have her see someone. We have a German refugee doctor here, Professor Steinreich. He is a child psychologist, and he specializes in trauma-affected children. He can't practice in the U.S. because he does not have a license to do so, even though he had his own clinic in Berlin before he fled Nazi persecution. We are lucky to have him here with us; we are able to employ him as a consultant. You will like him, and so will Anja, I think. He is here today, and I can introduce you if you'd like."

I thanked her profusely, and a short time later she introduced us to a kindly gentleman in his late fifties. He spoke very good English, and the best part was Anja seemed absolutely taken with him. He offered me the next two hours for a consultation. We went into a room with all sorts of toys, including children's musical instruments. We sat near Anja, while she prefered to explore the instruments. Seeing this, he smiled and said, "It appears she already has a leaning in life, it appears it might be perhaps toward music."

"Yes, she has shown strong interest in that direction. While we were in Prague, an uncle Jiri taught her to play octaves on the piano. My father teaches piano and has her under his wing. She loves it."

"How wonderful! But I must point out, however, that music is an inward event that the musicians share to communicate with us through their music. I want Anja to express herself in ways other than with music, however more comfortable she may be with that now. We will work on it with her."

Over the next two hours I told him the whole story. At one point, he was even moved to tears. He took his glasses off and, wiping his eyes, said, "Children pay a terrible price under those conditions, but in Anja's case, as heartbreaking as it is, her father gave her an extraordinary gift in giving her to you, how lucky she is, how very lucky. One of these days she will discard her mantle of silence and she will speak. I don't know how long it may take, but as long as she has you, she will do that." At that point, I had to dry my own tears.

Dr. Steinreich retrieved his schedule book. "I would like to see you both in two weeks, at which time I would like to do some simple testing. It will serve as a small indicator of how best to proceed. It is an honor for me to treat her, as it is to have met you." He stood and shook my hand, then he bent down to Anja and said, "I will see you again, Anja. So long for now." I thought it interesting that he did not say 'goodbye' but 'so long,' like an English *Auf Wiedersehen*. As we left, I felt relief that she now had two more healers in her life, one for her body and one for her psyche, and I hoped I was doing well as the one to care for her heart. I wished her father could know how well she is being cared for in a safe place surrounded with love, but, somehow, I think he knew that would happen.

UNSETTLING

IN THESE FIRST DAYS of being home again, I became aware of how much our reality was based in our perceptions of the moment, and the intrusion of strong memories can interfere with one's sense of reality. It had happened when I was in the elevator holding my first letter to Ernst; I was looking at his name on the envelope, concentrating on my happy memories of him. As I rode the elevator to the lobby, I suddenly thought that I could not put this in the mailbox because it is after curfew. When the elevator door opened, and I saw all the lobby lights on, the reality of no blackout or curfew jolted back into place. I found it hard to believe in the moments it took to cross the lobby, and reality was only confirmed when I stepped out into the street and saw that I was indeed home, where Anja and I could walk into a park without fearing signs of *Forbidden to Jews*. I had only lived under those restrictions for six months, but they had left their imprint, which emerged at odd moments.

I hurried to the corner mailbox, full of hope that Ernst would receive the letter soon. When I returned to the apartment, my father and mother were sitting by the radio, listening intently. The newscaster's grave voice delivered solemn news: "Germany had just invaded Poland, and all of Europe is on tenterhooks awaiting the further outcome of this action. Allied nations have yet to respond to this, Hitler has transgressed the trust given him. A peaceful resolution is now eagerly awaited but seems unlikely." The local newscaster came back on and said, "This concludes the report from our overseas correspondent. We will continue to report the news as it develops. Stay tuned for all the latest news." My father turned the radio off and lowered his head into his hands.

"Daddy?"

My father's voice sounded hollow as he spoke at the floor. "He's done it. Hitler has invaded Poland. All of Europe is at his mercy, and I am afraid he has none."

I sank into the couch, trying to comprehend what had just happened. I couldn't believe this is real. For one moment, I considered what Ernst had said about Prague early on, "We are here just to administrate it." But even I can't think that now, —invasion is just that.

"Daddy, what does this really mean?"

"I think it means war, considering the events leading up to this. It is another case of outright aggression, and it can't possibly be construed as anything else."

Thinking back now to when Ernst urged me to get out as fast as I could, I wondered whether he knew anything about this. He couldn't have. That had to be a high-level decision, not one shared with a paper-pushing lieutenant in faraway Prague. In addition to Ernst, I now also worried about Beata, Jiri, and Sabina, as well as Helen. As my feelings tried to catch up with this news, I struggled to reconcile them with a single intelligent thought. My father continued, "Poor Poland. Yes, this action probably means war in Europe." He looked over at me and said, "Thank God, Karin, you got out just in time."

Mother looked at me and said, "Karin, you don't look well. Are you alright?"

I stood shakily and said, "I will be, I just need to lie down for a bit." I went into my room and buried my face in my pillow to quiet my weeping. As I slowly regained my senses, I wondered again whether Ernst had known anything about what was about to happen. He seemed to hurry the whole process of getting us out of Prague so suddenly; I remembered that he had said, "You must use these within the month or not at all." At times he had been so sure he would never see me again, then but at other times he spoke so resolutely of coming to see me, as if he wasn't sure. Will I hear from him again? Will he get my letters? Surely that will happen, —after all, America is not involved. I tried so very hard to convince myself of that over and over again. I continued in this belief, I had to; I could not imagine Ernst in a war against America. I held onto the hope that the worst outcome might be that the army would send him to Poland to do paper work as he was doing in Prague. Of all things I wanted to hope that would be the worst that would happen.

It didn't take long, however, for that hope to be crushed. Just days after Germany's invasion of Poland, England and France declared war on Germany for its failure to withdraw from Poland. Is this what would divide Ernst and me in the eyes of the outside world? Surely nothing else would or could. Where would it end, and how and when would it end? My father was well informed; he read a lot and kept up with world events on a daily basis, so I would be sure to know what was happening overseas, whether I welcomed it or not. I would continue to write and wait for an answer.

When I put Anja to bed that night, my mother said, "Thank God she is here with you and us now." Then, to break the tension, she said, "I've been meaning to tell you we want to get a bed for her, one of her own. It can't be comfortable for both of you to sleep in your bed."

I wanted to say that, now more than ever, I wanted to keep her close. "I don't know. I'm not sure she would sleep in it."

"Maybe she could just nap in it to begin with," she suggested. That too was a remote possibility.

One evening, sitting at the dinner table, we heard loud sirens from police cars and fire engines. Anja's eyes widened and she put her fingers to her pursed her lips. She slipped out of her chair and ran off to hide. We heard her footsteps throughout the apartment, but when she couldn't find a hiding place, she climbed onto my lap, shaking and sobbing. My parents looked at each other and then at us with pity. My mother said, "Poor little thing! I can't imagine what she must have been through."

I comforted Anja and told her everything was all right. I took her to the window to show her nothing is out there. She took one quick look and burrowed her head on my chest where she sucked her thumb, reached for my hair, and slowly calmed down.

THE PIANO

AS SOON AS ANJA DISCOVERED my father's piano, she was eager to play her scales as often as possible. I shared with my parents how Jiri had allowed Anja to sit on his lap while he played, and had taught her the octaves. When I sat her up on the bench next to my father, she looked up at him as if for permission. When he smiled and nodded, she played her two-octave scale. He applauded when she finished. She smiled and moved over on the bench to make more room for him. She played the scale with her right hand again, and this time my father joined her with his left hand. That was the beginning of it. When he played *Twinkle, Twinkle Little Star*, she climbed on his lap and put her hands on top of his as he played, and her little legs swung in time to the music. My heart swelled with love and heartache for Beata and Jiri. My father sang the words softly, and singing, "how I wonder *who* you are."

My mother and I stepped into the kitchen to have coffee and a piece of cardamom cake. She looked at me and squeezed my hand, saying, "Thank you, Karin, for giving us this beautiful grandchild."

"It won't be easy, Mother."

"No, but it will be wonderful."

Next we heard one of the many Mozart versions of *Twinkle Twinkle Little Star*. When we returned to the music room, Anja was standing next to the piano bench, watching my father her eyes widened as if she were watching and hearing a whole new world unfold before her. I remembered what Dr. Steinreich had said about her leaning in life. From then on, she and my father were inseparable, both at the piano and away from it. When he sat down for his coffee and cake, he said, "I think she has a talent for it, and yes, and I'm not saying that just because she is my grandchild." He looked at me; a bit embarrassed, and said, "Well, you know what I mean."

"Yes, Daddy, I do."

New Events

WE WENT BACK to see Dr. Grace Hamilton for another check and to start Anja with her immunizations. Dr. Hamilton checked her over again, and then said, "I can start her on the multi-part immunization today for pertussis and diphtheria. The whooping cough and diphtheria vaccines are given in a series of three, she'll have to have two more. As I said before, since I don't see any signs that she has been given a vaccination for smallpox, she should have that as well. I'll have someone else in the clinic give her the shots, so that she doesn't associate me with pain."

I held Anja on my lap as a nurse wiped the alcohol swab on her arm. Anja watched her curiously, even as the needle was prepared. When Anja felt the jab of the needle, she cried out, "Karin!" She clutched my blouse and cried. My heart leapt in my chest. Grace smiled at Anja, "It's all over Anja, it's okay. We are finished." Then to me she said, "Now we know she can speak!"

While it felt wonderful that Anja said my name, I felt horrible because for the first time I have allowed Anja to be hurt. For any other child, a lollipop and a hug might make it okay, but I worried that her cautiously built trust in me was now broken, and we would have to find a way to mend it. We ate lunch in the hospital cafeteria before our next appointment with Dr. Steinreich.

We were in his office for just a few minutes before he said, "She seems upset. Has something happened?"

I told him about the shots and her reaction, but I was so upset with myself that I forgot to tell him she called out "Karin" in her pain and surprise. He probed further before I could remember to tell him. That was a big happening for Anja, and for me to have forgotten.

"You see, she showed you the lining of her mantle, and that is a big first step. You may not hear it again for a while, but hear it again you will, and hopefully not connected with pain."

Then he sat at a small table with Anja, where there was a collection of things. He showed her a set of small blocks with colored sections. He made a pattern with the pieces and then he motioned her to duplicate the pattern. She thoughtfully chose each block and one by one replicated his pattern, then she looked at him and waited. He smiled at her and patted her hand; she smiled back and touched his hand gently. Then he did similar things with pieces of paper, shaped blocks, always making patterns for her to follow and match.

When they were finished, he said, "All indications so far are that she is quite bright. A lot of activity is going on in that little head, to be sure. Now we want to try to have her express it in speech. I realize that the English language must be new sounds for her, making it a bit more of a challenge, but since that is all she will be hearing, she'll catch on quickly. Children are very adept at learning, and with a good ear they mimic easily, but until then it is vital that she begins to express herself in another way. I would like you to get her a large pad of paper and a box of colored wax crayons. Every day, I would like you to sit quietly, just the two of you, for as long as she will stay put, and encourage her to express herself on paper. In this way she is not dependent on speech but still she is expressing herself. Number each page in a corner in pencil in the order she makes them, and then I want you with her to hang them on your walls and doors. It is important for her to see that her efforts to communicate are appreciated. She will be proud of that recognition. The hope is that some speech will follow. It might be just a word or two, but whatever she says, repeat the words to her carefully when she does so that she is aware that expressing herself is a valued and now safe outlet for her thoughts and her feelings. Please bring some of them the next time you come to see me."

Then he went to Anja and extended his hand. When she put her hand in his, he shook it gently and said, "Thank you, Anja. I will see you again soon." To me he said, "In two weeks, maybe we can look forward to even a small change." I thanked him and we left. I felt that our appointments warranted an ice cream on the way home.

The following day I brought Anja into my bedroom after breakfast and presented her with a box of crayons and pad of paper. She looked at me expectantly; I waited briefly before opening the box and spilling out the crayons. I picked up a bright color and slowly doodled on the pad. I indicated that she could do the same. She picked out a crayon and started her own doodle. After a minute or two, her expression changed to one of concentration, and she started an inward journey of which I was not a part. As Dr. Steinreich predicted, she went on and on, and her hand movements swung larger and larger with each new page. Suddenly thoughtful, she put the crayon down and chose a new one. Her movements changed to make smaller shapes. She drew something tall with small circles attached. The shapes slowly clarified, one was a head with large eyes, and there was another head with even larger eyes. She circled that one repeatedly as if in emphasis. She filled page after page, and I numbered

205

them discreetly in the corners. When she finally tired of the activity, we worked together to hang them on the walls. She was delighted as I tacked up each one, surrounding the room with her pages. When my mother came home and saw the output she said, "Oh my, there has been a change in my absence." I watched as my mother took Anja in her arms and walked from picture to picture. My mother pointed at each one and then looked at Anja for an explanation. Anja only laughed until they came to the one with the faces. She looked away and reached out for me to take her. I wasn't sure if this would stir her to speech, but it certainly stirred a memory in her.

When my father had finished with his last pupil of the day, Anja ran to him. Within minutes, the apartment is awash in scales. All is right with the world again—but is it?

ONE DAY, MY MOTHER TOOK ANJA AND ME ON A LITTLE "jaunt" as she called it, to a nice department store. The racks of little girls' dresses in the children's department energized my mother. She looked them over and brought three of them over to me. She held them up to Anja and after repeated critical assessments and smiles, she said, "What do you think ladies? Which one shall it be?"

"Mother, it's a nice idea, but you know I can't afford it."

"No, but I can. Choose please!" I looked at the price tags, and she scolded me. "That is not the aesthetic choice that I want from you."

I sighed. "I'll leave it up to Anja then." She showed Anja each dress. She touched each dress with her little hands, but when she lingered over one, mother said, "That's the one! Now she needs a pair of shoes!" In the shoe department, Anja got a pair of little red leather Mary Janes and two pairs of socks.

Then we shared a sandwich at a small lunch counter. Anja was more interested in the dill pickle and chocolate milk. Then mother walked us up Fifth Avenue. When I guessed that she was heading to a large toy store, I said, "Let's not go in, Mother. She'll be overwhelmed."

My mother sniffed lightheartedly. "We are here because it is a grandmother's prerogative to indulge in such pleasures." There was no stopping her. Just inside the doors, there was a large promotional display of Beatrix Potter's books and stuffed animals. Anja was mesmerized. There were several sizes of stuffed Peter Rabbits. Anja gingerly reached out for one but could not reach it. My mother pointed to each size in turn, and when Anja pointed to the smallest one, mother took it down and handed it to her. Instead of looking it over, Anja hugged it tightly to her chest and buried her face in it.

"Does she have the book?"

I thought about all the days I had read this story to her. "We did, but I don't know what happened to it."

Mother picked up a copy of Peter Rabbit, and we went to the cashier. Anja wouldn't relinquish the stuffed rabbit, so the clerk had to come out from behind the counter to get the price tag. "Mother, how can I ever thank you?"

My mother just smiled at Anja. "You don't have to, Karin. She just did."

On the way home I watched Anja become the rescuer, rather than the rescued. Peter Rabbit was now safe in Anja's arms, protected from the evil Farmer McGregor. That night our bed was a bit crowded with Anja, Peter Rabbit, the book, as well as her new dress and her new shoes, which she insisted on keeping safe in their box.

She was now able to play two octaves with both hands, and from day to day I felt I was watching a tight little bud that held the promise to flower.

I held out hope for another promise, and I eagerly checked the mail every day for the letters that Ernst would have written to me. I didn't bother myself with the fact that even if he had written right away such a letter probably would not have gotten here by now. So far, not a word, but I wrote again, I would honor my promise despite the silence. Today I bought an anthology of sonnets and poems and wrote a dedication to him on the title page before sending it. Nothing would change this, despite the harrowing news from Poland.

WORLD'S FAIR 1939

AS A RESPITE FROM DAILY routine and anxiety over news from Europe, my parents planned a surprise for Anja and me. They took us to the 1939 World's Fair in Queens. If I had little idea of what to expect, Anja certainly had none whatsoever. The two huge iconic structures, The Trylon and The Perisphere, heralded the theme of the fair, "The World of Tomorrow." The world of today was perplexing enough for me as it was. We heard a replay of Albert Einstein's opening speech about cosmic rays. As a physicist he was not only looking farther into the future of the universe, but he also had a clear vision of what Hitler was espousing right here on earth when he had come to power in 1933. Albert Einstein was among those who saw what Hitler held in store for the future of all Jews. That is when he took his family and some coworkers and renounced his German citizenship, leaving Germany for the United States. Hitler had also renounced his own Austrian citizenship for German citizenship, although for different reasons.

At the World's Fair, we were agog at the enormity of it all. Of the many nations' pavilions, Germany did not participate, citing economic reasons, they were busy doing other things. There was so much to see that we returned several times, but we still did not see all of it. It was hot and the lines to get into a pavilion were often quite long, but just being on the site was exciting and tiring, and overwhelming, as The World of Tomorrow would also prove to be.

New Endeavors

WITHIN SOME WEEKS, and several needle sticks and trips to ice cream parlors, Anja completed her regimen of immunizations. Dr. Hamilton said, "Now that Anja has all of her shots, she can now safely play with other children."

On the same day, Dr. Steinreich told me about a woman, Ina Castle, who ran a small private preschool for children with special needs. "I have talked to her about Anja, and she welcomes a visit from you both."

"I do not have a job, so I can't possibly afford a private school."

"I brought that up with Miss Castle, and she is offering a scholarship of sorts. Please go and see her. She has done wonders with the children I have sent her."

Two days later, I stood before a brownstone house just a few blocks from where we lived. Gold letters on the door read, Castle Care. When I rang the bell, a man answered. He asked if I had an appointment, and with whom.

"I have an appointment with Miss Castle. My name is Karin Wilson."

"Please come in, she is expecting you."

I followed him down a hallway to a private office, where I was greeted by Miss Castle. "How nice to meet you Miss Wilson. I already know a bit about you from Dr. Steinreich, but please come in and sit down. Would you care to join me in a cup of herbal tea? I find it to be a nice pick-me-up at this time of day. It also calms one's nerves, or so it is claimed." She smiled and said, "But it is equally that the expectation of being calmed that actually calms a person, and this supports the illusion. I find that most of life is an illusion; some of it works for us, some of it doesn't, and some of it even works against us. It's all in how one brews it, it's all in the brew!" she laughed as she poured tea. I took an instant liking to her.

"I'm free for the next hour, so I would like to hear about Anja from you and how we might fit into her needs. Please know that everything you tell me will be held in the strictest confidence, so do not hesitate to share her history."

Fully confident in my sense of her and in Dr. Steinreich's recommendation, I proceeded to tell her Anja's story. At the end, she took her glasses off and rubbed her eyes. She looked at me and with a soft look and said, "I feel that Anja would do well here. She will feel cared for, and respected and loved, all the prerequisites for healing a young person who has had such an uncertain beginning. At least until you entered her life and brought her to this point. If I may say, I think you are a most remarkable young woman, to have taken on this great responsibility. Let us set up a time for you to come in with Anja so we can get acquainted. I think she may need you here at the beginning until she feels secure enough to be here on her own." Opening an appointment book, she offered me some days to come in with Anja.

I chose a day for another appointment, but then I felt compelled to say, "I must speak of the costs of her coming here. I am unemployed at the moment and living with my parents. It is hard for her to be left while I go out to look for work, but she is more trusting of my parents bit by bit. I have no idea what the tuition here might be, and I so hoped that I could work it off somehow with you until I can pay the fees."

"You are very conscientious for bringing it up. Dr. Steinreich told me about your situation. I have generous benefactors in the professional community, and they support us when the need arises with tuition. I am happy to say you are completely covered by a scholarship for Anja for as long as she will need it."

I was overwhelmed at this news. I collected myself enough to say, "I am grateful beyond words for this offer. Thank you so much!"

"You and Anja are welcome. I have some forms for you to fill out regarding her history. There may be a gap or two that you can't answer, but even her current information will be helpful."

I completed the forms to the best of my knowledge, and I hoped it was enough of a history about her problems, especially the one about her lack of speaking, to be helpful. When I gave the forms back to Miss Castle, she looked at them and said, "Excellent. We have enough to go on from here, thank you. I look forward to seeing you and meeting Anja on our next appointment." We finish our tea and she saw me out. Walking down the steps of Castle Care, I again couldn't believe my good fortune. At every turn, all the people I have needed had miraculously appeared and come to our aid. Surely there was some life force at play here, a guiding hand making it all happen as it did. I walked home barely able to feel the pavement beneath my feet, lost in wonder.

A few days later I returned to Castle Care, with Anja by my side. The man showed us into Miss Castle's office again. She and Anja looked at each other for a few moments, Anja with a nervous look in her eye and Miss Castle with a warm welcoming smile. She spoke gently to Anja, saying, "Hello, Anja. Welcome to your new play school. I know you will like us here and will make some new friends." Anja just stared at her, possibly only recognizing her name in all of Miss Castle's words.

Unfazed by Anja's lack of reaction, Miss Castle told me more of what the children do at the school. "I see you have brought her blanket and pillow; we already have a bin for her with her name on it where she'll keep it for nap times. We offer music and story time and art and singing in our program. We also work on manual skills development involving the children's imagination. At times we do field trips to the zoo and picnics in Central Park. As you may have guessed from our program, we aim to assist in the child's personal, social, educational, and emotional development. The approach and the results vary with each child, of course, according to his or her needs at the time, and to that end our classes are kept small. The leader of our program is Louise Vickers. She has a degree in early childhood development and education, and she is lovely with the children. She has just the right amount of exuberance to spur the little ones on to participate more fully to their true being. The children love her. I am also lucky to have a connection with an excellent teachers college, and their best students come here to do their practicum as helpers in our program. Once a month, I have an open invitation for parents to come together as a group. We discuss issues of interest to each other, mostly concerning their children. Those meetings occur the first Saturday morning of every month, and you are most welcome to join us. I think you might find it interesting, even if only to know that you aren't the only person with challenges as a parent. We have an ironclad rule that every child may only leave here at the end of the day with an approved adult. If it is not one of the child's parents, we will ask for identification to match your request.

"I think that covers it. Class meets from ten to two, five days a week. We serve a late morning refreshment of milk and a small cheese sandwich, and later a light lunch. If Anja has any special needs with regard to food, it will be noted. A few of our children do have food allergies. Now let me take you to the classroom. We allow new parents to sit by the door in the back of the room for the first few visits, as that may help Anja adjust."

We walked into the classroom. Miss Vickers came over to us and introduced herself, paying particular attention to Anja. She guided us to the shelf with bins, and I put her pillow and blanket in a bin labeled with her name. Anja was eyeing the group of seven children, and she drew herself closer to me. I sat down on the bench by the door, and Anja climbed onto my lap, still looking suspiciously at the group. She leaned into me and sucked her thumb. One of the little boys, who had been looking at her with interest since we came into the room, walked over to us. He addressed Anja, saying, "Hello, I'm Benji. What's your name?" Anja didn't respond, and I told him that she doesn't speak much.

"Oh, okay." He tried to take her hand to follow him, but she pulled it away to her chest. He then gestured for her to go with him. Anja just leaned harder into me. The little boy shrugged and smiled. "Okay, see you tomorrow."

Before he went back to the group, I said, "Her name is Anja."

He nodded and said, "Okay. See you tomorrow, Anja." He waved at her and went back to the group.

Shortly after Benji returned to the group, Anja slid off my lap and grabbed my hand. She tugged me toward the bins. She took her pillow and blanket from her bin and then pulled me toward the door.

Not an auspicious beginning, I told myself as we left Castle Care, but only for today I hope.

That evening, Miss Castle called me at home. "I heard about Anja's early departure today. Please do not be discouraged by that. It happens with new students sometimes. When Anja feels that it is a safe and fun place to be, she will relent and join in. It may take a few visits with you sitting in, and we might even need to try a few visits where you leave the classroom, but I know it will happen. Everyone looks forward to seeing Anja tomorrow."

"Thank you, Miss Castle. I was quite disheartened by how she reacted, but we will be back tomorrow." That was my note of progress for today.

There was still no word from Ernst. It is too early to have gotten anything yet, I tell myself, only half believing it.

THE FOLLOWING MORNING, ANJA FOLLOWED OUR morning routine until I packed up her pillow and blanket, at which point she balked. She refused to let me put on her coat. I decided to take a risk. I took the bag with her pillow and blanket and waved goodbye to her. I walked to the front door to leave. She quickly ran over to me, pulling me back inside and trying to close the door. I lifted her up and gave her a hug and a kiss, and then I walked over to her coat. She allowed me to put her coat on with little resistance. We walked the few blocks to Castle Care. When we came up to the brownstone, she balked again. I picked her up and carried her inside, and she didn't struggle. My quick sense of direct action seemed to be working. We were both discovering a new way of relating to each other.

Anja climbed onto my lap once I sat down on the bench by the classroom door. I hadn't put the bag with her blanket and pillow in her bin, thinking we'd be leaving soon anyway. Benji smiled and waved to Anja again. She looked away again, just like the day before. I waved to Benji, but when she saw that she pulled my hand down. Had I invaded her territory? I hoped so!

Before Miss Vickers started the day, Benji walked over to us. "Hello, Anja." She turned her head away from me just enough to see him from the corner of her eye. I think Benji understood what was at play here, and he simply waved goodbye and went back to the group. When Anja stood up shortly before the morning snack, I was happy that we had stayed longer than the day before. To my surprise, however, Anja took the bag with the pillow and blanket and hurriedly put it in an empty bin and then walked to the door. I quickly moved her bag into the right bin and then hurried to follow her. I figured this was a giant step forward, because this told me that she planned on returning.

WHEN ANJA AND I RETURNED TO THE APARTMENT, MY mother informed me that she had decided that Anja would have a bed of her own. I tried to convince her to save the unnecessary expense because Anja wouldn't sleep in it.

My mother was unmoved. "She will sleep in it when she is ready. I have done some window-shopping on the subject, so let's take her to look at them." Unable to stop my mother's momentum, we went to the bedding department of a nearby department store. My mother guided us to the favored bed, simple white wooden frame with clouds painted on the blue headboard. My mother laid down on it and urged me to do the same. I did, and Anja promptly tugged on my hand to make me stand up. "Mother, thank you for the effort, but she will have to make some of her own before she's ready for her own bed." We left the store without purchasing the bed, as I had predicted. One great leap at a time, first school and then the bed.

My mother saw it differently, however, because on Saturday morning the department store made a delivery at our door. Anja was having a cup of cocoa as the two deliverymen entered our bedroom. She quickly came to me, wanting to be lifted up out of harm's way. She watched the men assemble the bed, and then they left. My mother came in with packages of bedding and quickly made up the bed. When the sheets and blanket were neatly tucked in and the down pillow was fluffed and put in place, my mother looked at Anja and said, "I did the easy part, now the rest is up to you."

"Thank you, Mother." Anja and I are left staring at the new bed and its implications.

Desperate for any reason to leave the bedroom and its new challenge, I decided it was lunchtime. After lunch, my father went down for a newspaper and came back with the mail. He handed me two letters, saying, "They look at bit worn, and so do you! Here you are, sweetheart." I saw they were from Prague—finally!

I rushed into the bedroom and sat down on Anja's bed to open the letters. She promptly pulled me off the bed. I absently went over to my own bed and sat down to read the letters. The envelopes bore a stamp, *Militär Post.* I wondered why they did not go through the regular mail. Was the military censoring their mail now as well? I tore the both envelopes open to see which was written first.

2 September 1939

My dearest Karin,

I worry so about you now and what you must be thinking after September 1.

Do not worry, I am in Prague doing much less of what I have done. I may be transferred at some point, but for now I am here in quiet, lovely Prague. Everywhere I look, I see you. I ache for you more than you can know. The other evening, I went to the Hungarian goulash place where you and I ate, only to find it boarded up. The windows had been broken, and the owner is no longer here. I walked up the street and over the bridge to a sausage kiosk. I made a meal of their offerings and stood eating it halfway under their umbrella. It started to rain, and I left to walk back over the bridge, thinking of you sitting next to me by a warm fire at the inn, having a glass of wine and fresh bread with goose pâté. I often think of our other later visits there, just before you left, and those are much more heartbreaking for me now. I keep trying to project myself into a future with you, even as I am still here every day. I hope you are well and that Anna is happy to be home again with you. Please write as soon as you can. I await mail from you with a hunger you cannot imagine.

I send you all my love,
Ernst

4 September 1939

Dearest Karin,

Today I got your first letter.

You ask me where I am. I'll tell you.

I'm sitting on a park bench in Prague. I have just had lunch with you and Anna, and she is asleep on your lap. I have my arm around you, and your eyes are closed and your head is turned to the sunlight. I have just kissed you to be a part of your bliss, but I have startled you. When you opened your eyes, I asked you if you would come home with me now to Berlin, and to my great joy you said yes.

I hope you don't mind that I've changed the ending to favor me. I had to, because now I have to leave you and I must walk off alone into nothingness, because that is where I am without you. The only place worth being is with you. Every night when I try for sleep, I have those images with you with which I feed my imagination to make the darkness without you bearable. My heart aches for you.

I hope you are well, and even from here I continue to watch over you and the little one.

With all my love to you,
Ernst

I was relieved to receive his two letters, and to know we can write to each other despite the latest developments in Europe. That evening I wrote to Ernst, telling him that Mr. Wilson and I have parted and have agreed to a divorce, that the year apart was more than our troubled marriage could survive. Relieved of the deception, I went on to describe some of the resettling Anja and I had to do. We both needed hope that we would see each other again.

I heard my father quietly say to my mother, "I just want you to know that a little extra work fell into my hands today. On my free mornings I will be playing piano for a ballet class."

Before my mother could reply, I said, "Daddy, do you really need to do that on top of all your other students?"

"Karin, it's not a question of need. I want to do it."

I frowned. "It's because of Anja and me, isn't it?"

He shook his head. "It'll be something different for a change. I'm looking forward to it."

Anja pulled him toward the piano. He smiled and said, "Excuse me, Karin, but I'm being engaged!"

My mother whispered to me, "It makes him happy, can't you see that?"

I whispered back. "I think it's to keep up with your buying sprees for Anja. She is so little and, yet she has made such a big impact on all of us. I feel so responsible for all of it."

"Karin, look at me. Yes, has she made a big impact on all of us, but we would not trade it for all the tea in China. We are responsible adults, if you recall, so let us be that."

I nodded, grateful for my parents' generosity. "Speaking of being responsible, I need your advice on something." My mother nodded, and I continued. "At some point, Anja will ask, and I will have to tell her something about her father and how she came to me. I have all the papers and his letter to me. I want to keep them somewhere safe until that time comes. I thought I might write a letter to her as well, to keep with her father's note, telling her about my part in her being with me. Do you have any advice for me on that?"

My mother squeezed my arm. "I'm glad you are thinking about that. It is best to do it now and get it out of the way, while your memories are still fresh. I suggest you take all your papers and letters and address them to Anja. Then you can go to our bank and get a safe deposit box and leave them there until the time comes when they are needed. They will be safe and secure for all concerned. Just be sure to put her name on the access card as well."

I thanked her. "I knew you would know how I could do this. It's a load off my mind for now at least."

In the next few days I followed my mother's suggestion. I bundled up her father's letter to me with a letter sharing my side of the story of how that happened. I included the travel documents we were given to leave Prague, and I wrote about our arrival here in New York. I took my mother's red sealing wax and sealed the bundle. I wrote Anja's name on the outside of the packet. At the bank I reserved a new safe deposit box and put it all inside. I wished I could build my own steel vault around it for safety. Then I came home, a bit less burdened than when I left for the bank.

On my way home, I considered when Anja should be permitted to access this safe deposit box. Her twenty-first birthday seemed a likely target. I feared losing her, once she learned her true origin and that I was not her birth mother. Losing her and her love terrified me the most. She had steered my life since I was twenty-one; if she rejected me I would probably flounder for the rest of my life. My love for her was such that I would do or say anything to protect it. She had to know the truth one day, though—of that there was no question. I walked the long twenty-five blocks from the bank, reviewing my life . . . with Anja, my parents, Beata, Jiri, Sabina, and, of course, Ernst. After all, he did call us his little family.

ON THE FRIDAY OF THE WEEK I STARTED TAKING ANJA to school, Benji was waiting for her at the door to the classroom. As soon as I took her coat off, he took her hand and led her to the music circle on the floor. He made room for her next to him. She was perplexed but allowed herself to be led. She looked back over at me to be sure I would stay. I smiled and nodded at her, showing her that it was okay. The student teacher passed out the instruments.

Benji took a drum and a set of bells; he put the drum and the padded drumstick on Anja's lap. She did not know what to do when the student teacher said, "Okay, let's do *Mary had a Little Lamb*. One, two, and three . . ." When she gave them the downbeat, Anja was dumbfounded, but Benji put the drumstick in her hand and tapped the drum with it. She looked at him in confusion, but after he smiled and nodded to her, she tried it on her own. I was so happy at that progress. When they were finished, the children followed the teacher to the piano and sang songs. Anja did not sing of course, but she stood at the end of the piano keyboard, totally mesmerized. I had seen that look before. The next event was story time, and the student teacher read to them from a book. Anja smiled at me and gave me a tiny wave. She was making connections to bring past and present together. When they had naptime, Benji led her to the bins while the teacher put down padded mats with each child's name. When Benji and Anja came over to the mats he put his blanket and pillow down and told the teacher that Anja had to be next to him. Anja hadn't been laying down for more than five minutes when she sat bolt upright to check on me. I waved to her and she laid down again. Twenty minutes later they were served milk and a small cheese sandwich; once again Benji made sure they sat together. The next event was painting at their easels. Standing next to Benji, Anja hesitated while he started to paint on his paper. Benji made a few brush strokes on her paper, and Anja laughed and did the same on his. Communication was happening—whether by mimicry, confusion, or humor, it was happening. When it was time to go, a kind-looking lady came for Benji. I introduced myself, and she said, "It's a pleasure to meet you! I'm Hannah. You know, I hear a lot about Anja from Benji. It seems they have become good friends."

"Yes, he was truly wonderful with her today. He has made Anja's day here much easier." We said goodbye, and Benji and Anja waved to each other as we left. The next morning was Saturday, and after breakfast Anja ran for her coat and pulled me to the door. She wanted to go to school! How could I make her understand there would be no school on the weekend? I tried to take her coat and hang it up, but she held on tight.

I lifted her up and got the Peter Rabbit book and carried her to the kitchen table and began to read. She started to cry and then leaned on me sucking her thumb. This was a big setback, and an unexpected one at that. Sunday was not any better, despite our attempts to divert her attention as best we could.

Monday morning after breakfast, I got her coat and went to the door. She nearly jumped into it. I had to walk quickly to keep up with her. I didn't know her little legs could walk that fast. At school, Benji was waiting for her; I could barely get her coat off fast enough. Anja looked at me and gave me a push toward the door. Did she really want me to leave? I waved to her and walked out of the classroom. I stood outside the door, prepared for last-minute misgivings on her part. It never happened. The whole week followed suit. One afternoon I mentioned the Saturday and Sunday mornings of disappointment to Benji's mom. She said, "This Saturday morning we're going to the zoo. Would you and Anja like to come along? We could meet at the entrance. He lasts about half an hour and then we have a hot dog. Then we walk a bit more before leaving. All in all, it's a couple hours at the very most. What do you think?"

I eagerly accepted. "We would love to do that. It will be good for Anja to see that Benji is not in school either. I'll see you at the entrance."

Saturday came, and it seemed like a school day to Anja until we got in a cab. She did not look happy, but when she heard me say Benji's name she brightened somewhat. I could see Benji and his mother waiting as we got out of the cab. When the children spotted each other, all was well again. They bobbed along just ahead of us, Benji leading the way to his favorite exhibit, the monkey house. When I told her Anja does not speak due to being traumatized, she looked at me and said, "Benji was a bit like that too when he first came to Castle Care, but mostly he was not comfortable with the other children. It took a while, but he is fine now."

Hearing that, I guessed that perhaps Benji recognized Anja's distress on that first day and knew how it felt. Now the two of them were as funny to watch as the monkeys. Anja mimicked all of Benji's silly faces and hand gestures to the monkeys, who ignored them all as just another ruse to move them out of their captive lethargy. We chatted as the children walked along side us. She explained that she was not his mother, but his aunt. She didn't explain further, except to tell me that she was Benji's father's sister, and I did not probe, and neither did she.

We stopped at the hot dog stand and I handed Anja her first real American hot dog. It was a bit of a challenge for her to keep it in the bun. Benji helped her by squeezing the bun together while she took small nibbles. It was touching to see how caring he was with her.

The next week of school was as smooth as could be, and I found myself with several hours to myself in the middle of each day. The following Saturday morning, my mother took Anja to meet Benji and Hannah at the zoo while I attended my first Saturday morning parent's circle at the school. There were seven of us, and we did a round robin of our names. When I said I was Karin Wilson, Anja's mother, a man across the circle smiled at me. When it was his turn, he said, "I'm Aaron Garfield, Benji's father." He looked at me again, and we both smiled. The parents talked about different issues, some I was familiar with and others I was not. When the meeting was over, Aaron came over to me and said, "I know a bit about Anja from Benji. If you have time for a cup of coffee, perhaps we could get to know each other as well."

I heard myself say, "That would be nice, since they will be at the zoo for a little while." We walked to a small coffee shop and got to know each other a bit beyond our children. He went back to saying how happy Benji was to have a new friend.

"When I asked Benji to tell me about her, he hesitated just a moment and then said with a perky little smile, "She's cute!" We both laughed, and after that we were to become friends as well.

DURING OUR PREVIOUS MEETING WITH DR. STEINREICH, I asked whether Anja should see a speech therapist. Dr. Steinreich said, "I would like to hold off on that for now. She has had a lot to adjust to in a relatively short time. She has to deal with a new country and language, a pediatrician, a school, two new teachers, your parents, and even just being here to see me. Let us give her some more time before we explore yet another avenue."

I trusted his judgment, even above my concerns.

One afternoon, Anja and I had come home from school and were coloring with crayons. My father came home from an errand,

and Anja ran to him. She held out her hand to him and said, "Hello!" We all looked at each other in amazement.

"Well, hello, Anja." He picked her up and gave her a big hug. She beamed.

The next Saturday morning, I had a parent-teacher student progress meeting with Anja's two teachers. When I mentioned what had happened with my father, I heard the full story. It had become Benji's habit to interpret all of Anja's wishes and needs. When the teacher explained to Benji that, as helpful as that was, it had the effect that Anja would not speak if he continued to do this. They explained that Anja had to learn to speak for herself. He looked a bit put out as he walked off. A short time later, the teacher saw Benji and Anja standing apart from the other children. He said "Benji" and pointed to himself, and then he moved her jaw and lips with his fingers and said, "Say it!" He repeated it and she said, "Benji." He did it again and she repeated it. Then he pointed to her and said, "Anja, say it!" She did. The he put his hand out to shake hers and he said, "Hello." Again, he followed suit as before, putting her hand in his as he said, "Hello, Anja." When she did not repeat it, he said, "Do it, say it." Anja said, "Hello, Anja."

The teachers were quite surprised having seen that. I could not believe what was happening. Benji had found a way to get her to talk! I dragged my attention back to the meeting as Miss Vickers said, "I don't know that anyone other than Benji could have achieved that now. Anja seems to be happy with her new accomplishments. So, I would say that Anja is progressing nicely. She is more social now with Benji's continued guidance. He is a remarkable little boy, and they are great playmates together. Do you have any questions for me?"

"I did, before I arrived, but now I am so thrilled, they won't come to mind." We laughed, and then we scheduled our next parent-teacher meeting.

Anja's cycles of pantomime that had substituted for speech were slowly disappearing, word-by-word, daily now under Benji's rule for her of, "Do it, say it!" He tolerated little resistance from her, and she offered little. Her progress at the piano was no less astounding; her quickly budding talent awed my father.

When I came a bit early to pick her up on one Monday, I stood outside the classroom door and watched the class through the little window. The teacher was playing the piano as the children played some running and clapping game. I watched them all running around and laughing, like little crazed mice, and Anja was among them. When suddenly the piano stopped the children stood where they were and did a little clapping rhythm, when the teacher resumed playing they again ran wildly around until the final clapping ended it. I was so happy to see her take part in it all; she was adjusting at her own speed to be, a normal little three-year-old child.

She continued to progress under Benji's tutelage and the further guidance of Castle Care. One evening she went to her play bed and I heard her say, "Hello, Peter Rabbit." I peeked in to see her sitting on her bed with Peter Rabbit in her arm as she pointed to the open Peter Rabbit book. She was addressing the stuffed Peter Rabbit in her arm and pointed at him in the book, moving her fingers on his mouth. Happiness had me on the verge of laughter and tears.

Benji's aunt Hannah offered to care for Anja if ever there was a need for it. Now there was. I wanted to find work, and I hoped she could fill in when my mother was working with voice students.

I heard that an exclusive boutique department store on 57th Street was looking for sales help. When the personnel lady asked me if I had any sales experience, I said I had. I did not detail that by telling her that I was thinking of the lemonade stand that a friend and I had at the foot of her driveway when I was seven years old. At this point it seemed overkill to do so. I was hired; I was to be called as a fill-in for any salesperson in any department that did not come in to work that day. It sounded too temporary, but I needed something, so I accepted the position. I was called in two days later to work in the ladies' accessories department. As I acquainted myself with the inventory of beautiful scarves and shawls, a well-dressed and well-groomed lady asked for my attention.

"I would like your help, I need to have eight scarves as gifts for my volunteers. If I tell you their hair color, can you help me select them?"

"I'll do my best to assist you."

"Good, three are blondes, one is a red-head, two are brunettes of a sort, and two have black hair."

I slid the tray out with the scarves and she fingered them carefully. Some were silk, and some were rayon.

"I'd like all the same quality please."

"Would that be silk or rayon then?" I asked.

"Silk, please."

The silk was expensive but after choosing them, she asked, "Would you gift wrap them for me, and pencil in the hair color on each package? I would like them delivered to me."

After paying for them, she gave me her address, thanked me, and left. I'm not sure why—it could have been the word "volunteer"—but I connected that customer with my offer to help the Quakers once I was home. It was a fleeting thought that stuck with me through the next day, when I delivered the scarves to her Park Avenue address just off Washington Square. The doorman wanted to deliver the package, but I insisted it was to be delivered personally by me. He called up and then said to me, "Mrs. Mandel said to come up. She's on the fourth floor, apartment B."

The door to apartment 4B opened to a lovely entryway that led to a large living room, where Mrs. Mandel invited me to have tea with her in appreciation of my delivering her purchases. In one corner of the living room stood a beautiful baby grand piano. Seeing that, my creative wheels began to spin even faster than before. We talked a little bit about several subjects, but the important one of the work of volunteers kept surfacing. I told her briefly of my contact with the Quakers and how they helped relocate endangered refugee children. She said she knew little of The Friends Society but admired what she heard they did for children in Europe. I mentioned just enough about Anja and myself to peak her interest further. When I excused myself to leave, she said, "If ever I can be of help, please do contact me." She handed me her personal card and thanked me again.

The whole way home my mind came up with one idea after another. The one I liked most was the possibility doing a monthly musical event in her living room to an audience of invited paying guests. The money would go the Quaker's children's refugee fund. It was an audacious idea, but then, so were the times. That evening I called Thomas Brixley and explained my thoughts. I asked his permission to pursue it on behalf of the Quakers. He loved the idea and said he would help in any way he could. My parents were delighted to help as well. I sat down and wrote a proposal of the idea and sent it off to Mrs. Mandel. Some days later I got a reply.

"Miss Wilson, my piano has been standing idle far too long now waiting to be of service and pleasure for just such an idea. Please let us get together on this as soon as possible." That evening my parents and I gave further form to the idea. When the three of us met with Mrs. Mandel, she loved all of our ideas and was impressed with how we could answer every question she could think of. She agreed, and we started to get it working. She agreed to invite her wealthy friends and serve tea and finger sandwiches if we attended to the performing artists. Both my parents had colleagues and advanced students who would volunteer to perform. It was a go! Three and a half weeks later, we had a pianist, a violinist, and a tenor and a mezzo-soprano whom my mother accompanied on the piano. They did all their rehearsing at our house.

I arrived early on the day of the first performance to help and was introduced to Mr. Mandel and their son Joshua. Mrs. Mandel had thoughtfully rented gold and velvet chairs, which were arranged in the large living room space around the baby grand piano. There were fresh flowers and candles on the table with her elegant silver tea service, and there were beautiful china plates and platters of finger sandwiches. I was impressed by the elegance. Twenty people came, all commenting on what a nice idea it was.

Thomas Brixley came, and he mingled with the guests, making small talk or answering questions about the Quakers and their mission when asked. My father pulled together a nice program. The singers did a duet from *La Boheme*. Then the violinist played some Bach, followed by the young pianist with some Gershwin. My father played a couple Mozart pieces. It was so well received that a number of the guests wanted to know when the next one would take place.

After everyone had left, Mr. Mandel came in with a chilled bottle of white wine, calling for a celebration. Mr. Mandel asked me about Anja and her status. When I mentioned my concerns that she could not start a regular school later because I did not have a birth certificate for her, he invited me to come to his office later in the week for a more formal discussion about the problem. "My son Josh has recently joined our law firm. He is fresh out of law school with some innovative approaches to law." We thanked them for their hospitality and their help as they promised this evening was the first of more to come.

We went to Benji's house to collect Anja. She was fast asleep next to Benji, holding his pajama collar in her hand. Hannah said we could leave her and she would bring her over in the morning. Our lives were coming together in a way I never even imagined they could.

When I called Mr. Mandel's office to come and see him about Anja, he asked me to come in with my documentation, my passport and anything that I had for Anja. For a few seconds I felt some shades of Prague, but I shook them off. When I arrived for my appointment, his receptionist was expecting me. When she showed me into his office, Josh Mandel came in at the same time. Mr. Mandel wanted to hear the whole story as it applied to Anja. He looked over the few papers I had and said he would look into what could be done.

"The best of course would be for her to have a birth certificate, and a passport could follow. Leave it with me for now, and when I have anything to report I will be in touch." He made some notes, and he and Josh made some legal comments that went over my head. Soon after that I left. Hoping that something would come of it, I felt that if anything were possible, they could make it happen.

In the meantime, Mrs. Mandel and I were preparing for our next benefit recital. My father and mother lined up another winning program with the best performers available to them. We repeated our earlier preparations for our friendly paying audience. We were a hit once again. Thomas Brixley came to help us again, and he told me how much our efforts were appreciated by those in need of refuge.

CHANGES

A DARKER SIDE OF EVENTS also surfaced around this time. I awaited a letter from Ernst every day now. In early September, England and most of the Commonwealth countries and France had declared war on Germany. Following that, the United States announced its neutrality, while Canada declared war on Germany. The battle for the Atlantic was just beginning. Even with all of this, I wondered why hadn't I heard from Ernst since we are not at war with Germany.

One day in October I got a call from Thomas Brixley. He invited Anja and me to his place for a small celebration.

"Is it a birthday?" I asked.

"Better than that." he said.

Anja and I arrived looking our best for a mystery celebration. Entering his apartment, I was greeted with the wonderful smells of roasting chicken as he relieved us of our coats.

"It's quiet for a party," I said.

"Well, it won't be in a moment." He showed us into the living room. We were alone when he handed me a glass of wine and Anja a berry juice.

"Well, what shall we drink to?" As he said that Helen appeared with a glass in hand and said, "Let's drink to us!" I gasped in disbelief; we embraced and rocked in each other's arms between laughter and tears.

"Good heavens, good heavens!" was all I could say as we stepped back to look at each other. "When did you get here? How are you? What has happened? Are you here for good?"

She bent down and hugged Anja, who stared at her as wide-eyed as I did.

"Well, to begin with I got here two days ago. I'm tired but so happy to be here finally. I plan to go back to London to help gather the many loose ends there. What has happened? Well, right after you left, until the declaration of war, after September first, the Germans closed our contacts and arrangements to get any more children out. As sad as I feel about the curtailment, I take solace in the fact that we had nine good months of success in getting so many out. It was never enough, as we wanted to get them all out. I'll be staying here until I can go back, and I'll be done when they don't need me anymore."

Thomas gave a satisfied nod. "Yes, because I have some plans for her that do not involve a passport, an exit permit, or travel visa of any sort." He gave her a quick hug and said, "Ladies, this party includes food, so please be seated."

He lifted Anja onto a cushioned chair and tucked a napkin into her sweater. Then he brought in a roasted chicken and baked potatoes, with peas and carrots and salad. As he placed the dishes on the table, he said, "Leave room for desert!"

When all the dishes were on the table, he gave Anja a little pat on her head and said, "Now, we are ready to begin."

As he carved the chicken, I asked Helen, "Were you able to see Ernst before you had to leave?"

Helen nodded. "I did, and I have some letters for you that he entrusted to me rather than the mail."

"How is he? How does he look?"

"He looked a bit more gaunt since you last saw him on the train. He seemed sadder and quieter, but so do a lot of other people there—it is a sign of the times, to be sure. He was anxious over events and he looked troubled, except for when he spoke of you. He said, "Please give her my love, and please ask her to write as often as she can. I miss her letters." I told him I would, and I told him I knew you wished you could see him again. Then he said, "Yes, as in *Auf Wiedersehen*. Thank you and good luck to you Miss Arnsworth and I wish you safe travels home."

"He then gave my forearm a gentle squeeze and walked away."

Helen noted my sadness at her news, and she continued. "Karin, I won't be going back to Prague again. My work there is over, but I left with memories of good friends and colleagues, all of whom I hope one day to see again. Lieutenant Möller is one of those people." She smiled then, to help change the subject. "Thomas has been telling me of your fundraising efforts for the refugee children; you have no idea how that helps. What we do is costly on every level, human and otherwise."

The evening ended as it began, happy to see each other once again. Yet I could barely wait to leave and get home. Once home and with Anja asleep, I eagerly tore into the packet of letters from Ernst.

20 September 1939

My dearest Karin,

I must trust that this finds you well. I worry because I have not heard from you. Helen has to leave Prague, and she will bring with her my three letters to you plus something else for you. I have little news from my end other than I may be transferred, to where I do not know. I shall continue to write to you and I hope you to me— after all, my pen, now in your hands, does not like to run dry except from use.

Life for me is only less than half without you and even that little I have to work hard at. How is little Anja? I like that you changed her name? What does she think of that? Has she begun to speak now, even a few words? I would teach her to say, "I love you." And with that my dearest, I must say *Auf Wiedersehen*. I will be seeing Helen shortly and I want her to have this letter as well.

I love you with all my heart,
Ernst

Eagerly looking through the package of letters I feel something soft wrapped in tissue paper, when I open it I find a dark blue cashmere scarf. The note enfolded in it read:

15 September 1939
My dearest Karin,
I was home on a five-day leave in Berlin and I wanted you to have something of mine to keep. When you feel the need of a hug from me, please put my scarf around you and I will be there.

With all my love,
Ernst

I wrapped the scarf around my neck and buried my face in the ends of it. I could smell a faint trace of his aftershave. I sat still and closed my eyes, trying to see him before me. It was harder than I wanted it to be.

Another letter read:

14 September 1939

My dearest Karin,

I am writing this at home in Berlin, where I am still on leave for five days. At times we get such leave when we are about to be transferred. I am in my room, sitting in the middle of my bed, writing to you and wishing only that you were next to me. Some cartons containing my things from my old apartment surround me, and I wonder where I will be unpacking them later; whether that will be here in Berlin or in New York is entirely up to you of course. In thinking about New York, I thought I could go to the German embassy to see if they would hire me to translate legal documents. I am fluent in English and French, and I can work in both languages, so that poses a real possibility. Assuming of course you still want me in your life.

Please see the enclosed photos. I asked my father to take them because I want you to remember me in my private clothes instead of in uniform or even without any.

While the photos are black and white, I can tell you I am wearing dark blue trousers and a dark blue sweater. Blue is my favorite color, and I used to wear it most of the time.

I told my parents about you and I showed them your photo. They said you are not only beautiful but look compassionate as well; I heartily assured them you were both.

In Prague at work I met a nice colleague, Dieter Feltner. He is a fellow officer, but in communications, and because I am in supplies our duties often intersect. One evening after work, we sat in a tavern over some glasses of beer and commiserated on our sad lot of being without the women in our lives. Dieter is married and has two little boys, whom he misses greatly; at least he can get on a train to Cologne and be with them, while I languish alone in Prague without you.

Until I can hold you again, *Auf Wiedersehen*, my darling, Ernst

I looked closely at the full-length photo of his beautifully trim and fit body, and I ached for him anew. When I turned the photo over, he had written: To my dearest Karin, from your loving Ernst at home in Berlin September 1939. In bed that night I was overwhelmed with emotions as the tears pooled in my closed eyes.

A few weeks later I get another letter.

23 September 1939

Dearest Karin,

I hope you are well and keeping my pen well supplied with ink for all those letters I am awaiting from you. In the meantime, I have news that I have been promoted to *Oberleutnant*. In your military parlance that would be a first lieutenant, so I am finally moving up in the world. You didn't know I was only a second class lieutenant before, did you?

It may only be in preparation for things to come. Who knows? Dieter and I celebrated with something stronger than just beer. What is it like where you are now? I want to imagine myself in it with you. I am getting over a bit of a cold, but then that is to be expected without your warmth. Please write soon. I miss you, darling.

Yours,
Ernst

I wrote back.

Oct. 23, 1939
My dearest Ernst,

Congratulations on your promotion, though I must remind you that there never was nor ever will be anything second-class about you. Now maybe you will get leave to come and see me. How I wish! It was a happy surprise to see Helen again, along with your letters and your gift. Thank you so much for your scarf. It will give me many hugs until I get your next one personally. The photo is special, and I like it along with your comments, with which I readily agree! I am fine, other than missing you so much, and now I worry about where you will be transferred. Please keep me as current as you can on that. Anja is doing well; she speaks a bit now and is adjusting to her new circumstances as best she can. I think she is doing even better than I am at times. Please write.

Loving you,
Karin

Some time later, Benji's father Aaron invited me for lunch at his place while Hannah took the children to a puppet show. When I arrived, he apologized for the deli-style lunch, saying he wanted it to be efficient because he wanted to talk to me. He offered me a beer and some pretzels before lunch, and he then settled in for some conversation. He began by saying, "Since we have been getting to know each other, and while that has been mostly through our children, I wanted to take it a step further by telling you a bit more about myself. I was happily married to my wife Susanne when she suddenly became sick, stricken with encephalitis. She died when Benji was only four months old. I was inconsolable at losing her. If it had not been for Benji and my sister Hannah, I would have been totally lost. Hannah is single and helped care for Benji while Susanne was ill. When Susanne died, Hannah continued to take loving care of Benji, which she continues to do to this day. Hannah translates scientific articles and lengthy papers so she is able to work at home; her hours are at her convenience and more often than not at ours as well. It was only due to her that when I was finally able to, I delved into my work as a respite from the pain. I am a medical researcher, and sometimes I too can set my own hours. I wanted you to know this so that I could ask you about Anja's father as well." I poured the rest of my beer into my glass and told the tale as far as I dared.

"Anja's father was lost just before the war, while we were living in Prague. He was most likely taken without warning by the Nazis, as were so many others at the time that did not flee from Nazi persecution in time. He simply disappeared one day. Some relatives there cautioned me against making inquiries because it could bode badly for Anja and possibly even for me, so I sheltered Anja from a similar fate by moving in with a friend's relatives to keep the lowest of profiles until I could return to America. Anja was greatly traumatized by all these events, to the point where she stopped talking. With the help of the Quakers and a dear friend, I was finally able to leave Prague with her, and we finally sailed home to New York and my parents. Shortly after our return, with the help of more wonderful people, Anja was admitted to Castle Care. Benji bridged the gap for Anja, and they forged a comforting friendship. I think that brings everything up to date. Except for a few extenuating circumstances along the path to freedom. I too bore an inconsolable loss, but while yours was through an act of God, mine was of a more unforgiveable nature, an act of man."

Through lunch we shared a few other insights, all of a less probing nature, about being single parents. Later, as I reflected on the discussion at lunch, I thought about how I had described Ernst as a dear friend. I supposed that meeting him in the first place was a fortuitous encounter, so I felt I did not lie, I had simply withheld the intensity of it all.

ONE DAY I TOOK BENJI AND ANJA TO THE MUSEUM OF Natural History. Benji was anxious to show her his favorite exhibit, the dinosaur skeletons. Anja was more puzzled by them than impressed. We explored the museum, and when we came to a window display filled with butterflies from around the world, Anja was immediately transfixed. She stared at them for a while, resting her chin on her hands on the brass railing in front of the glass show case, completely mesmerized by the colorful display. Then I heard her whisper, "Papa Young." *Papillon*. I was taken aback at her memory of the word. Where in her past experiences with her parents did this reside? I leaned down to her and said, "They are called butterflies." She looked up at me and said, "Grandma calls you Karin and I call you Mama, but you are the same!"

I marveled at her keen sense of reasoning that at times spoke of her intelligence and perhaps even something more, something I may never be privy to.

Tonight, at dinner my parents talked about Colonel Charles Lindbergh's broadcast from September, warning against the agitation of the Western powers. The consensus at our table was that the Germans would cozy up to him even more now after that supportive rhetoric.

In late fall of 1939, concerns of a further military buildup in Europe by the Germans created many speculations as to the eventual outcome. They had by that time invaded Poland, Austria, and Czechoslovakia, and most reports from our overseas reporters were not encouraging as far as we could tell. We, not being in the war, could still get current events from Europe, but none of them put my mind at ease for Ernst's situation.

Now that we knew that Russia had invaded Finland, Stalin was considered the same as Hitler and Mussolini and the Japanese—he was another aggressor in the escalating events overseas. My father thought it was spreading like a wild fire out of control.

ANJA CONTINUED TO DO WELL AS I TRIED TO THINK OF my role as a parent in those days of uncertainty. So far, everything was going so well for Anja and me. I wondered if I would have the wherewithal to be a strong parent and do the right thing if any new challenges came our way. My parents had been our strongest supporters and helpers. I could never have done this without them.

Work was still a major concern for me; I didn't feel that a part-time fill-in job was enough. At times I felt like a newly arrived refugee seeking roots for a new life. If it weren't for the kindness of my parents, I would truly know what the term "displaced persons" meant. Nonetheless, my days are full attending to Anja and her needs, which at times includes Benji when Hannah or his father can't be with him. We trade times of caring for them as needed.

A WANTED ARRIVES

MY FATHER HAD JUST come back with the newspaper and the day's mail. He sorted the bills and paused over an envelope. Staring at it he said, "Here is something intriguing for you, Karin." As he handed it to me, I saw that it had been stamped from Juneau, Alaska.

"What in the world is this? I don't know anyone in Alaska."

I hesitated to open it, and my father said, "A new mystery in your life?"

There was no sender's name, only a P.O. box number. Inside were two pieces of paper. One was a short typed note that read:

> November 2, 1939
> Dear Miss Wilson,
> Enclosed please find a birth certificate for your daughter, Anja Wilson.
> I trust it will serve Anja and you well.
>
> A well-wishing benefactor

That was all. The other piece of paper was a documented birth certificate labeled NO RECORD OF BIRTH CERTIFICATE for female, Anja Wilson. Born on December 10, 1935, in the Territory of Alaska to Karin Wilson of New York City, State of New York, United States of America.

It was dated several weeks ago, and it had an official seal and a totally illegible signature.

It looked and felt genuine, but was it? When I said I would have to look into it, my mother said, "Why look a gift horse in the mouth?"

"If this is the real thing, I certainly need to know that."

I immediately called Mr. Mandel, who asked me to bring it and the note to him so he could look at it. When I did, he said, "This looks perfectly legitimate to me. You can use it."

"But who would have sent this to me, and why?"

"I can look into it if you'd like."

On the bus home, I began to wonder if Josh, Mr. Mandel's son and the newest member of the law firm, had put his innovative approaches to the law to use. It was just a thought, but one that I had to let go of the following week when Mr. Mandel confirmed that it all checked out to be valid. I still did not know who the well-wishing benefactor was, nor would I ever.

Once again, a big hurdle was overcome for Anja and me. Would there be others in the near and not so distant future?

SOCIAL

I WROTE TO BEATA and Jiri, more than anything to let them know I had not forgotten them. It was late in November, and the weather had turned cold. The biting wind met little resistance through my old winter coat and layers of worn sweaters. My mother made many stops to thrift shops to outfit Anja against the cold; I guessed the racks were bare of my size. Now I was sorry that I had left my Prague purchased warm winter coat behind due to its bulk for the trip home.

Aaron called to invite me out for dinner and a concert the following week. I hesitated at first, we had not done anything of a social nature, other than that one-cup of coffee, and a lunch at his place, but, I was sorely in need of some grown-up, non-parental company, so I said, "Yes, I would love to."

I was concerned that I had put it too strongly when he added, "Yes, it's a date." I hadn't meant it to be a date date.

Aaron took me to a nice little French café for dinner, and then we went to the City Center Theatre for an evening of George Gershwin's music. It was a nice evening, and at the end of it he said, "We should do this more often." I just smiled and thanked him, and so the evening ended.

Returning home, my mother made a few sly intimations that he seemed nice and more than casually interested in me. She even said he looked like a good catch. I made it clear that I was not fishing and that I liked things just the way they were.

The next big event was to be Anja's birthday party. According to her new birth certificate, on December 10, 1939, she would be four years old. That was a Sunday, so those who were invited would be sure to come. When I asked Anja if she had any friends to invite, she said, "Benji."

"Don't you have any other friends from school you would like to have?"

She simply said, "No." When I asked her if she wanted to do anything special on her birthday, it was clear she did not understand what I was talking about. *Had she never had a birthday celebration or party?* I wondered. Or was she just too young to remember?

Mother and I made a list: Benji, his dad, Hannah, and Greg. Alex was off skiing, and he wasn't a likely guest in any event; he surely would not have wanted to come anyway. We invited Mr. and Mrs. Mandel and Josh. Helen Arnsworth our dear Quaker friend and Thomas Brixley were out of town at the time. Eleven people were about the limit for our dining room table anyway.

The menu was a big roasted capon, thanks to mother's butcher. She kept him in her good graces by plying him now and then with pieces of her cardamom cake. We had baked potatoes and peas and carrots and a salad. Mother baked a chocolate cake. Dinner was to be at five, and it was clear that Anja did not know what we were doing or why. Daddy produced a few bottles of a nice wine and a good sherry, along with juice for the children. People arrived just before five, and Anja was thrilled to see Benji, who was all dressed up for the occasion. People put their presents on the sideboard, and my father handed the guests a glass of sherry as he made introductions. Before long, everyone was seated at the table, Benji and Anja sitting next to each other. My father made a short welcoming speech, and then dinner got underway. Anja looked around the table, still surprised by all the guests. After dinner, mother dimmed the lights as I came out with Anja's birthday cake, with four lit candles. As I walked toward her, she looked at me with great surprise as everyone sang happy birthday to her. For a moment she looked frightened. When I put the cake down in front of her, I said, "Anja, you get to make a wish, and then blow out the candles." None of that registered with her as she stared into the candlelight. I leaned close to her and showed her how to blow, but she pushed at me and continued staring into the candlelight. When they were burning down close to the frosting, Benji got up next to her and made a quick blowing sound, then he said, "Do it!" She looked at him and again he said, "Do it!" Then he bent down and they both blew the candles out. Everyone clapped and laughed with relief. Anja was perplexed by all of it.

Clearly this was the first birthday celebration she could remember. Where had she been the few years before she came to me? I would never know the answer to that. I cut the cake while Anja coveted the candles. After cake and ice cream, we gave Anja her presents. Benji gave her a puppy hand puppet, and his father gave her a kitten hand puppet. Hannah gave her a lovely children's book, the Mandels gave her a beautiful sweater, I gave her a pair of flannel pajamas. My parents gave her a piano book called *The Child's Beginner Book for Piano*. Greg gave her a pair of mittens and Josh, who only arrived after cake, gave me a bottle of wine and Anja a set of tickets for the carousel at Central Park. Anja was confused and overwhelmed by all of it, and we let her and Benji go into our bedroom to play. They immediately knelt on the floor with their elbows on the play bed to play with the hand puppets. All in all, it was a lovely evening. Later I tried to explain the custom of gift giving on birthdays, but she really did not understand it, but in the end did think it was a good idea. Benji would be four in February, and she would see then that birthdays happened to everyone.

The next day mother served Anja a piece of her leftover birthday cake after dinner. When she saw it, she ran into our bedroom and came back with the candles that had been on her cake. She stuck them all into her little piece of cake, then looked at me and gave a little blow. She wanted me to light them. There was so little of the candles left but she looked longingly at them, so I couldn't deny her. I lit the candles carefully, and when I made a blowing motion, she blew them out. Once again, she carefully saved them. It was puzzling yet touching to see.

CHRISTMAS 1939

MY MOTHER HAD BEEN making lots of shopping trips in preparation for the holidays—no surprise there—as this would be the first one to involve a grandchild. I hoped she wasn't going to outdo herself, but the chances were good that she would.

Christmas 1939 would have some somber overtones, however, due to the uncertain times in Europe.

My mother, Anja, and I prepared for the holidays by baking thin cookies in the Swedish tradition. We made crisp gingerbread cookies with her Swedish cookie cutters in the shapes of stars, hearts, and fir trees. We made little holes in them before baking so that when they had cooled we could thread red thread through them to hang on the tree. Mother brought out a box of tree ornaments from Sweden that she prized, and when Anja saw them she took a few and then quickly climbed up on a chair to hang them on the top rims of our lampshades. Mother thought she was so inventive. Christmas, like her birthday party, was a totally new event for Anja as it unfolded. When we all went to our favorite local Christmas tree lot and picked out a tree, Anja had no idea why a forest of them suddenly appeared in our neighborhood. To add to this confusion, she was perplexed when we picked one and father carried it home. When he set it up in our living room, she sat in front of it and couldn't take her eyes from it. After dinner we began to hang the ornaments and cookies on the tree. As predicted, Anja was totally confused. My father lifted her up as we handed her a few ornaments. It took a while before she would give them up, but with a few encouraging "Do it!" comments, she followed suit and hung them on the tree.

ON CHRISTMAS EVE THE FOUR OF US WENT TO CHURCH. Half the service was given in Swedish and half in English. The church was decorated beautifully, with fresh small fir branches tied onto the end poles of each pew with red ribbons and topped with candles. The service ended with the choir singing Christmas carols. Anja had been sitting on my lap until the singing began, at which point she stood up and, leaning on the pew in front of us, was enthralled. When they sang *Good King Wenceslaus* I felt tears backing up in my throat, and then when they sang *Silent Night* tears found their way down my cheeks. Christmas was different this year, so different, for all of us.

The butcher had informed my mother that he could not guarantee a Christmas goose for her—in fact, he wasn't sure he could get any. She made alternate plans for a pork roast. This year our Christmas Eve gift exchange would also be pared down because money was tight. Nonetheless, on Christmas Eve, after my father lit the candles on the tree, Anja ran up to him and stared at the candlelight. Then the gifts appeared, which surprised me as much as Anja. Mother had unraveled an old blue sweater of my father's and used the yarn to knit a beautiful vest for Anja. She had bought brightly colored buttons in the shapes of fruits for the front of it. Using the pictures in the book, my mother had also made a perfect copy of Peter Rabbit's jacket for Anja's stuffed rabbit. Anja was thrilled. Then mother handed me a big box from my father and her, wishing me a Merry Christmas. Astonished, I looked at them, "Go on, open it!" they caroled.

It was a beautiful, dark green, weather-resistant raincoat, all lined in rabbit fur!

"Mother, I can't take this!"

"I found it in the thrift shop in October. I could see it was your size and had to get it for you. You can't keep walking around in that old coat of yours. It is threadbare and unsuitable for this wintery weather."

It fit perfectly. I hugged my parents, thanking them. When I took it off, Anja stroked the lining. My mother grimaced slightly and said, "Please don't tell her what kind of fur it is—she may never forgive me!"

My father also gave me a pair of fur-lined leather gloves. "You can't keep your hands in your pockets all the time!" I gave mother a new coffee pot. To my father I gave some of his favorite pipe tobacco. He purred his pleasure at the gift, looking at my mother, who never let him smoke in the apartment. He gave Anja another music book, the first in a series called *Mozart for Children*. I gave Anja a pair of warm slippers.

For Christmas Eve dinner, we enjoyed mother's traditional menu of leek, bacon, and potato soup, along with a few shots of Aquavit. Then there was pickled herring, smoked ham, hard-boiled eggs, dark rye bread, and a strong dark beer. We finished with coffee and a wonderful lemon pound cake we all loved. Afterward we gathered at the piano. My father played Christmas carols, and my mother led the singing with her beautiful voice. I held Anja until she wriggled out of my arms and sat down next to my father, swaying to the music and trying to sing along. After we extinguished the tree candles, we cleared up the dishes and went to bed. In bed that night, Anja fell fast asleep next to me, while I laid awake, thinking of Ernst and wondering if he was in

Berlin with his parents with or without a Christmas letter from me. I had received no word from him in weeks.

A FEW DAYS BEFORE CHRISTMAS, I HAD CALLED AARON and extended my parents' invitation to Christmas dinner to him, Hannah, and Benji. They came over despite a heavy snow and temperatures that reminded me of Prague.

The Christmas tree and the decorations intrigued Benji. Anja sat him down in front of it and, as I was later to discover, she broke off pieces of the gingerbread cookies we had hung on the tree and the two of them merrily ate the cookies while we were busy with dinner preparations. When we noticed the cookie remainders dancing by their threads after dinner, we all enjoyed the humor of it well beyond its worth. We all appreciated the reminder that Christmas was about the children, after all.

On the day after Christmas, my mother and I had agreed to watch Benji while both Aaron and Hannah worked. When I came home from a quick errand, mother was in the kitchen. Looking at me, she shrugged and tossed a look into the dining room. I went in to see that Benji and Anja had cut and torn strange shapes out of newspaper, making a chain of sorts that they had taped around the backs of the dining room chairs so that they were all linked. I smiled. Clearly ,she had remembered the garlands we had hung in the pear trees in Prague. When I pointed out that we couldn't sit down to eat with them all connected, Benji and Anja crawled between the chairs and under the table and came up to sit in a chair. I laughed, relishing their inventiveness, even though we adults did not often fit into their plans. Our next meal was at the kitchen table.

Discoveries

A FEW DAYS LATER, MY FATHER PULLED ME ASIDE FOR A CHAT. "KARIN, WE NEED TO TALK ABOUT ANJA."

"What has she done now?"

"It is more a question of what I am doing. I believe that Anja has a rare musical talent, one that I am leery of directing without more of an expert opinion. She has been going through the books for children faster than even I anticipated. I have a colleague from music school that has made a specialty of teaching talented children. I need confirmation that I am not leading her astray. I would like your permission to have him hear her play and see what he thinks, see where I should be going in her instruction. His name is Anton Somes. He's very nice, and I'd like to invite him over for dinner, so he can meet her and listen to her play."

"Of course, but only with the understanding that I can't afford any lessons that he might want to give her."

"I just want his opinion."

"I'll leave it up to you, you're the expert on these matters."

THAT WEEKEND I MET ANTON SOMES. WHILE ANJA WAS busy rearranging her play bed, the four of us sat at the kitchen table and discussed the near future of our half-pint-sized girl's talent. My father began by saying, "I have a few obstacles that she and I need to overcome—actually, more I, than she. She does not know about numbers, so trying to talk about whole, half, and quarter notes is out of the question. In addition, her hands and fingers are so small that her reach is limited. At times she does some funny gymnastics with her hands and fingers to compensate," laughed my father. "She loves playing scales. She says they are running games for her fingers."

Mr. Somes asked, "Well, how does she learn a piece?"

"An interesting question. When I tell her I have a new piece for her, she wants me to play it through from beginning to end. Then she has it! She is able to play it. To test this ability, I played a song after her and purposefully played just one wrong note. She caught it and pointed her index finger at the key and said, "No!"

Mr. Somes' eyes widened. "Good heavens! You did tell me she is only four, am I right?"

"Yes, she is only four!"

"My youngest pupil is seven years old and does not come near to Anja's abilities."

My father positively beamed with pride. "I'll have her play for you after dinner. She is not at all shy when it comes to the piano."

After dinner we sat around Anja as she happily played for us. When she was finished we clapped, and she clapped right back. After dessert, Mr. Somes said, "As I see it, we are looking at a gifted little girl. I would be happy to guide her and you along what promises to be beyond our expectations. If you can bring her to me once a week, say at nine on Saturday mornings, I would be happy to work with her. No fee will be involved, since I believe she has as much to teach me as I do her."

So, began a whole new course of study for Anja and my father. I could not help but wonder whether her parents were talented musicians. I wished they could have seen her—then I thought that perhaps they could.

Within a few weeks, we thought Anja was ready for a recital. Anja was added to the program of one of the musical evenings at the Mandel's, "An Evening with Some Young Musicians." Mother couldn't have been more excited than if it had been at Carnegie Hall. Mother made Anja a dress of electric blue taffeta with big puffed sleeves and a silver taffeta sash, and she even ordered a pair of white leather Mary Janes for the outfit. Mother braided Anja's hair with strips of the leftover fabric entwined in them. Anja was thrilled by all the fuss made over her, never connecting it to a performance. The children who were to play all sat in the front row. They were arranged to play by age, with the youngest going first. When the announcement was made and her name was mentioned, Anja didn't budge. My father walked over to her and took her hand and led her to the piano. He decided to sit next to her on the bench, which turned out to be a good thing. Anja was so small that she had to stand at the taller piano, and she leaned back against the piano bench, so her feet can reach the pedals. Without my father as an anchor, the bench would have gone flying. When she was finished, he took her hand and showed her how to bow, as the audience clapped, none more enthusiastically than Benji, his father, and our family. Anja was thrilled and clapped right back at everyone. That was Anja's first recital, the first of many to follow.

TERROR

AFTER A TIRING WEEK of job hunting, I was looking forward to coming home to a cup of coffee, hugs, and a peaceful weekend with family. As I shut the door to our apartment, I immediately noticed the lack of piano scales from the music room and the sound of my mother's radio from the kitchen. It was quiet, too quiet. I called out for Anja, but there was no reply. My mother came out of my bedroom, stumbling as she came toward me. I looked at her bloodshot eyes. "Mother, what is it? Are you okay what's wrong? Is Daddy all right?" Shaking, and crying she said, "Anja is missing. Oh God please, please forgive me."

I sat her down and, holding her shoulders, asked, "What are you talking about?"

"She's gone, and we can't find her anywhere."

I got up and knocked on our neighbor's door. Mrs. Sherman kept canaries that Anja loved to listen to and watch. Mrs. Sherman told me she hadn't seen Anja today. When I said I would ask the Goldmans, because Anja liked to play with their poodle, she said, "The Goldmans left yesterday for a long weekend on Long Island."

I ran back into the apartment, and my mother was in a worse state than before. I ran to the elevator and looked around in the lobby, then I ran out onto the sidewalk. I dashed into the candy store, but they hadn't seen her; I got the same response at the magazine shop where she liked to look at the comic books. I went back home to find my mother sobbing, "It happened so quickly."

"What? What happened? Where's Daddy?"

She stammered, "Anja and Benji were playing in your room. I had just finished with my last student, who was talking to me, as she was ready to leave. Hannah arrived, carrying a suitcase. She said that they were going to visit family in New Jersey for the weekend and would be back Sunday night. Benji came out from playing with Anja. Hannah called to him, 'Hurry, Benji, get your coat. Your daddy is waiting for us, and we're already late!' She didn't even stop to put on his coat, and as he was being pulled to the door, he waved to Anja and said, 'Bye!'

"I was only partially registering all of this, as my student was still speaking. Anja stood there with a confused, scared look as Benji and Hannah left for the elevator. Then the telephone rang, at which point my student was saying goodbye, and just then your father called out to ask if I had change for ten dollars, as his student was also ready to leave. It was such a whirlwind all at once. When finally, everyone had left, I saw that the door was still open, so I closed it. I went to the kitchen and made myself a cup of coffee and set out a glass of milk and cookies for Anja. I called out for her to come and sit with me, and when she didn't, I called out again. Then I went into your bedroom, but she wasn't there. I looked in the music room; your father was folding up his music, but no Anja. We searched the apartment, but she was gone. We looked in the halls, we tried the neighbors, and we checked the lobby. We came back and sat down to figure out what to do. Your father decided that we had tried everything we could do, and that he would go to the police for help. He told me to stay home for when she returned. And then you came home."

"Where did Daddy go?"

She shrugged. "To the police. I don't know where, exactly."

Just then the phone rang, and I rushed to answer it. It was my father. He was at a nearby police precinct, and he told me to bring a photo of Anja. He gave me the address of the police station and told me to hurry. I ran to my room to get a photo, and then I ran to the elevator. When I arrived at the precinct, I saw my father in a state of distress that made me worry about his health. I met the police sergeant, who asked for a complete description of her and a photo. I sat down shaking; laboring for the breath to speak, when the officer said, "Please try to calm down. We'll do everything we can to find her. Little ones often just wander off on their own, which may be the case here as well."

His words were intended to calm me, but the phrase "which may be the case here as well" made me even more frightened. What else could have happened?

He asked again for the photo, and I handed it to him, saying, "It's a few months old." My father had taken it in Central Park on the carousel.

"We also need a description of her and what she was wearing today, along with her full name, her age, height, weight, hair and eye color, and any distinguishing marks or features. Is she Caucasian? Does she have any physical disabilities?" I only mentioned that she did not understand everything and has little delayed speech. "Thank you, Mrs. Wilson, we'll get onto this right away."

My father sat next to me and held my hand as I looked up at a large wall clock with a sweep second hand. It was now five o'clock.

My father estimated that Anja disappeared close to three thirty, or three forty-five, about an hour and a half hour since she disappeared.

It was a busy police station dealing with all sorts of people and their problems; I hoped mine was top priority. An hour later, the officer told us he had circulated an alert notice to all of the Manhattan police precincts. He suggested that we might want to go home to wait until they had word for us. No chance of that, we assured him. At seven p.m., my father called home for the second time to give my mother the status, as we knew it. When he came back, he said that we should eat something, so he would go out to get us a hamburger and coffee. I waved him off; my stomach was in no condition to eat or drink. When he came back, he had food for me anyway, but I shoved the food away from me and I shivered with the onset of new tears. Thoughts of how I could let this happen plagued me; her father never envisioned this particular scene when he had imagined other terrors for her. My head started to pound. I took two aspirin from my handbag and leaned back, closing my eyes. When I opened them again it was seven thirty on that big clock. I stopped the officer as he passed us and asked, "Is there any word, any word at all?"

"Not so far. It's a busy Friday night as usual. But I've got plenty of eyes out there looking for her." At eight p.m., my father again urged me to eat. My head began to throb again with a new flood of tears. I felt numb.

I heard my father speak to the sergeant, "Do you think she is all right? Is she safe?"

"We have to believe so, until we know otherwise."

At those words it is hard for me to even swallow. I started shaking, and my breathing was short and shallow. Daddy sat with his arm around me, saying, "We just have to wait."

"Wait for what? If she's safe, then why haven't they found her? If she isn't safe, why won't they say?" I watched the sweep hand make its circuit again and again. At eight forty-five marked five hours of waiting, five hours of terror. The pounding in my head was worse than ever. I closed my eyes, wanting to close off the rest of what I was thinking and feeling. I looked back at the clock, feeling that it had pinned me against the wall, to this bench. I closed my eyes again, only to hear a commotion outside the room where we were waiting. Keeping my eyes closed, I told myself not to speak until I was spoken to. I heard voices enter the room and small footsteps come running toward me. I opened my eyes, and all I could think was thank God, she is alive and safe. The gift had been returned to me. I grabbed her as she pulled herself, tired and scared, onto to my lap. She cried and sucked her thumb and pulled hard on my hair as if she would never let go again. I held her, hugged her and kissed her. I began to rock with her in my arms. I heard nothing else and felt nothing else but Anja, even though my father was embracing us both.

We are not yet free to go home. We must complete more paper-work, including a release form for me to sign. I did it all with her holding onto to me as if we were grafted together. I was shocked to see Ina Castle there. Between the police officer and Ina, I heard what likely had happened.

When Anja saw Benji leave with a suitcase and hurriedly wave goodbye, she must have feared that he was leaving her, and he would never come back. Her only memory of a suitcase was when we left Prague, never to return. In the confusion of the phone call and departing students, Anja slipped out of the apartment. Apparently when she went out to the street, trying to follow after Benji, she saw them leaving on a bus. She got on the next bus to follow them; it was a different line, of course, and it ended up an hour and a half later in in the bus depot in Harlem.

The bus driver took her to his boss, who called the local police precinct. The bus driver and the police made out reports. The bus driver seemed to remember her getting on with a crowd of people in lower Manhattan somewhere. Anja had not spoken the whole time, not even when she was asked her name. As more records were made of the incident, they took her to their precinct and photographed her, and she was then taken to a mid-town police station. As she sat on a police matron's lap, a ribbon was noticed around Anja's neck. The matron pulled it out from under her blouse and saw it was a school tag from Castle Care. They looked up Ina Castle as the owner and called her, telling her they had one of her students there and needed her help. Ina took a taxi to the station to discover Anja. What good fortune had led Anja, who had been on a field trip that day, to forget to turn in her tag? Ina could not remember where she lived except that it was close to the school. The police drove them to Castle Care, where Ina looked up Karin's phone number and address in Anja's files. They had phoned my mother from Castle Care, and she had confirmed it was Anja. Then they made their way over to our local precinct, where we were reunited after the terrifying hours of her disappearance. The cooled hamburger now fed a hungry little mouth.

After all the required reports were filled out and signed, we were free to leave. The police sergeant said, "We'll get you home faster on a Friday night than you can find a cab." My father sat in front, next to the policeman, and I slid onto the well-worn faux leather back seat with Anja as my frontal appendage. I wrapped my coat around her as Ernst had once done for me. Ina sat next to us. Ina sighed with relief and said how glad she was that Anja still wore her school tag after the field trip. They let us out first, and then the police car sped away to take Ina home.

When we walked into our apartment, I thought my mother would collapse with relief. We huddled together in the living room. My father spoke of installing a lock on the door that would be out of Anja's reach. The only words from Anja were tearful as she repeated, "Benji go way." We reassured her he would be back in a few days. She knew only too well about parting. I didn't know if she would believe us, if she could believe us. My father went down and got a pizza, a cream soda, and three bottles of beer. Daddy pulled himself together to play her favorite, *Twinkle, Twinkle, Little Star*; she leaned against me and fell asleep, still crying for Benji.

That night I thanked God for giving her to me in the first place and then, after borrowing her, returned her to me.

TODAY A LETTER FROM ERNST, THANK GOODNESS.

30 September 1939

My dearest Karin,

I woke up this morning with all my other thoughts for the day fogged by you. As I was shaving in front of the mirror, I saw you standing behind me, looking at me over my shoulder. I quickly turned around to an empty space. I put my hand up to the mirror to conjure you once again; I so desperately wanted to see you again. I waited before taking my hand away, only to see a soapy handprint left on the mirror. I could not bring you back because you are gone. There are times when I can believe just about anything now as the buffer to my reality. Again, you were gone of my doing, how I hated myself at that moment, even as I consoled myself that I had spirited you away to safety. I'm glad I had the power to provide it for you. I'm sorry to say I can't do so for myself.

Yesterday I heard from good authority that most likely I will be transferred out of Prague and into "full service," as it was put. That means only one thing; I will be transferred to the field of engagement. That is what armies are about. I fear the call, again one of no choice. Wherever I am, I hope I will still be able to get your letters. Please keep writing. My writing is my only lifeline to you.

Good night, dearest,
Your Ernst

I immediately wrote back.

December 28, 1939
Dearest Ernst,
I just received your letter from September 30. Why are letters taking longer and longer to get here? I wonder if it is due to censorship?

Please do not worry about my not writing to you, of course I do, and I will continue. I eagerly await your letters, too. I hope you are safe. Knowing that you are a supply officer, I hope you will never be in the line of fire, but somewhere in a supply depot away from danger. I try to keep up with the news from overseas, but it covers such a wide range of events that I worry when I don't know where you are.

It was so nice to see Helen Arnsworth again, she gave me what little news she knew of you and the package with your letters. The scarf could not have been a greater gift, unless you handed it to me yourself. Thank you for the cashmere hugs and letters that I read over and over again in lieu of any newer ones from you.

I am as well as can be expected, I have a part-time job as a sales girl in a department store. Anja is doing well at her school, and she is speaking more and more all the time.

I have not taught her to say, "I love you" because I am waiting to hear that from you in person.

Please be careful, and don't forget to write whenever you can.

I miss you so much.

Goodnight darling,
Karin

February 1940

NEW YEAR'S EVE came and went, delivering in its wake new anxieties for the war overseas as they unfolded day by day in Europe. I wondered where Ernst was; I wished I would hear from him.

While I kept busy with my part-time job, one day I decided to get a degree in library science. I sought a new focus for my future, and being a student required the discipline of time management to do all the reading. My English lit records from college favored me, and I was quickly accepted into the program. Anja's piano studies kept her busy, and Benji continued to be part of her focus as well. Aaron and I saw each other frequently to discuss our children, but he occasionally invited me out for dinner and a movie. I liked being asked out, but, even though I liked Aaron well enough, I hoped he would not make more of it. Ernst was the only man I could imagine myself being with for the rest of my life, as improbable as it was just then. Time would tell.

IT WAS A COLD FEBRUARY DAY AS I SCOUTED AROUND trying to find a few good presents for Benji's birthday. The rabbit fur lining of my coat makes being out on foot tolerable, for a while anyway. When I told Anja that we were getting ready for Benji's birthday party, she was delighted. Anja thought that a birthday meant that she would be getting presents. I had to explain the celebration to her, though I knew I had been unsuccessful when she said, "I'll let Benji play with my presents, too." I think that everything in her life outside of being clothed, fed, and housed before she entered mine was a mystery to her as well as to me. As bright and as talented as she was, her psyche had some vacant places yet to be filled. Even though she was so little, how can there be so few memories of joyous happenings in her life? She was a continuous mystery, but I was determined to fill any voids of celebrations for her. My mother was an overqualified ally in the endeavor.

We had a nice celebration for Benji, and we gave him more pieces for his log cabin farm and some animals he did not have. Anja put them on her bed just before he left, telling him he could play with them too. He was gracious about her possessiveness of his birthday gifts, so much more than I would have thought for a four-year-old, but then he was quite possessive of her as well.

Much to my surprise, I enjoyed being a part-time student again. Studying library science kept my mind from straying to Ernst so often, from whom I have not heard in a long time.

Anja made some amazing advances in her piano studies; we all wondered how she would develop her talent with time.

FEARS

====================

SO MUCH WAS GOING ON in Europe that my father feared we would not be able to stay out of the war. We were supporting and supplying our allies with the hardware they so badly needed to continue to defend themselves with. He said that what we were doing did not fit with the non-intervention pledge we espouse to ourselves and the rest of the world, and that the Axis countries would see it for what it was, an act of alliance. I hoped he was wrong, but he seldom was.

March 1940 brought further bad news; the Germans bombed a naval base near Scotland. German escalation continued with the alarming news that in early April Germany invaded Denmark and Norway. As frightening as this was, I was even more alarmed for Ernst. It had been some months since I had heard from him. Despite my father's in-depth news commentary, I had gotten into the habit of going to the Trans Lux Newsreel theaters; where for twenty-five cents I could see Europe alive on the screen for forty-five minutes. They changed the newsreels every Wednesday, when they switched over to the latest films. American photojournalists were able to film what was happening, to some degree at least, confirming that the war was as real as the faces on the screen. Each time I went, I left the theater with a darkness that I never imagined I would feel. I knew and loved someone who was caught up in what was happening. How was I supposed to feel?

Today as I was studying, Daddy came over to me saying in a subdued voice, "You might want to take a short break." He had just put down some letters from Ernst. Finally!

> 12 December 1939
>
> Dearest Karin,
>
> I am worried that I have not heard from you in a long time. The news from this side of the ocean does not in any way reflect my feelings. These are difficult times and I wish I were there with you and not here. I know that wishing won't make it so but it helps me feel differently about my situation, which I must do.
>
> How are you and Anja? I hope you are well and thinking of Christmas and more joyful things other than what is happening here. I wonder if you will have that crispy skinned Christmas goose. I hope you do! If so, take a bite of it for me, as that will be as close as I will get to a Christmas dinner this year.
>
> I love you and miss you more than feelings can put into words.
>
> Please write.
>
> Loving you,
> Ernst

His other letters were short as well, and I guessed that he felt he couldn't say more than he does. He wrote mostly about us; I didn't think the censors would see our love messages as anything critical except to us. His people were obviously censoring his letters; what else would explain the delayed pileup of letters?

April 12, 1940

Dear Ernst,

It was so good to get your letters, four of them at once. I think about you and wonder where you are and if you are safe. I watch the news from Europe and none of it is good. I wonder when the war will be over and when I will see you again. In a lighter vein, Anja invited her playmate over the other day, and when he saw the photo of the three of us on my dresser, he asked Anja, "Is that your daddy?"

"No, he is my uncle Ear Nest."

"Oh. Where is he?"

"He is in Prock."

"Where is that?"

"You go on a big train ride and on a boat and then a small train ride and on a big, big, big boat for a long time and then you are there."

"Far away."

"Yes."

They are so sweet, and I love listening to them. I hope their conversation gave you a smile as well. I must get back to my studying, which is a lot of reading and learning about cataloguing systems. It is not very entertaining, but I must learn it.

Be well my dearest, and do take care of yourself wherever you are.

I send you my love,
Karin

30 April 1940

My dearest Karin,

Your letter from April 12 arrived at a time when I needed to hear from you more than ever. I smiled more than I have in a long time when I read about Anja and her friend. I am so happy to be her "Uncle Ear Nest." How I wish we were still back in "Prock." She made the journey as far as I know it to be, to be with you I would travel whatever it takes for even a moment to hold you in my arms. "Ah, such stuff as dreams are made on." Shakespeare stole these words from me or just borrowed them so others could use them for their own dilemmas. Now too, it is time for me to put my head down for a short night. Tomorrow will not be a dream but more of a nightmare.

I am where darkness is the rule in spirit and behavior, and I fear there shall be more of it. I read the sonnets whenever I can to keep me in touch with feelings that otherwise would be dulled without them. Dieter and I try to cheer each other, we try more than we succeed, but the effort must be made. I am glad you are studying; while it doesn't sound like it has the poetry of the Bard, it will produce a result you are after. Right now I am at a loss for words, as so often happens these days. When we can, Dieter and I go for a beer and we sit silently, waiting for a lightness to happen in us. That generally eludes us, but that is just the way it is here. It is best I close now.

Love you,
Ernst

BAD NEWS

JUST BEFORE MY BIRTHDAY on May 13, mother and I were in the kitchen hashing over plans for a small celebration when my father came in. He was shaken by the news that Germany had invaded France, Belgium, Luxemburg, and the Netherlands. My mother gasped at the shock of hearing it, and I was left with only three words, "Oh, God, no!"

The room was quiet until my father said, "Now we are in it for sure, one way or another. There's no telling when or how, but it will happen, I'm sure of it."

On the evening of May 15, our overseas newscaster described the devastating German bombing of Rotterdam, Holland's major seaport. Can no one stop this? It seems we have to look to ourselves for the answer. Will aid ever be enough to do it, or will American blood be required?

Our vocabularies soon took on curious new words, like *blitz-krieg*, the *Maginot Line*, and the names of places that we were more familiar with on a schoolroom map than in the daily news. Where was Ernst? Had he been sent into the thick of it? After all, that is where supplies are needed, so his safety is surely in question. What am I to make of it all? If we go to war against Germany, what would I do? How would I feel? I watched my father pour himself a generous Scotch, saying, "Well, now that Winston Churchill is Prime Minister, he'll keep the bastards out, with our help of course. Someone has to stop them."

My father did not look at me as my mother said, "What about one of those for the ladies?"

As she put two glasses down in front of him, and he poured saying, "Well, old girl, we'll need to be fortified now, so bottoms up." He then put one of the glasses in my hand and said, "You'll probably need it more than the rest of us now." I only nodded and lifted the glass to my lips, as my tears doubled the volume on its way to my mouth.

My twenty-third birthday was a low-key event, except for the singing of *Happy Birthday*. Anja blew out my candles and handed them to Benji for safekeeping. My parents gave me a picture puzzle of the world with many hundreds of pieces. In my state of mind, I desperately wanted to put the world back together again as it was. I at least learned geography bit by bit in the days and weeks to come. Whenever I worked on the puzzle, Anja wanted to help. Her choice of disparate pieces refused to fit. She tried hard to make them fit, pressing them onto each other. When I give her two pieces that did fit, she beamed; she was so assured the world would be whole. Benji's father gave me a bottle of vintage wine, saying, "The French might wish they had this back right about now."

To which my father said, "Now, we can only toast them in appreciation."

Anja's present to me was an after-dinner recital. I was in total awe of her talent, and it reminded me that I needed to pay less attention to myself and more to her, who was not an item of news or expected letters, but a gift that kept giving back to me at times when

I least deserved it. My tears fell on my hands as I clapped. She ran over to me and said, "No be sad, mama! I play more for you." She ran back to the piano and played her favorite Mozart version of *Twinkle, Twinkle, Little Star*. She was just that in my life, a twinkling star that shone her light on me all the time. Because of her I knew I would survive whatever I had to face.

In the days that followed, in the spring of 1940 Holland surrendered to the Nazis. Days later, a new name of great distress to the Allies could be heard on the news: Dunkirk. The Nazis had pushed the Allied troops to the sea's edge of France in Dunkirk; their only hope of survival would come from across the English Channel, and come it did with small boats of every description, as English private boat owners braved the chop of the sea, the Nazi artillery, and strafing from the *Luftwaffe* to pick up the men as they waded out to the small boats. From there, the soldiers were ferried to larger ships that would take them back to England. In the week that it took to evacuate Dunkirk, thousands died. It was the worst mass horror we had heard of for the Allied troops. We also learned that, just fifteen miles off the coast of France, the Channel Islands were all that stood in the way of Hitler's ultimate goal, England. Our aid was more imperative than ever now.

In his prophetic way, my father said, "England stands alone now, but we will come to her side. It will take a lot of doing, but we are sure not to desert her. Roosevelt and Churchill speak the same language; their vocabularies may be different at times, we can be sure of that, but a common goal will know no deviance."

In a lighter moment, I asked, "Daddy, do you think they will forgive us The Boston Tea Party now?

"They will forgive us everything for the exchange of ships, planes, ammunition, food, and whatever else it takes."

"Our men as well?"

"That, too, if it comes to it."

Days later, Belgium also surrendered to the Nazis. In early June, the Nazis bombed Paris, and days later they took the French capital. I couldn't bring myself to write to Ernst; the flow of my feelings had been dammed up by the tide of war. I simply couldn't write. Soon Norway surrendered to the Nazis, and Italy declared war on Britain and France.

All of it was like some terrible disease that no one has any defense against, one that spreads like a plague out of control. The only help to come from us across the Atlantic was merchant ships loaded with supplies for the English, ships that were hunted by German U-boats and sunk at a frightening pace. How long can England hold out with these losses? How many losses will we suffer before we are pulled into this war? I think that the conviction behind our non-intervention here at home is weakening in face of the urgencies at hand.

OTHER NEWS

THE NEXT TIME GREG stopped by, he shared some troubling news with us. Alex had told him he was going to join England's Royal Air Force. In disbelief, Greg had said to him, "But you don't even know how to fly!" Alex's response was that he would know soon enough, according to a man he met at an air show. Greg reported the entire conversation as Alex had presented it, saying that Alex had been in the refreshment tent when the man approached him.

"What do you think of this?" the man asked Alex.

"What? The less than cold beer I'm drinking?"

"No, the air show."

"Looks like pretty exciting stuff. I know I couldn't do that."

"Well, we have something between their flying acrobatics and just flying. I'm sure you could do it."

"I don't even know how to fly."

"You could learn, the RAF is looking for young guys just like you. They'll teach you all you need to know."

"The RAF? They're the British, aren't they?"

"Sure are. They are also affiliated with the RCAF, the Royal Canadian Air Force. The way it would work for you is the RAF would first teach you to fly here in the States, and then you would go to Canada for more training, and then on to England for advanced training. It's an exciting life, socially and career-wise. I'll give you my phone number. Call me when you're ready to go, and I'll arrange the rest."

Greg said, "When he told me about it I reminded him that he had better reconsider this notion, since other brash ideas he has had in the past only lasted until he got tired of it and moved onto something new." Hearing this, I wondered if I had been one of those.

"He said his main reasoning was this, 'At some point I will be drafted into the U.S. army if I don't do this now. I sure as hell don't want to be a foot soldier in the infantry! I'll take my chances with the RAF; others are doing it and so can I.'

"I told him that if he is accepted, and does actually sign up, he won't be able to walk away if later he wants out. He'll have to stick it out to the end. He assured me he'd be fine and would not want to change his mind. After all, what could be more exciting than flying? And that was pretty much the end of it. He called the fellow, I should say recruiter, and Alex is now on his way to some training school in the south."

We were all taken aback, I especially, after his sudden departure from Prague and failure to return. A month later I got a letter from him.

> Hello again Karin,
>
> I guess by now Greg has told you of my momentous decision to become a pilot. So far, WOW! Lots to learn, to know and remember. It's not anything like architecture, except for a few angles. Ha! Lots of classroom time, with lectures in the evenings at times and even a few harrowing films of what not to do. The food is good, the

weather a bit hot, and the guys are great, but a few have dropped out already for various reasons. The instructors are top notch.

I know how busy Greg is, so I won't even ask him to write to me, but I wonder if you would, just once in a while. It would be nice—mail is a big deal here, and everybody looks forward to letters, so I hope I can look forward to yours as well.

Take care,
Alex

I felt as though I might become a wartime correspondent for both sides. That too remains to be seen.

SUMMER 1940

NEW YORK CITY was heating up, but things were even hotter in Europe. The Germans have begun to bomb London. It only took a few days before the British took the war to Berlin by bombing it. I hoped Ernst's parents are safe; I dared not think about Ernst right now, it was just too painful. It wasn't long before the Germans made London a prime target, but a number of other major cities were not spared the *blitzkrieg* from the *Luftwaffe*. We rejoiced over the news that the RAF was more than holding its own, but we wondered how long they could last.

I wondered if Alex would make it through his training to be a part of this. I hoped it could be over before then, because I couldn't imagine Alex in any of this at all.

With the Germans occupying Paris, we cringed at the thought that the beautiful city of light would become another victim to the darkness of war. War was raging in North Africa as well, and the question remained, what would the United States ultimately do?

I haven't had any mail from Ernst or Alex for a while, and going to the newsreel theaters is not quieting for me either. Things have become direr on every front, and still we sit at home, listening and watching it all from afar.

I got a call from Thomas Brixley to see how Anja and I were doing. He shared the troubling news that the German Foreign Office had turned down America's request for safe conduct for American ships to evacuate children under sixteen years of age from the war zones. He said, "I'm so glad you left when you did and that Anja is safe. I hope you are both settled into your new lives. If ever you need anything, you have my number, just call. Be well and take care."

IN AUGUST 1940, THE BRITS BEGAN TO BOMB BERLIN ON night raids. They suffered many losses, and retaliation reined freely. The Germans announced on September 30 that Japan, Germany, and Italy had signed a military alliance against the United States. A few weeks before that, a new government came to power in Japan under Prince Konoye, proclaiming a "new life" and a "new order" in Eastern Asia.

In September, President Roosevelt signed the military conscription bill, which allowed American men to be drafted into military service. The war was coming closer to us all the time.

On a beautiful day in September, Anja and I strolled in Central Park with my parents when Anja pointed to a little plaque on a bench that some family had donated. My mother read the plaque aloud. "I will hold your heart more tenderly than my own."

Anja looked up at me and asked, "What does that mean, Mama?"

"It means I love you so much."

She sat on the bench and asked us to sit with her. She had us link arms, and then she closed her eyes and said, "I love you so much."

Anja had a way of burrowing her feelings into you in a most surprising way at times; truth be told, she did this all the time.

November 1940

ON NOVEMBER 5, 1940, Roosevelt was re-elected for a third term. The uncertainty of Asia and Europe weighed heavily on him and us as a nation.

It was mid-November and we were thinking about Thanksgiving dinner. There is a sad edge to planning a celebration, because we knew that the inhabitants of Coventry, England, were not thinking of celebration, but of survival after two full days of German bombing. The disparity was sickening.

Thanksgiving came with a capon that successfully masqueraded as a turkey; we made enough of the trimmings to fill our guests and us as expected. I toasted everyone at the table with my own thanksgivings for those who were helping with the care of Anja when I couldn't.

It seemed heartless to be celebrating anything at the end of December, when we heard the devastating news about a massive air raid on London.

To escape the heaviness in our hearts my mother and I would go to Radio City Music Hall and treat ourselves to the sounds of the big bands. Glenn Miller was an all time favorite and Benny Goodman could make his clarinet wail in a way that would send shivers down my spine.

I liked Gene Kruper and Buddy Rich, drummers that could make your heart beat faster.

They buoyed our spirits with their music, jazz and swing time were some of our comforts as the year passed heavily, while the war in Europe raged on. Life here still required that I played an active part in Anja's life even as I attended classes, even though at times I enjoyed them second hand. My mother shared one of those times with me that she witnessed. One of the voice students had especially attracted Anja's attention, Anja asked if she could sit and listen during one of her lessons. They both gave their permission, and Anja sat quietly listening to the captivating voice of the young mezzo-soprano singing an aria in Italian. My mother accompanied her on the old spinet piano in the living room, where she gives her voice lessons. When the lesson was over, Anja clapped to the delight of the singer, who said, "My first appreciative audience!" Anja was so well behaved that she was allowed to be there the following day. To Anja's surprise, a young man joined the lesson. She watched and listened intently to the tenor as my mother directed the duet. When they were finished, Anja clapped to their delight. The following day, when the couple did not appear, Anja did, armed with her music and Peter Rabbit to the spinet piano. She leaned against the piano bench on the carpeted floor so she could reach the pedals. She opened her music on the stand, which she still couldn't read very well. She put Peter Rabbit next to the music and she began to play. Anja suddenly began to sing a made-up language in a falsetto. Then she said to Peter Rabbit, "Now you sing." When the request was not fulfilled, she sang again in a made-up language, but in the deepest range her voice would allow.

When she finished playing, she scolded Peter Rabbit for his lack of compliance, saying, "You must work harder." She folded up her music and tucked Peter Rabbit brusquely under her arm and left, the music lesson at an end. What never did come to an end was Anja's ability to overcome any obstacle in music, aside from the one with Peter Rabbit of course.

THEN IT CAME

ANOTHER YEAR OF GROWTH and development was coming to an end for Benji and Anja, and for us adults, as 1941 drew near to a close we all wondered what 1942 would catapult us into, on both the domestic and foreign fronts. How well prepared were we to face whatever would be asked of us? Life continued to delight in fads and fashions, songs and their singers. It was as though life took on a desperate tempo to counteract anything that put a damper on heightened spirits that seemed to be marking our lives in double time. Then it came.

ON SUNDAY DECEMBER 7, 1941 AS WE WERE IN THE HABIT of listening to a vocal music program that my mother liked. Anja was totally taken with a commercial for Hartz Mountain birdseed; the commercial had a canary that sang a sweet little song, and Anja always pressed her ear to the speaker for this treat. Today the program was interrupted by the announcer who told us in a distressed voice that the Japanese were bombing our naval ships and planes in Pearl Harbor, on the Pacific island of Oahu, Hawaii. We all stopped what we were doing in mid breath to listen to the limited information available at that moment.

My father said, "The handwriting was on the wall."

Mother said, "Yes, but it must have been in Japanese because we could not read it."

My father replied, "Yes, but we did have a bad translation of it earlier." Anja only wanted to hear her canary again. I think we all wished for that, in the hopes it could undo the attack on Pearl Harbor. I asked my father if he thought they would bomb the mainland, and if so how far in could they get. He doubted that the Japanese could reach the U.S. mainland, due to plane fuel consumption, but what was now happening was devastating beyond belief, as most of our Pacific fleet warships in harbor there were being bombed. Some of them had sunk, and others were totally disabled. The airfields with our many war planes were being bombed as well, all with a great loss of life. The war was no longer happening in just distant places, but shockingly the war has come home to us.

Later in December, a woman in my class told me about war plant hiring. The wages were high, and she had applied for a job at a munitions plant. She said she could come back to school later. I went to a placement office to inquire about work in a war plant. The woman mentioned all sorts of jobs. When I told her that I didn't want a job that was connected to killing, she looked up at me and said, "My dear, this whole war is about killing. Either you contribute, or you don't." When I got up to leave she said, "Hold on a minute, how about working for radio parts?" Radio parts sounded like something I could do and still sleep at night.

I nodded and said. "Yes, I can do that."

With address in hand, I entered the building of Ace Crystal Lab. The personnel director asked me how soon I could report for work.

"Tomorrow?"

"Tomorrow eight o'clock sharp you see Ted Holloway. Fill out these forms and bring them with you. Just so you know it'll be shift work, and we'll be running twenty-four hours a day, seven days a week at some point. We'll talk about salary tomorrow." He thanked me, and I left. Now, I too, was about to put my future on hold.

At home I looked over the forms I was to fill out. A lot of the usual information: education, past work experience, etc. Then there was a curious question: Did I have a criminal record? The answer of course was no. Obviously they weren't just taking anyone off the street. But they took me.

Mr. Holloway showed me around. The first thing I saw were large gunnysacks with the words *Product of South Africa* stenciled in black on each one. He told me they were crystals as big as large rocks in their raw state, and they were immersed in a carbon tetrachloride bath to clean them. Then a gemologist examined them to determine their axis to be cut into sections, after which they were mounted in wax onto a platform for cutting. He showed me how a large diamond blade slowly cut into the markings of the gemologist. The crystals were cut again and again until all of the markings had been cut. Then we came to a line of people who further refined the crystals with carborundum grinding wheels into smaller and smaller slices. He said my job would be to examine the final product, which would be a slice smaller than a microscope slide, for the slightest imperfections. The approved crystals were then ready to be put into the radios they were meant for.

He gave me an eye exam to see if I could spot the smallest of defects. Having passed this exam, he led me to the bench where I would be working. It had a small, highly illuminated box with a large magnifying glass mounted in the top of the box. I was to examine the finished crystals for the slightest defects. To impress upon me the required accuracy for this work, he said, "I want you at all times to remember that these crystals are put into the radios that are fitted into bombers and fighter planes and are relied on by the men flying them. A faulty crystal could endanger the lives of ten or more men in a bomber or the single life of a fighter pilot. I will be checking on your work at odd moments. If you have any questions, activate the red light to get my attention. The tray on the left of the light box holds the crystals to be examined, and the tray on the right is for the ones you have passed. Your rejects go into the bin at the top. I will give you a tray for you to practice on. I'll be by to see how you do. He switched the bright light on in the box and then left me to it.

I sat still, thinking for a few minutes of the bombers and fighter planes that would accomplish their missions to destroy the frightened humanity below because of directions to be given over the radios. I wondered if I could really do this just as he came over and asked, "Miss Wilson, do you have any questions?"

"No, Mr. Holloway. I just need a moment to focus."

He had given me a mixed batch of passable and non-passable crystals, which I successfully separated. He was pleased that I met the task. I was more conflicted.

On the bus home I wasn't so sure that giving up school and my part-time job was the right thing to have done. I thought of Alex in a plane, using a radio to receive information that would help him get safely home. Maybe one of my crystals would do that for him. That was the other side of the hot coin I would have to consider before dropping it.

THERE WERE MASSIVE GERMAN AIR RAIDS ON LONDON and other important cities, and now our non-intervention is no longer an issue of debate. War in the Pacific would take a toll we were ill prepared for; our home front was being mobilized into war time production to meet the demands of our own military, as well as those of our Allies in the Pacific and in Europe. It was a very tall order indeed.

My work took on a new energy, one I did not at all expect of myself even after seeing the newsreels of German troops on their lemming advances across Europe. I have not written to Ernst in a while, and I have also heard nothing from him.

On December 11, 1941, I had received the news that postal exchange with Germany had been officially severed. It was a shock to think that I could no longer write to Ernst and that I would not hear from him either. Ernst was now considered an enemy military combatant, so postal contact was forbidden. How long would this last? And how would he and I survive this vacuum? The war now had a stranglehold on all that was left to us, our feelings transcribed into words on paper. My despair deepened.

Raison d' Être

———————————

ONE DAY, AFTER SPENDING the afternoon with Benji and Hannah, Anja came home abuzz with excitement. Hannah indicated that she needed to speak with me, so we let the children play for a bit in our room while we spoke in the kitchen.

"Karin, I'm sorry to tell you this, but I think you will have a bit of an issue to handle this evening. Aaron recently bought a new electric alarm clock to replace his old wind-up clock, which Benji appropriated for his inventive use. He was toying with it when Anja came over today. He convinced her that it is a magic clock. He showed her he could change time by moving the hands back. He also told her he could move the hands forward into "wish time," and that all she had to do was to make a wish and it would come true. When her wish was to have her papa come to see her, little wizard Benji kept turning the hands forward until the alarm went off at 7 o'clock.

"See, your papa will come to see you at 7 o'clock."

"She got very excited to come home to be here when her papa comes to see her. So, she is sitting there till 7 o'clock to see her papa. I'm so sorry for the trouble this might cause you."

I was fit to be tied at this development, but I tried my best to hide my frustration. My mother said to Hannah, "They're just kids.

I'm sure Karin will work it out Hannah. Thank you for sharing this with us. I can't imagine we would ever have been able to guess at this particular game."

While we were talking, my father came home. He came into the kitchen and, before he really took in the concerned looks on our faces, he asked, "What's up with Anja by the front door? I could barely get the front door open because Anja and Benji are sitting on the floor, just inside the door. I had to push my way in . . . imagine my surprise when I saw them just sitting there! Anja only said hello and waved." My mother made a motion to shush him, and then gestured to get him to come closer. She gave him a very quick recap.

Hannah apologized again, then gathered Benji and went home.

The three of us pondered the problem for a few minutes. An idea struck me, and I said, "I think I know what I'm going to do. Just let me be alone with her for a while."

I sat down next to Anja by the door and put my arm around her.

Anja looked up at me with such innocent excitement that it nearly broke my heart. "Benji said my papa is coming to see me at seven o'clock. I heard the bell say so. I know he will come."

I kissed her head and said, "Sometimes we have to wait a long, long time to see the people we love, and it is even different and longer when they are in heaven."

Anja looked at me in confusion. "Anja, Benji made a mistake. When you hear the bell, it means to wake up your papa in heaven so he can look down and see you. Your papa is an angel now and his wings only let him fly in heaven. He can't fly away from heaven because that is where angels live. Come, darling, play some music for him. I know he will hear you and it will make him so happy that you are thinking of him and playing beautiful music just for him." I got up and held her hand as we went to the piano. She played so beautifully I didn't even hide my tears.

"Mama, is it seven o'clock now?"

"Yes, Anja. Your papa heard you, and he is so happy now."

She came and sat on my lap, resting her head on my shoulder and sucking her thumb. I thought that perhaps we have finally overcome some difficult feelings, once and for all. It wasn't what she expected, but it was what she accepted. I continued to be impressed by Anja's ability to make adjustments in her life, ever since I became one of those major adjustments. She would turn six in a few days, and life would continue to ask even more of her during her young years.

That evening after dinner, Anja was quieter than usual. During dessert, she thoughtfully asked, "Grandpa, when I play music and after I hear it, where does it go?"

"Well, I would have to think about that. That is a hard question to answer so quickly."

"Grandpa? Do you think the music goes up to heaven?"

I caught my father's eye and quickly nodded.

"Now, that you mention it, yes, I think your music might do just that, especially if someone special is waiting to hear them."

"Do you really think so?"

"Yes, dear, I really want to think so."

"Me, too," she said with the knowing confidence that only young children possess.

She got up and went to my father with her arms out for a hug. He took her onto his lap and she rested her head on his chest. She said, "Papa heard me." He kissed her forehead, and she sucked her thumb and closed her eyes. It was hard for all of us to get past this moment dry-eyed; we did many times like this with Anja. I thought of her father's letter to me, sealed in the safe deposit box, and I wished

I could know what he thought of all of this. Her happiness was at stake, so I was sure he would say he could hear every note.

After Anja was asleep, my parents said they thought my handling of the situation was a stroke of genius. "When her father gave her to me, he knew there would be at least one *raison d'être*. I don't know how many there may be, but I believe I've just used up one of them."

The three of us had a glass of wine and a few laughs as well as a tear or two before we said good night.

A FEW DAYS LATER, I STILL HAD NOT GOTTEN OVER THE effect that Benji's magic clock story had worked on Anja and our response to it. I decided to see Dr. Steinreich for his advice. He calmly listened to the whole story, nodding thoughtfully as I spoke.

"For young children, the finality of death is impossible to grasp. They reason it, in a mystical way, that they draw from what is near real in their world to something inexplicable, yet serviceable to assuage the longing which they do not yet understand is a permanent loss."

"I don't know how much of this was her own reasoning or that of Benji. His mother died when he was four months old, and when he was older and asked about her, he was told she is an angel up in heaven."

"Well, it would seem to me that perhaps they have both found a way to share their longing without the finality of death to disturb it. Children's knowledge and reasoning gets more sophisticated with time, and as they develop, they will deal with this differently. For now, I think you both are in a good place, and she has accepted what she is now capable of accepting. I hope you will as well."

I left Dr. Steinreich's office with the assurance that Anja and I would do and say what was needed in the present.

OTHER PLACES

<hr>

TODAY'S MAIL LAY on the kitchen table, among it a letter from Ernst, I was shocked to see it.

> 3 September 1941
>
> My dearest Karin,
>
> This is the first I have been able to write to you in a while. I await letters from you every day, but so far, no new letters from you. I hope all is well with you and Anja.
>
> I am in France now and I think I will be here for some time to come. I wish I were in New York or Prague or Berlin with you, anywhere but here.
>
> We are positioned outside a small village in the countryside. This morning I took a walk to get away from the supply trucks' diesel fumes. The landscape here is beautiful. After a short while I came to a rise that over-looked a valley with a vineyard. There was some early morning ground fog still nestled in the rows. I closed my eyes and imagined you standing next to me, holding my hand, and we were here in peacetime on our honey-moon. Just then two motorcycles came roaring down the

road near where I was standing, and they disturbed my daydream. I have a lot of those with you, and I intensify them when I take out your photo and look at it, unwilling to put it back in my shirt pocket where you now must live with me till the day your compass can give me different directions.

Karin, please keep me in your thoughts and even closer in your heart. I need to know that before this day ends, and a new one begins, for me, in this land where I am an unwelcomed stranger.

How is Anja? Is she speaking even more? What kinds of things does she say? Whenever I see children about her age, I miss her all the more, and you with her even more than that.

I send you all my love,
Ernst

This earlier written letter of his must have been in the delivery works before, when no exchange of letters took place. Will there be others that squeeze through?

I started going back to the newsreel theaters; I needed to see for myself what was going on in France. I saw lines of refugees carrying, pushing, and pulling wagons full of whatever they could salvage from the homes they were abandoning to the invaders. The civilians trudged on to places yet unknown to them, where and for how long, no one seemed to know. I tried not to associate Ernst with what I saw of the German soldiers in France, even though he was not there by his own choice. Still, it left a sting in me for all of it.

ANJA'S BIRTHDAY

ANJA HAD TURNED SIX, it was only once in her lifetime to do so and in mine as well. We had made it a celebration despite what is happening in the world, we had a nice dinner party, determined to brighten it for Anja. Anja and Benji still cooperated on the candle blowing and saving. Children are the hope of the world beyond what adults are capable of.

So much had changed in her life and mine since that fateful day in the bookshop in Prague in 1938. Sometimes I saw her looking in the mirror while she moved her hair around, studying a new effect. It was a surprisingly adult motion. Was she looking for a new persona, I wondered, while I was still figuring out her old one? She carefully chose what to wear for her birthday party; she wanted new ribbons for her hair as well. As far as presents were concerned, she now understood the difference between the giver and the receiver.

She continued to make extraordinary strides in music, and we were astounded at her nonchalance over it. It was so much a part of her that the work it entailed did not faze her a bit. She still had her moments when she got on my lap and rested her head against me and stroked my hair. I think we all have need of moments like that.

I opened a savings account in her name, a small assurance for her future needs. One would hardly recognize her now compared to how she was when we first arrived. I just hoped it didn't happen too fast because I still had so much to work out over having been given her not that long ago.

ALEX WROTE TO ME MORE OFTEN THAN I HAD THOUGHT he would. I tried to answer frequently, but I was never sure what would be of interest to him of my life. His by comparison was full of excitement, and he seemed to be satisfied to have chosen well for his temperament.

The musical evenings at the Mandel's were a welcomed relief, and I enjoyed helping in these social events.

I was despondent about my work in the radio crystal lab, thinking about its ultimate use as an instrument of warfare, but I also remembered German U-boats were attacking merchant ships in the Atlantic. I heard that they could at times hang around just fifty miles out at sea from New York City and along the entire length of the eastern coast, just waiting for our merchant ships loaded with fuel, train engines, planes, tanks, and spare parts, and food, medical supplies, ammunition, and other needed supplies to convoy across the Atlantic. One captured U-boat mariner said at times they were so close at night they could see the cars driving along the East River Drive in Manhattan. The losses were heavy, not only of the supplies but of the ships carrying them and the merchant mariners aboard them. Any doubts about the work I did had been dispelled by this heart-wrenching trend. We all had our wars to fight, and the work I did was mine.

The good news was that Ace Crystal had just hired another examiner like me. When Charlie heard that I had a little one, he said that since he was a bachelor he didn't mind taking my night shift. He had a limp and so was exempt from military service. A lucky offer for me since Anja still would not sleep alone. My mother had been taking on that night shift for me.

The Germans were bombing airfields and factories in England, and there were air battles and daylight raids over Britain as well. They had bombed central London, too. The British had since made a raid over Berlin. The German *Blitzkrieg* against Britain was massive. I wondered how much longer our allies could hold out.

We feared that it wouldn't be long before those convoys of goods across the Atlantic would also have ships with American soldiers being ferried over to England, despite the threat of the U-boats.

I had more opportunity to go to see the newsreels. They showed the bombing effects on London and the misery and deaths left in the wake of the *Blitzkrieg*. I was glad to leave the Trans Lux newsreel theaters, to be able to go out into the fresh and safe air before going to a house that was as whole as I had left it. One day I had a letter from Alex. He had passed all his exams and flight tests and was about to leave for Canada for further training. He was excited; I was less so, having just seen what air power can do.

WAR

PRESIDENT ROOSEVELT has declared war on the Axis powers, Britain joined us in declaring war on Japan, and on December 11, 1941, Hitler declared war on the United States. We were in it in all aspects. Men had been voluntarily signing up for the armed services all across the country as soon as Japan attacked Pearl Harbor; the outpouring had been enormous for all the branches of military service; hundreds of thousands of men had signed up. The draft had also been set for men from the ages of twenty-one to thirty-five years of age. Later, as the need arose, this was changed to include men eighteen to forty-five years of age. The hurried pace was alarming but necessary. Estimated for one year is the delivery of 50,000 planes, along with ships and guns and tanks, all part of our Lend Lease agreement. One of the planes is sure to have Alex's name on it. They were fearful times at best.

Anja and Benji were ready to leave Castle Care and go to kindergarten in another school. I met with Aaron about schools, sure that he would have been looking into them. He had, and the teachers of Castle Care and he had come to the conclusion that a small private school based on the Maria Montessori approach to education would be a good fit for Benji. The same school was suggested to me for Anja as well. We arranged a visit, and I liked everything about it except the cost. I was informed about scholarships and was told Anja was a favorable candidate for one. Aaron and I left happy about the school and what it offered; the only question was whether I could manage any extra costs. Aaron assured me that provisions could be made for anything I could not cover, but by whom I wondered? We both felt it was important for Benji and Anja to be together. I especially did not think that Anja would do well without him because she still depended on him for so much social and emotional support. We had all the meetings and arrangements taken care of for their attending in February 1942. We visited the school with the children, which they liked, but even so Anja held Benji's hand through the whole walk-through. Seeing that, Aaron and I knew we had done the right thing.

I received another letter from Alex, just before Christmas.

Hello, Karin,

Well, here I am, in Canada, in an accelerated program to further my training. The place in the States taught me how to fly, but here I am being taught to become a pilot. Very different, very, very different! I'll be learning navigation, formation flying, radio communication, mechanical stuff, as well as good sounds from the engine and some you'd rather not hear. I'm learning about the RCAF as a body of service, who's who and general physical workouts and lots of stuff too numerous to mention here. I'm looking forward to it; I've met some interesting guys from all over. Some know more than I do, and a few maybe a wee bit less. Creature comforts are good and so is the food. We don't have uniforms as yet, just one-piece jumpsuits, but the rest will come later, I guess once we make pilot. Today they urged us to make out our wills before leaving for overseas. They offered help if we needed it. Hell, I have news for them; I'm coming back, same way as I left, all in one piece. I'll be coming back to full employment; too, I'm sure. I'm thinking of all the architects that will be needed for new works then. This air force command is just an interim thing until I can do that.

That's about all from here. Say hi to Greg if you see him. Must run.

Alex
P.S. Note my new address.

We later heard that in November a U-boat sank the British aircraft carrier Ark Royal off Gibraltar I try to imagine what Alex must be thinking and feeling hearing that. Thankfully he still has a lot of training to go through from what he tells me.

No doubt he will be learning to use my radio crystals.

A big surprise today, a letter from Ernst that must have been hanging around for a long time somewhere too late to be stopped. I wonder if there will be more.

10 November 1941

My dearest Karin,

It has been a long time since I have gotten any letters from you. I hope all is well.

I am still where I was when I last wrote to you, and I am feeling worse about it as time goes on. Dieter explored the little village we are near and thought we should have a change from army food and eat at a little restaurant he found. A few evenings ago we went to the little family-run place with only about six tables. When we came in, the patrons who were already there stopped talking. We seated ourselves at one of the tables, and the owner came out to us. He pointed to a small chalkboard that showed the *plat de jour* of stewed rabbit. There was no other choice. We ordered and it came with a small glass of wine. Minutes after we were served, all of the patrons got up and left. It was their protest of our presence, not only in the restaurant but in their country as well. If the situation had been reversed and the French had invaded Germany, I know I would have felt the same. We ate in silence, paid for our meal, and added a generous tip, vowing never to repeat this experience. But of course, there will be others.

It is cold here, but not as bad as Prague. I hope my scarf is giving you some warm hugs, how I wish I could give them to you in person.

I have to get back to work, wishing all the while it were to a law practice instead of this.

Some things in life we have no choice about, this being one of them.

I love you with all my heart and miss you terribly.
Ernst

The contrast between the letters from Alex and Ernst was remarkable, and my feelings as well. I was concerned for both of them, but the degree of concern simply didn't compare. Now old mail is as welcomed as more recent letters. I promised myself I would answer Alex's letter when my spirits were better than they were just then.

I was relieved from my usual routine when Aaron invited me out for dinner one evening. He said he would like to see a lot more of me. When I said that working and keeping up with Anja was taking all of my time, he countered with, "I work as well, and have Benji to care for, but I don't see why it should rule out other parts of my life."

"I'm rather stressed, Aaron. I have a lot to deal with, and having a relationship is out of the question for me right now. I hope you will understand that."

"I do understand stress, but not making room in your life for someone like me is a lot harder to understand. I do not mean to put any pressure on you." He smiled. "At least not any more than I already have."

I smiled back and said, "Thank goodness for that, because I do value your friendship outside of anything more, right now."

"Well, Karin, I will hold out, you know. Do you know the saying, 'where there is a will there is a way'?"

I felt a sadness when I said, "Yes, I am familiar with that saying."

"Let's have a brandy on that to round out the evening."

Even though he saw me home, the evening was anything but rounded out.

As was another evening in Prague not that long ago.

EXCEPT FOR THE TALK ABOUT WAR, AND THE WAR WORK that we are fully committed to, life went on pretty much as it always had, except that the pace of everything had picked up due to the worries of war and our young men going overseas to fight, across the Atlantic and the Pacific.

Mr. Holloway introduced a new shift worker to Charlie and me. Sally would take the four P.M. to midnight shift, while Charlie was on from midnight to eight A.M., and I worked the eight A.M. to four P.M. shift.

New Year's Eve was more subdued this time for those of us with family and loved ones overseas. Nineteen forty-one had been a year of questions and great apprehension as the news reports from overseas flooded the media. Now we all wondered what 1942 would bring is on all our minds.

1942

STARTING ON JANUARY 7, German U-boats carried out an even more concerted offensive along the east coast of North America. From Canada to Virginia and points further south, they prowled in the dark of night thirty miles or even less at times from shore, awaiting the supply convoys headed for Britain. Stricken tankers at times could be seen aflame from shore. We did not know whether any ships filled with American servicemen were also on the way to Great Britain.

ANJA AND BENJI HAD SETTLED INTO THEIR NEW SCHOOL very nicely. While Anja had demonstrated greater independence in some areas, she still was very much attached to Benji. He appeared to be encouraging it as well.

I wrote to Alex, and he wrote back as frequently as he could. His last letter to me said he would be transferred after his exams. I assumed that meant he would be going overseas to England for the advanced training he was expecting. After seeing the latest newsreels and the aftermaths of bombings, I had new concerns for his safety as he moved further up the ladder of danger. More and more young men could be seen in the city streets in uniforms of the different services.

MAKING DO

I SAT DOWN WITH my mother and our new ration books to figure how our allotments were to be used among us. Thankfully we did not have a car, so gasoline and tires were of no concern. Sugar, coffee, meat, and shoes had priority over silk and nylons. We started going barelegged and applied a tinted lotion on our legs to resemble the look of stockings. With an eyebrow pencil we drew stocking seams up the backs of our legs. The nylons most available were for those who wore size five shoes; my mother and I were not among them; our size six feet did not fit them.

Mother said that if we were willing to give up using sugar in our tea and cereal, she could bake a cardamom cake once a month. We made the sacrifice. Mother made creative choices of meat at the butcher's shop; she went to him with a horseshoe in her bag for good luck and held it up to him when she was waited on. He often had off-stamp offers, otherwise known as under-the-counter offers. He claimed they were items not on the ration list, but at times it was questionable.

Anja needed new shoes badly, but she would not give up her Mary Janes, no matter how much they pinched her growing feet. Mother often cruised the thrift shops for her next needed size.

As for the rest of us, we made do with whatever we had. Some of my friends at work gussied up their appearances with Chen Yu's bright China Red nail polish, and lipstick, they were glad they were not a war effort item.

Those were the new signs that ushered in spring 1942.

GRIM EVENTS

THE GERMANS BEGAN an even more massive U-boat offensive along the entire east coast of the United States, lying in wait for convoys. The tactic was to follow them out into the ocean and then at night flank them on both sides of the convoy while one or more slipped between the ships of the convoy to release their deadly torpedoes. It was devastation en masse without enough countermeasures, at least for the time being. The news was taking a toll on me that I struggled to manage. I noticed that I had hit a saturation point and I was feeling numb. This past Sunday I went to church with mother, where I tried the power of prayer. The sermon was largely about forgiveness, but it was so hard to endow one's thoughts with forgiveness when the pastor asks for our prayers for all of the cathedral cities in Britain that the Germans are bombing. What will prayers do for the victims? Is there really a God watching over all of this? What would He say if we were to ask about His plan for all of this? I did not find this a place of healing and salvation, and I doubted that I would go again.

My twenty-fifth birthday was a quiet celebration. I had to work a long shift and was so tired that the wine with dinner put me to sleep even before Anja. I'm sure she was disappointed, as she no doubt had birthday candles to catalog. She played beautifully for me before I fell into the arms of Morpheus, though I would have preferred they were those of Ernst.

At the end of May 1942, we heard that a thousand British bombers hit Cologne in an air raid. I remembered that Ernst had told me that Dieter's wife and sons lived in Cologne; now I wished I didn't know that.

At the beginning of June, we heard that a mass murder of Jews occurred when they were gassed at a place in Poland called Auschwitz. Who could possibly imagine such an atrocity taking place? My heart was barren of all else but sadness at the news. Who could believe this of human beings? Did we or anyone else really know what was going on over there?

Or had human beings suddenly stopped being human? The world must make Germany answer for this after the war, assuming these deranged minds did not win the war. That could not be allowed to happen, no matter the cost to the nations fighting them. I felt terribly torn about Ernst.

OUR ATTENTION WAS DIVERTED TO NORTH AFRICA during the summer. On June 21, Rommel had captured Tobruk; we feared for the lives of our American servicemen there as the Germans mounted another massive offensive against the Allies. The newsreels were disquieting despite the sparseness of details about what is actually happening. I decided to stay away from the Trans Lux newsreel theaters, because I was always leaving with a churning in my stomach.

MR. SOMES THINKS THAT ANJA'S TALENT NEEDS EVEN more careful grooming. My father worked her harder than he was comfortable with after Mr. Somes' direction. Anja enjoyed doing her homework from school, and she and Benji often worked at it together. She had a few language difficulties, mostly with spelling, even though she was a voracious reader. The teachers felt she would overcome it with work and time, which sounded like a safe guess to me, knowing Anja. She also started having difficulties with numbers, which was puzzling because she had done well with that before now. There seemed to be a disquieting attitude developing in her that was hard to pinpoint. I hoped she would overcome it, but I decided to talk to Dr. Steinreich about my concerns.

I also was working hard because of overtime at the Crystal Lab. I tried not to imagine what the radios were transmitting as they flew over Cologne, and what the reconnaissance cameras showed if the bombers were on target, or nearly on, or off target and those who would have to go back again on a repeat bombing mission. There surely would be some survivors in Cologne from the first bombing who would not survive another raid. Civilians had to be paying a cost greater than that of the military. When I sat down to work, I first had to clear my mind of all thoughts and concentrate on the idea that these radios could save lives; otherwise I couldn't do this work.

ALEX

═══════════════════

ALEX WROTE AS OFTEN as he could, saying little about what he was doing, because of secrecy rules. He shared that he was moving up from where he was when he first arrived. I answered with family news and home-front events that surely paled in interest from what he was experiencing in England. In August 1942, we heard of the first all-American air attack in Europe. Here at home, blood donors were actively sought for their precious contributions; a sobering thought when we grumbled about our far less significant personal daily shortages.

In late October I got a letter from Alex telling me that he and his American mates were about to give up their Eagle Squadron patches and RAF uniforms because now they were being handed over to the Eighth Air Force of the U.S. Army Air Forces.

Dear Karin,

We are still in RAF uniforms, but they wasted no time in giving us forms to fill out for our new status. One of the offers is that we can take out a life insurance policy. I took that offer, just in case I should hit the dirt in an untimely manner, and you should know that I made you the beneficiary. I did it as my way of apologizing to you for the Prague debacle. I'm sorry that I stranded you there and for whatever difficulties you had to deal with because of it. I don't know what I was thinking back then, most likely just about my situation and myself. It was easy for me to do that because I thought you were so much smarter and stronger than I was. I guess I thought somehow you would manage and get out if you felt any personal danger. I was dismissive back then, so this is my chance to make up for it. I have been in touch with Greg about this and he is in total agreement with my decision. So I hope bygones will be just that, bygones. The upside of the changeover is that we will now be earning three times as much in pay as we did under the RAF, so I guess our beer consumption will increase as well.

Other than that, I now have to get used to the Americans and their antics. They are a rowdy bunch, especially when I want to get some shut-eye. I feel and sound like the Brits did about us when we first arrived. The bottom line is that we are all here to do the same job, to get this nasty war done and over with. We are coming into colder, rainy, and foggy days now when even a pint of warm beer can be rather comforting. Never thought I would think that. I'm on call, so I'd better say goodbye, for tonight anyway.

Alex

I was taken by his generous thought of me as a way of making up for Prague. I hoped there would never be a need for me to see a cent of that. I did not expect anything of the kind, and I'm sure he didn't either until this presented itself in the form of immediate decision-making. It must have been awful to live your life day-by-day or hour-by-hour, thinking that each one could be your last. I couldn't fathom how these young men did that, other than believing in their own survival, no matter what they are facing. I thought that fear and courage must have been meted out in equal amounts to them all.

A Big Surprise

I WAS AT THE SINK washing the Sunday breakfast dishes when the phone rang. My father answered it and then he called out to me, "Karin, come quickly. It's for you."

I was still drying my hands on the apron when I'm handed the phone. "Hello?" The voice at the other end steals my breath.

"Karin, hello. It's me, its Ernst."

"Oh, my God!"

"I've been trying to make this call for weeks. I have three minutes and then they will cut me off. How are you?"

"I'm okay. Are you alright?"

"Who was it that answered the phone?"

"That was my father."

"Are you living at home with your parents now?"

"Yes, I am."

"That's good news. Are you divorced now?"

"Yes, I am. Where are you?"

"I'm so relieved to hear that. I'm in France."

"Are you safe?"

"Relatively so. We get bombed every now and then, but that is to be expected. I would be a lot better if we could write. Karin, please keep writing letters and save them for me. I want to know what you are doing and how you are. I'll do the same, and when we see each other we can exchange them to fill in the lost time. How is school?"

"I'm taking a break from my studies. I found a job. I needed work."

"What do you do?"

"I make radios."

"Maybe if I turn one on here, I will hear *Begin the Beguine*, then I'll know it is one you made." I couldn't say that mine relayed no music of any kind. "How is the little one?"

"Anja is fine."

"Oh, Karin. Just hearing your voice, I can almost see you and feel you in my arms. I miss you terribly." He paused as his voice started to tremble. I heard him take a deep breath before he continued. "I have your photo in my shirt pocket, facing my heart. I have another one of you in the sonnets you sent me; I keep it as a bookmark for that special one. Karin, I miss you so much, at times I can hardly stand it."

He had to pause again, and in the precious time we had left, I tried to help him. All I could find to say was, "I love you, Ernst. You are in my thoughts and I hope this war ends soon so we can be together again." I wanted to say more than that, and I wanted to say it differently, but that didn't happen.

He said, "I love you darling, I love you, I—" The connection was cut off.

My hand shook as I hung up the phone. It was a miracle that he could even call; it reminded me of his mantra, "Where there is a will, there is a way." I closed my eyes, sifting through my memories. I saw him in his uniform, and then I saw him in bed with me at the inn, when he put his ID tags on the night table. He had smiled and said, "Don't worry about my ID tags. If I die of happiness here, only you will know the true cause."

Tears welled up in my eyes as my father came over to me. "Was that who I think it was?" he asked quietly.

"Yes, it was."

His reply was gentle and caring. "One would hardly know there is a war on at times."

I held the end of the apron up to my eyes and went back to the sink in a daze. All I could think was, "Thank God he is alive."

THE NEXT DAY AT WORK, CHARLIE GAVE ME AN UPDATE when I relieved him at the end of his shift. "Be extra sharp today. We have had a flood of flawed crystals. Look at my rejects and you'll see what I mean. Good morning, and, good luck."

I looked at some of the crystals in his reject pile. I spotted tiny rice-shaped or tear-drop flaws that looked like air bubbles. Holloway came over to me and said, "I'm checking down the line to see where it's happening. I want everyone to take a break until I discover the problem."

I walked into the lounge, but the acrid smell of long overheated coffee dregs drove me away. I paced the hallway until Holloway called us all back.

"Listen, everybody. Scrap this last batch. There was an error early in the determination. Use the time to clean your equipment and take an early lunch. By then we should be up and running again, hopefully!"

We lost three hours of work before I was passed the first of the new batch. When I slid the first crystal into my viewer, I wondered if I would hear *Begin The Beguine* or just the sounds of bombers headed for the day's target. Ernst said he was safe, but who is and who isn't in a bombing raid? Holloway came over to me, "Come on, Karin, times a' wasting. Let's get on with it." I carefully searched the next one of the new batch for even the slightest flaw. There were none, and I felt a shiver go through me as I put it in the passed box and reached for the next one.

Rationing

===

THE MEAT FARE for late October 1942 left a lot to be desired as I watched mother unpack the haul from the butcher with great surprise. She had a pile of pig's tails. When I looked at her she said, "I will make a gourmet delight of these, I promise. It might even become one of your favorites."

"Yes, mother, one of my least favorites."

Dinner tonight delighted Anja, who gleefully sucked on the little gelatinous segments of the tails. My father and I had to admit that there was apparently nothing that my mother couldn't make delectable, even though we all agreed that areas above the tail were more appreciated. The boiled potatoes and carrots tonight were delicious as always. After this we knew that mother must have had a surprise up her sleeve for the upcoming Thanksgiving, Anja's birthday, and Christmas dinner.

THANKSGIVING DINNER WAS A MEDLEY OF HOLIDAY standards along with some unexpected surprises. Mother's horseshoe at the butcher surreptitiously delivered two ducks for our table. Mother was so good at roasting them; it seemed a crime to cut into them, they looked so perfect. After the roasted potatoes and vegetables made the rounds, my father stood and lifted his glass to toast everyone, with an additional mention to remember those who could not be present. He looked pointedly at me and smiled sadly before he sipped his wine. We eagerly cut into our share of the duck, but as we tasted it, the faces around the table took on a decidedly different flavor. Mother was aghast; the ducks had such a strong fishy taste that we couldn't eat it.

Daddy said, "I think you should leave your horseshoe home next time. I'd say these are wild ducks shot from some blind somewhere in the marshes by someone dealing in the black market. I'm sure they were costly, even with ration stamps, and most definitely to our enjoyment."

Mother looked down at her plate, coughing; she apologized for her misguided stealth. We laughed and toasted her with another glass of wine. She responded with good cheer, saying, "I hope the apples for the apple pie were not shot down from some tree out in the wilds." More laughter dissolved the duck issue.

In our family, one of the biggest food concerns was the availability of coffee. At the end of November, we were allowed just one pound every five weeks. My mother continued her ideas of stretching our food staples by buying one pound of chicory for every pound of coffee and blending the two. It not only stretched our supply, it was delicious. There would be more cutbacks to deal with as shortages of goods and food dictated.

Shortly after Thanksgiving, I wrote my first non-deliverable missive to Ernst.

December 1, 1942

My dearest Ernst,

I am still reeling from hearing your voice over the phone. I can't believe that you somehow managed to do that. "Where there is a will, there is a way." Your catch phrase says it all. It was so hard for me to hear your voice and not be able to see you. For a brief moment I felt that maybe this war was not all that terrible if you were still able to get a call through to me. But of course, I know the facts. Now I am sitting here with my eyes closed and remembering when you first held my hand, at the concert. I am sure I fell in love with you then.

I hope you are safe and well. It feels good to be back living with my parents, and I am forever grateful for all the help they are to me with Anja. She can be a handful at times, especially when she is determined about an issue. She is more beautiful than ever. She is so very talented as a musician; it will be interesting to see where that takes her later as an adult.

We have some food rationing, which has its ups and downs, such as when my mother came home with pigtails for dinner. My mother is an excellent cook and she made even this taste better than you might imagine. For Thanksgiving she felt especially favored when she came home with two ducks. They were beautifully roasted, but when we tasted our first bite, they tasted so strongly of fish we could not eat them. They must have come to her butcher from some unapproved source, likely one that operated in the foul marshlands outside of the city. We must not complain; I know there are people in Europe who are starving, who would have eaten these ducks with relish. I am so lucky to be here and home again where it is safe. I have only you to thank for that, my dearest.

Tonight, I send you all my love,

Karin

I slowly folded the letter and made room in my dresser drawer for it and the many others that were to follow.

December 12, 1942

My dearest Ernst,

Two days ago, we celebrated Anja's seventh birthday. I wish you could see her now; she is so smart and talented and beautiful. I hope you will be able to see her before much more time passes.

It is rather cold here today; I hear it is cold there as well. I go to a newsreel theater where I can see what is happening in some places in the world. Sometimes I hope that maybe I would see that the camera has caught you on film, but then that would mean you are a prisoner of war and I am not sure you would like that. If that were to happen, however, at least it would take you out of the war and so you would be safe.

Good night, darling,

Karin

Neatly folded, I placed it in the drawer with the first one. I wondered how many there would be before we were together again and could exchange them.

AT THE END OF DECEMBER 1942, WE HEARD THE DEVAS-
tating news that in 1942 German U-boats sank over one thousand
Allied cargo ships sailing in convoys in the Atlantic. We were told
this maritime massacre began on January 12 and continued mostly
unchecked all year. In the summer of 1942, the U-boats struck at
night on the surface, with guns and torpedoes sinking freighters and
oil tankers with shocking ease. Many of these ships were sunk within
sight of our shores. We were greatly saddened to know that so many
merchant seamen were lost in the effort to get goods and supplies
to our fighting allies in Europe. Why were we not able to stop these
U-boats that operated just off our eastern shores? There must be
a reason.

ALEX IN ENGLAND

TODAY THERE WAS a letter from Alex.

> December 30, 1942
>
> Dear Karin,
>
> I hope I get a letter from you soon, because I would welcome your news and anything about Greg that you can share. He is coming up short on letter writing.
>
> Yesterday I did my first flight over the English Channel. It looked peaceful enough from the English shoreline but once I was flying over the water, I could see that France is only some twenty-two miles away across the water, a jittery prospect to say the least. I dared not look at my knuckles. Today we have heavy overcast and rain; no flying, which means we have time for letter writing and beer drinking if nothing else. Some of the young ladies who were attracted by our RAF uniforms became less enthralled when they saw our Eagle Squadron shoulder patches that branded us as Americans. Of course, once we have said just a word or two they don't even need to see the patch to know who we are. They have a saying

about us, "You Yanks are overfed, overpaid, oversexed, and over here."

The last of those certainly applies to me—oh well, so be it.

I'm off now for one of those beers at the local pub before I pack it in for the night.

Warm regards,
Alex

January 5, 1943
Dear Alex,

It sounds like you are hard at work in and out of the classroom. Socializing sounds a bit slim, but I guess when you're that tired, sleep is more attractive.

I'm hard at work doing my bit for the war effort, as are so many others. With so many men away, women are taking up the slack in all fields. I hope that Greg is not called up; he is in his residency at the hospital and he won't be fully qualified until he has completed it.

Anja looks forward to this year in school and new challenges in her music. She is amazing in all aspects. Motherhood is an eye opener for me, just when I think I have understood her latest phase, she enters a new one for me to decipher, and few clues are offered.

It has been cold here, and a bowl of hot soup after standing in line to board an already crowded bus after work makes soup something I look forward to.

I hope you are being fed well to help ward off your bouts with the cold and damp. Before I get into a warm tub, I want to look over Anja's homework so we can both rest easy.

Until next time,
Karin

In late January, while I was eating my breakfast, the radio announced the first U.S. bombing raid on Germany at Wilhelmshaven. I looked it up in the atlas and was relieved to see that it was not near Berlin or Cologne. At the same time, I had concerns for Alex. This morning when I went to work it was with a heavy heart, thinking that it might have been one of my passed crystals that aided the air raid. I have to find a mindset that will not drive me crazy so that I can find some peace in all of this, but I can only wonder if there is such a mindset.

I REALIZED IN LATE MARCH THAT I HAD NOT WRITTEN A letter to Ernst in some time. On the other hand, within a five-day period German U-boats sank twenty-seven of our merchant ships. I simply cannot pick up that pen.

New Moves for Anja and Other News

WE MET WITH MR. SOMES to hear his views on Anja's progress. He felt that she needed a well-rounded, concerted program of study. Mr. Somes had spoken with the people at a conservatory that accepted outstanding young students. He asked our permission to set up an appointment with them to discuss her entrance.

In addition to the constant issue of money, I was concerned about her age and the impact that such a focused program might have on her emotionally. Mr. Somes suggested having a trial period, which made good sense.

We had an appointment to meet them with Anja for her entrance audition. As we waited, Anja patiently wove her fingers in and out as a distraction until we were led into a room with a piano. She was invited to play anything that she especially liked. While she played, the two people who were observing made notes on a clipboard. Then they asked her to play something of their choosing. When they gave her the sheet music, my father said that Anja did not sight read. He asked if he could play it through once for her, at which time Anja would play the piece. They looked at each other skeptically, and then nodded their approval. When he was finished, my father got up and let Anja sit at the piano. She sat for a moment, and then played it flawlessly. They made more notes and then asked us a few questions.

One major concern was that she did not sight read, but they were impressed that she was able to play it after just hearing it, let alone hearing it just once. We went into an office where they told us they were interested in having her as a student in their youth program, which met every Saturday.

I was so relieved to hear that she could still stay in her school; I had worried what would have happened if she were separated from Benji all week long. I'm not sure she understood what her going to the conservatory meant. My father worried about the pressure she might feel in this august environment. As it turned out, every Saturday Anja happily marched into the conservatory with my father in tow and was treated to a new divergence of her musical abilities. She accomplished it with great relish, and I think she sensed the pleasure of her teachers as well. I was thankful once again for a scholarship in the youth program. I think my father was proud and a bit relieved that she was in this program rather than limited by what he or Mr. Somes could teach her.

Anja kept up her school studies, perhaps only because doing her homework and practicing without fail meant she could spend time with Benji.

I wasn't sure where all this was going, but I hoped I would be up to the task to support her, whatever it turned out to be.

THE BATTLE FOR THE ATLANTIC TURNED AROUND IN May, with the Germans now being the hunted, but there was still a heavy cost to men and supplies. Thank goodness that Ernst is not a submariner. Between April and June 1943, we sank 100 U-boats due to improved technology, and the Germans finally gave up the Atlantic wolf pack hunts.

ONE EVENING WHILE OUT AT DINNER WITH AARON, HE started talking about the inconsistencies in life. I couldn't help but think he was talking about me when he said, "Funny, isn't it, how we can become innocently yet deeply involved in something, just because life has put it in our path?" I nodded as I took a sip of my wine, thinking how that is exactly what happened with Anja and Ernst, innocently, yet now deeply involved in my life.

Today I watched the newsreels, which showed German and Italian troops surrendering in North Africa. The British bombed the Ruhr. Dönitz suspended U-boat operations in the North Atlantic. It appeared that the Germans were losing their grip as the aggressors in some areas. I was especially happy over the news of the U-boat suspension in the North Atlantic. Hopefully more of our convoys would make it over safely with the supplies and men needed by the Allies. I hoped desperately that this might lead to a winding down of the war, though I feared it was only a time to regroup for its continuation, since the Germans still had an encompassing foothold in Europe.

While the tide had turned, and the Allies were winning sea battles to some degree, it came at the tragic cost of fifty thousand merchant seamen who lost their lives, while seven out of ten German U-boat crews never made it back to base. It was only after the war that we learned that, of the forty thousand German U-boat mariners who went to war, thirty thousand never returned home. The lost lives among Allied pilots and their crews were still to be counted, along with the land forces and the navy. The civilian losses would be higher.

I hoped that all of this death and devastation would leave a more peaceful world for Anja to grow up in, one where she would never have to give her child away to keep him or her safe.

Sometimes I still saw her father as he stood by the counter in the book shop, chatting as if to just pass the time, when all the while he was sizing me up for Anja. How little I knew, and in some respects still do.

TODAY ANJA DISPLAYED A NEW ASPECT OF HER AUTODIdactic abilities. I came home from work to find Anja and my mother at the kitchen table with apples all over the kitchen table. Anja held a whole apple in front of her, and she asked my mother to cut another apple in half. Anja asked her to cut another one into quarters, and so on until one of the apples was reduced to sixteen pieces. Anja knew the words but not the concept of them, so she had found a way to visually imprint on her memory the value of musical notes as they related to each other and the whole. It was surprising that she developed this concept. She was smarter than I ever was at her age, when I too, had trouble with numbers, but of course she couldn't have inherited it from me. She was an amazing seven-year-old, and my mother agreed because Anja had made it possible for us to have an apple pie. As my mother wryly pointed out, "It will give her another chance to ingest and digest the numbers." We were all happy with Anja's accomplishment.

Happy News

ON A SUNDAY IN JUNE, Greg called to ask if he could stop by with a visitor. When he arrived, his guest was Dr. Grace Hamilton, Anja's pediatrician. They came in and we stood there for an expected moment before Greg introduced Grace to my parents. When mother showed them into the living room, Greg announced, "I want you to be the first to hear that Grace and I are engaged!"

Congratulations flooded the air. My mother said, "I hope you know, Greg, we consider you as part of the family, and it now seems as if the family has just grown. I love big families! Welcome to ours, Grace."

My father said, "This calls for a glass of wine, as least." My father is the family dispenser of spirits, which he offers with enthusiasm to anyone whether their state may be high or low.

After a glass of wine, Greg said, "I'm taking my fiancé out for a celebratory dinner, and then I'll go and write the good news to Alex. I'm glad you have met each other and can share in my happiness with this lovely, lovely lady."

Sad News

IN JULY, WHEN I CAME HOME from taking Anja to play at Benji's, I came into the kitchen and saw Greg at the table with my mother standing by his side. She had her hand on his shoulder as he wept behind his hands over a paper on the table. As I look at the troubled scene, my father came over to me and with his arm around my shoulders led me into the living room. He softly said, "Greg just got a telegram to say that Alex has been killed."

I heard the words, but they did not register. I stared at the floor, unable to react. My father sat me down on the couch, then he sat next to me without speaking. Eventually he said, "Let's hope it was quick. The telegram doesn't have anything to say of the details except that he was killed in action in the performance of his duty. We hope we will hear more, but probably should not expect to, given the times and conditions." My father hugged my shoulders and said, "I'll leave you to absorb the news in privacy."

He got up and walked back to the kitchen. I sat there wondering why I did not have an outburst of tearful sorrow. I thought perhaps it was because I could not believe it; he felt as alive as ever to me. I had a barrier of disbelief that the news could not surpass. I went into the kitchen where my father was pouring some stiff portions of scotch.

Greg stood and put his arm around me, saying, "It wasn't supposed to happen this way. His craving for adventure should have seen him into a long and happy life. He often said how grounded he felt with you, and yet he knew at the same time that he was out of your league for anything permanent. He did love you in his own way, Karin. I'm glad he knew you and that you trusted him as far as you did."

My father handed each of us a glass as Greg sat down again. He said, "He was my kid brother, and for the first time that I can remember, he was excited about something when he joined the air force, more than anything he had ever done before. I even tried to discourage him from doing that, but he was determined. He has paid a terrible price, and I wish I had been more persuasive with him, but now none of that matters."

My father poured more scotch and said, "You can't blame yourself even in the slightest for his decision. He did what he wanted to do, and it made him feel fulfilled. You have to honor that, Greg. He would have wanted you to."

My mother tried to lighten the mood by offering to make us some hot food.

Greg shook his head. "Thank you, Mrs. Wilson, but I need to go back to the hospital. Grace was in a patient conference, so I couldn't talk to her then, but I need to see her now. Thank you anyway." He gave my mother and me a hug. He gripped my father's upper arm as they shook hands, and he said, "Thank you for the shoulder and the scotch."

"We're all here for you, Greg. Take care."

A FEW DAYS LATER, RIGHT AFTER LUNCH, MR. HOLLOWAY jumped up on a table and said, "I want you all to hear this. I have good news. Our production quota numbers are in for June, and you met them. Congratulations! Now let's see if we can top those for July. We want to keep up a steady supply so our young men in their flying machines can keep talking and listening without a pause. Thank you all." Then he clapped his outstretched hands to us as if he were herding chickens. "Let's get back to it, folks!"

I sat at my workstation and felt a lump in my throat as I thought of Alex. I wanted to know more than just that he was killed in action. I wanted to know where and how he had died. Just then I felt Mr. Holloway behind me. He asked, "Is there a problem, Karin?"

"No, thank you." As I lifted the first crystal under my magnifying glass, I thought about how Alex would not be using another crystal. My vision doubled, I blew my nose, and dabbed at my eyes, and then I focused again on the crystal under the searing examination light.

The memory of Winston Churchill, when he spoke before The House of Commons in 1940, came to mind: "Never in the field of human conflict, was so much owed by so many to so few." He was referring to the RAF fighter and bomber command efforts to defend Britain from persistent German attacks. He paid a great tribute to men like Alex who had given their lives for a cause that meant so much to so many. We later heard that the RAF Costal Command that was in charge of protecting convoys flew more than 80,000 sorties.

BECAUSE GRACE WAS ON DUTY IN THE HOSPITAL, GREG was free to eat with us. My father went to get Chinese takeout. When he came back with more than half a dozen boxes, my mother said, "No wonder the Chinese are starving; it's all over here." Mother made tea and we ate our way through carton after little white carton of Chinese food. Each box had the name of the dish written on the top in Chinese. My father read them off to us in imaginative Chinese to our delighted applause; it was just what we needed to lighten our spirits. When we were done eating, he produced a handful of fortune cookies. We each took one and read it aloud. Greg's fortune read, "You will soon have a light heart." My father's read, "You have family blessings," while my mother's read, "You will make much of little." We laughed. And mine announced, "You will meet a tall, dark handsome stranger." To which I said, "Thank you, but I already have!"

SAD MISSIVE

SOME WEEKS LATER I received a registered letter from the U.S. government informing me that, as beneficiary of a life insurance policy from Alex Forman, formerly of the U.S. Air Force, I may now redeem this policy with the enclosed check for ten thousand dollars. I was shocked at the amount. It was a great fortune for me, to be sure, but at the same time I wondered if the U.S. government deemed ten thousand dollars as the total value of a man's life. Being reminded of Alex's death and the check amount, both had me in suspended disbelief. Alex had never mentioned the amount of his policy, but this huge amount of money could make a big difference in Anja's life, and to some extent in mine.

I wanted to be sure that Alex had talked to Greg about this in more detail than he had written to me. I left several messages for Greg to call me, and when I finally spoke to him about it, Greg was in total agreement and he did know the amount.

"As a doctor I know that I will never want for a meal or a roof over my head, so I hope you will have some of the same assurances now."

My shoulders drooped with the weight of this benefit. "I feel guilty about having this."

"Please don't. It was his wish—he wanted you to have it, and so do I. End of discussion, Karin. Now, I have to get back to work, we will be in touch."

I too had to get back to work, and two days later as I sat at my workstation I suddenly broke into tears. My crying brought Mr. Holloway over, who then called Edna from the office over to me. Mr. Holloway sat at my place and worked to keep the flow going. She walked me into the empty lounge and tried to comfort me. I struggled with the idea that I would never again see or hear from Alex. Meeting him and going to Prague with him, which resulted with Anja and Ernst being in my life, was a deep connection between us. Without him in my life, none of the rest would have happened. We certainly weren't a love match, but there was a friendship there, even with its ups and downs. I think getting that check was the tangible proof that made me realize I had only memories of him left, that he was gone forever. It hit me all at once, as I realized while working on the crystals, that he would never need one again.

Edna made me a cup of tea and asked if she could help in any way. When I told her what happened to Alex, she said, "Not all of our radio crystals find their way home with our pilots, but it's what we do and what they do that matters. Karin, stay here and rest for a bit, and when you feel up to it, going back to work will surprise you. You may well find you have a renewed energy now for all those unknown airmen who now need what you do."

She squeezed my arm and left me alone. I drew strength for her comment and from the strength in her. I washed my face with cold water and went back to work; I worked without emotion, only a drive to produce what was so sorely needed.

A week later I deposited most of the insurance money in Anja's savings account, keeping enough aside to pay for larger expenses, one being tuition for a private summer music camp for young gifted musicians in the Catskill Mountains. She would stay away at this camp, away from Benji and me for a few weeks in the summer, at a time when she was ready to do that.

It was good to come home today to my parents and Anja. Their company comforted me. That evening I wrote one of those letters to Ernst.

> August 1943
>
> My dearest Ernst,
>
> Tonight, I wish I could lie in your arms and not feel anything except your love.
>
> Today I was inconsolable over the death of a friend who was a pilot in the air force. He was killed over the English Channel. His name was Alex Forman, and he left me a legacy that touched me deeply. I will use it for Anja's well being and future needs as she grows up.
>
> I feel guilty that I am only talking about myself, even when my thoughts for your safety worry me greatly. How I wish we could actually send our letters to each other now, so I could dwell on the loving comfort of your words. The ones you know are the ones I need!
>
> Good night, my darling,
> Karin

The weeks and months moved slowly for me now, and if it weren't for Anja and my parents, I would surely be more depressed. Anja and Benji were so inventive in each other's lives. They did their homework together and played together, never tiring of each other.

There were times when Anja played some of her favorite music for Benji, and he simply sat and watched her with interest; I think he was as astounded by her talent and ability as the rest of us were.

I STAYED AWAY FROM THE NEWSREEL THEATERS FOR A long while, unsure whether I could handle the sights that the newsreels showed. Eventually I did go, and I saw an Allied air raid create a firestorm in Hamburg. More recent newsreels showed Germans evacuating Sicily and American daylight air raids repeated on two cities in Germany. They also included a short clip of the winners in a dog show in England. It must be events like this that keep the people's spirits from flagging in their otherwise perilous times.

Saturday at dinner, my father said he had a little talk with one of Anja's teachers at the conservatory. "As skilled as she is in playing back a piece after hearing it only once, she must apply herself to sight reading. As she is doing it now, she only sees that 'the notes go up or down,' as she puts it. The instructor suggested that it would be a big help if I helped her with that at home."

He continued, "Neither Anja nor I look forward to this, knowing her resistance from all the previous attempts we have made. She will do it in her own time, I'm sure."

Doing It

IN A WEAK moment I thought of asking Benji to use his method of instruction with Anja. At that point I hadn't dismissed the idea of involving him, given how well it worked in the past. Who am I to argue with success?

November came upon us quickly, and mother and I are once again thinking of the holidays. Thanksgiving will have to go by the ration books. A turkey is almost entirely out of the question, especially since my mother decided to skip the offerings of our butcher. One day she saw him leaning on the edge of the scale with his prominent belly to increase a customer's meat weight. He was caught by the customer, but my mother had already decided to take her business elsewhere.

The new butcher was more principled when he told mother he was putting people's names in his book for turkey orders. We would have to wait to see what was available to him, and thus to us, closer to the holiday. As it turned out, we got lucky and were given a young turkey. My mother and I knew how to make the most that of on Thanksgiving.

THE ACE CRYSTAL LAB FACILITY RAN DAY AND NIGHT, holiday or not. Charlie once again took my shift on Thanksgiving, so I could be at home, while Sally continued to struggle for perfections on her shift.

This year we had Grace at our table along with Greg, as well as Benji and his father. Aaron and Greg gave us bottles of a good wine, with which my father toasted all of us. Once again, he made a special toast to those absent from our table tonight but not from our hearts. When he sat down, mother quickly announced that to avoid any possible hunger at the end of the dinner, she made an apple pie and a pecan pie, which was greeted with moans of appreciation. After dinner Anja gave us a little concert; you could have heard a pin drop, everyone was in awe of her talent and ability. Despite the heaviness in our hearts, we still had so much to be thankful for this Thanksgiving.

ON DECEMBER 10, 1943, ANJA TURNED EIGHT. I GREETED this event with mixed feelings, simply because she was growing up so quickly, too quickly. We had a lovely dinner of her choice: roasted chicken, baked potatoes, a salad of tomatoes and onions, and of course birthday cake. Mother and I made a fanciful cake in the shape of a piano keyboard. With white frosting we marked the keys, and we cut up licorice sticks for the black keys. We placed eight candles, one on each of the octaves, and two more at the ends of the key-board. She was thrilled and laughed so much she could hardly blow out the candles. She did manage it, however, and these candles were not saved. For her birthday she wanted a new dress and a white pin-afore to go over it. This time it was my choice, and she loved it—her wish was granted, and she was even happier that Benji liked her dress and pinafore. He gave her hair barrettes and a zipped leather pencil case. Aaron gave a generous gift of two tickets for a piano concert at Carnegie Hall. My mother gave her a purse, her first handbag, and when she opened it she found a new one dollar bill in it, a small comb, a mirror, and a hankie. My father gave her some blank music notebooks and some special pencils to notate notes with. Hannah was nursing a bad cold so had stayed at home, but with Benji and Aaron she had sent two beautifully illustrated books about an eight-year-old girl who sought adventures. Greg gave her a card that said, "When we both are free, I invite you out to dinner in a restaurant of your choice, just the two of us." She loved that. Grace gave her a diary book with a little key, explaining that she can write all her secrets in it and no one will ever see it, because she can lock them up. Anja raised her eyebrows and with a special smile said, "I think I know a few." At that, I wished I did too.

CHRISTMAS IN 1943 WAS A QUIET AFFAIR, BUT NOT WITH-out the joy of having the children decorate the tree and baking cook-ies. Benji had permission from his dad to come to church with us on Christmas Eve. He and Anja entertained themselves during the Swedish part of the service. We had been given music sheets with the music and the words to the carols, and when the singing began, Anja began to sing, but Benji, not knowing them, did not. I heard Anja say to Benji, "It's easy, just listen to the music and sing the words, and when the black notes on top of them go up, you sing high, and when they go down you sing low." He looked at her and laughed. Then she said, "Now, sing, do it!" He giggled, and followed her instructions after her second command of, "Do it!"

Benji, Aaron, and Hannah were invited for Christmas din-ner as well. My mother made a pork roast, then thinking that not everyone would eat pork she managed some roast chicken as well, but as it turned out the chicken remained untouched We had a nice evening and Benji even asked Anja to play for us. It was touching to see how proud he is of her.

As 1943 drew to a close, I thought about how Ernst and I had been unable to share a word between us for the past two years. The war seemed endless, and at times I dared not wonder whether he was still alive. So many lives had been lost on both sides already, and it would continue until this terrible war ended. These days when I go to work and when I turn that harsh light on, I become an automaton; I do not allow my feelings to surface.

This year we spent New Year's Eve at home as usual. My father said, "I hope this will be a happier new year for all of us, both here and overseas." We hugged each other and then sat quietly into 1944.

1944

MY FATHER'S WISH was not to be, however, as we heard that the Germans and the Allies were still fighting it out in Italy. It went on and on, and then in March we heard that the German army had invaded Hungary.

Today it was recorded that the British had dropped 3,000 tons of bombs during an air raid on Hamburg, Germany. First, they dropped explosive bombs that blew off the roofs of houses, then they bombed the water mains, and then they dropped incendiary bombs that created a massive firestorm, incinerating thousands of people. Scenes that defy beliefs. The report did not say the number of lives it cost flying the planes, except that we have come to know those numbers are the costs of war as well. No peace was in sight.

ANJA WAS DOING WELL IN SCHOOL AND MY FATHER continued to take her to the conservatory every Saturday morning. She had learned to sight read some, and she was making great strides in her studies there. I wished I were back studying at school again, but that would stay on hold as long as the war effort was on.

I was almost looking forward to my birthday in May this year, thinking that I would have more than one martini to replace an otherwise lacking glow. Turning twenty-seven was nothing to howl about it, nor was being unmarried and having a daughter with no prospects of giving her a father and me a husband. I thought I should be allowed to emit at least one banshee howl. I still had two months to consider that.

Tonight Aaron invited me out for "An evening on the town," as he put it.

We had dinner and then he took me to a nightclub for drinks and dancing. Before the first sip of our martinis, he raised his glass to me and said, "To us!"

I felt a slight smile on my face, and all I could say was, "Yes, we seem to do a lot of this, I've noticed."

"No, not nearly enough," he replied.

We watched couples dancing, and soon he extended his hand as an invitation to dance. I took a large sip of my martini and followed him to the dance floor. The band launched into a new number without pausing at the end of the last one. Aaron extended his arms to me, and we stepped into the music of *Heart and Soul*. I knew the lyrics, and they were all about Ernst and me. Now I wished I had finished that martini to help me through this, but I hadn't, and so it didn't. I felt a lump in my throat as I tried to make my feet obey the music, to make myself obey the reality of whom I was dancing with. I couldn't explain why I went out with Aaron; he wanted it to lead to something more, but I didn't. I feared that it speaks poorly of me to suggest hope where there was none.

WE HEARD ON THE NEWS THAT JUNE 6, 1944, WILL BE known as a day in world history unlike any other. We sat close to our radios to hear of the Allied invasion of some 160,000 troops who had stormed the beaches of Normandy, France. In doing so, they had to run past their own wounded and pass over their dead comrades lying among the deadly German Atlantic Wall structures on the beaches. Some French people in the seaside houses watched in disbelief as landing barges disgorged wave after wave of Allied soldiers into the raging waters, only to be gunned down by the Germans on top of the high bluffs. There was carnage everywhere, in the water, near the water's edge, and on the beaches. Few Allied soldiers had made it through unscathed.

Later we learned that this heroic landing came at a horrific human cost. More than seventeen thousand Allied soldiers were killed, wounded or went missing during the battle for Normandy, as were some nine thousand German troops. Some 12,200 French civilians had died as well, and many more were severely wounded. This was just the beginning: the human price paid to fight for freedom from tyranny was astronomical!

I knew then that they were on their way to Ernst. I said a prayer for all of them.

Later in June we heard other frightening news. Hitler had poised 3,350 tanks and 650,000 horses on the Soviet frontier. A massive invasion was feared. I hoped once again that the fighting might deescalate in Western Europe—after all how could Hitler maintain two major fronts at the same time? By 1944 Germany failed to manufacture the trucks and jeeps needed to mobilize her troops, while the U.S. and British forces were well equipped for troop movements. It also came down to the ever-changing number of troops.

Another hot day in July drove me into the air-conditioned newsreel theater. Today I saw lines and lines of the many hundreds of enemy prisoners of war, trudging in despair toward an unknown destiny, while Allied troops on the same road walked and drove in the opposite direction, to where the prisoners had come from, unknown destinations for the Allies as well. Only once did the camera catch the faces of a few German officers, but Ernst was not among them.

The next reel had me stiffen myself in my seat as the reel entitled 'Marching to the Tune of the Collaborators.' The title was superimposed over a scene of some half-naked women being marched down the center of a city street. The narrator told us these were the women charged with collaborating sexually with German soldiers. They were called *Collaboration Horizontale* in France, and as soon as the Allies freed a town from the Germans, self-appointed vigilantes of the town took the defenseless women and shaved their heads and painted a swastika on their foreheads and then pushed them to walk the cordon of their town's people, who shouted and laughed as they humiliated them. In other places, these women were dragged into city squares and had their hair shaved off in front of jeering crowds, then stripped naked or nearly so. They often had swastikas painted on them as well before being beaten up. Seeing this, I wondered whether I, too, would have had to endure this if I had stayed in Prague. It sent a shudder through me. I had read that many of the women granted sexual favors to the German military, particularly the officers, who had money and access to foodstuffs. Many of these women had children whose cries of hunger haunted them, their husbands either off at war or killed or imprisoned during an occupation and no longer there to care for their families. Among them, to be sure, were some prostitutes simply plying their trade equally. A mother does whatever she has to do to save her children, and this is what many of them were guilty of. At the time, there was little intervention on their behalf. While many people condemned this treatment later on, they had done nothing at the time, even while they were sympathetic to the women, even as some of the women carried babies in their arms or held onto their young children. It was only much later that it came to light that this abuse was doled out to at least twenty thousand women in France alone. The real number was probably much higher, because it was estimated that members of the *Wehrmacht* had fathered eighty thousand children just with French mothers. We learned much later, after the war had ended, that across Europe German occupiers fathered eight hundred thousand children. They were children of war, not to be ignored.

I SURVIVED TURNING TWENTY-SEVEN A FEW MONTHS ago, but what I did not survive well was what I saw one day in late July, when the heat was so intense I again went into the nearest Trans Lux newsreel theater to escape the heat. In the dark, air-conditioned interior, I saw a film of a greater darkness that made my blood run cold. Films of piles of bodies discovered in Nazi concentration camps and ovens with half-burned corpses as the Allied soldiers entered the first of these camps and searched for survivors. This camp was just one of many later discovered by the Allies. I looked at the screen and wondered if Anja's father was among them. Suddenly I felt a welling up of my insides and light-headedness, and I knew that I was going to be sick to my stomach. I ran toward the Ladies room, but I had only made it as far as the lobby when I became sick. An attendant came over to me and put his hand on my shoulder and said, "You're not the first this has happened to." He got me a glass of water and told me to rest and not to see the rest of the films.

When I came out of the theater I took a taxi home, not trusting my legs to get me home without further incident. No one was home when I got there; I was relieved, because I could not speak of what I had seen. I went into my bedroom and took the photo of Ernst, Anja, and me off my dresser. In doing so, I saw for the first time what he had written on the back, "My dear little family, Prague, 1939." I put it in my drawer and closed it as the tears ran down my face and onto my hands that were pressing the drawer shut. I wished I were someone else—anyone else, just not me. I felt that I was destroying something beautiful in my life, as the beauty of those many thousands of lives had been destroyed, and their survivors were never to see or feel the same about a German or his country ever again. I poured myself a daddy-sized scotch and sat at the kitchen table. I waited for I don't know what to change in myself, if it ever could. Having seen those camps left an irreconcilable hole in my heart where Ernst once was. Will I ever be able to let him fill it again, if even just in memory?

Just then happy laughing sounds entered the apartment. They sounded surreal compared to what I was feeling. My parents and Anja were the only sounds and sights that could heal me. My father said, "I see you had a running start without me. Are you all right?" All I could do was to shrug my shoulders. "Ah, one of those days," he said.

TODAY ANJA ASKED TO BORROW ONE OF MY HAIR BANDS. I told her which drawer they were in but by accident she opened the wrong one, the one with my letters to Ernst and the photo of the three of us. When she turned the photo over she saw, "My dear little family, Prague, 1939." She came to me in the kitchen and held the photo out to me, asking, "Is this my papa?"

"No, dear, you know that is Uncle Ernst."

"Do you have any pictures of my papa?"

I was still good at fabrications, and I said, "No, Anja, not a single one. The house we were living in burned down with everything we owned. I had been out food shopping with you and when I came home I saw the house in flames. All I had with me was you and some groceries."

"Is that how my papa died?"

"No, dear, he died early in the war and we never saw him again."

"Did he love me?"

"Oh, yes, he loved you so very much, more than anyone else in the world, he told me that many times."

"Did he love you, too?"

"I'm sure he did."

"I wish I had a picture of him."

"You do, Anja. Every time you look in the mirror, you will see your father's beautiful face and eyes, you look so much like him."

"I do? I'm so happy."

"So am I, every time I look at you."

"Mama, which color hair band should I wear? The red one, or the purple one with the sparkles on it?"

"I think you should choose sparkles. It matches your personality."

She laughed and put the red one and photo back in their drawers. At times it takes so little to assuage a large heavy issue in a young child; they can move on more easily than we can as adults. I was so thankful that the letter from her father was safely in the bank and not in my drawer, because there could not have been an alternative explanation for that. This was not the time in her life or mine for that disclosure.

349

THESE JULY DAYS WERE EVEN HOTTER AT ACE CRYSTAL Lab. We did not have air conditioning, and we could not use fans because such air circulation might blow dust particles onto the crystals being worked on. I worked a lot of overtime lately to cover when Charlie was rehearsing with his Dixieland band for an engagement. By the time I left work my eyes were smarting from the sharp glare of the hot examining light. When I got home my mother placed cold cucumber slices over my closed lids. I think I heard them sigh with relief.

The best part of next week would be on Sunday, when we were all going to hear Anja play in a recital at the conservatory. My mother as usual had a program of preening for Anja, and now Anja had a few ideas of her own, one included my purple hair band. Anja insisted the stage lights would enhance the sparkle while mother tried to convince her that she was the sparkle. I let them verbally duke it out to nearly both their satisfactions. That is how this family did things, a problem that might surface was talked and worked into the ground and buried in favor of an amicable solution. Anja was a new mix in this, one to be reconciled with on her occasional vociferous outcry of injustice, at which time our family court usually rested its case.

Today, when she came out on stage, Anja kept her eyes on the floor and walked with purpose to the side of the piano. It felt as though I were seeing another Anja. She faced the audience briefly, then turned and sat down. For a moment she just went to that place where this all comes from in her, as if to summon it; then she was all business, and she put her hands on the keys and began to play. She had no music in front of her. It was all in her head and heart, and she was totally transported to the point that I thought perhaps she actually became the music itself. My mother was right; she did sparkle to greatness in her playing. Hearing her play, I never stopped wondering what might come of her talent, to what heights might she rise and where might it take it her. She was eight years old then, and so relaxed about it all. After the recital, some adults approached her, waiting to speak to her while she was overexcited about a wrist gardenia that Benji had given her and helped her put it on over her hand. These hands of hers that played with a feeling that came from some great depth in her that only she was privy to, all this seemed to fall away when it came to Benji, whom she saw as the great sparkle in her life.

Benji's dad, seeing the people waiting to speak to her, tried to have Benji step to his side, but Anja held onto to his hand and kept sniffing the heady fragrance of the gardenia. A few people leaned over and spoke to her and gave her some flowers, and she was surprised and thrilled by this. But not once did she let go of Benji's hand. I caught my mother's eye, and we both raised our eyebrows at the scene and smiled. My mother came over to me while all this was going on and said in my ear, *"Ein Wunderkind!"* I knew of course what that meant, and my mother had put her finger on it perfectly. The German saying made me wish that Ernst were at my side and loving her as much as we did. At that thought I was distracted enough to have missed the further activities. Eventually I saw my mother putting Anja's jacket over her shoulders and I heard Aaron say he wanted to treat us all in celebration of Anja's recital. My father was still talking to one of her teachers when he waved to me to come over. He introduced me to this teacher. As he shook my hand he said, "Thank you, Mrs. Wilson, for sharing your lovely daughter with us. She is a treat to teach and constantly surprises me."

"Thank you, at times I think I have little to teach her any more, and yes, she surprises me as well, a surprise gift to be sure." We both laughed and then said our farewells. There was a little breeze in the air, just enough to be refreshing, on this heady evening sparkled by Anja.

JULY TURNED OUT TO BE A MONTH OF UNEXPECTED events; another German military attempt to assassinate Hitler has failed. Not all prayers get answered.

As American soldiers landed on the island of Guam in the Pacific, short newscasts described their desperate attempts to drive out the Japanese. Surely the worst of it was kept from us as the fighting and dying continued unabated as they moved from one island to another of the Japanese-held Pacific Islands. We were being stretched for men and materials on two fronts and our war bond drives continued aggressively in reminder of those efforts, along with the pleas for blood donations. I signed on as a Red Cross Blood Donor card member; every eight weeks I gave a pint. I just wished my mother would forgo the liver and onions on those days.

In lieu of letters from Ernst, I have been in regular attendance at the newsreel theaters. We were introduced to Operation Cobra, the Allied breakout past Normandy. Where was Ernst? Was he still in France? If so, I feared even more for his life. We had no further news of the Allied advance. It will come, I am sure, but at what cost?

Today, after all these months of seeing each other at Ace Crystal, Charlie told me he had a brother fighting in the Pacific theater of war, which widened as one island after the other was engaged in heaving fighting. Prayers were in order for our men, who not only had to fight the Japanese, but the jungle heat and the ever present danger of Malaria, along with diseases and debilitating dysentery, all of which diminished a man's fighting strength. But they went on and on despite the drawbacks.

I turned to one of my drawbacks as I wrote:

July 28, 1944

Dear Ernst,

How I wish I knew where you were right now. I hope you are safe and away from the fighting that is going on in places in France. It is hot here and today when I came home from work Anja had me lie down while she put a cold wet cloth on my face, saying, "It is body air conditioning!" She is so sweet and thoughtful. She even said that when my father takes her out for an ice cream, she will get one for me, too. All I need now is you and our little family will be complete. I hope that you have time to read the sonnets I sent you, and that they are "surviving the rigors of military life." My dearest, I hope you are as well. I often imagine what our life will be like together, maybe we'll have a little boy with blue eyes and as handsome as you. All I want is you!

Take care and be well my dearest,

Karin

I now have to flatten the pile in my drawer with each new addition.

New Adventures

WE PACKED A PICNIC lunch today and made an exodus from the heat of the city streets into the shade of Central Park. We found a nice sheltered spot and spread our picnic blanket, breathing the cleaner, cooler air before we ate. Benji was with us and ate his first liverwurst sandwich. We enjoyed rusticating outside our usual kitchen table meal times. My father cleverly offered us some well chilled white wine from his thermos bottle, as drinking in public was otherwise not in fashion. After lunch, Benji and Anja hunted for little grass daisies. When they came back to the blanket, Anja made a little wreath of them and they took turns wearing it. I rested back on my elbows, and upon closing my eyes I was back in Prague on another blanket in another park, savoring the words, "I am falling in love with you and I don't know how to stop it." I rolled over onto my side and felt a deep longing. I wished I could hear him say those words again, with him next to me. I wished I knew where he was and what he was doing; perhaps for all concerned it was best I didn't know.

My days of crystal gazing are endless; I worked six days a week now, and on my Sundays off I just wanted to hide my eyes and myself behind sunglasses. I was getting enough sleep, all things considered, but there was a weariness in me that followed me throughout the week, such that on my Sundays off it is difficult to have the energy and the upbeat mood to enjoy spending the time with Anja. I felt that events surrounding the war had caught me up and were pulling me along without any consultation as to whether I was capable of handling what was being thrown at me. As I looked back over the last handful of years, it all had started when I left with Alex that morning to board the SS *Stimins*. I guessed the powers that be must have taken a page from Benji's book of instructions, the one that said, "Do it!"

MY FATHER TOLD ME THAT HE HAD ENTERED ANJA IN A citywide youth music competition. He hoped that I would approve of this, because he had already submitted the application. He described a series of prizes for winners. When I asked him what Anja thought about it, he said she had just shrugged and gone back to doing her homework.

I hesitated. "I'm not sure about this."

"Well, she doesn't seem to be either. I'll talk to her about it in more detail and we'll see."

"Daddy, I don't want her to be pressured into anything she doesn't want to do or doesn't understand the meaning of."

"No, of course not. It will be her decision all the way."

Anja didn't decline when this was all clarified with her, so on a hot Saturday morning early in August; we made our way to the competition venue. There were a lot of children with their parents, all a bit on edge in anticipation of the event. Anja sat with us and looked around and then at us and shrugged. Shrugging seems to be Anja's latest preferred reaction to an ambivalent opinion of anything.

A man came out on the stage and read off the names of the piano participants. When Anja heard her name, she looked at us and smiled and shrugged. So far, so good I thought.

They were called up one at a time, in alphabetical order. We had to sit through quite a few participants; she was the last and only W to be called up. I gave her a hug and said, "Have fun, darling."

She smiled and said, "I always do." She waved at my father as he blew her a kiss. Then she slid past me and walked up to the stage. The host shook her hand and introduced her to the audience, and then he walked her over to the piano. She looked up at him and smiled, and he nodded and walked away. Anja sat down at the piano and looked at the keys for longer than I thought was normal, then she put her hands over the keys and closed her eyes for a moment. She looked up and then down, as if her fingers had found their way from her memory and her heart, she leapt into a superb rendition of Mozart. When she was finished, she got up as the audience applauded and hurriedly walked to the wings. The host took her hand and walked her back to center stage for her applause, which had continued unabated as she first left the stage, then redoubled when she came back out. She looked around at the audience, and then she smiled and shrugged and made a little curtsy. She looked up at the host as if to say, Okay, I did it, now can I go? The host smiled and gestured that they could leave the stage. Our family sat there, once again in awe of our little girl, who harbored a gigantic talent that flowed from her as matter-of-factly as breathing . . . only she took everyone's breath away in doing it.

We watched as all the participants came out on stage and were again applauded. Each child was given a small bouquet of flowers and a card. They were then led off-stage to go to their parents to await the announcement of the winners. The judges in the front row consulted their notes and each other. It didn't take them long; in fact, just some minutes later the host appeared on stage to announce the winners.

"Every year when we hold this competition, it is so hard to choose from all the wonderful young musicians, but that is what a competition is about. This year it was even harder due to some bigger age differences than normal. So, I won't have you wait a moment longer to hear the outcome for this year."

The third- place prize was announced first, and it went to a boy who had played a trumpet piece wonderfully. Second prize was awarded to a girl who had played the violin. Both were older than Anja. Everyone held their breath as the host said with a happy voice, "And the first prize goes to Anja Wilson!" There was applause from everyone, even the non-winners, in recognition of her amazing talent.

"Would Anja Wilson please come up to receive her prize?" Anja and I looked at each other, and she just grinned and shrugged. I urged her to stand up, and I gave her a hug and said, "Sweetheart, you did it!" She laughed, and I nudged her to go up on stage for her prize. She squeezed past me to my father and took his hand, saying, "Come, Grandpa, we won a prize." I could see his eyes tear up as he took her hand. The two of them walked to the stage, and he left her to go up alone but stood close by and smiling he blew her a kiss. The host took her hand and walked her to center stage. He gave her a beautiful bouquet of flowers and announced the prize as a weekend visit to a summer music camp. She looked at the host and clapped excitedly, and then she clapped at the applauding audience. She gave the host a hug and ran to my father, finally showing more than a shrug's worth of joy.

Anja's first competition was over, and there would be more. When we came out, Benji and his father were standing by the door waiting. Tickets for the event had only been given to family members due to the size of the venue. As soon as we got through the doors, Anja said loudly, "I did it! I won!" Benji ran over to her and gave her a hug. My father positively glowed; he hadn't stopped smiling since the announcer had called Anja's name. My mother said to me, "What a *Wunderkind* you have there."

I replied, "No, Mother, *we* have here!"

When we got home, we put the flowers in water, and my mother and I laid out the spread of food we had prepared in anticipation of the event. Nobody was willing to admit it, but we all had expected that outcome. Benji and Anja went off and played as they always did. This talented little girl just did whatever came naturally to her, on and off stage. My father handed each of us a glass of cold beer, which he lifted to us and said, "Consider it champagne. Here's to our darling little Anja." I wished her parents and Ernst could have been with us, too; that would have miraculously turned the beer into champagne.

When I went back to work on Monday, I was still bursting with pride. I told Charlie about Anja's triumph, and he congratulated me on his way out the door. I sat down to discriminate between radio crystals that would either work a radio or would not. Here, there were no second- or third-place performers—they all had to be winners.

ON A FRIDAY, TWO WEEKS AFTER THE COMPETITION, Anja and I were on the train going to the music camp up in the Catskill Mountains. It was a beautiful ride through the lush emerald green mountains of New York. Anja was so excited she kept asking, "When will we be there?"

When we finally arrived, we were met by a Mr. Rosen, who told us how excited everyone was to meet Anja. He drove us to the camp office where we met Miss Connor, who ran the camp. She lost no time in telling us about this beautiful estate, which had been given by the owners as a memorial to their talented daughter who had died in an accident when she was young. Miss Connor said they felt fortunate to be able to share this beautiful setting with other talented young musicians. Mr. Rosen and Miss Connor drove us around the property, pointing out a tennis court and a swimming pool, after which they dropped us off at the guesthouse where Anja and I would be staying.

We had a lovely room with a bathroom, and there was a bay window that looked out over well-tended gardens. Anja was thrilled. Mr. Rosen came later and drove us to the dining hall, where Miss Connor introduced us to the campers, adding, "And we hope that Anja will feel up to playing for us tomorrow night in the auditorium." That came as a surprise and Anja smiled and shrugged. We were applauded and sat down at Miss Connor's table and had a nice dinner. After dinner, three girls about Anja's age came over to us and, introducing themselves, asked Anja if she would like to play with them. Anja looked at me for approval and I nodded. We followed them to the large veranda, where they played cat's cradle. It was new to Anja, but she caught on quickly with her nimble fingers and she had a lot of fun. I sat on a cushioned wicker chair and gazed over the velvety manicured green lawns, and I wished that Ernst were at my side. Just before sunset, the girls walked us back to the guesthouse. Anja's new friends gave her a hug and then ran off. Anja was happy. The guesthouse had some chairs and a swinging settee on the porch. Anja enjoyed this swing, humming some tunes as she rocked back and forth. As it got darker, some hungry mosquitoes found us and I decided it was time to go inside. Just before we went in, Anja pointed into the growing darkness and said, "Look, Mama! Look at that. What is it?" Fireflies had come out to dance in the night air.

"They are sometimes called lightning bugs or fireflies."

"I like lightning bugs better. How do they do that?"

"They have a small light in their tummy that they can turn on or off."

"Oh, how can they do that?"

"Come, dear. We can watch them from the bedroom window without being bitten by mosquitos." And thus, Anja learned that the beautiful and the not so beautiful lived side by side.

We slept well, and when Mr. Rosen came to take us to breakfast, he told us that the campers had free time to play or do whatever they liked on Saturday mornings until lunchtime. I walked to the pool with Anja, and we sat watching the children paddle around. There was a young lifeguard about 17 years old who kept a steady eye on the swimmers.

Anja looked pensive when she asked me, "I wonder what I should play tonight?"

"How about doing a shortened version of the piece you played for the competition?"

"Sure, I can do that." Anja was relaxed as she got up and walked to the pool's edge. She stood there; watching the swimmers, when suddenly a boy came running up to her back and, with both hands, pushed her into the pool. Anja had never been swimming before and she disappeared from sight. I ran over, kicking off my shoes and jumped in after her. I was frightened by what I saw, because she had made no attempt to surface. I grabbed her, and her eyes were closed, when suddenly the young lifeguard jumped in and took her from me. He hurried out of the pool with Anja and laid her face down on the grass. He turned her head to the side and began to work the water out of her. Anja coughed hard and then spit up water. The lifeguard carefully watched Anja, and then asked me if we were staying at the guesthouse. He carried her to the guesthouse and knew the room we were in. He sat her down and asked her if she was all right. She shook her head no, but the lifeguard smiled a little, which I took to be a good sign. He told me to give Anja a warm shower and wash the chlorine out of her hair and then to get her dry and warm and into bed. He would see to it that some saltines, hot broth, and some ginger ale were sent up to her, adding it will warm her and settle her stomach. I thanked him, and he left. I gave us both warm showers and got her into bed. She was shaken by what happened to her.

"I want to go home, Mama. I don't want to be here."

"Maybe you'll want to stay after you feel better."

"No, I want to go home."

Just listening to her and looking at her I could see how necessary that was.

Miss Connor came to us, most apologetic for what had happened.

"He is a troubled boy and has gotten into trouble here before, but never anything like this. I have called his parents to come and take him home."

"Miss Connor, I'm sorry to say that Anja wants to go home as well."

"I understand how she feels. I will give you a voucher so that she can come back any weekend she wishes to."

I packed up our wet clothes and we prepared to leave. Mr. Rosen took us to the two o'clock train back into the city.

Anja either rested with her head on my lap or sat holding my arm the whole trip home. I had called my father to tell him of our return, and he was there at the train station to meet us. She started to cry when she saw him, and when we got home she said, "I want to see Benji."

She cried when Benji walked in, and we heard her tell him, "I think I died." Those words shot through me. Now I wish Miss Connor had not told us about the family's little girl who had died. I wondered whether Anja may have identified with her. Then I thought that it might not have mattered that much, considering how frightening it would be to be shoved into the water that way. Anja slept in my bed that night and held onto my hair, two things she hadn't done in a long time.

In the days and weeks that followed, she became increasingly occupied with death and dying, so much so that I went to see Dr. Steinreich. When he heard what happened he said, "As for her being submerged in the pool, I can tell you there is something called the Reptilian Brain Response. When young children are submerged in water, especially cold water, this response sends signals throughout the body and brain, and these impulses are warnings that set into motion a powerful set of brain and body responses. It is automatic and tries to protect them from physical harm. It works when it can in young children, while awaiting rescue, so it sounds as though she was safer than you could know as a frightened mother. We can also thank that young lifeguard who put his training into practice. Now, having said that, we are still left with the question of Anja's growing concerns with death. I think her pool experience raised emotions in her over the death of her father. But I would like to see her soon, so she and I can talk about it."

Some days later I led her in to see Dr. Steinreich. When she came out of his office she had a small smile on her face, and I knew I had done the right thing to have him see her.

At dinner that evening she said that maybe when she is older she would take swimming lessons. I'm sure I had Dr. Steinreich to thank for that result. My mother said, "We'll have to get you a pretty bathing suit for that." That certainly peaked her interest, and daddy in his supportive way said, "Maybe I can learn to swim at the same time."

All's well that ends well, I thought, at least on this side of the ocean.

FIVE YEARS OF WAR IN EUROPE

IN THE MIDDLE OF August 1944, we learned the Allies were moving into southern France. I have added fears of that news. Later we heard that the Allies had liberated Paris. I supposed the lights would go on again now in some places, but not in all. I saw newsreels of burned and destroyed equipment that the retreating Germans littered all over the roadsides. After five years of war, the Germans were on the move to keep distance between them and the Allies, but for how long? Four million German soldiers were killed, wounded, or taken prisoner; I can only hope that Ernst is not among them. Hitler had amassed a new army of civilians, which he called the *Volksgrenadiers,* or the People's Infantry. They are grandfathers, prisoners, youths, misfits, and men from occupied countries who were pressed into fighting for the Germans. The Germans now kept radio silence. Berlin was being bombed relentlessly.

> September 1, 1944
>
> My dearest Ernst,
>
> I fear the news from Europe. Where in heaven's name are you? Are you still in France, and if you are, where? How I wish I could get another phone call from

you. I know that would be unlikely, as conditions have changed and not for the better since your call to me.

The really good news I can give you is that Anja has won a first prize in a big citywide music competition for young people. She is amazing, how I wish you could see her. How I wish I could see you. I hope you are well and safe. Please take care of yourself and help to answer my prayers. I am well; I work long hours but then so do a lot of people these days. I miss you.

Loving you,
Karin

We were well into September when I went to see the latest newsreels. Films showed the weary Allied soldiers who have liberated Boulogne and Calais; I hoped yet again that these were the early signs of the war drawing to an end. The guarded figures of the loss of life are unimaginable. I hope we don't have to see another winter of war.

WE ARE FEELING THE SHORTAGES OF RATIONED GOODS even if we line up early for our allotted share. Why do I even mention this? We here at home have lights and heat that can be turned on, food to eat, and warm, safe beds to sleep in, when people in Europe have none of those assurances and necessities. I can't imagine the worry that mothers there have while their children's lives are in peril and fear starvation and the ceaseless continuation of this war, year after year. I am so glad little Anja is here with me where we are safe. There are many people to thank for that, but for me one in particular, an enemy combatant, as he is now considered, who cannot even receive my letters. Despair is my only response to it all.

In October we heard that Athens had been liberated and strange reports that Rommel had committed suicide. Why would one of their great generals do this? What was going on?

In November the Axis forces surrendered in Greece. This year we would have even more to be thankful for at Thanksgiving. Many of us hoped these events overseas were the beginning of the end, but the fighting was far from over.

November 10, 1944

My dear Ernst,

I hope you are safe and well. The news that we get here about the war in Europe is not in favor of the German military, just the opposite. I hope you and I share the same prayers for a resolution and an end to the war. We have plans, you and I, which need to be worked out to make them a reality. Let's start with how we should get married. I grew up in the Protestant faith, but my attendance leaves much to be desired. I observe Christmas, mostly because of the music and how pretty the church looks decorated with candles and greenery.

I wonder where you place your faith. I'm sure with what you are going through in this war; it must be greatly tested for belief, if for nothing else.

I am fine with city hall!

I wonder what we should wear?

I want a plain gold band on my finger, but not too narrow, so it does not escape notice.

I hope you will want to wear a ring as well, so as not to escape notice!

Ah, darling, hopes and dreams, we must hold on to them, until they become a reality.

Tomorrow is another workday, so I must go to bed. I am sorry that it is not with you.

Good night darling,
Karin

December 10, 1944

Today we celebrated Anja's ninth birthday. I saw how excited she was at the prospect of growing up and morphing into becoming a teenager. She was far more ready for that than I was.

I could see that Benji was as well in some respects. I had a long day at work and thankfully mother once again took up the slack in my absence. I feel that time is sliding past me at a pace I have yet to digest. Anja was most excited at getting a new pair of shoes, but not just any pair of shoes, these were penny loafers. My father had gotten two very shiny brand new copper pennies for her to put into the slots on the tongue of the shoes, all the rage among her contemporaries.

She now joined the trendsetters in her age group.

BATTLE OF THE BULGE

IN DECEMBER WE HEARD about something called the Battle of the Bulge. It began December 16, 1944. Hitler sent a quarter of a million troops across an eighty-five-mile length of the Allied front, from southern Belgium into Luxembourg. In the cold winter weather, German troops advanced some fifty miles into the Allied lines, creating a deadly bulge that pushed into Allied defenses, diminishing thoughts here at home that the end of war was near.

We saw films of some of our soldiers in lightweight uniforms trudging wearily through thigh-deep snow in places, trying to stay alive in the midst of enemy fire coming from all directions. There seemed to be no front line of engagement. We saw our soldiers lying in the deep snow, looking lost and afraid to move or not to move, caught in the deadly web of the terrible cold and the terrible fear of the enemy awaiting them just ahead in the frozen whiteness.

There was little enthusiasm for Christmas that year, not with what we knew American soldiers were going through overseas. Young children here needed the assurances that Santa Claus has not forgotten them; the Salvation Army had so many of them posted around the city, ringing their bells for contributions for the needy, and there are many. Christmas carols can be heard in many places in anticipation of the spending season. Thank goodness for children; without them, we might have forgotten to feel any joy at this time of year.

Charlie and I were working long hours, as new government contracts ratcheted up the demand for radios in the new planes. I often cringed at the thought of their use, but then I would close my eyes for a few seconds, take a few deep breaths, and focus on the next crystal. This was how I endured. At times I thought that surely these had to be the most irrevocable memories of my life; but there had been others, and I survived them, as I knew I would once again.

I came home from work to find that Santa's little helpers had been busy making Christmas cookies with my mother. This year Benji had been recruited to help. For dinner, we had veal sausages, boiled potatoes, cabbage, and salad.

Then our whole entourage, led by my father, went to our favorite Christmas tree lot. A jolly Italian man and his family ran the lot, they cut the trees in New Jersey and brought them into the city. This year, however, the man sat alone, removed from his customers, while his young son helped the customers. The man sat on a wooden crate with a brown paper bag in his hand, from which he drank from the enclosed bottle . As he lifted the bag to his mouth, I saw that he wore a wide black band of mourning on his coat sleeve. His youngest son, about fifteen years old, sold us our tree this year. When my father asked him who had died, he looked away and said, "My oldest brother, Mario. He was killed in France." The word 'killed' bit into me as if it were acid. When my father paid him for the tree, the young man said, "Thank you, Mr. Wilson. I wish you and your family a merry Christmas."

My father replied, "Thank you, and I wish you and your family peace in your hearts. Please give your family our condolences, and say hello to your father from us."

"I will." The boy promised. That was the heaviest tree we ever had to carry home from the Martinelli family.

ONCE AGAIN, WE HAD THE CHILDREN TO THANK FOR dispelling the gloom we felt. My father helped out in that department as well, making a dent in the Christmas Aquavit for the three of us. I had a second one as well, trying to do my part. I sat at the table and watched as Benji and Anja laboriously fed the red thread through the pre- made holes in the gingerbread cookies. Anja said, "Mama, close your eyes." I did as she wished, and I felt Anja put something around my ears. Benji snickered. She told me to wait, and I heard her run out of the kitchen, when Anja returned and said, "Okay, Mama, you can open them now." She gave me the hand mirror from our room, and I saw she had hung gingerbread stars on my ears, where I also saw a tired, sad but smiling face needing to admire her efforts. When I gave her a hug, she nibbled a little bit of the star. She did not know it, but she had taken a much larger piece of me five years ago, and I was to wear her for the rest of my life.

On Christmas Eve, our family went to church as usual. Benji stayed home with a cold, so it was just the four of us. I listened intently to the pastor deliver the Swedish part of the sermon, for the little I could understand of it, and then to the English version. We again were given the sheet music with the carols and the small quartet accompanied our singing. When we sang *Silent Night*, I had a sharp pain in my chest that caused me to double over. I sat down and gasped for my next breath, and I felt ill ,when Anja sat on my lap and sang. How strange . . . that had never happened to me before. I hoped it was not the early signs of the dreaded tuberculosis. I felt drained on the way home and decided to skip dinner and go to bed. I assured my concerned parents that I would be all right after a good night's sleep. My troubled sleep was anything but good. I blamed it on putting in long hours at work and was glad that Charlie sat in for me on Christmas day.

My family had put off the traditional exchange of gifts on Christmas Eve so that I could share it with them on Christmas day. I felt a bit better but still drained from the previous night. I was able to help my mother with dinner preparations, and Aaron came over with Benji, who felt better just by seeing Anja.

My father insisted that Aquavit was the Viking cure-all, especially at Christmas time. My father dispensed a dosage to me that gave some credence to his belief. The roasted capon felt nearly as good. In some days we would see the end of 1944, and we could only wonder what will happen in 1945 that might be different from the previous five years.

IN JANUARY 1945, THE BATTLE OF THE BULGE RAGED ON with heavy loss of life on both sides due to relentless fighting and the bitter cold weather. Then it was suddenly over. The Germans had withdrawn from the Ardennes. More than seventy-six thousand Americans had been killed, wounded, or captured in this effort. The Allies had regained the territory they held in early December. How could so little progress justify so many lost lives? I had been avoiding the newsreel movies; I could not abide by what they have to show from either side. I constantly worried about what might have happened to Ernst. Was he wounded, or captured, or, I feared, even worse than that?

I continued working, and the only consistently uplifting time for me were the concerts at the Mandel's home. I was happy to see a very pregnant Helen, with Thomas excitedly awaiting their first baby. She had a new glow about her as we talked of the old days when we first met each other in Prague. I had to be reminded of them, they felt so distant. She thought that Anja was the crowning glory of her efforts way back then.

1945

ON A COLD DAY late in January 1945, my father handed me a small packet. He said, "You have friends everywhere." I didn't recognize the sender's name, a Lieutenant Elsie Summers, R.N., U.S. Army Medical Corps. On opening the packet, I saw a letter.

> Dear Miss Wilson,
>
> I am a U.S. Army nurse serving overseas. I was on duty in a U.S. Army field hospital in Belgium when our medics brought in a wounded German officer. We did what we were able to do before we sent him back to a German medical unit. Before doing so, he asked me if I would send you the enclosed packet of letters that had been written to you over time. Since I was about to take a short compassionate leave, I promised to do so. Please find the letters enclosed. My thoughts are with you and I wish you well.
>
> Lt. Elsie Summers, R.N.

All I could think was, "Thank God he was alive." I was so thankful to this nurse for connecting Ernst with me once again after all this time. I was deliriously overjoyed. Thank God, I repeated to myself. Looking back at the package I saw another letter in an unfamiliar handwriting.

27 December 1944

Dear Miss Wilson,

My name is Dieter Feltner; I served with my friend, Ernst Möller. It pains me greatly to have to tell you that he lost his life on December 24 in Belgium. I don't want to leave you with just those heart-breaking words, so I will tell you what happened.

On 20 December, Ernst was sent two new replacement recruits, one a young boy barely thirteen years old, and another one, an old man. The boy was terrified from the noise and threat of the artillery and mortar fire we exchanged with the enemy, while all that separated us from the enemy was a wide field. The boy often cried out for his mother and never stopped being terrified. On the 24th, while Ernst and I were talking near my bunker, the boy in his panic and confusion suddenly ran out in the wrong direction onto the field, toward the enemy. Ernst was the first to see it and he ran after the boy, bringing him down to the ground. As that happened, Ernst was shot by a sniper. Our men had the uninjured boy crawl back to us while Ernst's sergeant and I pulled Ernst back to us through the snow. When the sergeant and I got Ernst back we found that he was bleeding heavily from his chest. He was shaking badly. I held his hands as he tried to say something, but he could not get the words out. After some labored gasps, he was gone. His is the most intolerable loss of the war to me; he was my best friend. I'm sure that the last words he was trying to speak were for you. He spoke so lovingly of you, and how he was going to New York to be with you. He and I agreed that, if anything should happen to one of us, the other would write to our loved ones. Today it is my sad duty to keep that promise.

When our medic finally got to us, he said there was nothing he or we could have done for him; it had been a fatal chest wound.

Ernst's sergeant said he and his men wanted to bury him. In giving them permission, I told them of an orchard I had seen nearby. It had a hedgerow around it, with an inner path all around the grove within. The sergeant got a pick ax to break through the frozen ground, and then he and his men dug a grave for Ernst just inside the hedgerow in the orchard. We carried Ernst in his blanket and lowered him into the ground. One of his men had been a seminary student and said the 23rd Psalm, and then the men and I stood by the grave, where we sang the first verse of *Stille Nacht*, or *Silent Night*. Then an amazing thing happened. After we marked his grave, the men reached into their pockets and took out candle stubs. They put them in the softly mounded earth and lit them, then they stood at attention and saluted him. After a few moments, they took the shovels and their rifles and solemnly walked back to their posts. I remained to see the candle flames swaying in the slowly encroaching ground fog. It was a surreal moment, as we honored a good man. These candles that the men put on his grave were the ones they lit at night in the bottom of their foxholes to hold their hands over for just some seconds to keep them from freezing. This gesture said more than words that his men respected and admired him.

Before leaving his grave, I took a small handful of the newly dug earth, which I have enclosed here with his letters. I thought it would be of help to you to have something of where he is.

Miss Wilson, my heart goes out to you for your loss and sorrow. I am glad that you can read his enclosed letters of his time out here. He wanted you to have them, though they are a poor substitute for the man himself.

I send you my deepest feelings for comfort at this time.

Most sincerely yours,
Lt. Dieter Feltner

I sat numbly looking up at the familiar things in our living room but recognizing nothing. I went to the window and looked down at the street, as life out there continued as if this had not happened. People walked their dogs, pushed baby carriages and carried their groceries, buses stopped to let people off and take people on, while across two oceans people were killing each other, doing what was now normal for them. I thought about how they too began and ended their days, many never to begin another one, my Ernst among them.

I untied the rest of the packet and looked through the stack of papers. I saw my letters to him, well worn by repeated folding and fingering. I found the page with my note to Ernst from the book of sonnets I had sent to him. The book was not there, another casualty of war. Shakespeare would know how to get through that. My thoughts were bordering on the bizarre now, and given what I was feeling, it was a wonder I could even think of anything as my heart gave way to mourning for what I had only had the smallest taste of. I found the photo he had kept close to his heart. There were other letters there, bent and tattered at the corners, but clearly, they were the letters Ernst had written and saved for me. My mind couldn't think on that right then, and I strangely thought about how I never did get to tell him that Anja left her silent world behind thanks to a German Jewish refugee doctor who specialized in traumatized children. Ernst would have liked to have known that.

Stunned, I walked into my bedroom and put his dark blue scarf around my neck. I took his undelivered letters with the packet of earth and his photo of us, along with my unsent letters and his gray woolen blanket, and I got into bed, covering myself completely. In the darkness I inhaled and exhaled our lives together as I wept a requiem for love. I held his scarf ends to my mouth to muffle my cries. Slowly I caught my breath and rolled over to my other side, the cool side that was foreign to the one I had just come from. I don't know how long I had lain there when my mother came in and touched my shoulder. When I moved the blanket away from my face, I saw it had become as dark outside as it was under his blanket. All I could say was, "He's gone, Mother. He is lying in the cold ground somewhere without me."

"No, Karin, he'll be with you, in your heart, in your thoughts, surely not as you want him, but he gave you love and joy for the short while that you knew each other. I know he'd want you to go on without him. That is how it is when you love someone." She reached over and took me in her arms and rocked me as I did with Anja when she lost her papa. As if she knew, my mother said, "Think of Anja when she lost her papa, and her terrors, and look at her now. She is back in a happy life again. So, it will be for you, too, and we will all help you get there as well." She folded up the gray blanket and put it on top of his letters. My mother bent down and kissed me, whispering, "What can I get you, dear heart? What can I do for you?"

"Nothing. There is nothing."

"Daddy and Anja will be home any time now, and dinner is ready. Will you have a glass of wine with me, before they come home?"

I didn't answer, but she left and came back with two glasses of wine. I pulled myself to a sitting position and took the glass from her. I felt so bereft of myself, as if all feeling was dulled into numbness, so that I had to concentrate just to swallow the wine. My mother put her hand on my foot saying, "You won't always feel this way, Karin. It will get better with time."

"How much time and how much better?"

"It will change. It will be different in time, and you won't feel the sharpness of the sting that you feel now." I contained an angry, despairing unvoiced retort, thinking, what does she or anyone know of what I feel? I put Ernst's scarf, the packet of earth, and the photo in my bottom drawer on top of my letters to him and his pen, covering them with his blanket; it was the first tiny step to nowhere.

Time began again when Anja and Benji and my father came into the apartment. I heard Anja say, "Shush, Benji, don't spoil the surprise for my mama." My mother took our empty wine glasses and said, "I'll head them off. Come out as soon as you can."

A few minutes later, I washed my face with cold water and stepped back out into my life. When I entered the kitchen, Anja ran over to me and gave me a big hug without even looking at my face. She is so instinctive in everything she does, both on and away from the piano. After dinner, Anja said, "Close your eyes, Mama, and don't open them until I say." I heard her open the refrigerator door and the rattle of plates, then, she said, "Okay, Mama you can look!"

In front of me was a perfect cannoli.

"We went to the Italian bakery and I got to choose!" I thanked her for the perfect surprise, looking at her lovingly as she beamed with pride. The cold creamy custard of the cannoli was the best antidote offered to cool the fire in my chest. After dinner, Benji and Anja sat down to do their homework, and it was quiet once again, except for the occasional rubbing sound of the eraser. How I wished I could erase what I was feeling. It would be a long time before my feelings faded to a ghost image like pencil marks after an eraser had done its work.

After I saw Anja to bed, I took the packet of letters from Ernst, half afraid to read them, because then I would know they would be his last words to me. I could not change that, much as I wanted to, so I picked up the first one and read.

12 December 1941

My dear Karin,

Today I was told, as you must have been as well, that we cannot exchange letters due to declaration of hostilities between our two countries. It has nothing to do with us. We are still and shall forever be who and what we mean to each other. I want us to keep writing even though we can't send them, but as I do, I will keep them for us as a diary to tell of the time that must pass before we see each other again. I hope that you will do the same. I'm still in France, and I do what every soldier on either side does, trying to stay uninjured and alive day by day. I do not see any signs of this fighting coming to an end soon. Right now it is really an air war, and I feel sorry for the poor souls on both sides who have to climb into their cockpits and hope that the day will not be their last.

It has been cold and rainy, and the ground has become mud that would like to suck the boots off any soldier taking more than a few steps. Today, Dieter, my friend, bought a bottle of wine and a hard sausage, which we drank and ate to quell our disgust at being here instead of home with our loved ones. For me that now means that I would be with you in New York. I have some paperwork to do now, so I had best say goodnight to my dearest.

Your loving Ernst

13 December 1941
Dear Karin,
I heard that your President Roosevelt has declared war on the Axis countries. I had hoped that outright war would not be the result of some previous hostilities; I don't know what it will mean from here on in. Peace can be the only solution.

It has gotten cold where I am, and even the occasional few glasses of wine with my friend Dieter fail to warm our spirits. We usually talk about the war, since that is all we really know about here. Since I can't get letters from you, I treasure each one I get from my parents and a few friends with news from home.

I have twelve men under my command, and at times I feel like a father to them. They look to me for hope and assurance. I wish I had someone like that as well. My commanding officer only needs a monocle and a riding crop to complete the picture of a comic version of an officer of his standing, but there is little of comic relief where I am.

Many civilians tried to flee the area before they were caught up in the fighting. Those on the farms with animals stayed to tend to their livestock, and they live in their cellars, by day and night. These are fearful times for everyone.

I hope you are well, my love to you and Anja.
Ernst

19 December 1941
My dear Karin,

It has been raining steadily for the past two days and now it has become a mix of rain and snow, which makes it even colder. I can't tell you how often I think of our winter in Prague and how I wanted to shield you from the cold. I imagine you inside my winter coat, a memory I treasure and hope I will relive again one day. I hope you are warm and well where you are with little Anja. I am still where I was in France, and as supply officer I am busier than ever. Dieter is busy as well, and we haven't had much leisure time for a glass of wine together, as we are bound to our duties first and foremost. It is late at night here now and I have had little sleep for the last two days, so I will try for some hours now. With you in my thoughts, hopefully I will find some peace for sleep.

My warmest love to you,
Ernst

21 December 1941

Karin dearest,

As I write this it is with uncertainty as to my situation here. We were told this morning that the command is now under entirely new direct leadership, it will now be under Hitler and we fear what that will mean. Dieter and I can only hope for the best while we fear the worst. Today we are enshrouded in a heavy fog, where we can't see ahead of us. Could that be a metaphor for the change? Only time will tell.

I'm sorry to have so many words of dismay for you, but I can only write of what I know, little as it is, and of what I feel here. How I wish I could get at least one letter from you. Sometimes I dwell on the most I could wish for, which is to have you lying in my arms. Both will have to wait for another time. Until then, my dearest, you have all my love.

Ernst

13 January 1942

My dearest,

I hope you had a nice Christmas with a crispy goose or maybe a duck to enhance the holiday festivities. Here, Dieter and I belted down a few shots of schnapps, after which we ate with our men and shared the rest of the schnapps with them until the bottle was bone dry. I can tell you we did not eat anything with a crispy skin, much to our disappointment. Officers are fed better than the men, but Dieter and I know the value of our own comradeship with them, so we eat with them. We heard that there is a new offensive being launched against the Allies in the Atlantic. I know what that means, and I thank God that you and Anja are not on a ship on the Atlantic. It makes my blood run cold for those who are. I wonder what this New Year will bring us; my hope is for it to bring us together.

All my love to you,
Ernst

March 1942

My dearest Karin,

It is now three years since I first met you on that March day in Prague. When I walked into the book shop and saw you, I knew right away something special was happening to me. The past three years have not dulled that feeling for me, and I hope it hasn't for you either. I don't feel that time is on my side, but I must trust that you are keeping my pen in motion for me.

I am being transferred along with Dieter. That is all I can say now; we are on the move to a more advanced position. I wish I could advance my position out of here, but that is not to be. I am so cold here. Today I even found a live cockroach hiding in my food. Even he looked for warm shelter, I flicked him off into the bushes, where he'll have to survive like the rest of us, or not.

Karin, how are you? What are you doing now? And how is Anja? Please dance with her in your arms to *Begin the Beguine*. I want us to remember that time, so long ago. I have not been reading the sonnets, which once gave me such joy to read. Now those words only add to my heartache for you.

I love you Karin,
Your Ernst

April 1942
My dearest Karin,

At times I am at a loss for words and cannot sit down and write even a few lines to you.

In March the RAF began bombing us heavily here in France. I hear they have heavily bombed Essen and Lübeck, as well. Dieter told me he heard they are also bombing Hamburg without mercy. We are on the move here, but none of it makes much sense. I wonder if it does it to the planners and the plotters, but I know it does not to our dying and wounded.

As for myself, you might not recognize me or even want to. I haven't shaved in about ten days, and a bath is something we only dream about. Food and medical supplies head my list of needs, but my many requests go unfilled. The reason given is heavy Allied bombing of the rail lines. That may or may not be the case; we surmise our supplies are going to the Eastern Front, where the need is the greatest.

Karin, enough of war talk. If I were shaved and bathed, I would hold you in my arms, no matter where we might be, but preferably in New York. How are you, and how is our little Anja, our fledgling Mozart? I miss you terribly. Dieter says I suffer more from the effects of love than I do from the war. Well, that remains to be seen. I must go now; I send you all my love.

Ernst

31 May 1942

Dearest Karin,

How I wish this terrible war would disappear like a morning fog. I am sad today; for Dieter, my best friend here has just heard that yesterday the RAF bombers attacked Cologne with more than one thousand planes. Cologne is where his wife and his two sons live, and he is inconsolable with worry. Even with his position in communications, he is unable to get word to or from Cologne. He is constantly on his wire trying to get through. I pray for his family and for Dieter.

In total contrast to the events around us, it is a beautiful warm day. It looks as if the world could not possibly make and contain such terror, I can smell a sweet drift of Honeysuckle flowers blooming somewhere nearby. I know them because my mother grows them in her garden. I wonder if she can smell them today as well. I have not heard from my parents in some time now, so I hope they are safe. How I wish I could hear from you, even a few words. My only consolation is that I know where you are.

All my love,
Ernst

15 June 1942
Dearest Karin,

Today is a happier day. Dieter got through to his wife's brother, who is a high official in the Cologne police department. Some days before the bombing of Cologne, he took Dieter's wife and sons up to the mountains, where they have an aunt who has a goat farm. Dieter said, "I can just see my wife tending goats while fretting about her manicured fingernails. They are safe, though I'm sure my wife is not happy that there is no phone service to the farm." Dieter laughs at this, a true laugh, not the derisive laughter of soldiers, and it is the sweetest sound I have heard in years. When she asked her brother how she would know it is safe to come back to the city, he simply said, when I come for you.

Later on, I had fun with Dieter. I said, "Dieter, let's go celebrate, it's my birthday today."

He said, "No, it isn't, Ernst, unless you have more than one in the same year."

"Ah, Dieter, it is the birth of a new day!" We went to a nice restaurant, or what was left of it anyway, determined not to be put off by rude attitudes from three other German officers. We had what passes for a good lunch these days, a small consolation for our real hungers.

Karin, dear, I would rather do anything instead of writing these diary letters only to be seen by me, at least for now. There's no way to know for how long.

With all my love,
Ernst

30 September 1942
Dear Karin,

It has been a long time since I have been able to write to you. We have been dodging some heavy fighting, and my supplies are not getting through. This evening our cavalry came along leading thirty or so horses into the woods for the night. Dieter said, "Maybe your supplies are arriving in their saddle bags."

How I wished they carried what we need. I went over to them—it was nice to stand among the horses and smell their smells instead of the acrid smell of the cordite from our guns. A few of the men came over to me after grooming their horses and asked about water. I thought it was a strange idea to have men up on horses, a big moving target for the enemy. But Hitler saw fit to have six hundred fifty thousand horses for front-line duty, all for the Eastern Front, an attest to his continued madness.

For me it was nice to stroke them and look into their large trusting eyes as they flicked their ears and looked at each other for company. Dieter had gotten a message for their leader, who read it, shook his head in disbelief, and called his men to him. Other than that it was a nice break for me from the usual insanity of the day.

I looked at myself in a mirror today and dared to wonder if you would love or even like what I saw. I had best stay away from mirrors, for now anyway.

Loving you,
Ernst

October 1942

My dear Karin,

I have just returned from daring to make that phone call to you. After trying for three weeks, I finally got through to you. It was a miracle to hear your voice. I have been plagued by not knowing how you are and with whom. I had to call. I was at first dismayed when I heard a man's voice answer the phone, but I was relieved to hear you say it was your father and that you are divorced and living at home with your parents. That put my mind and heart at rest, though hearing your voice and not being able to see you and hold you did not. Still, I am glad for those three minutes we had.

I recently confided in Dieter, my best friend, a notion I have been entertaining. I told him I heard that some German prisoners were being sent to America to wait out the war. I said that if I were to give myself up, that could happen to me as well. I figured I would risk being shot, maybe once in the back by German soldiers and then again in the front by the Allies. Dieter said, "Seeing that you are an officer, the Allies might think you are worth something for information you might have."

We thought on that for a moment, and then he reconsidered. "But then, upon hearing that you know nothing, perhaps they would shoot you." We laughed and went on about our business.

Not on my way to America to love you,
Ernst

27 October 1942
Dear Karin,

I am so glad I have not been sent to the Eastern Front, where the chances of dying are a certainty. Our troops who survive are slowly making their way back, sorely defeated. These are bad times no matter which front one is on; only some are more terrible than others. Dieter talks about his wife and little boys, and I talk a lot about you. It helps me to keep you real rather than only a memory.

I'm quite busy these days. The war office has its own idea about what we need and what I order, and what I get is just a slim version of the need. Dieter has his own little supply line he taps when needed, which keeps us in schnapps and the occasional smoked sausage. Once we even had nearly fresh bread and some cheese with an unintended moldy crust. He shares all of it with me, and

I am lucky that, when we are transferred to a new place, supply (that's me) and communications (that's Dieter) move out in tandem. Dieter is amazing in that his supply of schnapps remains largely uninterrupted. How he does it, he laughingly won't divulge, not even to me. The only thing that would really raise my spirits would be to hold you in my arms. Did I ever mention to you that Dieter and I have an arrangement between us, that if anything should happen to one of us, the other would contact our loved ones? I want you to know that, just in case.

Well, darling, I am going to have a bite to eat maybe and maybe try for some sleep, I'm sure both will be a disappointment to me.

Goodnight darling,
Ernst

13 May 1943
Karin dearest,

It has been a long seven months since I have written one of these undeliverable letters to you. It has been four years since I last saw you, and I still cannot forget you. But maybe you have moved on in your life without me, which would only be normal for you. Here, there is no normal, only my love for you, which I hold on to every day in hopes of being with you again. That is all I can believe in here where I am.

I am sitting here at a crossroads, awaiting my supply trucks. I have been waiting for hours now, but so far nothing. I have taken your photo out of my shirt pocket and I can't stop looking at you. I have these many past months tried to read the sonnets, but it would be like asking a beautiful fragrant flower to bloom in a dark sewer. I feel I don't even want to look at the words for fear that I would sully them. From what I have seen here, I feel I have become part of the sewer of mankind. I am sorry, darling, I don't wish to upset you, but if I were to write of my life here in detail it would be too upsetting for both of us.

It must be nice this time of year where you are. It should be here, but it isn't. I haven't heard from my parents in months. I can only hope and pray they are well. I must go and see if Dieter can raise my supply people on his radio.

Loving you,
Ernst

14 July 1943
Dearest Karin,
I have not been able to write to you earlier than this, as we have been on the move. I am now a little outside of Lyon in France. I wish I could say that I am enjoying the delicious Lyonnais food, especially its famous *Tripe à la Lyonnais*, but I can't. I'm sorry to say that the only tripe I have seen here in the countryside is that of war-torn cows lying about with their tripe exposed to the elements and flies. The things being done here by the SS occupation forces are an atrocious affront to everything one can describe as being human. Dieter and I keep to ourselves

as much as we possibly can. It pains me to have to requisition our foodstuff from the already beleaguered local population, leaving them with little for them to live on. But that is not the worst of what is being done here. I cannot believe I come from the same country where the perpetrators come from. If there is a God, He has a lot to answer for by allowing what I see and hear to happen. It is only when I look at your photo that I feel I can go on one more day.

What are you doing today? What are you wearing? And how can sleep well without me?

I must go, I am being called for.

With all my love to you,
Ernst

November 1943

My dearest Karin,

I see it has been five months since I have written a letter to you. It has taken me that long to be able to write to you again. Time here hangs heavily for everyone, including me; I can't believe that we are facing yet another winter of fighting.

Today I saw children hitting chestnut trees with boards and long sticks to knock some stray chestnuts onto to some tarps they laid on the ground to catch them. I fear this will be their only food today. If anyone knows who is eating what here, it is me.

The weather is turning colder here, not at all surprising given the chilly events happening here as a daily routine.

I wonder what little Anja is eating today. I'm sure she is well cared for by you, I only wish I could care for you and her myself. Will I ever see that day, I often ask myself.

Dieter and I have to content ourselves that our families are safe, his in the mountains away from the city and you and Anja safe but in a faraway country. How I wish I were there with you. I wonder if you will ever even see these letters. If there is any hope of that, then I have no choice but to keep writing them.

Goodnight my darling,
Ernst

24 December 1943

My dearest Karin,

My God, another Christmas, another winter without you. Earlier today Dieter and I took a short walk and came across a family in their barren barn kneeling in front of a *crèche* scene that they had set up on the hay-strewn floor. Dieter and I paused for only a few seconds, so as not to disturb or alarm them. I said I thought this would be their only Christmas celebration. As we walked on, Dieter asked me if I was religious. He volunteered his thoughts on that when he said, "I was, until I got here." That is all we said.

I try to envision you and your family in front of a Christmas tree, with candles and decorations, and I try to imagine myself standing next to you with my arm around you. Forgive me; I have to stop writing this.

Merry Christmas darling,
Ernst

February 1944
Dearest Karin,

We are now into a new year, though little has changed here since last year, except many more have been wounded and many more have been killed. I'm sure that is so for both sides.

How I worry about you, and especially about us. It has been nearly five years since we last saw each other on the train and I said *Auf Wiedersehen*. Now it really does feel more like goodbye, with its sound of finality. I worry that there is no room in your heart anymore for what I have become, an enemy soldier. My worst fears for us are that you have met someone else and have given up on me. That is what I feel about us on my worst days here; on my better days, I look at your photo and try so very hard to believe that I will see you again and hold you again. It has a dream quality to it, as if when I look up to see you, you recede further and further into the distance beyond where I can go. Yesterday I took out the sonnets and read those words I have trouble remembering, and even that was as if I only imagined us. Dieter says I am losing my grip, that after more than four years; you are becoming my dream world. Dieter has a bottle of wine he wants to share with me. Then I will think of us, sitting in an inn on the outskirts of Prague.

Dieter is calling me, but I wish it were you.

Until then,
Ernst

April 1944
My dearest Karin,

Sometimes I wonder why I write these letters. But you must know that Dieter and I have promised each other that if something should happen to one of us, the other will send our belongings to our loved ones. I love you and I will do so despite any turn of heart you may have about me. Dieter thinks we might be transferred soon; to where and why and for what remains to be seen, but we dread the worst. I think nearly anywhere will be better than this hellhole. Taking food out of the mouths of children and their families is not my idea of soldiering, yet that is what I am forced to do as a supply officer.

Today I picked a few wild flowers and pressed them into the pages of my favorite sonnet. I wish I could have put them on you. How are you, darling? What are you doing? Are you still working? How is our little Mozart? I'm sure she doesn't even remember who I am. I ask myself, do you?

Loving you,
Ernst

June 1944

My dearest Karin,

The Allies have just landed in Normandy, and while I am some distance from them, I know at some point I shall see them. I am still here outside of Lyon, and I wish I were not. Now that the Allies have arrived en masse, things are sure to go worse for us. We hear there are heavy Allied bombing raids just beyond Normandy. We may be transferred closer or further from the fighting, but it is not known by us at this point.

You are in my thoughts.

Loving you,
Ernst

August 1944

My dearest Karin,

We left Lyon last night, but we do not know yet where we are going. My parting thought here is that all who will think of Germans when this war is over will have only hateful memories of us. We heard last month that another assassination attempt was made on Hitler's life, again by his own senior officers, but we had no good luck in that. Conditions here are not good for anyone. Dieter just told me the Allies have invaded southern France. At times defeatist news like that is late getting to us. A morale issue, I'm sure.

The only hope I hold onto is for us.

Loving you,
Ernst

October 1944

My dear Karin,

We have been on the move since we left Lyon; things are not going well for us. We heard that the Allies are on the move as well; they have already liberated Paris and our armies are out of Boulogne and Calais, which have been liberated from our occupation. Further disturbing news for us is that Rommel has committed suicide; we have trouble believing that. All our news is secondhand and often comes to us well after the fact.

You are my only good thought these passing weeks and months. I have some twelve men under my command here, and I think I must go now and do some handholding among them. How I wish they were your hands.

Forever in my heart,
Ernst

November 1944

My dear Karin,

I am somewhere near the border of France and Belgium, and if we are headed for the Ardennes I fear the worst is yet to come. We are stopping for the night and it has become bitter cold. We have to make do the best we can. Up until now I have not told you that I am at the front, actually the front is all around us, and sometimes we even surprise each other, especially in the dark, as we do not normally expect to see anyone but one of our own. Of the twelve men under me, I have lost two. I don't know how I will be able to write to their families. One boy was only eighteen, and the other had just become a father for the first time. Both men died because of an unintended nighttime encounter with a single Allied soldier. I have ordered my men not to move out of their foxholes at night; even a trip to the latrine can be deadly. No one knows where anyone is anymore, or why.

Karin, dear, I can't say another word to you right now.

Loving you,
Ernst

December 1944

Dearest Karin,

I'm not even sure of the day or the date anymore, and I even question the year. There have been so many of them without you, of that I am sure. There is nothing here to mark the time except for the fighting and the dying, but even that blurs together because it is happening constantly.

I hope you are well, warm and dry and well fed and safe, even though I am not. I feel only a state of dissolution, and when I look around me I see only a forest of men who have been cut down and left to freeze where they fell, men of both sides. The extreme cold here is punctuated by the sudden swooping of carrion crows that perch on the bodies of the freshly dead, pecking on their wounds to release their steaming innards for their own survival. For those creatures that haven't died here, they must desperately seek out and take what can offer life. My only solace in seeing this is that their loved ones can't see them lying here, only that they will get some words from their war departments that their loved ones died valiantly in the service of their country. Those empty words will conceal these scenes.

Karin, dear, I should not be telling you all this, but I do because I want you to feel something of me, anything at all, just please do not forget me.

Loving you,
Ernst

12 December 1944
My dear Karin,

I am sitting in Dieter's communication bunker so that my stiff cold fingers can hold and move a pen. I have never before been in cold such as this; neither have two of my men who have been evacuated to medical services with frostbite of their feet. I'm sure their swollen, black-ened feet will not see front-line duty again, or any other kind of duty. We have heavy snow, which does not stop the artillery and mortar fire from both sides. Dieter tells me he heard on the hot wire that we could be getting replacements, but when and how is a mystery. Dieter offered me a dram of schnapps to celebrate the news. How he squirrels away a constant supply of it continues to be a mystery. I have to go and check on my men, since that is all I can do for them these days. The Allies have bombed our supply routes, leaving us in desperate need of everything, as I am of you.

My love to you,
Ernst

15 December 1944
Dear Karin,

I have warmed my hands so that I can write to you now, because I fear I may not be able to later on. I'm in my foxhole now. Being here makes me feel like a strange unfurred animal living in the wild by having to dig a hole in the ground to be safe, all the while knowing my only safe warm home is with you. How I wish I could feel your warmth beside me. Right now, the unexpected quote from Keats comes to mind, "Touch has a memory, O say, love, say, what can I do to kill it and be free?" My greatest torment here at times is when I think of us at the inn; with that memory, I can barely move the pen now.

Loving you,
Ernst

18 December 1944
My dear Karin,

For a while we were in a state of no man's territory. The Allies pushed us back some kilometers from where we were, and we held that line for a time. Then a reversal took place so that we were right back where we were earlier. To my great surprise I even found my old foxhole. It appears that an American soldier had used it after we were pushed back. I pulled out the old fir tree branches to replace them with some fresh ones, and I found two empty paper wrappers of Wrigley's Spearmint chewing gum and an empty package of American cigarettes called Lucky Strike. It is alarming to know what close quarters we are forced to do our soldiering in. I'm glad he is gone.

I am in a small hamlet outside of Bastogne. Something called the Battle of the Bulge has occurred; the fighting on both sides is fierce. We have once again been urged to have our men take a drug called Pervitin; it is a stimulant that can push a man beyond his normal capability of performance. It is highly addictive and I have ordered my men not to take it. Dieter tells me his two runners have been on it for a while now, and he barely recognizes them as being the same men. They now run through rain, snow, and sleet as if it weren't happening. Their demeanor has certainly changed since they have been on it. They will have to fight the aftereffects once they are no longer issued it. It is a terrible incentive to keep fighting.

Dieter called me into his communications bunker today.

When I came in I saw a cage of carrier pigeons, and Dieter introduced me to Hans Warner, their handler. I walked over to the cage of cooing pigeons, and Dieter asked me if I knew anything about these birds. In a whisper I said, "In bubbling butter with mushrooms and onions and a splash of white wine, they sauté deliciously." Dieter looked at me and grinned. He said, "Keep that to yourself. I'll see you later." What I said would have more meaning for you when I tell you it has been nine days since we have had any hot food.

I have things to do, so I must say,

I love you,
Ernst

22 December 1944

My dearest Karin,

It will be Christmas soon, another one without you. Today I got an early gift. You should know that in German the word *Gift* means venom or poison. A corporal from headquarters delivered it to me. I was given two new replacements from the *Volksgrenadier*; the corporal handed me their paperwork and after a snappy salute he turned and left me to face the replacements. The newly formed *Volksgrenadier* is Hitler's replacement army in place of his depleted one. They are an assembly of rag-tag assorted military men from occupied countries, many of whom speak no German. But it also included German civilians, young boys and grandfathers and even some criminal types not fit to be in everyday society. Standing before me was an underfed, underdeveloped boy wearing a soldier's jacket. The sleeves hung limply at his sides, his hands were well hidden in the too-large sleeves of the jacket; the shoulder seams hung just above his elbows, and the jacket ended below his knees. It would take two or three of him to fill out this jacket. His tattered laced-up shoes were held closed with bits of string and the only thing that nearly fit him was the cap on his head. His paper work said he was sixteen. He was no more sixteen than I am. My sergeant stood by as I stared at this child, his pale frightened face devoid of any childhood. If this is our new army, God forgive us. Ruefully I asked, "When was your last birthday?" He sputtered, "Two months ago." My sergeant curtly reminded him to address me as sir.

"Two months ago, sir."

"And how old did you turn on that birthday?"

"I turned thirteen."

My sergeant again reminded him to add sir. I held my hand up to my sergeant to forgo the additions. Above the constant noise of artillery and mortar firing from both sides, I stepped closer to the boy and said; "You are to stay at the sergeant's side at all times. You are not to say anything or do anything or go anywhere unless you are told to do so. Do you understand that?" Just as he was about to answer, my sergeant took a menacing step closer to him, and the boy uttered a frightened "Yes, sir." Above the noise of the shelling, I instructed my sergeant to keep him in his sight at all times. He gave me a quick glance of disapproval, but he then took hold of the near empty sleeve of the boy and pulled him along to the sergeant's foxhole. I now turned my attention to the second replacement, who was old enough to be the boy's grandfather. I said, "This must seem strange to you."

"No, sir, not really. I was here about twenty-five years ago in the Great War, the war to end all wars. The killing and the dying seems the same now. Back then, there were thirty-eight million causalities before it was over, military and civilians of all sides. The only difference

I see now is that where we had trenches, which were like communal graves, you now make individual ones with these foxholes. Sir." He saluted me, which I returned, feeling like a child next to this man who was here to see history repeat itself so tragically once again in his lifetime.

His dirty uniform fit him well enough, and he knew how to handle his rifle. I told him to keep his head down. I called one of my men to help him dig a foxhole through the frozen earth.

Through the din of the artillery I heard Dieter call me to his communications dugout. I wished it were for a much-needed shot of schnapps; instead, he gave me the troubling news that his two runners have been captured.

"I fear less for their conditions as prisoners than I do for what they will have to endure being cut off from their supply of Pervitin. That will be awful for them, and they won't be the only ones."

We sat speechless in his dugout until his radio equipment signaled him. I left and came out to softly falling snow. I went to check on my sergeant, who was enlarging his foxhole to accommodate the young boy, who stood by his side shaking and crying with his fists balled up under his chin and his arms pressed against his chest. I walked away from the desolate scene as the thundering of the artillery and mortars continued to invade everything and everyone they met. If there is a hell, this place surely is the model.

My dearest, I dare not let myself think of you while I am in the midst of all this. Tonight I will lie in my foxhole with my hand over your photo and plead with you to keep me in your heart.

I love you,
Ernst

23 December 1944
My dearest Karin,
Here, in the ominous predawn darkness, only my memory tells me where my men are dug in across the blanket of deep snow and cold. It has been quiet for a while now; I hope it does not signal an advancement of the enemy troops, because my men are exhausted from the heavy defensive fighting of the past days. It so often feels that all this will never end, and if it does it may be with our last breath. I wish I could see you now, more than in my mind's eye. To see you and hear you would be worth my last breath. There, the stillness has broken, I must go.

Loving you,
Ernst

THE FRONT LINE — 23 DECEMBER 1944

SNOW LAY THICK while cutting winds blasted us from the northeast. The morning sky was a dark heavy blanket over us when I walked into Dieter's communications dugout to get his thoughts. Dieter looking at me and grinned. "Isn't it a bit early for a shot of schnapps?

"It may not be after I ask your advice. It's about the boy. Aside from driving my sergeant crazy with his constant crying and calling out for his mother, the boy is a danger to himself and to the rest of us. The enemy won't have to see us as a target, they'll hear us. I have written a letter to the commander requesting the boy's removal from our front line. Please read it aloud so I can get the full impact of my request." Dieter looked at me with apprehension as I handed him the letter.

COMMUNIQUE
From: Lt. Ernst Möller
To: Commander Eichler
Re: Removal of recent replacement Kurt Stuts
Honored Commander:
It grieves me to appeal to you about the young boy, Kurt Stuts, recently sent me as a replacement. This frail, untrained, and extremely frightened boy turned thirteen

just two months ago. He is completely unable to tolerate the artillery and mortar fire, among other loud sounds. I have had to billet him with my sergeant in his foxhole to keep him from wandering. He sobs and cries out loudly, and he is clearly a danger to himself and the rest of us. He is not front-line material and I take it upon myself to request he be sent home. He is not soldier material. I owe it to you and my men to take this step to continue as a fit unit of defense. This boy in our presence makes that impossible.

Respectfully yours,
Lt. Ernst Möller

Once read out loud, I fully realized the step I was taking. I asked Dieter, "Well, what do you think? Will he have my head for this?"

"He might if he could, but he can't spare a single officer. He may later demote you to rank of private."

"What else do you think?"

"I think you put the case clear and up front to him. What are your plans for this letter and the boy?"

"I want to send the boy and my letter, along with my sergeant, to the commander. I hope that will be the end of it."

"But returning a gift to the giver at Christmas is not pro forma," Dieter joked. "But then, neither is this Christmas."

"Dieter, help me out. Please hold on to the letter just in case I change my mind."

"If you do or you don't we both need a shot of schnapps now, aside from celebrating Christmas Eve tomorrow."

24 December 1944

My darling Karin,

Tonight will be Christmas Eve. I wish for peace on earth for us all, and I hope you will remember me. There is no peace where I am, so my thoughts turn to you for comfort and joy.

I have dozed fitfully during what passes for the night here; my young replacement must have cried himself to sleep. Most of the time he cries out for his mother again and again. I think we all at this point also cry for our mothers, only we don't give voice to it. I think it is about 4 a.m. now. It is so white and quiet. Only minutes ago a small dark bird flew into a bush near my foxhole and sang a short sweet song, and then it left as quickly as it appeared. I think it was a message from you; the way the dog in Prague beckoned me to see you. It is so dark and quiet, and I have the feeling I will be with Mozart soon, sitting in a tavern with a tankard of bitters. I will tell him about an evening in Prague when I sat next to you and held your hand with my heart bursting for you to the strains of his string quartet. I will tell him how out of my nervousness for you I bored you with my pedantic stories about him. He had a twisted sense of humor, and I think he will be amused when I tell him that. I know I will be in good company when I tell him all about you, because he prized love above all else. He will turn green with envy at every detail that I will minutely describe about you. I also think I will see, off in the corner by a leaded bull's-eye bay window, Shakespeare sorting through a sheaf of papers, the beginnings of some new sonnets. I wonder if

I can entice him with a new tankard of ale to write one just for us. He has caught my eye and I know he is reading my thoughts.

My dear Karin, as you can tell I do believe in the inevitable outcome of where I am now. I still carry that title page with your handwritten dedication to me, close to my heart. If you can dance with words, I should be allowed to embrace you with them, my darling Karin, but searing words that come to mind now are those of Keats in a poem he wrote entitled, 'When I Have Fears That I May Cease to Be.' I take them as words of prophecy. I have some German words I want you to know and remember from me: *Du bist meine Liebe für Ewigkeit!* I wish you a good night, as I too will try to bed down once again with you as I close my eyes.

Your loving,
Ernst

The last two sentences of his last letter to me brought his letter up to my lips, and I held it there until I could no longer. My mother had studied German, and she translated his German as "You are my love for eternity!" Other than *Auf Wiedersehen*, which was never to happen again, this was the only German I was ever to learn, to know the meaning of, feel, and remember. I would never forget those words.

Everything I had of his and us I put away in my bottom drawer. The photo of the three of us I kept in the upper drawer with my personal clothes. We would not be going anywhere, just resting together.

Other families would save photos of their loved ones as well. The Battle of the Bulge was the most costly action ever fought by the U.S. Army, which suffered more than seventy-five thousand casualties. Their families now had those dreaded telegrams as the last news of them, as did the families of the other thirty-five thousand Allied soldiers. As many as one hundred thousand German families also had their photos and telegrams.

And the war was not yet over.

WHEN I GOT INTO BED AND MY HEAD TOUCHED THE pillow, I felt it swimming with images of us in Prague. I could hear Ernst speaking to me in scenes I had so often replayed in my mind. Now I had other images of him as a soldier trying to stay alive, and then not alive because he had to save another child. He knew that he would be seeing Mozart and Shakespeare that day; he also knew he was saying goodbye and not *Auf Wiedersehen*. He had taught me the difference because he knew it would come to this. I opened my eyes to look at Anja fast asleep in her bed. It gave me comfort that I too was able to save a life from the war and that all I had done to make it possible was to love Ernst more than he and I were to know. When the swirling images stopped, I closed my eyes and waited for peace.

ANOTHER RITE AT THE FRONT

AFTER HAVING LAID ERNST to his eternal rest, I walked back to my dugout and sat down in the dim light, listening to the pigeons cooing. I reached into my drawer and poured myself a schnapps. Lifting it to my lips, I said, "Here's to you, Ernst, dear friend and best soldier ever, rest in peace." There was nothing warming about the schnapps, so I put my hands in my pockets where I felt the letter Ernst had written to the commander. I could do something to honor Ernst; I called for his sergeant along with the boy to my dugout. I had never seen the sergeant so sad and tense as he came in pulling the boy by the jacket. He saluted me and said, "At your service, sir."

"I want you to take this letter along with the boy to the commander, and then report back to me." His outstretched hand shook, perhaps with apprehension or the cold, or maybe both. He pocketed the letter, saluted, and left, dragging the boy behind him.

The wait for the sergeant's return seemed interminable. I turned when I heard the canvas door cover rustle. The sergeant saluted me and said, "Mission accomplished, sir."

"How did that go?"

"When the commander read the letter, he pulled the boy in front of him. He had flushed with anger when he said to me, 'Tell the lieutenant to report to me immediately.'

I know the commander had liked Ernst, but this did not bode well now.

"I said, it grieves me to say sir, but Lieutenant Möller is dead."

"What do you mean dead?"

"He was shot by a sniper when he ran to rescue this boy, who in his fear and panic ran toward the enemy instead of to the rear of our lines." The commander turned his back to me, but I could see the letter shaking in his hand. He suddenly reached out and struck the boy so hard he went flying. Without turning, the commander said, "Get back to your post, sergeant."

"I left, fearful for the boy, but I knew there was no other recourse."

"You are right. Thank you, sergeant. You completed a difficult mission for all of us." I reached back into my drawer and now we both put a dent in the bottle.

AFTERWARDS

WE HAD ONLY BEEN together for those short six months in Prague before he had made our escape possible. Now all that was left to me of the past five years were letters and that out-of-the-blue phone call, the last time I was ever to hear his voice. Our feelings never waned in all that time. I recalled the Christmas Eve service, when I sat in church with my family and felt that sharp pain in my chest. I now know that I felt that as he lay dying in the snow. Now his voice was denied me, but not his love. Whenever I thought of him, it felt as though my blood stopped circulating. Everything within me wants to stop so that I can feel his hand in mine and his lips on mine.

I fell into darkened spirits; one day was no different than the next. At times I would lie down and listen to Anja playing scales. There was something about her rapid runs that I liked to listen to. They had a happy quickening sound, one that my mind and body needed reminding of.

SEVERAL MONTHS LATER, AARON CALLED TO INVITE ME to celebrate his belated birthday. It was only at my mother's insistent urging that I accepted. He had made reservations at a supper club.

They featured a wonderful singer, and I enjoyed her repertoire of songs until she sang the introduction to *Night and Day*. I knew the lyrics and tried to steel myself against the feelings it would awaken in me, because they described Ernst and me perfectly.

I had to turn down Aaron's offer to dance to it, which would have been more than I could handle. Aaron was gracious about my shortcomings until he said, "You will need more time, but I hope not more than I can offer you." I lifted my refilled wine glass and nearly drained it all at once. A Cannoli would have helped as well. When he saw a small smile on my face, he said, "That is a sign of hope." All of this was just too early for me, and I think he knew it, too, but not why. I wished him a belated happy birthday, to which he said, "Happiness has boundaries." I couldn't wait for the evening to end.

An Ending

═══════════════════════════

IT WAS MARCH 1945 when we heard that the U.S. forces had crossed the Rhine River. The Germans retreated into Germany.

At the end of April, we heard that the Soviet forces had entered Berlin. Hitler was finished, and so was the war.

On May 7, 1945, General Eisenhower accepted the German's unconditional surrender at Reims, France. The Germans also surrendered to the Russians in Berlin.

My God, finally, the war was over, but only in Europe. Why did it have to take my Ernst so close to the end?

May 8, 1945, was declared Victory in Europe Day. The city was filled with the raucous sounds of those celebrating. It was the day the Germans gave up the fight, nearly six months after Ernst was killed. If only he had not been sent that young boy replacement, he might still be alive. If only.

I put the radio on a music station and I drank a cold beer, all to dull the wild celebrants in the streets.

War still raged in the Pacific.

Today Mr. Holloway got up on the table and made a general announcement. "There may be some cutbacks due to the lessening of government contracts, and cutbacks will be affected by seniority. We all know that the planes and their radios are still needed, especially in the Pacific, where the need for them is far from gone." We have a few cuts in hours but other than that it seems to be business as usual.

When I went to work the next day, Mr. Holloway jumped up on the table again and announced that no new government contracts were in the offing, so some layoffs would begin as of now. This dramatic event made the heat of the day even hotter, at least for those who did not have seniority status. I gave my spot in the queue to Charlie so I could go back to school to get my degree, a goal I had set for myself and would accomplish.

ON MY WAY TO THE NEWSPAPER STAND TO GET A COPY of *The New York Sunday Times* for our after breakfast reading, I noticed that there were more gold star banners in the windows of families that had lost a service member in the war. Some had more than one gold star for the multiple family members lost in the war. I had heard of families with even three, though the greatest loss in a single family were the five Sullivan brothers who lost their lives when the ship they all served on sank in 1942. Victory in Europe or the Pacific would only mean a loss for these families for the rest of their lives. How could they bear that? I could not imagine their pain, nor did I want to. I had my own to bear.

ON MY BIRTHDAY, I LOOKED IN THE MIRROR AND ASKED the image, "How did I get to be twenty-eight? I have a nine-year-old daughter, and that should suffice for the time being, since I haven't provided her with a father or me with a husband. That observation is getting to be old hat. Maybe I should lay that aside until I once again believe in miracles."

BEING NINE YEARS OLD CAN HAVE ITS UPS AND DOWNS, as we were to discover one evening as we began our bread pudding dessert. Anja asked if she could stay overnight at Benji's tomorrow. I asked her what the sleeping arrangement would be. She looked at me and shrugged.

"That's no answer, Anja."

"Why?"

"Why? Because you and Benji are growing up and you should not be sleeping in the same bed anymore."

"Well, boys and girls do."

"Not at your age they don't. Only once you are a grown adult and can make mature decisions. Until then, no!"

Anja looked deep into her pudding and said in a low voice into the dish, "*Molto rigoroso.*"

My father said sharply, "Anja, apologize to your mother." When she didn't, he said in a sterner voice, "Apologize, right now."

Then barely looking at me, her voice quavered, "I'm sorry for what I said."

My father said, "Anja, you are not to use your Italian music terms for anything else except for your music."

She quickly got up in tears, ran into the bedroom, and shut the door. My mother stopped me from going after her, saying, "Let her be for a few minutes so she can work it out and sort her feelings."

"Daddy, what exactly did she say?"

"She said *Molto rigoroso,* meaning, very strict."

"Daddy, was that so bad?"

"We have to nip this talking back in the bud. She is to be respectful at all times to you and to us. We must set the behaviors on the proper course. She is growing into herself more and more, and I want her to be as proud of that as we are."

"Thank you, I too need guidance for her in that direction. Now I'll go in and smooth some ruffled feathers."

When I came in, she turned her back to me and was still visibly upset. I gently rubbed her shoulders and said, "We all have to learn the same things as we grow up."

"Did you, too?" she asked tearfully.

"I'm sure I did, and Grandpa probably said the same thing to me."

"I'm sorry, Mama. I really am."

"Okay, darling. We've learned that lesson, now let's go see if that bread pudding needs more vanilla sauce."

My mother was at the sink already when my father came over and stroked our backs and said, "The pudding needs more vanilla sauce."

AFTERMATH

ON A VERY HOT DAY in august, Victory in Japan was announced.

The decision to end the war with Japan came with the shocking cost of hundreds of thousands of lives taken by atomic bombs dropped by the United States on the Japanese cities of Hiroshima and Nagasaki. An estimated two hundred twenty-five thousand died in the initial explosions, and radiation sickness was to claim many more lives through the following weeks, months and years. The decision was made to drop the bombs to stop the war, otherwise it was estimated that at least one million Allied soldiers would have died, along with uncounted Japanese lives. This drastic measure was needed to bring the war to a halt and avoid that alternative.

People were jubilant across America, and Times Square was once again the hub of celebration as it had been for Victory in Europe day. I removed Anja and myself from all the noise and commotion and went to the beach, where we found a tree-shaded area near the boardwalk. We sat on our blanket and listened to the waves of the Atlantic Ocean lull us to a more peaceful place to escape the madness of it all. Anja and I both lost our loved ones in the war, and we both were left with lingering memories of them that would never end.

Good News

IN LATE AUGUST Greg stopped by to tell us that Grace and he were planning to get married in September. The news put my parents in a heightened mood, saying, "Of course you will have to clear it with Grace, but we would love to have the reception here at our house."

Greg was speechless until he said, "We have no plans for that, our only plans are for City Hall. Grace's father lives in Puerto Rico, where he is a fruit exporter and is now involved in some legal problems there and can't leave. Her mother recently remarried, and they are in Mexico on their honeymoon, looking for a second home there."

My mother, seeing a clear path said, "Well, if Grace agrees, we are your surrogate family, after all, and we can do this. I think we can handle up to fifty people." She looked to my father for his surprised nod of approval.

"What a generous offer! I'm sure Grace will be thrilled. It would be mostly our friends and colleagues from work, nowhere near fifty people, I'm sure."

Greg was eager to tell Grace about the offer and virtually ran out the door. Shortly after we all sat down for a planning session. They gave us the date, and we planned the food and reception that was to be our gift to them.

My parents did the food and I was to be the booze lady. I felt a bit typecast in the role, but with the help of my father, it all worked out smoothly. He taught Anja to play *Here Comes the Bride*; we heard it being practiced several times every day until the wedding. I'm sure Wagner would have smiled if he could have heard her.

When the day finally arrived, they came to our apartment directly from City Hall. They were positively in a state of euphoria. Greg wore a dark blue suit with a white shirt and a blue and silver tie. Grace was beautiful in a crème-colored suit over a soft rose silk blouse, and she wore a headband of fresh baby's breath and carried a bouquet of all white flowers. She was radiant, and for a brief moment, I wished it were I in her position. We had a glass of champagne and then they went off for a long carriage ride through Central Park while we made the final touch- ups to a long table in a niche in the living room with delicacies of every description, as much as the still-in-place current rationing would allow.

My father and I did a great job with the liquid refreshments, and he had insisted on French champagne, enough at least to toast the bride and groom.

Anja looked lovely in a beautiful flowered dress, and my mother and father dressed for their parts. I wore a dress that looked like it came from the same bolt of cloth as Anja's. We were all party-ready as their friends began arriving. Benji came looking handsome with Hannah. She said Aaron was in Chicago for a meeting. I was glad; otherwise it could have been awkward to have him here.

All in all we were just over twenty-five people, a comfortable number for our space. Anja was taking one last look of herself in the mirror when I went to pour her a glass of milk. With my head in the refrigerator, I said, "Anja, you must have this before you eat. I am even putting some of Grandma's strawberry syrup in it for you."

I shut the refrigerator door and turned around ready to hand her the milk when something unexpected happened. I came face to face with a man who rendered me speechless. With a warm smile, the man said, "Thank you for the offer of the spiked milk, but I was rather hoping for a sip of champagne in honor of the occasion." He reached his hand to me across the table and said, "I should introduce myself. I'm Jean Daniel Martineau, but please just call me Daniel."

I put the milk down and shook his hand. I felt at that moment that our chemistries compounded. After we shook hands he just stood there, holding my hand and smiling that soft smile. "The little girl that the milk was intended for made a bee line for the living room, where all the excitement is." For me the excitement was right here across the kitchen table. Still holding my hand, he raised it over to the end of the table and said, "Shall we go find her? By the way, is she yours?"

"I'm Karin Wilson." That was no explanation, but conversation was not coming easily from me as I had become chemically speechless. We walked into the living room and stood there watching the activities. He turned to me and asked, "Is your husband here as well?"

My heart cringed a little at this question. "No," was all I could say.

"Or Anja's father?"

"No, neither."

He smiled and said, "I know where I can get us something to drink." As he stepped away, I saw that someone he obviously knew stopped him, and they spoke briefly. I watched him as he stood there talking, carefully taking in his good looks. His eyes glistened as he spoke, and that alone would have done it. There was something so beautifully masculine about him as he stroked his hair back with his hand and held it there for just a moment before he engaged in further conversation. He was beautiful to look at. It was not a face across the room, but a face across the kitchen table that had caught me up. *Something wonderful is happening to me*, I thought. I only hope he can discover it for himself.

He came back with two glasses of chilled white wine; I guessed he thought this might be a loosening solution for my awkward conversation. As we stood there sipping the wine, another fellow I noticed looking at me from the end of the room walked over to us.

He smiled at me and said, "Hello, my name is Zac. And you are?"

Daniel quickly interrupted. "This is Karin Wilson, and we're engaged."

Zac said, "You don't keep a big secret like that from a good friend. When did that happen?"

Daniel looked at me with that smile and said, "About twenty minutes ago." Looking back at him, I felt the wine loosen my imagination, and I saw him as a handsome matinee idol about to star in a new episode, one in which I hoped to be his co-star.

Zac looked at me and said, "You have to be careful of this guy, Miss Wilson. He charms all the ladies with that phony French accent of his. Don't fall for it!"

Daniel shook his head in mock sadness. "I'm sorry, Zac, but your advice came just a little too late."

"Yeah, I guess I should have been here twenty minutes ago."

Daniel turned to me and said, "You have to give Zac a wide berth. He's in radiology, and that makes him radioactive."

Zac smiled. "Yes, so you can find me in the dark!" They both laughed; I am still unnerved by it all and can only manage a smiling nod.

Zac then said to me, "Speaking of a wide berth, do you see that lovely lady at the end of the room? That's Sadie, my heartthrob, talking to Dr. Willard McKenzie, that tall, good-looking much-touted, orthopedic surgeon who's got it all. He's independently wealthy, has a fabulous apartment, a showy car, and I won't even mention his sailboat that sleeps eight. Now, tell me what does he have that I don't?"

"In a word, he has Sadie!"

"Touché, Daniel, thanks for reminding me. Well, you two probably have lots to talk about, so I'll just toddle off for now."

As soon as he walked away, Daniel looked at me apologetically and said, "Of course, I only meant we were engaged in conversation." I managed an embarrassed smile.

My father played an attention-getting chord and everyone turned to him. Anja sat down at the piano and played *Here Comes the Bride* as Grace and Greg made their entrance from the kitchen. They walked over to my parents, where my father handed them each a glass of champagne and said, "We all wish you a long and happy life together, and we are so glad that you are beginning it here among friends and family." My parents raised a glass of champagne to toast the teary-eyed Grace as Greg put his arm around her and nuzzled her with a kiss. Everyone raised their own small glass of champagne, and the festivities took off. We had moved the furniture against the walls and rolled up the rug to make space for dancing. We lowered the lights as Mother lit the many candles on her piano and on the buffet table, and then my father played a waltz for the newlyweds' first dance. After the first few moments, Greg said, "Please join us, everyone."

Daniel took my hand and said, "I think that means us." When he put his arm around me, I felt that chemistry compounding again and again. Usually talkative, I remained speechless. I couldn't decide if I should move forward or backward, and I wasn't thinking of the dancing. I was taken unawares by my feelings, feelings that I had been so sure I would never feel again. But now in Daniel's arms they emerged and there was nothing I could do about them. Helen was right about the way love happened, and I had little say in the matter.

My father played some of his favorite Ella Fitzgerald records, and the dancing continued. When we sat out a few dances, Daniel said, "I'm extremely busy this week, but I would love to see you again. Could you meet me for lunch tomorrow in the hospital cafeteria? I could be there at one." Without any thought, I said, "Yes, I can do that." I wished I had said it with more enthusiasm in my voice. I started to feel self-conscious again, so I said, "Please excuse me. I'll gather up some plates and glasses for the next round of use." When I got up to collect them, he followed and helped, and then we went into the kitchen. I was surprised by his willingness to help as I washed and he dried. All the while, he looked at me with undisguised interest.

"You know, I did this same thing one summer in a restaurant when I was in high school. Only this is far more pleasant doing it with you."

"I did something similar on a freighter one summer, and there was nothing pleasant about it, inside or outside of the galley."

"You intrigue me more and more by the moment," he said, and we laughed.

"I think I was just the victim of circumstances." I wish I hadn't said that, and I hoped he did not think that I implied him.

"We all are to some degree, at one time or another in our lives."

Now I hoped that didn't imply me.

We took the clean glasses and dishes back to the living room, after which he turned to me and took my hand, saying, "We should reward our good works with a dance." I followed his warm, inviting smile to the dance floor. This time he held me just a bit closer and we danced to the softness of Ella's voice again and again.

At one point, my mother and father came in with a beautiful cake. Anja came running over to me, "Mama, there are no candles on it! Why is that?"

"I guess because it is not a birthday cake."

"When I get married I am going to have candles on my cake!"

We watched as Grace was handed a knife and made the first cut. She laughed and said, "Now I know why I never became a surgeon—I'd get frosting all over the place!" Laughter and applause followed from her colleagues and friends.

Daniel said, "Karin, come, share a piece of cake with me." I felt in some way I already had. As the party went on, I saw my father and Dr. Steinreich deep in conversation. They looked like men of the world. I felt Daniel was one of them as well, at least of my world. I wondered what was going on in his mind when Anja addressed me as "Mama." It hadn't seemed to send any ripples through him, and it did not alter the moment nor disturb the chemistry between us.

I watched Anja and Benji dancing. They were so sweet with each other, and I thought that there would one day be candles on their cake.

The evening slowly ended, but Daniel and I did not—we were just beginning. I was sure of that when I walked him to the elevator. When the door slid open, he leaned down and kissed my cheek. Stepping into the elevator he said, "Tomorrow, one o'clock in the cafeteria." He held his hand up to me as a last goodbye, and then the door closed. As I walked back into the apartment, my mother's words came to me. Yes, perhaps I would indeed feel happiness again.

A Beginning

THE MORNING AFTER the reception, my mother and I took a break from the cleanup. As we sat down, my mother was less than pensive when she said; "I think it was a nice reception for everyone, don't you?"

"It was lovely, Mother. You and Daddy did a great job. It couldn't have been nicer for them."

"Well, I hope the next reception we do here will be yours."

"I don't see that on the horizon just yet."

"From where I sit, I would have to say you have to put your more receptive self out there."

"How so?"

"Be more engaging! Take Aaron, for instance. I think one nod from you would do it."

"I don't love Aaron. He is just a friend, and more as Benji's father than anything else. I have, as you say, 'put myself out there.' If I had married Alex I would be a widow now, and if I had married Ernst I would also be a widow. My prospects don't seem too likely from where I sit."

"If you go on thinking that way, your future will continue as Mrs. Anja, as it is now. While on the subject, I noticed that handsome

French fellow was attentive to you. I also noticed that you were somewhat less than responsive to his attentions."

I blushed. "Mother, you do make a lot of nothing."

"What I saw was not nothing, and I hope you saw something, too. I promise not to say another word on the subject." I laughed. She frowned playfully and said, "Yes, for today, and with great restraint."

Mrs. Anja? When I heard those words, I was taken aback. My mother often was economic with her words to clearly deliver her message. In this case her words cut to my core. That message was to be pondered by me again and again as time went on.

I GOT TO THE CAFETERIA FIFTEEN MINUTES EARLY TO BE sure to get a table, one at which I would learn more than I knew now.

Suddenly I saw him rushing in, his white coat flying as he dashed around looking for me. I stood up and waved, and he rushed over. He gave me a quick kiss on the cheek and said, "How nice to see you again. I'll get us lunch. The day's offering is meatloaf or tuna salad."

"Tuna salad, please."

"Coming up."

I watched him hurry to the line, which now can't move quickly enough for him. I was touched by his eagerness as he took out his wallet well before being waited on. He came over with a tray of two tuna salads, and putting one in front of me he said, "They were ready and quick, but then I made a choice on your behalf. I hope you like iced tea?"

"If I didn't before, I will now." We laughed and began our lunch. I looked up at him and said, "Your friend Zac said you charm the ladies with your French accent."

"You left out the word 'phony.'"

"Well, I was charmed by you before you even said a word."

"Now I'm the speechless one." We both laughed.

"To clear up that accent question, I can tell you that both my parents are French and I was born in Paris, where my father taught history. One day I overheard a conversation my parents were having, it was one that was to change my life in ways I did not know. My father said, 'I have something important to say. I have read Hitler's two volumes of *Mein Kampf.* I can tell you that Hitler takes his misshapen ideas and gives them form, from an armed and military Germany to inciting the national will of the people to support and carry them out. Anti-Semitism is cloaked at first in strange analogies to the animal world, which he then directly applies to humans. He is a clever seller of his disguised ideas that clearly emerge from his dangerous thinking.' My father went on to say that he felt this could easily erupt into another war in Europe. When Hitler became chancellor of Germany in 1933, my father's fears had been further renewed.

He reminded my mother that when he was a soldier in the French army during the Great War, he saw and did things that he never ever wanted me to experience. "I want us to leave Europe and go to America. Your sister is happy there, and so we can be as well." Up until then my mother listened quietly, but she was not happy with the idea of leaving France for America. My father's defense was, "Juliette, we have only one son, and this will be our gift to him." They had other things to say, but for me, after hearing all this, the thought of leaving what I knew and my friends troubled me no end. After numerous trips to the American Embassy with forms filled out and medical exams approved, four months later we were in Le Havre boarding an ocean liner bound for New York. By now I had mostly given up my hesitation and became caught up in the new adventure.

"We enrolled in English lessons aboard the ship; both my parents spoke English, but my classroom English needed work. I met other young people on the ship whose parents had my father's thinking. The day we sailed past the Statue of Liberty, my father said, "Look, Lady France welcomes us." My mother looked at him and then at me with a wan smile, not so thrilled by the events ahead. "So, that is where the accent comes from. I think I have just about lost it anyway." I smile at him, shaking my head no.

"This is the longest uninterrupted lunch hour I can remember in this cafeteria. Now that I have given you my life's history, I want to hear yours."

As I opened my mouth, a bell sounded to alert the staff of the hour.

"Oh, that signals back to work for me. May I call you?"

I hurriedly wrote my number on the cashier's receipt as he got up. He kissed my cheek again, and when I look surprised he said, "That's very French, you know." He smiled and took the receipt. He paused and said, "Thank you for having lunch with me." Then I see his back as he rushed off, a scene that was to replay itself more than I could have imagined.

THAT EVENING, DANIEL CALLED TO SAY HE GOT OFF AT midnight, and he asked if I would meet him for breakfast in the cafeteria tomorrow at 7 a.m. before his next shift. I agreed.

"Great! Same table, yes? See you there. I'm sorry, I have to run now."

I sat at the same table and saw him leave the line with a tray of two breakfasts. He put the tray down and kissed my cheek. I smiled as he put our breakfast before us. As he sat down, he said, "I hope you like scrambled eggs. Now, there is so much about you I would like to know." My mother's words were beginning to resound through the conversation.

"You finished work at midnight, and now you are here again for the 8 a.m. shift. That seems strenuous to me. Is it for you as well?"

"It's part of the job. I've gotten used to it, except for those times at 6 A.M. when I have to forfeit another few hours of sleep." He laughed.

The humor escaped me, but what did not escape me was his ability to adapt to the unusual.

"Now, tell me, how will you spend your day, a bit more tired than usual I suspect, since I got you up so early."

"I have a war job, which I am about to give up so I can pursue my studies in library sciences. I'll have a degree when I'm done."

"What sort of work were you doing?"

"I inspected radio crystals that went into war planes. It took its toll on me, so I had to get used to that."

"What are your immediate plans now?

"To go back to school full-time for that degree."

"I don't mean to pry, but where does little Anja fit into all of this?"

"I'd like to leave that for another time."

"Yes, of course, I wouldn't want that to be interrupted by the shift bell."

He went to get us a second cup of coffee, and when he returned he asked, "When can I see you again? I'm off tomorrow at 8 p.m. If you'd like, you could meet me here. I only live three blocks from the hospital, so we could spend some uninterrupted time together, if you'd like to do that."

"That sounds possible."

My mother would be proud of me at those words. Daniel said, "Great! Please meet me inside the main entrance at 8 p.m." He got up and kissed my cheek, leaving just as the 8 a.m. bell went off. I saw he had only eaten half his breakfast; his attentions were across the table from him rather than on his breakfast.

The next evening I stood inside the main entrance to wait for him. I saw him talking with another white coat, and then he turned and, with a big smile, he hurried to where I was. We went out into the evening air, and he unexpectedly took my hand and said, "I am only three blocks from here." He was only three heartbeats from me, as I felt my hand in his, and I tried not to breathe too hard of the night air.

When we got out of the elevator of his apartment building, he dug for his keys in his pocket. He looked at me with a small smile and said, "Don't expect too much." Opening his door, he stepped aside and with a sweep of his hand said, "Welcome to my humble abode."

I was nervous as I heard myself say, "Said the spider to the fly."

He laughed and said, "Now, you are one step ahead of me."

My still nervous reply was, "I feel I am one step behind you."

Closing the door, he said, "I'll close that gap." He kissed me on both cheeks, in the European fashion, and then with another kiss, he said, "In France we always greet someone that we know with a kiss on each cheek, but if we especially like them, they get that third kiss." He gazed into my eyes and whispered, "I think I still need to close that gap." Then he gave me a quick, gentle kiss on my lips. I wasn't expecting that, and I don't think he was either. He straightened and cleared his throat, saying, "Let me give you the grand tour of my cha-teau." It was a one-room studio apartment. Along one wall were sev-eral bookshelves packed from floor to ceiling, in front of which was a long desk piled with papers, with a reading lamp bent at an acute angle from his last use. "Leaving my study now and moving smartly along," he stepped to a niche that had a couch and a coffee table covered with medical journals. "We are now in the living room." Next, just a few steps away from the couch, on the other side of a large window, he said, "And here is the sleeping chamber, which doesn't get nearly enough use. I also have a tiny bathroom and a closet kitchen, and that, mademoiselle, concludes the tour, but included in the cost of admission is a crisp dry martini made by the humble renter of this vast expanse of space." He bowed and said, "If it pleases the lady to be seated." He walked me to the couch, but before I could sit down he put his arms around me lightly and gave me another quick kiss. "Please do not interpret that as a plea for a gratuity; it was entirely gratuitous on my part and I hope you are not offended."

I sat down, saying, "Not at all. I am just a bit speechless."

"Well, yes, I am getting a bit used to that about you." While he collected his journals into one pile on the coffee table, he smiled and said, "I did not expect the tour to end this way, though I certainly wished it would. Now I had better go and make us those extra frosty martinis."

I leaned back and closed my eyes as I felt the weight of being there. My mother would have been very proud, but I was a bit shaken by all of it. Daniel came over with a tray that held a martini pitcher, two glasses, and a plate with toast squares and French Brie. He put some cheese on a toast and handed it to me, saying, "You should have something with fat in it before you drink alcohol. It helps to line the stomach, to handle the frosty onslaught of a joyous martini. That was lesson number one in medical school!" He laughed, "We indulged in that advice, even at times when it was only lab alcohol—or I should say, especially when it was lab alcohol." He smiled at me and raised his glass to me, saying, "May this happen again and again."

We sipped our martinis, and then Daniel pressed on. "Karin, tell me about yourself."

That was a sobering request, and at first all I could think to say was, "Where shall I begin?"

"Wherever you wish and whatever you are comfortable with."

There was so much I wasn't comfortable with; it was hard to decide where to begin. I surprised myself when I started speaking of taking a class at the university in 1938.

Three hours and two martinis later, I said, "This must never be mentioned, because Anja does not know of her father's letter to me. I fear it would devastate us both if she were to know that, at least for now."

"No, of course not, your story is safe with me. How strange that I left Europe to avoid a war, and that you left here to go over and walked into that same war. Thankfully we are both sitting here, though my life seems like a walk in the park compared to what you went through."

"I have heard it said that destiny only gives us the life we can handle. At times I think I was overrated for my assignment."

He took my hand and looked into my eyes, saying, "But destiny also willed us to meet for a reason."

"Yes, indeed." I smiled and said, "I only hope she hasn't overrated me again."

"Not a chance, I'll make sure of that. I also see it is late, so let me take you home."

Back in the night air, my breathing isn't as hard as it was earlier. Daniel held my hand as he hailed a taxi. When we got in the taxi, the driver asked, "Where to?" That was my question as well. Daniel looked at me, and I told the driver my address. We sat back as the driver sped us to my home. In the dark of the taxi, I felt Daniel take my hand and hold it. He leaned back and closed his eyes, saying, "We're on our way."

THAT NIGHT I FELT I BETRAYED MY MEMORY OF ERNST. He was the last and only man to have kissed me, and tonight I unwittingly stepped out of those shadows. I wished I felt it to be freeing. Daniel was so nice and easy to be with, and I knew I wasn't that way for him. How was it that I was able to tell him about myself, and so many of my life's events since 1938, but never once did I mention Ernst. I was still lost in shadows that were darker and less revealing of myself than I wished. It was clear to me that Daniel would have to take the lead because I, as yet, could not.

TODAY WAS MY LAST DAY AT ACE CRYSTAL LABS. CHARLIE was glad that Mr. Holloway gave his approval to allow him to assume my seniority position. Mr. Holloway handed me an envelope with my severance pay, plus a bonus. He also gave me another envelope with a letter of recommendation for my job performance. I hoped I would never need that again, but the money was welcomed. My next step was to go to the university admittance office, where I officially registered as a full-time student, thanks to my parent's offer to support Anja and me so that I could move ahead to independence.

I CAME HOME TO A CONTENTIOUS DISCUSSION BETWEEN my father and Anja. It centered around her desire to take on a piece by Brahms. She had to take my father on as well, who defended his opinion that it was a difficult piece, presenting new challenges that she had not yet dealt with. It was an eye opener for me that Anja had become more assertive than I expected. My father came out of his music room and shut the door saying, "She has a stubborn streak that is hard to reason with." We could hear her attacking the new challenges without mercy.

He shook his head and said, "I give up! She'll come to her own realization of the challenges."

I had no business taking any part in this because I lacked the knowledge to do so. Twenty minutes later she came out of the room in tears, saying, "I can't do it."

My father put his arm around her and said, "One day you will be able to, just not today."

She wiped her tears and said, "Maybe tomorrow or the next day."

I gave her a hug and said, "Sweetheart, that is very wise of you."

She looked at me as if I had made an error in judgment, but then she said, "I should have listened." When I agreed, she changed the subject. "Benji is coming over; we are going to see a Fred Astaire and Ginger Rogers movie. Grandpa is taking us. Do you want to come, too?"

"I would love to!"

We sat in the dark theater watching the two most harmonious people move to rhythm and music that stirred the imagination.

Later Anja convinced Benji they should take dance lessons. There was little Anja could not convince one to do. My mother was energetic about finding a good dance studio for Anja and Benji. After many inquiries and meetings, she found one run by a couple who took dance instruction seriously even for the younger ones. Anja and Benji were signed up.

EVEN THOUGH I DID NOT SEE DANIEL THIS PAST WEEK, he called me nearly every day.

One day he called to say he would like me to meet his parents. I was surprised and before I could comment he said, "Can you meet me on Wednesday evening at a French restaurant called Chez Midi on the west side? We can meet at six. I know it is early but it will be quieter then. It is popular with the French community, and they tend to eat later in the evening."

WHEN I PANICKED ABOUT HOW TO LOOK, HOW TO DRESS, or how to act, my mother said, "Just be yourself and you'll be so impressive."

I looked at her and said, "I don't know who that is anymore."

"No, but I do!" she replied.

When I walked into the small restaurant, Daniel saw me right away. He slid off a bar stool and came over to me. He embraced me with a kiss and said, "They haven't arrived yet, but I have a table for us." He pulled the chair out for me, and for a panicked moment I wanted to leave. Then I felt the chair at the back of my knees, and I lowered myself to a position of vulnerability. When I looked up at Daniel, I saw him wave to a couple by the door. They acknowledged Daniel's wave and approached the table.

After a round of three cheek kisses between parents and son, I was introduced with handshakes to Mr. and Mrs. Martineau. His mother Juliette was an attractive woman in a classic European way. His father, a bit portly, was a self-assured man who, after giving me an evaluating look, made me feel welcome. Then he said to Daniel, "We should order wine."

"I've done that already," Daniel said.

The waiter came over with a bottle and showed the label to Daniel's father. The waiter then opened the bottle and poured a little into his glass. Mr. Martineau sampled the wine and nodded, at which time our glasses were filled halfway. A waitress came over with a plate of hors d'oeuvres, and when she had left, Daniel lifted his glass and said, "Here's to us." Both his parents said, "*A notre santé.*" His father broke the slight awkwardness by saying, "The tripe is done to perfection here." I never wanted to hear that word again, and I must have winced because he said, "Of course, it's not to everyone's taste." He was observant.

Daniel helped me when he said, "I'm going to have the *coq au vin.*" I wondered if he did that for my sake, thinking that chicken in wine would be more acceptable to me than some of the less common French items on the menu.

"That sounds good, I'll have that as well." I answered. Daniel's parents ordered the tripe. Daniel smiled and poured us more wine, and then we began to chat. His father said, "Jean Daniel tells us you were visiting in Prague when the invasion happened. That must have been frightening for you."

"Yes, it was, when I realized I couldn't leave when I wanted to."

His mother said, "How awful that must have been. It must have taken a lot of courage to come out of it as you did."

"Yes, but many people helped me, so it wasn't all my own doing. Among them were the Quakers."

Mrs. Martineau nodded. "Oh, yes, I have heard of their efforts. It is an admirable organization."

Mr. Martineau said, "Has Jean Daniel told you why we left France when we did?"

"Yes, he has. That too was a courageous choice you made at that time."

Then we moved on to professions. Daniel's father taught history, which I knew, but I was impressed to learn that his mother was a bacteriologist of some note from a famous institute in Paris. She was currently working for the New York City Board of Health. His father was teaching history at a private preparatory military academy. My studies were lauded as the curator of the vast pool of knowledge collected by visionaries through the ages. Daniel's career was pretty much recognized as an exceptional foregone conclusion, and all three of them were pretty comfortable with that.

We ended our dinner with a selection of cheeses, after which his mother said, "It is good to see that the French are able to make and export some of their fine cheeses again. We have missed them."

His father added to this by saying, "Some of them were still being made regionally in France during the war. The Germans bought a small amount locally, but generally they appropriated the products for themselves, so I'm sure the French are as happy as we are to enjoy them once again." His small and informative history lesson had our attention.

Then his mother looked to Daniel. "And what is this week's schedule like for you?"

"Packed on all accounts. It looks like I'll hardly leave the hospital this week."

His mother looked at me and said, "It speaks legions of your patience to put up seeing so little of him a lot of the time."

I gave her a small smile. "It helps that I'll have to keep my nose in the books, but we do see each other, mostly over a meal in the hospital cafeteria."

His father mumbled into his wine glass, "How romantic."

The waitress rescued the table from more of the brooding father atmosphere putting a plate of *petit fours* on the table, along with coffee that kept me up watching the wee hours of the night on the clock. We finished our first meeting on a lighter note, discussing pastries, until we were interrupted by the waiter with the check, which he gave to Daniel's father, which may or may not have been French custom. I thanked them for a lovely evening and a wonderful dinner, and then we went through a round of triple kisses to say good night. Daniel's parents hailed a taxi, while Daniel and I walked a block before hailing our own taxi. As we waited for a cab, Daniel asked, "Your place or mine?"

"You choose," I said.

Daniel gave the driver his address; after all, this whole evening had not been planned by me and was not in my hands, even less so as I entered his place with a few misgivings.

He poured us each a tall glass of water, saying. "A sobering end to the evening."

We sat down, and he looked at me cautiously before asking, "So, what did your think of my parents?"

"It was a little awkward, not knowing what they would think of me."

"That aside, what did you think of them?"

"I think your mother is nice and empathetic, and your father seems to be much in command of himself."

Daniel laughed. "Yes, you are right on that. At times he is that way with others. He is a good man at heart and does care for others, despite his aura to the contrary sometimes. I know my parents well enough to say I think they liked you."

"But why would that matter?"

"It does to me. I only briefly met your parents at the reception, but from all that I saw, and from what Greg and Grace say, they seem like wonderful caring people, and you certainly are the result of that."

"They are that to be sure, but I have stumbled and bumbled my way in life. As much as they tried to be my cautionary speed bumps, I still raced on blindly to an uncertain course."

"I hope I don't step in front of you, it could be disastrous for both of us." He laughed. He put his hand on mine and said, "But I'm sure it won't be." With that assurance, we left his apartment and Daniel hailed a taxi for us and saw me home.

STUDIES

TO THE SOUND of Anja's scales, I sat down and organized my books and schedule as a full-time student. This week we were to visit some local libraries to see how information can be disseminated on a smaller scale while still following the master plan. At the end of the week, we would go to the library of all libraries, the main branch on Fifth Avenue and 42nd Street. When we walked past the two stone lions that flanked either side of the steps, they felt like guardians of the citadel we were about to enter, the bastion of all the knowledge and learning in the universe. We assembled inside the main entrance, where a guide led us through the passages of designated disciplines. It was so awe-inspiring that we were more or less speechless until we were seated in our classroom again.

Our instructor said, "Well, now, any questions?" We answered with a collective soft moan, then she said, "This is the realm you are about to enter, so put your thinking caps on because this course will not be a piece of cake or a walk in the park. You will be working hard for the degree that will allow you to become part of this elite system of knowledge gathering, storing, and disseminating. Good luck to all of you. Let us begin." I had learned some of the preliminaries earlier when I attempted to do this, before I stopped classes to work at Ace Crystal Labs. Now there was no war, although I had a few skirmishes of my own to get through: Anja, Daniel, and the haunting shadows of my memories. In the coming months I would march my way through my lessons, some of which were interesting and others not very, but still necessary.

ANJA'S PROGRESS WAS REMARKABLE, AND MY FATHER allowed Anja to practice the Brahms piece only after all her other practice and homework was completed.

My parents kept to their word to support me through school, including with the expenses that Anja incurred. This was no small commitment, and I was grateful to have the life insurance money to fall back on.

Daniel and I managed to meet now and then between our schedules, mostly over a meal at the cafeteria. One day he called and asked to see me at his place after dinner. That had a slightly ominous ring to it. When I arrived he said, "First of all," And he kissed me. "Second, I think we have come to a crossroads of decision-making. I want to lay it all out for you from my side. I am a pediatrician, and in my work with children who have suffered rheumatic fever and have been left with damaged hearts, I have immersed myself in that area. Pediatric cardiology is a relatively new area of specialty, I have given myself over to it, to learn all that I can access from experienced cardiologists and other related specialists. Aside from that, my time is now divided between the pediatric ward, the clinic, and the rotations we are all required to do in the ER. That is why I am always tied up at the hospital. I wish I had more time to spend with you, but I haven't. I think of you, quite a lot in fact, which brings me to my next subject. I would love for you to live with me."

In disbelief I was left speechless.

I knew his offer was serious, when he said, "Karin, this is not the time to be speechless."

"You're right, Daniel." I gathered my thoughts and my strength, afraid for where this was heading. "I don't see where Anja fits into what you have just proposed. You know Anja's history and her needs. She is thriving in our loving family. My father is her mentor for the piano, and she is accustomed to spending much of her time with my parents. As I see it, there is no room here for Anja, let alone for a piano, which is a must for her."

Daniel nodded. "I have given all of those points some thought. I need to be no more than three blocks from the hospital. Seeing that the housing shortage makes a move challenging, I intend to go to all of the apartment buildings in a three-block range to meet with the superintendents. I will tell them what we need, and I would offer them a month's rent as a finder's fee."

"That is very generous of you, and thoughtful, but the fact remains that Anja and I would be sitting alone night after night without you."

"Karin, I am sorry to say that this is one aspect that I cannot change, at least not in the immediate future. If you could see those precious little ones who need medical care and science to speed up a solution for their damaged hearts, you would understand my position."

"Daniel, I understand it now—I do—but I also have a precious little one who needs my family life and me to thrive."

Daniel's shoulders slumped, but I could tell that he wasn't all that surprised with this outcome. "I see this as a bit of an impasse, Karin. For the time being, I so would like you to stand still long enough for me to love you for now, and we can see what comes into our uncertain futures."

I smiled warmly at him. "I can stop moving for that long."

He smiled back at me and said, "That's all I ask." He kissed me tenderly and said, "I think we should celebrate with a Martini." Two Martinis later, we are were in his "bed chamber." Gin and emotions have moved us to that pivotal point of love making, when suddenly I pulled back. We were both quiet for a moment, when then he said, "Don't worry, Karin. I'm okay with whatever is happening. I suspect a broken heart is at play here, and I think I know how to fix that, if you'll let me try." I burst into tears, when he took me in his arms, and whispered, said, "It's okay, it's perfectly okay."

There was nothing perfect about it, and it wasn't okay. Ernst was the only man who had made love to me, and just now he had stepped out of the shadows to remind me of that. I lay in Daniel's arms for a long time, and I felt the shadows receding, as if Ernst understood how badly I wanted my war to be finally over.

Daniel asked, "What can I do? What can I say?"

"You have done all of it," I murmured.

"I think we'll have to take it from there, don't you think?"

"Yes, I do." And as Daniel and I made love that night, the pain of losing Ernst became bittersweet as that wound finally began to heal. As the shadows dissipated, I found the daylight blinding.

LESSONS

THERE SEEMS TO BE ROOM in my life for yet another surprise. Daniel announced that he was going to attend a medical conference in Chicago, and he asked if I could arrange to come with him. It promised to be a chance for us to have some private time together, away from our busy schedules. I agreed that we were much in need of that, so long as I was able to arrange Anja's care with my parents. My parents of course agreed, but Anja seemed a bit leery about my leaving her for more than just a few hours.

WE FLEW FROM NEW YORK TO CHICAGO, WHICH WAS IN itself an adventure for me. We checked into the conference hotel and I luxuriated in our private room. We arrived on a Wednesday so Daniel could register and gather information for the opening of the conference on Thursday. He came back to our room excited about the list of names of some of the lecturers. We had dinner in the hotel and later fully enjoyed the privacy of our room. Thursday morning we had an early breakfast, he left me to attend the lectures he had signed up for. There was a luncheon for attendees in the ballroom, but guests were not permitted. Daniel suggested that I explore

Chicago on my own for the day, and we agreed to meet for dinner at six.

Armed with a visitor's map and a list of sights for tourists, I explored downtown Chicago. I went to a wonderful museum and ate lunch there, and then I headed out for some window-shopping. Having forgotten my nightgown, I splurged on a frothy lace one the likes of which I imagined a newlywed bride would wear night after night. When I got back to the hotel, I found a note from Daniel saying he would be delayed because he had been invited to have drinks with some of the people he wanted to talk to. At half past eight he returned to the room, apologizing for being so late. We went down to the hotel restaurant but found we could not get in without a reservation. We left the hotel and found a small diner a few streets away; they were out of a lot of the items on the menu, but they offered to make us sausage and eggs. We resignedly ate a repeated breakfast. Daniel was tired but mentally stimulated by the day's events. We got back to the hotel at ten, and we were completely exhausted. My new nightgown never made it out of the pink tissued box.

Friday morning we had an early breakfast, and then he said he was going to join some people for coffee before the conference began. He asked if I would I mind getting the breakfast check, and then he'd see me for lunch. I watched him walk away; he might as well have been wearing his white coat as I saw him disappear into the crowd. I sat in the lobby and watched the people who came and went. Eventually I went up to the room to shower and preen for lunch. Daniel came up at one and said they were serving sandwiches in one of the conference rooms, if I cared to join him. We walked into a stuffy, crowded room, waited in line for some sandwiches, and then stood there eating until he dashed off to his next event.

Saturday was like Thursday, and I was on my own by 8 a.m. I decided to call home to see how Anja and my parents were doing. My mother answered the phone. "Excitement, excitement, excitement! I am to remind you that Benji and Anja have their dance recital on Sunday at 3 p.m. Be prepared, she is counting on you being there. Here she is."

"Hello, Mama! I'm so excited we are having our dance class recital tomorrow. You have to be here. We will be all dressed up and there will be live music and lemonade and cake. You can't be late. I'll see you there! Love you more, bye, bye."

My mother came back on and said, "I guess you got the message. It's being held at the dance studio. I know you are planning to be back Sunday late, but try to be here. Love you darling, bye!"

I went down to the crowded conference rooms to look for Daniel, but I couldn't find him. I went back up and called the airline. They had only one cancelation on a flight to New York, which left at 4 P.M. that evening. I took it. I packed my things and left Daniel a note.

Dear Daniel, I'm sorry I could not find you earlier. I have gone back to New York. Anja needs me. Call me when you're back. Love, Karin.

I got home weary and tried out, but Anja was so happy to see me that it was worth the exhaustion. Hours later, Daniel called. "Is Anja all right?"

"Yes, she needed me."

"Well, actually I did, too. As a surprise I made a reservation for us tonight in the hotel's Starlight Lounge for a candlelit dinner and dancing. Instead I had a room service sandwich and a beer and will watch a late-night movie, the classic *Brief Encounter*. I had planned for breakfast in bed on Sunday as well. I'm so sorry it is not happening."

"So am I, so am I."

"Don't worry about it. I'll call you when I'm back. Take care. I love you, Karin."

"Good night, Daniel, sleep well. I'll talk to you tomorrow." I hung up. I unpacked my things and put my frothy lace nightgown, still in its box and wrapped in pink tissue paper, on the top shelf in the rear of my closet. I thought, if man's best-laid plans can go awry, so can a woman's.

The apartment was awash with excitement in the morning, and I found myself watching it as if from afar. My father said, "Thank goodness you are here. The girliness going on here has made me realize how useless maleness is at a time like this. The planning and carrying on for this event is astounding."

I too felt useless but from a different vantage point. As Anja's mother, I was remiss in not taking the lead in her big event. My mother was on top of it all; she had made a dress for Anja, which I thought was a bit grown up for her, but Anja loved it. My mother had done up her hair as well. The topper was when I saw Anja stand between my mother's knees, in front of my mother's vanity. She was applying something on Anja's lips—no, not lipstick too! Mother saw my disapproving look. "Its not lipstick, dear, its only Tangee." Tangee was a slightly colored lip balm that could well pass for lipstick on a ten-year-old. "It'll give her a soft glow." My mother's words were not as placating to me as she intended them to be, but I did not want to rain on their parade, so I did not say anything. Since I felt like an invited bystander, I kept my thoughts to myself.

Fully preened, polished, and Tangeed, Anja led the way as my father hustled us into a taxi. When I looked over at my "little girl," a small shudder went through me, as if she were off to her wedding.

When we arrived at the dance studio, Benji, Aaron, and Hannah were waiting for us. Without a word, Benji took Anja's hand and we followed them into the studio. Chairs lined the walls for all the family and friends, and we sat down together as Benji and Anja walked hand in hand to check in for the recital.

There were several mirrored balls suspended from the ceiling. The piano had a large vase of beautiful flowers on it, and an empty chair and music stand awaited the violinist.

A colorful husband-and-wife dance team that had retired from professional competition to teach ran the studio. Mrs. Cleary introduced her husband and herself as the sole instructors who oversaw not just dance instruction but aspects of health, grooming, and grace for their pupils.

She then introduced all of the students as each couple stepped forward to the applause of the onlookers. The dancers were seated on the opposite side from us. When the pianist and violinist took their places, the lights were lowered, and the mirrored balls slowly rotated. The first group, which included Benji and Anja, took their places and awaited the moment to step into a waltz.

I watched Benji and Anja breeze past us as light-footed as a pair of butterflies on the wing. Suddenly Anja's dress, her hair, and even the Tangee all fit in place as the mirrored balls caught them in flight. Mother looked at me and smiled, as if to say everything was as it should be, and that was wonderful. Anja had music in her feet as well as in her hands, and Benji was there to be part of all of it. We watched them do the Fox Trot, followed by a type of square dance. That marked the end of the six weeks of lessons that Benji and Anja had completed.

Next to perform were the pupils enrolled in the four-month course. They were announced as a group of contemporary and Latin dances. We watched them do the Samba, the Rumba, a Two Step, and finally a Jive. Anja watched them with sheer admiration. Then they all did the Charleston, which ended the recital. Mrs. Cleary did not miss a beat when she announced any six-week pupils who wished to do so could now sign up for the four-month classes. Anja from across the room vigorously pointed to herself and Benji. It was a *fait accompli*—my Saturday afternoons were now spoken for. As I stood in line to sign her up, I was glad I had also stood in line for that four o'clock cancelation seat from Chicago to New York. Some joys held their precedence in line. Anja came over and took my hand and said, "Thank you Mama. Thank you, thank you." We mingled over lemonade and pound cake, and I watched our little Fred Astaire and Ginger Rogers stare at the older dance couples, knowing that in four months they would be one of them.

A MONTH LATER I WAS EXCITEDLY LOOKING FORWARD to a candlelit dinner invitation from Daniel. It took that long to finally arrange a work-free evening for the two of us. I splurged on a luxury trip to the beauty salon. Made up and dressed, I was applying the last touch of cologne when the phone rang. It was Daniel, calling to say he had been called in to the hospital and so wanted to change the plan for the evening to dinner in the cafeteria. I had never been more disappointed by his change of plans. I left the house angry and sad, but by the time I got to the hospital cafeteria, I had made peace with myself, knowing it was not his fault that he was called in to work. I found a table and waited. Soon he rushed over to where I was sitting.

"I'm so sorry, Karin. I just called and canceled our reservation. I'll make it up to you as soon as I can. I'll get us dinner—tonight its pot roast or chicken."

"I'll have the chicken, something I can identify with tonight."

He gave me a quick kiss and then ran to the line. When he came back with the tray he had a cup filled with mashed potatoes and in it a birthday candle. He put it down between us and smiled apologetically, saying, "After all, I did promise you a candle light dinner."

I tried to return the smile, but I couldn't. We were nearly finished with our dinner when he was paged. He leaped to his feet, gave me a kiss, and said, "I'll call you." I watched his white coat flutter as he hurriedly exited the cafeteria. I sat there looking at the unlit candle in the mashed potatoes, feeling sorry for myself. I was on the verge of tears when Zac suddenly appeared by the empty chair opposite me.

"May I join you? I heard his page." When I nodded, he sat down. "Ah, he was kind enough to leave me his salad and dessert, as well as a beautiful deserted lady. If he comes back, I'll replace the salad and dessert, though that's unlikely. I wish I could do something for the deserted lady right now. By the way, you look most lovely tonight, Karin. I wish you had been my date."

"Right now, so do I." I gave a reluctant smile, but he didn't.

Zac sat forward in his chair. "Daniel is my best friend. I know him well. We are all professionals in this building, but Daniel is different, he is a professional professional. He is married to his work, and he is truly devoted to it. I don't want to speak out of turn, but I must say that the best you can hope for with him is to be his mistress, the one who will always have to step aside for his true love."

I put my empty fork down and looked at him blankly. He quietly said, "Ah, I see it was to be a candlelit dinner. Here, allow me." He gave a hollow laugh, but I couldn't match his attempt to cheer me up.

"Thank goodness I'm in radiology. I come as close to being a nine to fiver as a doctor can be, which means I am free to see you home if you wish."

I wished. We got up and left the table, leaving the candle to burn itself out.

ONE DAY NOT LONG AFTER THE DISASTROUS CANDLELIT dinner, Daniel and I sat in the cafeteria having another of our ill-fated dinners. He was paged within minutes of sitting down with our food. I nodded glumly, knowing what that meant. He got up, kissed me, said he was sorry and that he would call me.

A few minutes later, Zac appeared as if the savior in some melodrama. "Ah, yes, I too heard the page. Want some company?"

"Sure. Tell me, don't you have a home to go to?"

Zac shrugged. "I do and I don't."

We chatted casually, though it felt like we were both avoiding the obvious topic.

"I'll see you home if you'd like," Zac offered.

"That would be nice, if you don't have anything better to do."

"It's not a matter of better. It would be my pleasure."

We got a cab, and Zac asked the driver to stop about a block sooner than necessary. As we walked toward my building, he asked, "Is there a place nearby where we can stop and have a beer?"

" Yes, Nick's Lounge is just around the corner."

We sat at a corner table and ordered two tap beers and a bowl of peanuts. Zac loosened his tie and said, "This feels better." He sipped his beer and looked at me like he wanted to say something. Eventually he said, "So, tell me, Karin, how are you?"

"Busy. I'm a full-time student at the university, and I have a little one to keep track of and everything that implies."

"How is it going with you and Daniel?"

"As far as plans go, it's hit or miss. I took your words to heart, you know, about Daniel's work and that marriage and my role in it." I sipped my beer, and when I put it down, Zac leaned over and dabbed the foam from my upper lip. After a moment to consider what he'd done, I said, "It's hard for me to see how we are going to get to know each other with so little time together."

Zac clawed some peanuts from the bowl. Gazing out across the pub, he ate them thoughtfully. Then, lifting his glass, he looked at me pointedly and drank several swallows of beer. He wiped his mouth with the side of his hand and asked, "So, how do you feel about that?"

I was puzzled by the direction of conversation. It seemed altogether pointless. "There's nothing he or I can do about it. It's just our status quo, I fear."

Zac cleared his throat. "Do you love him?"

I nodded.

Zac nodded back. "Love can be a fearsome thing at times. I'll tell you my quest. In the past you have heard me mention Sadie. My current situation is also a status quo, but with a twist. She's been madly in love with Willard McKenzie from orthopedics for a long time, with one not so small problem: Willard is not in love with Sadie. He was, however, in love with a handsome naval officer whose eight by ten photo sat openly on Willard's bookcase. Sadie and Willard hung out together as a ploy of public deception for his real affection. Sadie loved Willard enough to go along with it. Willard's friend had served on a warship in the Pacific when a Japanese submarine sank it with no reported survivors. Telegrams were sent home, and his sister, knowing of her brother's relationship with Willard, came from California to tell Willard in person. After hearing the news, Willard became more and more morose to the point where he stopped working. There were great concerns for his welfare and for his career, all of which were realized one day when Willard shot himself. Sadie was beside herself. I now had concerns for her safety."

Zac paused for a few more gulps of his beer. "Willard's sister moved into his apartment. One day, she called Sadie over to help her. When Sadie arrived, she was told to be prepared for a shock. When she walked into the living room, there was Willard's friend, sitting on the couch. He was a sallow, hollow-cheeked wreck of a man bearing little resemblance to his photo, but it was him. After his ship was sunk, a Japanese fishing boat had found him half dead days later, floating on a large piece of the ship's wreckage. They pulled him out of the water and turned him over to their authorities, which barely patched him up and put him in a POW camp. He was released after the war, and then he was sent to a military hospital in California where his sister lived, and she watched over him until he was well enough to travel to New York to be with Willard again. She did not have the heart to tell him about Willard. Imagine his surprise when he arrived at Willard's apartment and found his sister. In his devastation at the news of Willard's death, he walked slowly through the apartment, room after room, in a state of bare recognition. Then he left, as if in a trance, and he went back to California with his sister, who could continue to care for him.

"Sadie came apart at the seams at this, and she was now afraid to be alone. She asked me if she could stay with me for a little. I took her in, but it was not what I dreamed it would be. I gave her my bedroom and I slept in my study. I made all the meals and cleaned up after her, while she stopped going to work, stopped keeping herself clean, and stopped talking to me. She took to drinking as well. A few days ago she told me that one of the nurses she knew from their floor was recently divorced and that she would be moving in with her. When she left, she left me a note on a crumpled envelope from the wastebasket. It just said, *Thank you, Sadie."*

"Oh my God, I'm so sorry. I didn't know."

"No one does, except Daniel," Zac said..

I reached my hand out to him, and he took it in his. After a moment, he said, "Misery loves company, but I would love you without any misery." He pulled his hand back and finished his beer. Then he said, "I sometimes think that love has got to be one of the cruelest things we were made to feel. I promised to see you home. I should do that now."

We walked around the corner to my building. At the door he leaned forward and kissed my cheek. "That's for everything, Karin. Good night."

He turned to hail a taxi. I watched as he climbed into one, and I found it hard to walk into my building alone.

The next day Daniel called to say he was off at eight that night, and would I meet him at his place? When I got there, he greeted me with a big hug. Then he stepped back to look at me, and stepped back in to kiss me. "Martinis are just about ready." I followed him to his kitchenette, where after extra-vigorous shaking of the cocktail shaker he poured two drinks.

Handing one of them to me, he said, "You better take this before I sip on that one, too." He followed me to the couch, saying, "It feels like I haven't seen you in ages, How are you?"

"Busy, but then you know what that's like." I smiled, but he did not.

"The page turned out to be a false alarm, so I went back down to the cafeteria to see you, but you were gone. I called, but your father said you were not home. Where were you?"

"I saw Zac in the cafeteria and he offered to see me home. We stopped for a beer at a place around the corner from my building."

"Yes, I know. I talked to him about that today, so you would not have to." He raised his glass to his lips, looking at me.

"Daniel, do I sense some jealousy here?"

He shook his head. "Caution."

I looked sharply at Daniel. "Are you cautioning me?"

"No, I would never do that, Karin. I'm being cautious. Zac is too vulnerable these days, and I just don't want anything to happen that the three of us would regret."

Now I shook my head. "No danger of that," I said.

"There is always a danger of that," Daniel said, rather darkly.

We finished our martinis, and then made our way back to his bedchamber. Tonight I felt that the spontaneity had given way to placation. When I was back in my own bed, I thought about Daniel and his attitude, and how he really wanted it all. And why not, when he can could have it, because for me he was still that face across the kitchen table.

WE CONTINUED IN THIS FOR QUITE SOME TIME. ONE evening he came over and had dinner with us, to my mother's great pleasure and Anja's curiosity. During dinner, Anja asked, "Mr. Daniel, do you play the piano?"

"No, I don't. I do play the guitar a little."

"What do you play?"

"I like classical music. As demanding as it is, I keep after it."

Anja laughed, recognizing the little agonies of those words. "Next time when you come, would you please bring your guitar we could play together?"

"I'll tune up my courage and do that."

Anja took to him without question, and he dutifully brought his guitar the next time he came over. Before Anja could program the entire evening, my mother said, "Dinner first, Anja. One always has dinner before a concert." Anja smirked.

As soon as dinner was over, Anja took Daniel by the hand and said, "Follow me." He did as all the rest of us have done, which was to follow her commands. They disappeared into the music room. I heard her open the piano bench lid, and she said, "Maybe you use a pitch pipe instead of the piano?"

With his A in tune, they talked a little and then they began to play. They were a little off at first, but then they came together. They played longer than I expected, and I felt a pang or two of jealousy over sharing the little time Daniel and I had together.

Reading my mind, or perhaps it was clear on my face; my mother shrugged and said, "I'm calling them in for dessert now."

As they came into the kitchen, Daniel wiped his brow and said, "I thought she might be an amateur; I gave it my best but mostly failed to keep up with her."

In a vain tone that highlighted her innocence, Anja said, "You'll have to work harder and then we'll get better."

He laughed, "That is what I do all the time." He looked at me with a pointed smile. It seemed Anja had already developed concrete plans for him; I should take a page from her book. He was so nice with her, my little rival.

ANJA WAS BACK TO SERIOUS WORK AND SO WAS I. THE standstill between Daniel and I continued along the same path, and we were both acclimated to it. My studies kept me on my toes, especially when impromptu quizzes were sprung on us. Instructors did this because such quizzes were a good marker of how *au courant* we were in our studies.

When I used words like "impromptu" and "*au courant,*" I had to laugh at the irony of how these words applied to my love life. The subject of becoming Mrs. Martineau never came up, and the offer to become his flat mate was not revisited. Daniel dealt in the real and factual world of outcomes, while I was still looking for something as being more than a glorified roommate or a mistress taking second seat to a man's career.

My mother happened to mention the other day that I was born on Mother's Day. It seemed I was destined for that role from early on. As far as I know, there is no Mrs. Day.

Anja continued to do well in school, and she was even more remarkable in her music studies. Her teachers already speculated to some extent about Anja having a professional career as a pianist. Anja had become much more self-possessed as she grew. She is serious about almost everything, including Benji, who was becoming more aware of their combined destinies. He had sought her out at the age of three, and she was holding him to it.

My parents, bless their hearts, rolled with the punches. Without them in our lives, I'm not sure Anja and I could do any of this. My father has been a wonderful father figure for Anja, something I hadn't been able to provide for her so far.

The Martineau dinners at Chez Midi happened now and then. They followed a formula every time. We would rehash the same conversations each time, with a few new anecdotes added before we would part with the three-kiss exchange. Then Daniel would hail us a taxi, but he would no longer ask, "Your place or mine?" We would arrive at his apartment, the forgone conclusion to the evening. He would then take me home, and his last words would be, "I'll call you." He still set my chemistry in motion whenever I saw him. Quaker Helen was right; I had little to say about it.

I had a mended broken heart, and I had ventured a rocky road of love. Even with the unexpected pitfalls, I had survived because at every turn of the road Anja was there to point the way home. As long as I keep prepared and stay *au courant*, I will master the impromptus as they appear.

One night, we went out to dinner, and the evening followed the formula as usual. Throughout the date, however, I could feel that something was different. When Daniel made our usual martinis before the evening's end, he said, "I have something to tell you." That made me anxious and excited at the same time.

"A month or so ago, I applied for a very interesting research project in my field. Today I got word I have been accepted to join the team."

"Oh, congratulations! Will you have just that, or will you keep all your other work as well?"

"As of now, I'm not sure. There is another small problem, a more significant detail. The project is in San Francisco."

What I felt when I heard those words was nothing small.

My breath caught in my chest, and my mouth fell open. "San Francisco? For how long?" I stammered.

"Probably close to a year."

"A year? God no, what's going to happen to us?"

"We can write to each other, and we can talk on the telephone. Maybe you'll see your way clear to come out to visit me. We can do this. I love you, Karin, and I don't want this opportunity to be the end of us."

This was the first time in recent memory that I can remember him saying he loved me, and it came just as he was about to leave me for a year. His assumption that I would simply endure whatever he planned in his life made me angry. Suddenly I felt some of my chemistry for him decompose from where it had been just minutes earlier.

Then I lost my temper and said, "Will I have to go to a psychic to figure out when I can make contact with you? Will she tell me that an intervening request is cutting her off?"

Between my slurps of gin, I realized that my anger was making me say stupid things. I stopped and caught my breath. Then I asked, "When will you leave?"

"In about a week."

I put my glass down, and I spoke stiffly. "I'm sure you'll call me before then, but right now I have to leave."

"I'll take you home."

"No, I can manage." I put on my coat and he came down with me to get a cab. As I got into it, he leaned down near me. Without turning around, I said, "Goodbye, Daniel." I had meant to say good night.

I pulled the door shut and fell back into the seat. The driver asked, "Where to, Miss?" I thought to myself, yes, that was my question as well. Then I gave him my address.

DISSOLUTION

I FELT LIKE A THROWAWAY that was coming apart at the seams. When I got out at Perry Street, I walked around the corner to Nick's Lounge and sat at the same table where Zac and I had sat. I ordered a martini and just sat there. I looked around at the lounge signs that advertised the brands available for one's refreshment. I remembered the things Zac said when we were here. The ones that had seared my memory were, "I sometimes think that love has got to be one of the cruelest things we were made to feel." That was exactly what I was feeling. I didn't know how I could walk into the apartment feeling like I did just then, compared to how I felt when I left it earlier. I'm not the same person anymore. Daniel was a part of my life an hour ago, and now he wasn't. I refused to write letters again; that may be his solution, but I would not live that way again. We were finished. It had happened to me once again. The waiter came over and asked if I wanted anything else. In a doleful moment, I wondered where I would begin. The ads for refreshment blurred as I finished the martini, and when I left I over-tipped the waiter. I walked around the block several times before entering my building. When I reached the elevator, I took a deep breath and once again entered the home of Mrs. Anja.

Coming into the apartment I hear my father giving a late lesson. There was a note on the kitchen table for me from my mother, "Anja and I are at a rehearsal. See you later."

I felt my life was just one big rehearsal for a still unplanned event. I dropped my handbag and coat on my bed and burst into tears. Part of me hoped he would call, but he didn't.

Daniel did call a few days later, asking if I would come over to his place after 7 p.m. I answered with a blunt "yes," I couldn't talk to him just then because I was studying for a test. The only thing I hadn't learned at that point was how to avoid or change that fatal flaw in myself so that I did not have to keep picking myself up from the depths of one emotional dilemma after another. I'd had these few days to simmer down, to no avail; I could only hope I would be more mature by 7 p.m. What are the chances?

I used my key ring to knock on his door in place of my trembling hand. When he opened the door, I wanted to run away, but I just stood there until he took my hand and led me inside. Without the benefit of gin, coffee, or water, he got right to it.

"Karin, if I had my rathers, this research project would be right here in New York. But it isn't, and I can't change that. Leaving you for a year is no less painful for me than for you. Medicine is what I do; I don't call the conditions of where or when. I was hoping you would understand that."

I tried to keep myself calm as I replied. "Daniel, I don't really know how painful this is for you, but for me it will be devastating not to see you for a year. Seeing you as little as I do has been hard for me, even though I know what medicine means to you. For me it has been bad medicine, and I am afraid I am beyond healing. I need a presence in my life of warmth and love, one I can count on, and not someone to give me scraps of it now and then. I hope you understand my feelings. What are we to do, you and I? I think we have come to the end of us being us, such as it has been."

"Karin, I wish you didn't see it that way. People do adjust to conditions even more extreme than this."

"Daniel, I have been in those extremes, and I can't do it again."

"Karin, I will keep in touch with you, and we'll test those waters. You may be stronger than you think."

"Time will tell, but now it's time for me to go. Aside from this one, I have another test tomorrow. I will think of you and I will miss you, but I am accustomed to that."

He stepped up to me and hugged me. He said, "This is just an interlude, it is not the end." He kissed me and I left.

I counted each day leading up to his departure. He did not call me, and I did not call him. I guess the interlude had begun. I hit my books and studied hard.

A week later I got a picture postcard from San Francisco. The message read, "I have arrived. I miss you! Love, Daniel." Three weeks later I got a short letter, but he had forgotten to put his return address on the envelope.

About a month later he called. He told me in detail about the project, his living conditions, the weather, and the scenery. Eventually he asked, "How are you?"

"I'm busy as usual, trying to adjust to what needs adjusting to. Other than what you told me, how are you?"

"I'm fine, but of course I miss you. I haven't had a martini since my last one with you, if that says anything."

"I guess it says research demands total sobriety."

"It has been good talking to you, Karin. We should do more of it, but I have to go now—duty calls."

"Thanks for calling. Goodbye, Daniel." We hang up.

Three months have gone by without a call. At times I still miss the page-interrupted meals in the cafeteria, but not nearly as much as I thought I would.

Friendship in Remiss

I OFTEN SAT at a far corner table after work and ate my dinner with reading material at the ready should I see Karin walk into the cafeteria. She always sat at the same table, and she either would or would not be joined by Daniel at 7 p.m. Just seeing her was my reward. Neither of them ever saw me as I watched their drama unfold, as he was so often paged. It was only rarely that I worked up the courage to go over to her after he had left and offered my seemingly incidental greetings. When I did I always left with her as soon as I could manage it. For me it had become a triangle that would dissolve a long friendship, especially when I would at times see them leave together. I knew my motives were questionable, but I refused to seek an answer.

At the hospital, our professional paths rarely crossed; unless I was called down to do his fluoroscopic imaging on his rheumatic fever patients. At those times we would chit chat the way friends do while waiting for something to happen; in this case we waited for one of his little patients to choke down a wad of barium sulfate that would serve as the tracer for the image he was interested in seeing on the big screen that I manipulated for his viewing. I felt an added tension when I sat in front of the screen as I directed the equipment and he stood behind me watching the images over my shoulder. I often had the shuddering feeling that he could see through me as well.

CHANGES

SEVERAL MONTHS AFTER Daniel left, I got a phone call on a Sunday morning.

"Hello, Karin, this is Zac. I haven't seen you in a while. How are you? Before you answer that, can you meet me for brunch? I'm sure your neighborhood has a better place for that than mine. May I meet you in front of your building in half an hour?"

So far I hadn't said anything more than hello. Mother was busy at her sewing machine, and my father and Anja were working on a new piano piece. Who would miss me? I hadn't been out for brunch since I can't remember when, so I said yes.

I had to wait in front of my building for just a few minutes when a cab drove up and deposited Zac on the sidewalk. He stood there at the curb looking at me for a long moment, then walked over and said, "Hi, Karin. That was a good idea you had about us having brunch." He gave me a quick kiss on my check and said, "Lead on to the best brunch place in the Village."

We linked arms and walked to where I knew that brunch was a big deal on Sunday, which might even be said for us on this whim of his.

We enjoyed our meal with light and easy conversation until he asked whether I had heard from Daniel.

"Well, I got a picture postcard, and a short letter, all within the first month and a phone call some time later.."

Zac nodded. "I got a picture post card and a detailed letter about the research that has him excited. He said it was the best decision he has made in years."

"Then I guess I wasn't one of them."

He looked at me kindly and said, "He told me that he misses you and that the year will go by quickly enough before he sees you again."

"That remains to be seen," I said stiffly

"What have you been doing since I last saw you?"

"Well, I went into a state of angry grieving over the San Francisco business, but I have adjusted some over that. I am working hard to get my degree, and then I'll see what cards are dealt me."

"How is your little girl doing?"

"She is doing just fine." Happy for the change of subject, I laughed and said, "She has her future husband all lined up, and she is already on a career path. All in all, I could learn a lot from her." Realizing that Zac was working hard on his end of the conversation, I asked, "Zac, what's going on with you? Are you feeling better than the last time I saw you?"

"Oh, yes, much better, thanks. I am more relaxed, more accepting of my lot in life. I'm even enjoying work again, and life looks better now than it did before. Karin, what do you say I give you my number, so the next time you have that good idea for us to meet for brunch, you can call me. I have your number, so I can confirm."

I wondered how he got my number, but I set that aside because this was exactly the lighthearted conversation I needed. We were finished when the waiter asked, "Would you like anything else?"

Zac looked at me, "Karin?"

"No, thank you, I'm fine."

When the waiter left, Zac said, "I would say you are more than fine, but then I have always thought that." I smiled, grateful for the compliment. Zac paid the waiter and we left. Out on the sidewalk, Zac asked, "Is there anything else you would like to do today?"

"I'm sure if I put my mind to it I could come up with lots of nice things to do on a Sunday, but I have to go back home to study. I have been distracted from my course work, and I have even been cautioned about it."

"If you should need a break from the books, please let me know. We can explore some of those nice things you mentioned. For today I'll just have to settle for walking you home." We linked arms again, and at the door to my building he gave me another quick kiss on my cheek. "That was a good idea you had, Karin, going for brunch. I hope to hear from you soon."

I took my door key out, and he put his hand up in a goodbye gesture as he walked down the street to find a taxi.

TWO WEEKS LATER, ZAC CALLED AGAIN. WE HADN'T been in touch since that brunch.

He said, "My answering machine had a message from you, something about brunch today?"

I laughed and said, "Must have been another Karin. I'm just about to have breakfast."

"Don't! I can be there in fifteen minutes." He hung up.

Fifteen minutes later, I went down to find him on the sidewalk, looking at his watch. "You're late! Are you always so late when you make appointments? I'll overlook it this time, but let's go. I'm starving." I didn't even have time to laugh before he gave me a kiss on the cheek and took my hand. We talked and laughed as we walked to the brunch place. It was crowded, and we had to wait in line, pressed near the wall to make room for the people leaving. He put his arm around my waist and held me close to him. When I raised an eyebrow at his behavior, he pulled an innocent look and said, "I don't want you to get trampled by the heathen hordes." We laughed again.

When we were finally seated, he said, "I'm glad you called. I'm sorry, but my answering machine was a bit garbled. Had you said anything else after practically begging me to take you out to brunch?"

I just looked at him and started laughing.

"Okay, don't take it so hard. I won't put you on the spot, not this time anyway."

WE WENT ON THIS WAY FOR SOME TIME. HIS SENSE OF humor was a breath of fresh air, and it brought about a change in the weather pattern in me from dreary days to sunny skies, and I now looked forward to his calls.

HE CALLED ONE SATURDAY SAYING, "I HAVEN'T BEEN TO the zoo for ages! Thanks for inviting me to tag along with you and Anja. What time did you say we should meet? It'll be more crowded on Sundays, but I'm at your beck and call. If I recall, you said I should be at your place at ten, and we can go on from there. Good planning, Karin. I'll see you then!" Before I get my laughter under control, he had ended the call. He left me no out, and realized I didn't want one.

Anja and I stood in front of our building as a taxi pulled up. Zac said something to the driver, and then he got out and came over to us. He said hello mostly to Anja, although I did get a kiss on my cheek before he led us back to the taxi. Anja watched him with great interest; I wondered what she saw. I wonder less about what I see, as it is taking shape with each passing week.

At the zoo we walked with Anja between us, each of us holding one of her hands as we ambled from animal cage to animal house. Zac looked at me with a smile every once in a while saying, "This was a good idea you had." I burst out laughing.

Anja asked, "Mama, can I have a hot dog please?" We sat on a bench while she tackled her hot dog.

Zac said, "After this, let's go to this French bistro I know near here." Anja looked at him and nodded her agreement. Once again, what choice did I have?

At the bistro, Anja asked, "Do they have snails?"

Zac looked at the menu and said, "Yes, I believe they do."

"Good. I want snails. Benji says the French eat snails."

I felt a bit sidelined in all of this as I watched Anja eat snails, while Zac held the shells for her with the provided utensil.

"Mm, good," she said. Zac looked at me with a bit of a wince and shrugged.

Zac and I had omelets with mushrooms. When they arrive, Anja took my plate and picked out the mushrooms with her fork. "I don't really like mushrooms, Mama. You know that."

This had definitely turned out to be an Anja outing. I gave Zac a hard look and asked, "Are you sure it was me who called, or was it maybe Anja?" Zac shook with silent laughter.

And so, we went on, and phone calls were made to my number with plans that were confirmed to his.

IN THE FIVE AND A HALF MONTHS SINCE DANIEL LEFT, I had heard little from him, a few phone messages, which was typical of our difficulty in aligning our availability, a few picture postcards, nothing more sustaining than that.

Then I got a call from Zac, who said, "Daniel is arriving on Thursday, and he asked if I could put him up. He goes back to San Francisco on Sunday. Just so you know, if he asks about you, I will be honest. It may just be best not to call me while he is here. I'll talk to you after he has left on Sunday. I send you good thoughts." When I agreed, he hung up.

This was the first I had heard about Daniel coming to New York. When he called me Thursday night, I tried to act surprised.

"I'm here on a hurried trip to pack up my things from my sublet. Friday I'll be in the hospital with my colleagues. Saturday I'll have lunch with my parents, and I'd like to have dinner with you Saturday night. Can you meet me at Chez Midi at six? I'll make the reservation. I go back on Sunday. It will be so good to see you again. Well, until Saturday at six, take care. I'll see you then." That was all. I wasn't asked, nor did I have a chance to have a say in the matter.

When I got there, Daniel was just finishing a drink at the bar. I took him by surprise, and for a moment he looked as though he was trying to remember who I was. Then he said, "Good God, it's good to see you! I'm glad you could make it!" He then moved me along, saying, "Our table is ready." I wasn't, and I wondered if he was.

After we were handed menus, we stole a quick look at each other. He ordered the tripe and I had a soufflé, something more expansive than substantive, something more fitting for the ensuing conversation.

"Well, tell me how have you been? How is school going?"

"I'm adjusting. School is a bit of a chore at times, but I'm getting through my courses on schedule. How are you doing?"

"The research project is demanding, but mostly because I have to coordinate with three others who have different work habits. All in all, it is going well. The head of the department is going to start a pediatric cardiology department at the end of the year, and he has offered me a position there. It is a dream come true for me, and I will get in on the ground floor development of this new service. It won't be easy, but I am prepared for that."

Hesitating, he asked, "What are your thoughts about that?"

I pushed my plate away and looked at the items on the table to compose myself. Finally I said, "My thoughts are that this is the end for us, but I suppose I saw that coming."

He quickly said, "It doesn't have to be, Karin! You could come out to visit me once in a while, and we could write and I could call you."

"This long-distance relationship doesn't sound long-lasting to me. I still want a presence in my life that is warm and supportive and available, not something that will fade away with time. I just don't see us in your picture, or I should say, I don't see me in it. Do you, really?"

"It all depends on what you want."

"Daniel, I am not the only person involved in this decision. This is more complicated for me than it is for you, and it always has been. I think we are two people who should never have met as we did; our lives do not mesh, something that we overlooked or ignored at the beginning. I'd like to hear how you are from time to time, and I think that's how it will have to be.

His face was serious when he said, "I had hoped for more."

I nodded sadly. "So did I, so did I."

We finished our wine and left the restaurant. He took me home for the last time, and on the sidewalk, he put his arms around me. He kissed me politely and said, "Take care of yourself. I wish I had done a better job of it."

I will remember the feeling of both for a long time, then he turned and walked away.

I was emotionally spent as I put my key in the door. Once in the lobby, I just sat down and cried, a fitting end.

SUNDAY EVENING, ZAC CALLED, "HOW ARE YOU?"

"I'm somewhere between devastating and devastated."

"Can I see you tomorrow? If you know of a nice restaurant in your neighborhood, you should invite me to come and have dinner with you. You should tell me to meet you at six in front of your building."

"Yes, Zac, I can confirm that right now. It will be nice to see you again."

"That is the nicest thing you could have said to me. I'll see you at six."

I HAD ONE OF THOSE PRE EXAM IMPROMPTU QUIZZES IN class, so I would know where I was in my studies. It turned out that it was more of a continuation of my weekend. Anja had to study for a math test, which caused a lot of tears for her and for my father. I washed my face, brushed my hair, put on some lipstick, kissed my family, and headed to the front door of my building. Zac stood there with a bouquet of Parma violets. He said, "I couldn't decide on colors, so I went monochrome."

"Violets, how lovely, how expensive, how I love them!"

I buried my nose in them, and Zac took the opportunity to kiss my forehead and say, "They're soft and fragrant and lovely like you."

He did that to cheer me up, and to be honest, it helped, quite a lot.

"There is a nice little place near here that excels in comfort food," I offered.

"I knew I could talk you into it." I laughed; when I did he hugged me, saying, "There is something about your laugh that is addictive, Karin. I just want more and more of it—I can't get enough."

As we walked to the restaurant, Zac stopped and turned me to look at him. He puts his arms around me and kissed me tenderly. He said, "It's an addiction treatment. Remember, I'm a doctor, I know about these things. I know what works and what doesn't. It's okay to keep walking now. If you should swoon, I'll catch you."

I leaned into his arms again and said, "Zac, I thank God for sending you to me as my agent of rescue."

"Yes, I have been assigned that role by the deity above, expressly to care for you. I am sworn to fulfill that honor."

I laughed at his ridiculous words. "We sound like something in a movie."

"Oh, I know that one! It's the one where the guy gets the girl, right!"

As we finished our dinner Zac said, "Let's talk about it and get it over with. So, he stayed at my place, making me feel uncomfortable about it all. He talked a lot about the research and his excitement about the job offer. I of course didn't say anything about you; he was pretty closed on that except to say that he planned to meet you for dinner on Saturday. I helped him pack up his things on Sunday, and he said, 'It's not looking good for Karin and me, I'll have to see what happens.'"

"That's about all he said. I could tell he was sad and disappointed in your response. He didn't talk about it more, and I didn't ask. I knew better than to try, because my feelings would have gotten in the way. I was glad to see him leave on Sunday; although I also felt I had betrayed an old friend. I did not choose my feelings about him, and I especially can't help my feelings about you. I'll leave it there."

I put my hand on his across the table. "Zac, you did not steal me away from Daniel. We gave each other permission to separate from where we had been."

"I wish that made me feel better."

He held my hand as we walked back to my building. He stopped and said, "Well, Karin, I look forward to another confirmation call, as soon as you are ready for one." He quickly kissed me and stepped off the curb into a cab. I held my hand up as the cab drove away.

I realized that I, as well had stepped off a curb in my life.

I CAME HOME FROM SCHOOL EACH DAY WITH ONE GOAL in mind, escape. At times I poured myself a good portion of wine or whiskey and took it to my room. I lay down on my bed, still dressed. I finished the drink, not in a social way but in a hurried, medicinal way, and then I went to sleep. I escaped my loveless life, my war work, my studies, and my non-parenting of Anja. I was sinking into a dark and lonely place that I feared going into as much as I did coming out of.

One afternoon my mother was waiting for me in the kitchen when I came home.

"Sit down, Karin. I want to talk to you. Daddy and I have been worried about you for some time now. You come home, and at times have a stiff drink, and go to bed; sometimes you sleep through dinner until the next morning, still dressed. If you haven't noticed, Anja has been spending more time at Benji's lately than she has here. When I spoke to her about it, she told me she feels unloved and neglected by you. I agree with her. As much as Daddy and I love to care for her, she needs you above anyone else. I know this business with Daniel has taken a toll on you, and we feel we have let you have the time you needed to recover from the break-up. Now, Karin, we need you back with us."

I felt the façade of normalcy crumble at my mother's words. "Daniel was my last hope for happiness, such as it was. I gave it my all, and now there isn't anything left of me that's worth saving." Mother pulled her chair next to mine and put her arms around me as I sobbed.

"Not worth saving? Karin, whatever gave you that idea? You have thrown yourself away to feelings that are not worthy of you. Anja needs your love, and so do we. If you can't pull yourself out of this, you should get professional help. You and we can't go on like this. Call Anja to come home for dinner and spend the evening with her. You both need that now."

Anja came home and immediately threw her arms around me. She just stood there, holding me without saying a word. Mother handed us aprons and said, "Okay, ladies we're having hamburgers with onions, tomatoes, and lettuce on kaiser rolls."

"Grandma, don't forget the fries!"

My mother laughed. "That's right! We are doing the works tonight."

"Can I have a cream soda, too?"

"Tell Grandpa we'll need two cream sodas and three beers."

"And potato chips?"

"Okay, Anja, we are gilding the lily tonight."

When the three of us had arranged dinner on the table, my father said, "Oh, how grand! We have company for dinner tonight!"

It was the best hamburger I ever ate, and it was one of the best evenings I could remember in a long time. After dinner we played Anja's favorite made-up card game, Slap It. Tonight she broke one of her steadfast rules, however, when she let me win!

My heart swelled with wonderful feelings of motherly love as I realized that Anja was returning a big favor; she was taking care of me, saving me from myself.

One evening Zac called, out of the blue as if he knew I needed him. He said, "I hear there are two beers set out at Nick's Lounge with our names on them. I'll see you there in fifteen minutes. Hurry, before someone else claims them."

SITTING IN NICK'S LOUNGE OVER OUR NAMED BEERS, I asked Zac a question that had been on my mind for some time. "Zac, why do you couch your invitations to me the way you do? Why don't you just come out and ask me?"

Zac smiled a little sheepishly. "Two reasons. One, I want you to feel some lightheartedness, because life can be hard sometimes. Two, I'm always afraid that, if I come right out and ask you, you might say no."

"I like your surprises, Zac, and I would not say no."

"I never know if your feelings for Daniel might get in my way." Zac shrugged. "They could, you know."

"No, they couldn't," I said firmly. "Daniel and I are passé, gone, as in finished."

"Are you sure?"

"Yes, absolutely."

He reached for my hand, saying nothing for a moment. Then he said, "I feel safer now."

I squeezed his hand in mine. "So ,do I, Zac."

A FEW DAYS LATER, ZAC CALLED. "KARIN, I INVITE YOU and your daughter to my place for lunch on Sunday. Can you make it?"

I accepted, and then I warned, "She has a healthy appetite, you know."

"Yes, so do I."

The cab dropped us just off Madison Avenue at a beautiful old townhouse. As we looked at the few names, I realized that I was just discovering Zac's last name: Emerson.

I rang the bell, and we were buzzed in just as he opened the door for us.

"You found it, I see." He gave me a quick kiss and leaned down to shake Anja's hand, saying, "Hello again, Anja, I'm Zac. Please follow me."

He led us into a beautiful spacious living room with a large window at the far end looking out over a garden. Anja gasped and very nearly shouted, "Oh, look Mama, a baby grand piano!" She turned to Zac and clasped her hands together. "Mr. Zac, can I play it? Please!"

Zac laughed at Anja's imploring sincerity and said, "Yes, if you'd like."

She grew serious and said, "I have to wash my hands first." Zac looked at me and smiled as he showed her to the bathroom.

She came back, still wiping the backs of her hands on her blouse. She slid onto the bench like an old professional, which I supposed she was, and she began to play.

Zac's jaw dropped. "Good heavens! I was expecting Chop Sticks, not Mozart." He took my hand and said quietly, "I'd like to listen, if that's okay." I sat down beside him on the down-filled leather couch. He was mesmerized by Anja's playing.

When she finished, Anja said, "Thank you, Mr. Zac. That was exciting."

"Yes, it certainly was! When did you learn to play like that?"

"I was born with it," she giggled, "but I have had some help."

I examined the piano, now that Anja was done playing. While I couldn't play well, I still knew my way around pianos. "Zac, this is an impressive piece of living room furniture."

"Thanks. It was a gift from my mother on my twenty-first birthday."

"I suspect there is a story behind that," I said with a smile.

"There is. I had been taking lesson since I was seven. In my senior year of high school, I said I wanted to go to the music conservatory to study music. My father said, 'I won't fund your half-cocked schemes of having a career in music, but I will if you choose medicine.' My mother thought I should follow my passion, but I ended up following my father's wishes. He's a well-known surgeon, you see. I went into radiology, where I have less renown. I never became the concert pianist I dreamed of being, but I have found out I am rather good at both."

Anja said, "I'm going to be a concert pianist someday."

Zac bowed and said, "Then I will be in the front row, applauding you." She laughed. Then he brought us into the dining room to a table laden with the best of Zabar's delicatessen, the likes of which is not often seen or available these days. Anja's eyes brightened at the sight as she wriggled into a chair. She rubbed her hands together and said, "I'm ready!"

After lunch Zac asked Anja if she knew Boogie Woogie. She giggled and said, "No. What is that?"

"Let's go wash our hands and I'll show you."

She hurried back and sat at the piano with him. He played Boogie Woogie for her, and she laughed at the musical antics as they played together. She was good at even this.

Magic was happening there and I was happy to know I was a key part of it as I watched this lovely man become part of our lives.

ANJA'S LIFE HAS BECOME BENJI, MUSIC, AND BENJI, MUSIC, and school, and dance classes. There is no doubt that the warmth and stability of our family is giving her a grounding that keeps her on a path toward a happy and secure life, which is essential for a child prodigy. I continued on that path alongside her, determined at all cost to see her flourish in whatever life destiny had in store for her, even at the possible cost of my being "Mrs. Anja" on occasion. The testament, the one that I have given myself to, is the one that lies sealed in a bank safety deposit box.

We all have our destinies.

ACKNOWLEDGMENTS

Great thanks to Nina Wolsk—without her help, encouragement, advice, and love, I would still be struggling.

To Julie Bentzon, who never fails to let 3,000 miles of Atlantic Ocean deter her from support and suggestions with loving encouragement.

To Laura Henderson, my chief guru who not only held my hand but led me through the minefields of cybernetics, saving me many times over.

To Jimmy Woods Corwin, whose kindness and warmth are supporting.

To Maja Henderson, who hears my distress over my computer illogicals before I have even voiced them, and saves me with her infinite knowledge and patience.

To Patrick Gibson, for his telepathic instincts that have saved me from cyber meltdown.

Special thanks to Scott Henderson, who, long before I took pen to paper, recognized in me the storyteller that became a writer.

To Janette Turner, my constant mentor and reminder, who encouraged and supported me in believing that writing is what I am meant to do.

Mary Conley, my dear friend who makes me laugh when I am closer to tears, insisting that I write the great American novel; To Kizzie Jones and Thom Wert, without whose friendship and support of my writing and their generous help I would still be questioning myself; Lindsay Baumhefner and her husband, two people the writer gods sent to me as a warm surprise in appreciation of my writing.

Research is the arm that drives the hand of a writer, and I thank the following people who helped me get the facts in order: Louis Fiset, secretary of the Military History Society, and his colleagues Dan and Al, for their help and interest in supplying me with some of the more obscure facts; and Derek O'Brien of the RAF Museum in London, England, who so kindly answered my request regarding the RAF and the RCAF during World War II. Many heartfelt thanks to the Quakers of The American Friends Service, who allowed me to tell some of what they did during World War II.

Many thanks to my publishing team, especially Karen Maneely.

ABOUT THE AUTHOR

Ingrid Wolsk was born in New York City. Having grown up in a lonely childhood, she later longed for adventure and travels. Even as a young child, she had a strong feeling for storytelling, when she wrote poems and very short stories. Later in life, she lived abroad for ten years absorbing experiences that at times would find themselves in her writing.

She has worked many different jobs, both in and outside of the arts.

The Secret of Anja is her first novel. She is now working on her second novel *Camp Henley*. She also has a flash fiction piece, *A Screech of Warning*, available on Amazon Kindle, which is listed under her maiden name of Andersen.

Ingrid Wolsk lives outside of Seattle, Washington, and has two daughters.